THREE ASSASSINATIONS

One Family's Tragedy

Three Assassinations
One Family's Tragedy
Copyright © 2022 by Cheryl P. Weiner

Additional copies may be ordered from the publisher for educational,
business, promotional or premium use.
For information, contact ALIVE Book Publishing at:
alivebookpublishing.com, or call (925) 837-7303.

Book Cover and Interior design by Alex P. Johnson

ISBN 13
978-1-63132-167-2

Library of Congress Control Number 2022654321

Library of Congress Cataloging-in-Publication Data
is available upon request.

First Edition

Published in the United States of America by ALIVE Book Publishing
an imprint of Advanced Publishing LLC
3200 A Danville Blvd., Suite 204, Alamo, California 94507
alivebookpublishing.com

PRINTED IN THE UNITED STATES OF AMERICA

10 9 8 7 6 5 4 3 2 1

THREE ASSASSINATIONS

One Family's Tragedy

CHERYL P. WEINER

ABOOKS

Alive Book Publishing

WHEN YOUR STORY PROVIDES A GLIMPSE
INTO YOUR FAMILY'S PAST,
IT ALSO REVEALS YOUR FAMILY'S HERITAGE

In memory of my parents
FRANCINE and MILTON
and my brother IRWIN

Prologue

On December 24, 2006, with family surrounding her hospital bed, my mother, Francine Edith Stroll, lay dying. Her small private room, crowded with family from around the country, had come to say goodbye.

Since it was Christmas Eve, the hospital provided a trio of carolers who strolled the corridors singing beautiful hymns and festive holiday songs for the patients and their caregivers. As the carolers passed by my mother's room, the musicians saw what was transpiring and apologized for disturbing the family in our moment of grief. I told the carolers how much my mother loved to sing and dance and asked them to continue playing their music.

The three men came into the room and began a rendition of "Hark, the Herald Angels Sing." As the music filled the small hospital room, the blanket at the foot of my mother's bed began to twitch. The puzzled nurse lifted the blanket and saw that my mother's feet were moving rhythmically to the beat of the song. It was absolutely magical.

Ten minutes later, Mom took her last breath. I had been sitting alongside her when she passed and I leaned over and kissed her forehead.

"We all love you so much," I whispered. "Rest in peace."

After my mother died, it took me several months before I could face packing up her belongings. When I finally walked into her bedroom, I could still smell hints of her perfume floating through her closet. I felt her presence.

Her eyeglasses were still on her nightstand next to her

notepad and pen. I gently picked them up and held them close to my heart. When my father came into the room, he put his arms around me and we both began to weep.

When I began to pack up my mother's clothes, shoes, and array of purses, I uncovered several cardboard shoeboxes sealed with rolls and rolls of scotch tape. Each box was carefully labeled in my mother's beautiful cursive handwriting. Gently, I pulled out each cardboard box and began to sort through the contents of my mother's memories, my mother's life, my family's past. I glanced over everything immersed in the old photographs and letters written on the fragile, yellowing paper.

A black mourner's ribbon, a prayer card, and newspaper articles about a violent death. And so many names . . . Jack . . . David . . . Lewis . . . Adela . . . Mary. Some I recognized, some I had never heard before.

And finally, I came upon a small white piece of paper that had been torn and folded into a six-by-six square. My mother had written along the top: "I am finally ready to tell my story. I'm going to call it *Why Was I Born?*"

I settled back against the bed and began to read.

PART ONE
Odessa, Russia

Odessa was founded in 1794 by Catherine the Great. The city was scouted by a Neapolitan mercenary, named by a Russian empress, governed by her one-eyed secret husband, and built by two exiled French noblemen. Odessa was created and developed out of nothing but a vast, flat landscape and the Black Sea.

Odessa is where Francine's story begins.

David

Nicholas

Chapter 1

Lewis and Edith
Odessa, 1867

The city center of Odessa was energetic, frenetic, and bustling with the business of trade, shipping, and exchange. Horse-drawn carriages busily passed up and down the decaying streets as families performed their daily routines. As the wooden carriages travelled over the wide, cobbled streets, clouds of dust billowed into the air.

Outside the center, the streets were lined with beautiful swanlike branches of acacia trees providing shade for the citizenry of Odessa. The acacias' perfectly shaped yellow and white blossoms whiffed to the heavens. Beyond the trees, rows of houses, each plastered in vibrant colors, reflected sunlight from the glistening water of the Black Sea.

July 20, 1867 dawned a typical warm summer day. A special sense of excitement and a feeling of hope filled the yellow stucco two-story house where Lewis and Edith Kaufmann lived. The couple had been married for three glorious years and prayed they would be blessed with a large family. But as each year passed, Lewis and Edith worried they might never have a child.

The Jewish Sabbath began Friday evening when the sun went down, signifying a day of prayer, rest, and time spent with family. However, for the Kaufmanns, today was far from typical. Edith Kaufmann had endured a restless night and was certain that today would be their mitzvah. Today, Lewis and Edith would be blessed with life's most precious gift, their firstborn child.

Edith sat in a floral-patterned wing chair, huddled in the corner of their bedroom. With her hands supporting her enlarged belly, she anxiously waited for the sun to rise. She needed to get up and walk around the small room. As she placed her hands on the carved wooden frame of the chair, she supported her awkwardly shaped form. She slowly got up, steadied her swollen feet, and began pacing back and forth across the room. The wooden floorboards creaked with each step. Edith did not want to awaken her husband, but there was no way for her to lighten her gait.

When the cramping began to intensify, Edith gingerly sat down on the edge of their marital bed. She looked over to Lewis sleeping peacefully, placed her hand on his arm, and called out his name.

"Lewis."

At first he did not respond. Then Edith spoke a bit louder and lovingly nudged him. Lewis slowly opened his eyes. He focused and saw Edith sitting on the bed.

"What is it my dear?" asked Lewis.

"I think it is time for you to get Bashra."

Lewis gasped. "Are you sure?" Before Edith could reply, he stammered, "Of course. I'll go right now!"

Lewis started to head out the door when he heard Edith's hearty laugh. "Lewis, you need to get out of your nightshirt and get dressed."

Bashra Lebovitz lived about one kilometer from the Kaufmann home. Lewis thought about running to her house, then realized he would exhaust himself before he was a quarter of the way. Instead, he went behind the house to the small stable and hitched his horse to the covered carriage. Lewis knew Bashra would be at home on this Sabbath unless, of course, she was busy delivering another new life.

When he arrived at the small, faded, blue house, he banged on the door shouting, "Bashra, Bashra, Edith has sent me. It is time, it's time."

With one swift move the door opened and Bashra pulled

Lewis into the kitchen. "Is she sure?" Bashra asked. "This is her first time and she might just be anxious."

"She is certain."

"Then take this stack of clean cloths and my boiling pots. I'll be right back." Bashra left Lewis at the door while she collected her birthing smock and medicinal herbs. Then she stuffed everything into her satchel.

While Lewis waited, he grew more and more nervous until he was dizzy with fear and anticipation. Edith had already suffered two miscarriages, and he did not think he could bear the pain of a third. He stepped outside to get some fresh air as the front door swung open and Bashra exclaimed, "*Poydem, poydem!* Let's go!"

Arriving home, Lewis heard Edith moaning. He cringed each time he heard her whine. Bashra pointed with her index finger and demanded, "You stay here, Lewis. Give me my towels and my bag." She glared at him. "Edith will be fine."

Lewis paced back and forth, flexing and stretching his limbs. He wanted to comfort Edith, but knew he could not bear to see his wife in pain. His job was to be focused and stay calm. He went outside, sat down on the front step, cupped his hands over his eyes, and began to pray. Tears of joy and worry trickled down his face as Bashra came down the stairs.

"Lewis, it will be many hours, possibly the entire day before your child will appear. Why don't you go to the synagogue and pray? All the men will be there, wondering where you are."

The tone in her voice was firm and unyielding. "Besides," she added. "Edith does not want you to hear her groans! Go along now. I will take good care of her."

Lewis nodded his head in agreement and left for the synagogue. As he walked numbly along the streets, immersed in deep thought, he hadn't even realized he had walked right past his destination.

Images of the past and thoughts of the future rapidly flowed through his mind. He thought about the first time he met Edith. He remembered that April day with perfect clarity. It was shortly before his Bar Mitzvah. He had just turned thirteen. In the Jewish tradition, he was now considered a man. His only thoughts were of the new responsibilities and duties he would be assuming not only to his family, but also to his faith. Falling in love and getting married one day was a distant and formless image.

But all that changed in an instant. Lewis had been rehearsing his Torah reading from the pulpit when he looked up and saw the shadow of a young girl and an elderly man standing under the entry threshold. The man was at least six feet tall and wore a black top hat that added a few more inches to his commanding stature. The pair walked into the sacred vestibule of the temple.

The man took his hat off, revealing a beautiful, beaded kippah, the traditional Jewish brimless cap. Then he proceeded towards the pulpit. Lewis had never seen this man before, but it was obvious that Rabbi Jacobsky knew him well. The two men embraced, taking turns kissing the other's cheek.

"Doron, my brother, what brings you here all the way from Vienna?"

"I had some business in Yalta and decided to bring my daughter Edith with me. I wanted her to have a special birthday celebration in your beautiful city. She is turning eleven in a few weeks." Doron pointed toward the back of the synagogue where Edith dutifully stood.

The sun crept through the open wood door and its rays seemed to turn Edith's blonde hair to gold. Looking into Edith's eyes made Lewis' heart beat faster. He was breathless. His hands trembled ever so slightly. He gingerly walked toward her. She was so beautiful. Her deep, blue eyes glistened as she turned her head towards him.

"Lewis, this is my niece, Edith," the rabbi said. "Would you mind stopping your rehearsal and taking her for a walk? My brother and I have so much to talk about and catch up on."

Lewis could barely speak. "How do you do, Edith? I am honored to meet you."

Edith turned her head shyly towards the floor. "I am honored to meet you, too." She reached out her hand and placed it in his. Lewis took a deep breath. His heart was pounding. A sense of calm enveloped his soul.

Lewis looked into Edith's eyes and asked, "Would you like to take a walk?"

"Yes. I would like that very much," replied Edith.

"Is this your first time in Odessa?" Lewis asked.

"No. I have been coming to Odessa with my father for several years now," Edith said with a smile. "Odessa is so beautiful. Have you ever been to Vienna?"

"I have not," Lewis replied.

"You will definitely have to come. Vienna is a magnificent city. I'm sure you will love it."

The two of them spoke for several hours as they walked in the spring sunshine. When it was time for Edith to leave, Lewis asked shyly, "Would it be all right for us to correspond from time to time?"

"Yes. I would like that," Edith replied, just as shyly.

Over the next four years, as Lewis and Edith returned to their daily lives, the young couple corresponded on a fairly regular basis. Every time Doron traveled to Odessa, his beautiful daughter accompanied him. With each encounter, the young couple's love for each other grew stronger, and these became the most important moments in their lives.

During those years, Edith blossomed into a flower of grace and beauty. Her body was slender, firm, and alluring. Her sunlit, golden blond hair fell past the nape of her neck like floating clouds hovering over the horizon. Her skin was soft as a hummingbird's feather and her eyes were a subtle and exquisite blue.

When she looked at Lewis, there was no denying the love they shared.

Lewis was made powerless by his love for Edith. At the end of each day, he memorialized his thoughts of her in his journal. Some nights he would fall asleep with his head resting on his wooden desk, with pen in hand. Each night, as daylight turned into darkness, Lewis imagined the life he and Edith would soon be sharing.

Finally, that joyous day arrived. Lewis stood shaking at the front of the newly completed synagogue as the rabbi walked through a side door and took his place behind the pulpit. All eyes turned toward the back door as Edith walked steadily down the aisle. She wore a simple white satin gown with long sleeves and was clutching a bouquet of acacia blossoms.

As Edith and Lewis stood underneath the chuppah, the canopy where Jewish marriages are performed, Lewis felt himself growing dizzy with joy. He whispered under his breath, "And now my life with Edith truly begins."

As the rabbi recited the traditional prayers, Lewis and Edith stared into each other's eyes. After the service, the blissful couple celebrated their marriage with family and friends. Wine was poured freely into crystal glasses and a banquet of food was meticulously placed on several round tables. Hours later, when the festivities came to an end, Edith and Lewis went back to their new home and consummated their love.

Now, three years later, Lewis waited with anticipation for their child to be born. The infant entered the world a few minutes before midnight on Saturday evening. It was a complicated and painful delivery. The baby's first cry was piercing and strong. After Bashra cleaned up the infant, she placed him into Edith's arms and went downstairs.

"Lewis, come meet your son."

They were the most glorious words Lewis had ever heard.

"A son!" Lewis babbled. "Is he healthy? How is Edith?"

Without waiting for answers, he ran up the hallway stairs, slowing as he passed into the dimly-lit bedroom. He saw his son, swaddled in a blue and white blanket as Edith was placing the baby up to her breast. Lewis bent down and kissed his son on his head, then kissed his wife on her lips. She opened the blanket ever so slightly, and Lewis kvelled with pride and pleasure at his first glimpse of his baby boy. They would name him David.

David's dewy skin was the color of the first snow of winter. He had a full head of light brown hair and his hands appeared unusually large for such a small bundle of life. His toes curled tightly into a ball when he cried out for his mother's milk. When he opened his eyes, Lewis saw they gleamed a deep, dark blue. David had his mother's eyes. Most surprising, David smelled like the gentle fragrance of the acacia blossoms.

As Lewis sat beside his wife, his dreams for his son floated in and out of his head. What would the future hold for this precious boy? Would his son want to take over his mercantile store? Or, maybe David would take a different path and become a musician, an engineer, or a doctor.

Whatever his path, Lewis prayed that David's life would be full of love and prosperity, and free of hatred and judgment. He prayed God would bless him with many more children, but that prayer would remain unanswered. Edith and Lewis would never have another child.

For Lewis, life took on a richer new rhythm. He spent the mornings with Edith and David, and at ten o'clock, he would punctually walk to his mercantile store. He would spend the rest of the day selling his beautifully handcrafted violins and Edith's custom designed fur coats.

Edith spent her days strolling through town, then taking David to the mercantile. While David napped in his small cradle, Edith was able to continue designing her coats made from the pelts of the silver fox. Edith's fur coats were well known throughout Odessa, and word of her designs was starting to spread through other parts of Russia as well. It was a joyous time for the Kaufmann family.

Thirty-five days later, the town buzzed with excitement and anticipation. The American steamer, *Quaker City,* was due to arrive in a few weeks' time. Mark Twain, the famous American novelist, was reportedly on board. It was rumored that the Tsar planned to personally greet the arriving celebrity and passengers.

As the weeks went by, the happy furor in the town grew stronger every day. The townspeople made long-needed repairs to the outsides of their stucco houses. Acacia trees were pruned, and colorful fresh plantings were meticulously placed throughout the city.

The cobbled streets were repaired, and the holes made by the horses' hoofs and carriage wheels were filled. Workers blazed a new walking path toward the famous stone stairway etched out of the landscape, and more wooden barrels for ice cream were placed along the streets. The town sparkled and the townspeople bustled with anticipation and pride.

Then, on August 25, 1867, the *Quaker City* steamed into port. It was a glistening summer day, and the sky was a light turquoise. Standing at the pier, Lewis watched Mark Twain step onto Odessa's soil at the end of his twenty-four-hour Black Sea crossing. The men, women, and children of Odessa clapped and cheered as Twain disembarked.

Lewis had heard that one of the main reasons Twain took this voyage was to see Odessa's famous stone staircase, built in 1841, connecting the seaport to the city center. This magnificent cascade of stone steps was one of the most brilliant staircases in the world. After disembarking the ship, Twain walked to the famous steps. As he approached the staircase, he stared in disbelief at the infinite number of stairs that looked as if they led to the heavens.

When Twain reached the very top of the staircase, he looked down toward the sea and scanned the streets below. The two-hundred steps, which he had just climbed, seemed to have vanished. "What an engineering and architectural marvel," was his comment.

As Twain continued his exploration through the city streets, he observed the vibrant businesses and the beautiful display of goods from local merchants. He also saw and sampled sweet wine being sold in wooden buckets. Then he tasted refreshing ice cream flavored with honey from the barrels.

The chatter in town that Alexander II would be greeting Twain in Odessa turned out to be false. Instead, the Tsar sent his twenty-two-year-old son, Alexander III, in his place. Lewis was delighted by the change of plans.

Alexander III had been to Odessa with his father numerous times over the years and during those trips, the Tsar and his son, along with their entourage, had often visited the Kaufmann mercantile store. It was common for the Tsar to select several handcrafted violins as well as other instruments and take them back to St. Petersburg. On several occasions, Alexander had even asked Lewis to play a sonata on the violin.

This latest visit with Mark Twain turned out to be the most memorable of all. Twain wandered around the shop marveling at the handcrafted instruments and beautiful fur coats. Then Lewis escorted Alexander and Twain toward the back of the store. There he proudly displayed the hides from the silver fox. He would be using those pelts to make the fur coats the Tsar recently requested for the royal family.

"My father will be very pleased with these skins. They are magnificent," Alexander said with a smile.

"I'm glad you approve. My wife is almost finished with the design, and I will begin working on the coats very shortly."

While Alexander browsed through the store, he saw Edith sitting at her desk with David in her arms.

"What a beautiful child," Alexander said. "What is his name?"

"David," Edith said shyly.

"May I hold him?" Alexander asked.

"*Da*, yes," she replied.

Edith reluctantly put David in Alexander's arms. No one except Lewis and herself, and of course Bashra, had ever held her son.

Alexander smiled down at the baby boy. "My wife, Minnie, and I are praying that we too will be given a son. May I bless David?"

"We would be honored," Lewis answered.

Alexander kissed David and gently placed him back in Edith's arms.

"*Spasibo.* Thank you," Alexander said.

"*Eto moya chest.* It is my honor," replied Edith proudly.

When Alexander and Twain left the store, Edith and Lewis looked in each other's eyes.

"One day, I will tell David about the day the famous writer Mark Twain and the future Tsar of Russia came into our store when he was just five weeks old," said Lewis. "I will describe to our son how Alexander cradled him in his large muscular arms. I will share with him the kindness and gentleness Alexander showed as he looked into David's eyes. We will always remember this day, Edith."

At first, Edith was too moved to speak, but then she said, "Yes, we will."

What neither family knew at the time, was that eight months later, Nicholas II would be born, and the two boys, David and Nicholas, would one day foster a unique friendship that would connect the Kaufmanns and the Romanovs for years to come.

Mark Twain loved the city of Odessa. One of the more interesting comments Twain wrote during his visit was:

The many mercantile stores in this beautiful city had an interesting mix of goods. It was quite amusing because one sold fur coats and also sold violins. And if you bought a violin, you had to buy three furs. What I also saw was that the streets were filled with men, women, and children. Some were Italians. Others were Greeks. Many were Jews. But they were all Ukrainians and Russians. I felt completely at home when I visited Odessa.

Twain had wanted to spend as much time as possible in Odessa, but his trip was suddenly cut short when he was told that the Tsar wanted to meet him and the other Americans at his palace in Yalta. Hearing this news, Twain and the rest of the American passengers hurried back to the ship.

When the *Quaker City* steamed out of port, the townspeople watched the ship move farther and farther toward the horizon until the remaining speck of what was the stern of the steamer disappeared.

Lewis followed the news about Twain's journey. Over the next couple of weeks, the paper reported more than a thousand Russian citizens had rushed toward the harbor to greet the passengers onboard. When the *Quaker City* set anchor in Yalta, the enthusiastic and roaring crowds jostled for position to view the Americans departing from the ship.

"Welcome," they shouted.

The crowd cheered as the applause reverberated through the cobblestone streets. As the passengers disembarked, rows of four-wheeled, covered carriages waited to take the Americans to the Emperor's summer palace in Livadia. The Tsar had built the palace six years earlier as a gift to his wife, Marie.

Anticipating his meeting with the Emperor, Twain prepared a short speech for the Tsar. He completed his narrative shortly before the ship set anchor. Twain's speech was hand-delivered to the Emperor with the hope that he would be permitted to read his written greeting. Much to Twain's pleasure, his request was granted.

Twain, who wrote with ease, humor, wit, and brilliance, was

overheard expressing anxiety about addressing the Tsar of Russia. But as he walked into the main foyer of the palace, with his fellow passengers standing behind him, his jitters appeared to have vanished:

> *To His Imperial Majesty: Alexander II, Emperor of Russia: We, a handful of citizens of the United States—have no excuse for presenting ourselves before your Majesty, save a desire to offer our grateful acknowledgements to the Lord of a Realm which, through good and through evil report, has been the steadfast friend of our Native Land.*
>
> *We could not presume thus to present ourselves did we not know that the words we speak and the sentiments we utter, reflect the thoughts and feelings of all our countrymen: from the green hills of New England to the snowy peaks of the far Pacific. Though few in number, we utter the voice of a Nation.*

"*Spasibo*. Thank you, Mr. Twain. I would like to personally tour you and my American guests around the palace," said the Tsar.

"We would be honored," replied Twain.

Inside the palace, the walls were a soft white with ornate cornices and high, curved, plastered ceilings. The arched floor-to-ceiling windows were adorned with off-white and gold satin draperies, reflecting the sunlight that brightened the furnished interiors. The numerous formal rooms throughout the residence displayed exquisite large watercolors painted by world-renowned artists. The Tsar enthusiastically described the frequent galas and festivals that were celebrated on the black and gold marble floors.

After the tour, the Tsar invited everyone for breakfast in one of the many elaborate dining rooms. He served lemon tea and *sushka*, a sweet-tasting cracker, to his guests.

When Mark Twain returned to America, he was bombarded

with questions about the Tsar. "What was he like?" asked re-porters.

"He was very tall and spare, and a determined-looking man, though a very pleasant looking one, nevertheless. It is easy to see that he is kind and affectionate. There is something very noble in his expression when his cap is off," Twain explained.

What Twain could not know at the time, was that over the next fifty years, thousands and thousands of the men, women, and children from Odessa would call themselves Americans. David Kaufmann, the infant boy Mark Twain saw in Lewis Kaufmann's shop that summer day in 1867, would be one of them.

Chapter 2

Nicholas II
St. Petersburg, May 1868

It had been brutally cold over the last couple of months with record levels of snowfall. Even though it was May, winter was still lurking through the clouds. However, the weather did not deter the rugged and determined people of St. Petersburg. Crowds of Russian men, women and children huddled in groups, anxiously awaiting the impending birth of the Tsar's first grandchild.

Alexander III and his wife Maria, whom he affectionately called Minnie, were staying at their palace in Tsarskoye Selo near St. Petersburg. Maria's personal doctor and her midwife had been at Maria's side for the last three days. The infant had been expected to arrive several weeks earlier. Today, however, there was serious chatter that the infant would be born before the day's end.

Finally, church bells rang joyously throughout the city as the newest Romanov made a vociferous and boisterous entrance. A celebratory roar from the Russian citizens erupted throughout the streets.

"*Welkam, welkam,*" cheered the crowd. A few minutes later, the official announcement was made. "It is a boy. It's a boy."

Alexander quietly walked into his wife's chambers and stared at the tiny infant. The baby was slight in size. His hands and feet were small, even for an infant. He had a full head of brown hair, the color of his mother's. His eyes were a deep dark blue, the shade of the sea at dusk.

Maria handed the infant to her husband. "I give you a son named in your brother's image."

Alexander looked into his son's eyes and whispered, "Nicholas, my beloved son. One day you will be the Tsar of Russia."

Chapter 3

Lewis and Edith
Odessa, 1868

When the news reached Odessa that baby Nicholas had been born, the sound of roars and clapping reverberated through the stucco walls of the village houses. The church bells rang five times, which meant the newest Romanov was a male. Alexander III and his wife had a son.

The ensuing yelling, clapping, and merriment seeped through the cracked walls and awakened Lewis. Groggily, he rubbed his eyes.

"Has the Empress given birth?"

"Yes. And the baby is a boy."

Lewis smiled. "Remember when Alexander came to Odessa and held David in his arms? He said that he too was praying for a son. Now that his prayers have been answered, I wonder if he will name him Nicholas, after Alexander's brother."

"I do remember that," Edith said as she gazed down at her baby's drooping eyes while he sucked her abundant milk. "What a loving tribute that would be," she mused.

Lewis sat upright. "Edith, I am going to open the store early today in celebration. Not only is this a good day for the royal family, it is also a good day for Russia." Edith smiled in agreement as Lewis kissed David on his forehead.

Not much changed in Odessa over the next thirteen years. The seaport remained vibrant with shipping and trade. Another primary school was built and a small Jewish temple had been recently completed near the outskirts of town.

The one thing that had changed significantly was that more

families began immigrating to England, Spain, and the United States. Those who went to America usually had relatives sponsoring their family members.

Lewis Kaufmann had no desire to leave his homeland. His children were thriving and his store was prosperous. Many people from outside of Odessa would come to the mercantile just to purchase one of Lewis's violins or furs from the silver fox.

Over the next thirteen years, Alexander continued to come back to Odessa during his travels through the Russian Empire. On those visits, Lewis and Alexander developed a friendship that neither would have ever expected.

Their love for music created a strong and mutual bond. Whenever Alexander visited the Kaufmann mercantile store, the two men would pick up their violins and play a symphony of Beethoven, Vivaldi, or Strauss. As the music drifted, the notes floated into the air. During those years, their friendship behind the hand-carved doors created an unspeakable bond between them.

As Nicholas got older, Alexander would bring his son with him. Now, David and Nicholas followed suit by fostering their own relationship. The young men swam in the Black Sea. They climbed the stone staircase and ate ice cream out of the wooden barrels. They corresponded often, and always looked forward to seeing each other. The Romanov family continued to visit Odessa, and David and Nicholas's friendship continued to thrive.

David, now almost thirteen, was turning into a man. He was doing well in school and looked forward to helping his father in the mercantile. His Hebrew lessons were going well and he was excited about his upcoming Bar Mitzvah.

Chapter 4

Alexander II
St. Petersburg, March 13, 1881

Sunday morning was always a lazy day for Lewis. Edith, however, was up extra early preparing an elaborate breakfast of eggs, biscuits, and fresh strawberry jam. Lewis smelled the aromas of the morning meal as he walked into his son's room. David, now fourteen, was propped up, reading in bed. As the door creaked upon, David closed his book.

"David, I need you to help me in the store today. It shouldn't take too long," said Lewis. "Let's have breakfast and get our chores done first. We can go later this afternoon. Looks like today is going to be a nice day."

"Sure, Father," David replied.

At around three-thirty, as Lewis and David were just about to walk into the shop, they could see something was very wrong. Crowds of people were walking briskly, yelling and crying.

"Tsar Alexander II is dead. He was assassinated! He was assassinated! Oh my God!"

"Father, what's happening?" David yelled out. He stood motionless as his father turned and locked the shop's front door.

"David, we need to go home now," Lewis said quietly. David nodded, not saying a word.

Lewis was numb. As they walked home in silence, he reflected back to that summer day in 1867 when Alexander III and Mark Twain had walked into his shop. Lewis would never forget how Alexander had held David in his enormous arms and kissed him on the top of his head. Now the torch would be passed on to him. Alexander III would now be Russia's Tsar.

Lewis didn't realize he was crying. He quickly wiped his

eyes and looked down. He whispered, "the Tsar was a decent man." Lewis began to pray, not only for the Romanovs, but also for his own family.

The news of the Tsar's death sent shock waves throughout Russia. As the official written announcement began trickling into the bustling town of Odessa, a thick, black cloud of despair loomed over the seaport. The gruesome and unimaginable details of the assassination were posted in St. Petersburg Square, and notices were published throughout the country for all Russians to read:

It was a typical Sunday morning for the Tsar. His routine was to travel by carriage to the Mikhailovsky Manege for the military roll call. But on this fateful Sunday morning, a bomb was thrown at the carriage, killing one of the Tsar's Cossacks. The Tsar was mortally injured and his body brutally mutilated. He was immediately taken to the Winter Palace in St. Petersburg where he was given communion and last rites before dying later that day.

The assassins were identified as Nikolai Rysakov, a twenty-year-old revolutionary member of the left-wing radical organization Narodnaya Volya. The other two bombers involved in the assassination were Hryniewiecki and Yemelyanov. The Tsar, who was born on April 29, 1818, was just shy of sixty-three years old when he died. He had ruled Russia for twenty-six years.

Lewis's unspoken fear and dread was that this horrific tragedy would change Alexander forever. How could it not? He could not imagine the pain, terror, and anger Alexander must be feeling. Lewis also feared that Alexander's grief and rage would now set the tone for his reign and he worried what would happen next. He hoped his concerns would prove to be baseless and untrue.

Lewis went to the synagogue to pray and David accompanied him. As the two were about to enter the temple, David asked anxiously, "Father, what is going to happen now?"

"Alexander will take over his father's position as the next Tsar," Lewis said, trying to sound confident. "Do not worry, David. He is a good man. Everything will be fine." Lewis heard the waver of trepidation in his own voice.

"Let's light a candle for the Romanov family. We need to pray God will take away some of the pain and help his heart heal," Lewis said softly.

When they got home, Lewis went for a walk across town to the famous steps, remembering with longing when Mark Twain had climbed them. He sat down on a stone ledge and put his hands over his eyes. Fear and heartbreak overcame him, and he allowed himself to cry.

As Lewis sat at the top of the staircase, he looked back toward town and began reflecting on the fallen Tsar. What a man he had been. He had done so much for his people. No wonder he had been given the moniker "Alexander the Liberator."

The Tsar had emancipated the serfs and abolished capital punishment. He had reorganized the courts and created elections for local judges, as well as implementing many other social and progressive changes for all Russians.

Sadly, many of those changes had angered a significant part of the population, which had fueled many assassination attempts over the years. The Tsar had evaded the bullets in the past, but this time his luck had run out.

Over the following days, those who witnessed the horror told their accounts. The chief of police and the chief of the Emperor's guards, who were in the sleigh behind the Emperor's carriage, gave graphic accounts of the March 13 attack.

I was deafened by the new explosion, then burned, wounded, and thrown to the ground. Suddenly, amid the smoke and snowy fog, I heard His Majesty's weak voice cry, "Help!" Gathering what strength I had, I jumped up and rushed to the Emperor. His

Majesty was half-laying, half-sitting, leaning on his right arm. Thinking he was merely wounded heavily, I tried to lift him, but the Tsar's legs were shattered, and the blood poured out of them. Twenty people, with wounds of varying degree, lay on the sidewalk and on the street. Some managed to stand, others to crawl, while still others tried to get out from beneath bodies that had fallen on them. Through the snow, debris, and blood, you could see fragments of clothing and bloody chunks of human flesh. The Tsar, who was bleeding to death, was holding on for dear life. He was swiftly put on one of the sleighs and taken to the Winter Palace. His legs were torn away from his body, his stomach was ripped open, and his face was mutilated beyond recognition.

On March 15, 1881, at age thirty-six, a grief–stricken Alexander III ascended the throne. As the firstborn male, Nicholas II, became "Tsarevitch," heir apparent to the throne.

The royal family moved into the Winter Palace in Gatchina. Fearing a terrorist attack against him and his family, Alexander delayed his coronation. With a heavy heart, Alexander III was crowned in Moscow on May 15, 1883, a date he preferred to forget rather than celebrate. Alexander's heart was broken. His anger, grief, and pain were immeasurable. He wrote in his journal, "I do not consider that day a holiday and do not accept any congratulations."

The Empress also described the coronation in a letter to her mother.

On those days, we morally experienced such strong inner excitement, that it seemed that an eternity had passed. I felt just like a sacrificial lamb. Sasha, genuflecting, read a wonderful prayer, and his voice was completely calm and strong. Everyone wailed, and this was so solemn, stirring, and at the same time, so touching! For me, this was the same feeling you experience immediately after giving birth; that is the only thing I can compare it to. I regarded it all as more like a production of one of Wagner's operas, in which we were playing the main roles.

Something happened to Alexander the day his father was murdered. He was a changed man, a man he himself could hardly recognize. Once a gentle lion, he had turned into a man of cold steel. Every minute of every day he feared for his life and the lives of his family. He carried a monstrous burden, a burden that ate away a piece of his soul with every breath he took.

In Odessa, shortly after the assassination, Lewis's fears came true. At first there had been innuendos that a Jew was behind the Emperor's assassination. This proved to be completely false, but the mere suggestion propelled a wave of anti-Jewish riots throughout the Russian Empire.

Lewis knew that the Jews in Odessa were proud people. They were resilient. They had dealt with hatred and fear for their entire lives. Lewis wasn't under any illusion about the blame placed at the feet of the Jewish people. He was concerned and saddened by the riots. He prayed no one would be injured or killed. He sat down at the kitchen table as Edith handed him a cup of tea.

"Lewis, are we going to be alright?" she asked him.

"Yes. Do not worry. Alexander is a good man," he replied. "He will follow in his father's footsteps and that is a good thing. This is a sad time for all of us. The Tsar was a good and decent man."

Edith turned and walked toward the sink. She didn't want her husband to see her tears.

Lewis walked over to his wife, wiped her tears, and stroked her hair. "Edith, we have each other. We have our son. He is healthy. Do not worry. We will face all our challenges together. I will always take care of you and David."

Chapter 5

Alexander III
St. Petersburg, 1882

In St. Petersburg, the murderers who killed the Tsar were captured and publicly hanged. They proudly admitted that they were members of the revolutionary group called the People's Will, and Alexander executed all those who were directly or even remotely responsible for his father's death. This included the leaders of all terrorist revolutionary groups throughout Russia.

Alexander's revenge did not end there. Horrified and enraged by his father's assassination, he introduced some harsh security measures to fight terror. He empowered the police to enhance stronghold tactics and increased censorship of the press. He went after the liberal People's Will group, obliterating any remnants of its membership and affiliations. The Tsar, wretchedly furious and unbridled, blamed all dissidents for creating an atmosphere of unrest and fear. Leaving no group untouched by his wrath, he eventually turned his focus on the Jews.

When riots broke out in primarily Jewish cities throughout Russia, Alexander's answer to the unrest was to silence the crowds and to corral the masses. He did this by instituting powerful and brutal restrictions called the May Laws, specifically directed toward all Russians of the Jewish faith.

The May Laws of May 15, 1882, stated that Jews could live only within towns and no longer within villages or in the countryside. Jews living in villages had to leave their homes immediately and move into segregated areas. Furthermore, Jews could not receive mortgages, hold leases, or manage any land outside of town. Jews were also restricted from operating any businesses on Sundays or on Christian holidays.

A number of other laws were also soon implemented. These imposed strict quotas on the numbers of Jews who could study in high schools and universities. Jews who were not already in universities were barred from even applying. Limits were also placed on the numbers of Jews who could work as doctors and lawyers. Many Jews were expelled from their government jobs.

The May Laws of 1882 sent shock waves throughout the Russian Empire for all Russian Jews. Odessa and Kiev felt the waves of hatred and fear the most. Russian Jews began reassessing their future and the safety of their families. Many began to flee.

Lewis was concerned but remained resolute. He would not leave his home. He would not leave his family and friends. Odessa was his home, and he would never leave!

Chapter 6

David
Odessa, 1882

Lewis could not get the thought of Alexander out of his head. It was so difficult trying to reconcile the image of a cold and frightening monarch with the gentle music-loving man he had known over the last fifteen years.

He remembered those many afternoons when Alexander would come into the shop with his entourage while his Royal Guards watched the front door. During those visits, the two men discovered their shared love for music. Lewis was an accomplished violinist and Alexander was an accomplished musician who loved playing the French horn. Over the years, when Alexander would return to the mercantile, he would always pick out several instruments. The two men would play beautiful music inside the cracked walls of the shop.

Like fathers, like sons, David and Nicholas also fostered their own friendship over the years. Since they were so close in age, they had many things to talk about and many things to share. Their correspondence with each other became a regular and routine ritual.

Over the last several years, while the Tsar had been conducting official business elsewhere in the region, Nicholas would travel to Odessa accompanied by several Royal Guards. He would always visit Kaufmann's mercantile store and spend time with David. The two young men would spend the entire day together climbing the famous stone steps at the end of town, sharing stories about their lives and dreams. On many occasions, Nicholas and David would listen to Lewis play his violin while Edith accompanied her husband on the piano.

As the years passed and the two boys grew into men, David and Nicholas looked forward to hearing about each other's adventures. At the time, neither father objected to their son's friendship.

Lewis knew that his relationship with Alexander would now change significantly. He knew and understood how hatred and grief could change a man to the point of being almost unrecognizable. The one unanswered question, which would play over and over again in Lewis's head, was whether his friendship with Alexander would now be a blessing or would it be a curse. Lewis prayed it would be the former, but deep in his heart he knew that it would more than likely end up being the latter.

At fifteen, David had grown into a strong, intelligent, well-educated young man. He understood the repercussions and consequences of the Tsar's assassination. He also understood the changes that might occur to his beloved homeland, especially in towns like Odessa where there was a large Jewish community. As an optimistic and overly confident young man, he was certain he and his family would be fine, and that his family's business would continue to thrive.

Lewis did not share the same optimistic view. He knew, in the cavern of his heart, that hard times were looming for them. He also knew that difficult decisions would need to be made, not just for his family and friends, but also for businesses, communities, schools, and places of worship. These were precarious times. Nothing was certain. Nothing could be taken for granted. Circumstances had changed dramatically, and now there was much fear and uncertainty throughout Odessa. Lewis also knew he could not ignore that fear, as uncertainty bred hate and blame.

Over the next several weeks, as more and more news of the Tsar's assassination arrived and the gruesome details began to unfold, David became increasingly concerned about Nicholas. He couldn't begin to comprehend the pain and grief Nicholas and the entire Romanov family was dealing with. David wondered whether his friendship with Nicholas would or could ever be the same again. It was not something he felt comfortable talking about. He kept his thoughts to himself and would talk to his father about it when the time was right.

Things started changing rather quickly in Odessa after the May Laws were enacted. Many families found themselves making very difficult decisions to ensure their future. Lewis and Edith knew that they needed to guarantee David's future. It was time to put words into action.

The single most important decision that Lewis had to make was decided in the Kaufmann home around the wooden dining room table, a table Lewis had carved by hand as an anniversary present for Edith. Lewis and Edith were alone in the house when he decided to bring up the subject. Lewis slowly approached his wife who was sitting next to the window, knitting.

"Edith, please sit at the table with me," he said.

She looked anxious. "Are you hungry? Can I fix you something?"

Heavily, he shook his head. "We need to talk. We need to talk about David's future."

Edith looked away. Lewis took her hand in his.

"Edith, we have to make a very important decision. I know this decision will break our hearts. I have given this much thought and I believe that this is necessary for our son's future. We need to send David away to Vienna. He will live with your parents and continue his education. We will know that he will be safe."

"How will we live through this?" she whispered as she began to sob.

"*Mit got 'hilf.* With God's help," replied Lewis.

It was a decision that tore through Edith and Lewis's hearts and ripped through their souls. David was their only child. But they both knew it was the only decision they could make.

When David returned home later that night, he came into the dining room and saw his parents sitting at the table, pale and still.

"What's wrong with Mother?" he demanded.

"Sit down, son," Lewis told him heavily. "Your mother and I have something to tell you."

David could not sleep that night. He kept replaying the scene with his parents over and over in his mind and felt washed by tides of conflicting emotions. He was not unhappy at the thought of living with his grandparents. They were generous and interesting. His *bubbe*, Penelope, was an artist, and his *zayde*, Ephraim, was a lawyer. It would be a safe and stimulating life being with them. But on the other hand, he was a man now, and he wanted to stand shoulder to shoulder with the other men in his town, helping them to fight injustice. More importantly, he did not want to leave his mother and father.

David's thoughts continued in an uneasy swirl, making him feel light-headed and sick. He thought about Vienna and all the adventures he could experience there. He recognized this chance for the generous gift it was. How could he turn it down? He had always wanted to be an engineer, and now he would be able to achieve that goal. His world was suddenly expanding with end-less possibilities.

But as the night wore on, he felt guiltier and guiltier. What if the political situation worsened and his parents were in danger? He could not ignore or erase everyone's concerns about the changes and restrictions that were being imposed on the Jews. Living in Vienna, he might not be able to get to them in time. He tried not to think about all the different scenarios that could occur during his absence and prayed that his parents would be safe.

No, he could not be so selfish. His mind was made up. He could not leave. He was his parents' only child and it was his re-sponsibility and his honor to take care of them. He would not abandon them, no matter what the cost. David was finally able to get to sleep.

Early the next morning, he went downstairs to talk to his father. He sat in his usual place at the table, waiting for his father to begin speaking. Lewis hesitated for a moment, then said, "David, you will be travelling to Vienna to continue your education."

David wanted to interrupt his father but knew better of that. He listened intently as his father laid out the details of his upcoming journey.

"You will be living with your grandparents," Edith interjected.

David loved his *bubbe* and his *zayde* but he also knew this was a fight he would never win. His father had decided this was what needed to be done and there would be no further discussion. He knew what his parents' motives were; they wanted him to have a secure future. He realized that this was an opportunity he could not refuse. This was a gift, a very precious gift. He would go to the university, study hard, and make his parents proud.

Then David's thoughts shifted to his university studies and his temporary home. He thoroughly enjoyed learning about mechanics and was very accomplished in mathematics and equations. His world was expanding with endless possibilities for a bright future.

As the moments and hours passed, David felt guiltier and guiltier about the excitement he was feeling. He knew he needed to settle down and control his emotions and his thoughts. When he refocused, he quickly changed his mind—*again*. There was only one right decision; he could not leave his parents. He was too worried about their wellbeing and safety. He was their only child. It was his responsibility to take care of them. He would not leave them, no matter what the cost. David walked back downstairs to talk to his father.

"Father, thank you for this opportunity. I know you are doing this for me out of love, but I will not leave you and mother. It's my responsibility to be here for you and I will not shy away from that, no matter what the sacrifice."

Color crept into Lewis's face. He turned away from his son. He was proud of David for his unselfishness and courage. But this was not David's decision to make. There would be no further discussion. Lewis spoke sternly.

"David. This conversation is over. You are going to Vienna. You will not speak another word about my decision. Do you understand?"

Reluctantly, David answered, "Yes, Father. Can I be excused?"

"Of course," Edith replied

David went to his room. He sat down at the small desk in his bedroom and pulled out his writing pad. He dipped the pen Nicholas had given him for his thirteenth birthday into the inkwell and began writing Nicolas a short note:

My friend,
My parents are sending me to Vienna to study at the university now that the May Laws forbid me from pursuing my education here in Odessa. I will be living with my grandparents and leaving my home and my family. How can something like this happen? I know you have suffered a terrible loss, but to . . .

David stopped writing. He held the letter in his hand and ripped it into small pieces. He sat down on the edge of his bed. He didn't want to leave his mother and father. He didn't want to leave the family home. Exhaustion set in and he fell into a deep sleep.

Chapter 7

David and Adela
Vienna, 1885

On a hot and humid summer day at the end of August 1882, David went to the train depot with his father and mother. He carried one suitcase and pulled his small steamer trunk behind him. His suitcase was filled with his clothes and personal belongings. The trunk contained gifts and fur muffs made for his *bubbe* and *zayde* and his cousins in Vienna. David hand carried, in its case, the violin that his father made him for his thirteenth birthday.

Edith and Lewis held hands. They looked at each other, each holding back tears. Lewis squeezed Edith's hand to assure her that everything would be fine. Then he turned to his son and spoke. "David, make us proud."

Edith handed David a cloth sack filled with freshly baked bread, cured meat, dried fruit, and rugalach, David's favorite pastry.

"My only child, you are my heart. You are my breath. Come home to us," she said in a low whisper.

She kissed her son on both cheeks and he did the same to her. David shook his father's hand and Lewis grabbed David by the shoulders with a vice-like hold, pulling him into his chest. He squeezed his son and whispered goodbye. As David boarded the train, he was drained of all feeling and emotion. Then he closed his eyes and fell asleep.

The journey was long, arduous, and at times, grueling. When David arrived in Vienna, his grandfather awaited him. As David stepped off the steel platform with his suitcase and steamer trunk, he heard his grandfather yelling his name.

"David, David. You have arrived. You have arrived."

David could not see him, so with his travel documents in his leather pouch, he headed to customs. He walked through a gate that led to a security checkpoint. That is when he heard his grandfather's voice again, "*Ikh bin da*. I am here." The two men locked eyes with one another. There was joy in their faces. David knew this was where he was supposed to be.

As David settled down into his daily routine, he was somewhat conflicted. He was happy to spend quality time with his grandparents, but sad having to leave his home. He worried about his parents and was also a little homesick. As the days passed, his excitement overcame any doubt that this is where he was meant to be. Just thinking about his life in Vienna sent shivers up his spine.

Music had always been an integral part of David's life. So, when David saw the flyer posted in the university quad, he was excited to attend the concert. As he slid into his seat, the girl sitting next to him smiled and David smiled back.

The warm fall night turned magical under the brilliant stars. As the chamber quartet began to play Debussy's *String Quartet in G Minor*, David's eyes strayed again and again to the beautiful girl seated next to him. When the conductor raised his baton, a frisson of electricity passed between them. After the last concerto was finished, Adela and David talked for several hours. At the end of the evening, David knew that he had found the love of his life.

David asked Adela if he could walk her home. As they strolled through the university grounds, David learned Adela was an accomplished cellist and pianist studying music at the Vienna Academy of Music. He also found out that Adela had gone to private schools and spoke German, Yiddish, and English. Their conversations, usually in English, were effortless, fun, and insightful. David and Adela quickly became inseparable.

Adela's upbringing had been very different from David's. Her father, Isaac, was a successful lawyer. David's father was a shopkeeper. But both families shared their love for music and their love for family.

David shared his stories about his father's relationship with the Russian Tsar and his own friendship with Nicholas. Adela, mesmerized by David's admission, pummeled him with numerous questions.

"Did you ever meet the Tsar?" Adela asked.

"My father told me that a month after my birth, Alexander III came into his store with Mark Twain. Twain was intrigued by the fact that my father made handcrafted violins and sold fur coats made from the pelts of the Siberian silver fox. My father and Alexander were both musicians, so I guess they talked about music."

"David, you don't just talk about music with the future Tsar of Russia!" David just smiled and shrugged his shoulders.

"Tell me more. This is unbelievable," Adela exclaimed.

When David told her about his own friendship with Nicholas, Adela was truly astonished. And again, David just smiled. Adela continued peppering him with more questions about their friendship.

"What was Nicholas like? Did he speak multiple languages, did he . . ."

"Slow down. I'll share everything with you," David said in a loving tone.

After a few minutes, Adela looked into David's eyes, tilted her head, and with a slight flutter, asked one more time. "Please tell me the story." Then he started telling her the tale.

"Over the years, when a Romanov would come to Odessa, they would come into our shop," David began. "When Nicholas got older, he came with his father, Alexander III. Nicholas and I were about the same age. I was nine months older. I know this will sound strange, but Nicholas and I became friends."

"This is unbelievable!" Adela exclaimed again. "Tell me more."

As David shared his story about his friendship with Nicholas, he felt a real sense of intimacy with Adela. He trusted her to be the keeper of this knowledge, and that trust continued to grow as their relationship continued to flourish.

The young couple talked constantly, discussing everything from world events to the kind of flowers they wanted on their wedding day. They talked about how they intended to raise their children. David wanted at least four sons and Adela wanted at least six children, three girls and three boys. She would always jest and say, "Three are for you and three are for me."

They talked about the dreams they shared for the children they would one day have. They both wanted them to be strong and independent. They wanted their children to stand by their beliefs and be faithful to their Jewish heritage. But most importantly, they wanted their children to share their love for music.

Over the next several months, David and Adela were spending almost all their time together. They attended every concert they could fit into their rigorous schedules. They agreed that music was a powerful aphrodisiac. Several weeks later, after an evening listening to a concert of Mozart's music, as Adela's eyes gleamed in the moonlight, she asked, "Are you free Sunday to join me and my family for dinner?"

David beamed. He knew what an important step this was in their relationship. He said bravely, "Yes, of course. I would love to meet your parents."

David decided not to ask any more questions. He knew what she meant. Adela wanted to introduce him to her parents, her father, Isaac, and her mother, Sarah. David was looking forward to that day. He was ready to commit to a serious relationship with Adela. He loved her. He couldn't wait for Adela to meet his parents. For now, he would have to be patient. But he was

looking forward to bringing Adela to Odessa one day. He shivered with excitement. David knew his parents would love her
as much as he did.

The following Sunday, David and Adela arrived at the Goldman home. The beautiful stone chalet, trimmed in intricate decorative wood, was breathtaking. The red brick steps to the front
landing sparkled from the sun's rays. As the couple walked up
to the porch, Isaac swung the door open.

"We have been waiting for the two of you. Come in," he said.
Adela went in first and kissed her father on his check. David
reached his hand out. Isaac's grip was firm.

Sarah came out of the parlor and hugged her daughter, and
then she whispered, "David is very good-looking."

Isaac interjected, "David, I've heard so much about you, I feel
as if I have known you forever."

David responded, "I feel the same way, sir. Adela shared
many stories with me about you and Mrs. Goldman. I'm very
happy we have finally met."

"Adela, why don't you give David a tour of our home and
then join us in the garden?" suggested Isaac.

"Of course, Father," replied Adela.

The Goldman's home was beautiful. The rooms were large
and welcoming. Beautiful artwork was displayed in every room.
After the tour, the couple walked out to the garden and joined
Mr. and Mrs. Goldman. They talked for hours, and David felt as
if he were home.

On Sundays, when David would visit the Goldman home,
the talks around the dinner table were always vivacious, interesting, and enlightening. At times they were even heated. Isaac
challenged David, insidiously engaging him intellectually in
ways that expanded David's world. It was exhilarating, and
David looked forward to those feisty discussions.

The next couple of years seemed to fly by. David completed
his studies and it was time for him to return to Odessa. Before

he left, there was still one more thing he needed to do. He was going to meet with Adela's father and ask for his daughter's hand in marriage. David knew it would be several years before they could be married, but he was determined to make sure that Mr. Goldman would give his permission and his blessings.

David hadn't been at the Goldman home for several weeks because of final examinations, but this Sunday, he was determined to have the talk with Isaac. When he arrived at the Goldman's home, David checked his pocket to make sure the ring was secure in the small satin pouch. As he walked up the three steps to the front porch, his hands began to sweat. His heart began to flutter, and there were drops of moisture dripping down his sideburns. He checked his trouser pocket one more time and then knocked on the front door.

"David, good to see you again. We have missed your visits the last couple of weeks. How did your final examinations go?" asked Mr. Goldman.

"Very well, sir."

"Come in, David. Dinner will be ready soon."

"Thank you, Mr. Goldman. Is Adela home yet?" David asked.

"Yes. She is upstairs. Let's have a talk. Sit down, David," Mr. Goldman said in a firm voice.

David followed Mr. Goldman into the sitting room. He was doing everything he could to stop shaking as he sat down.

"David, what are your plans now that you have graduated from the university?" Mr. Goldman asked. "I know that you have obligations to meet at home, but I want you to know you can always work for me if you decide to stay in Vienna."

"Thank you, Mr. Goldman. That is a very generous offer, but I must return home. My parents are having health issues and they really need me. It is my responsibility and my honor to take care of them."

"I understand, David, but what are your intentions with my

daughter?" he asked.

David wasn't prepared for this question. He had rehearsed this moment a dozen times. He had wanted to be the one to bring it up first.

"I love Adela. I will never love anyone else. I want to ask for your permission to marry her. I couldn't bear to live my life without her. I know that I must be able to provide for her. I can certainly take over my father's business and that is what I intend to do when I return home. Eventually, I hope to work for the railroad. That has been my dream since I was a young boy. With my engineering degree, my dream may one day become a reality."

David paused. There was a moment of stillness and silence before David spoke.

"Mr. Goldman, do I have your permission to ask Adela to be my wife? We may have to wait several years before we can wed and I can offer her the life she deserves. I will always take care of Adela. Your daughter is my life, my soul, and my heart."

Isaac didn't respond right away. David was afraid to take a breath. When Isaac stood up, David's instinct was to do the same. Isaac held out his right hand, and with a firm grip, he shook his future son-in-law's hand.

"David, I will be proud to call you my son," Mr. Goldman said as he stepped back. "You have my permission to ask Adela for her hand in marriage with one condition. You must be able to provide for her before you can consummate your love. Now, let's go into the dining room and have dinner."

"Thank you, Mr. Goldman. I will not disappoint you."

"David, you can call me Isaac."

David could barely eat. He kept rehearsing what he wanted to say to Adela. When the dishes were cleared from the table, David asked, "Mr. Goldman, may I take Adela out to the garden?"

"Of course David, as long as that is what Adela wants to do?" Isaac replied.

Adela smiled. David pulled out her chair, then the two of them walked out the French doors that led to the garden.

David had chosen an exquisite pearl ring that was set in a four-prong, rose-gold setting. Pearl was Adela's birthstone. The two of them sat down on a stone bench surrounded by roses, carnations, and edelweiss. David inhaled the sweet, scented air as he was awed by the beauty of the setting. He reached for Adela's right hand and gently put hers in his. Then he began his rehearsed speech.

"Adela, I will always love you. I can't promise you much today, but I promise I will always take care of you. I will always provide for you and will always be there for you. I promise that I will be the best husband and father I can possibly be."

David went down on one knee.

"Adela Goldman, will you accept this ring as a token of my love and commitment? Will you marry me and be my wife?"

"Yes. I will," Adela said, tears forming in her eyes.

The two embraced. David took the ring out of his pocket and slid it on to Adela's finger. Isaac and Sara, who had been looking through the glass doors, came outside and congratulated the couple.

"We have been waiting for this day for quite some time," said Isaac. "David, we welcome you into our family. Our home is now your home. I look forward to meeting your parents when we visit Odessa. I am so proud of both of you. Let's toast to a long, beautiful life, and lots of grandchildren. Now, let's go into the sitting room and open a bottle of schnapps."

Isaac kissed his daughter's cheek, shook David's hand, and then gave David a bear hug.

The next several weeks were bittersweet as David prepared for his return to Odessa. After securing his passage, David sent a letter to his father:

Dear Father,

I am staring at a star-filled sky as I write my homecoming note. I am returning to Odessa by rail. Father, when I left Odessa, you not only gave me the precious gift of a university education, you also gave me the opportunity to expand my world and find the love of my life. When I boarded the train in Odessa over three years ago, I carried a suitcase and a knapsack of food mother baked for me. Today, I return home to you with love in my heart for the woman who will become my wife.

With much love and gratitude,

David

On July 30, 1885, with heaviness and joy in his heart, David boarded the train back to Odessa. Once he returned home, he would make arrangements for Adela to formally meet the rest of his family.

As the train pulled into the familiar station, David saw his father waiting for him on the train's platform.

"*Tate*! Father!" he exclaimed.

Chapter 8

Lewis and David
Odessa, 1887

It had been two months since David had come back home from Vienna. Lewis and Edith were ecstatic to have their son back. David knew this was where he needed to be. He wanted and needed to take care of his parents, but his heart ached to caress the love of his life.

As David sat at his wooden desk in the back of the mercantile store, he visualized what life would be like married to Adela. His mind drifted with beautiful images of the children they would have together and the adventures they would share. His skin tingled as he envisioned the future they would create. It was an exciting time for the young couple.

David, now nineteen, was stringing some of Kaufmann's newly-carved violins when a knock at the front door jolted him back to reality. He got up to unlock the door, expecting to see a customer, but to his shock and amazement, there were Royal Guards and Cossacks outside! David froze as the Tsar walked into the mercantile store with Nicholas following behind. The visit was unannounced and unexpected. The Royal Guards and Cossacks, who were accompanying the royals, stayed outside and did not enter the store. David put the violin down and saluted the Tsar.

"I will get my father," said David, but before Alexander had a chance to speak, Lewis was already hurrying down the wooden stairs. To his relief, Alexander was smiling and spoke first.

"Comrade, I have returned to my favorite furrier to make a request. Do you still have that bottle of vodka that I brought you on my last visit?"

Not trusting his voice, Lewis saluted the Tsar and nodded. He sighed with relief, and then gestured toward the stairs.

"Maybe it would be best if we go upstairs," said Lewis, who was not certain what this visit was about, and did not want the conversation to be overheard.

The Tsar turned toward David. "It's good to see you again, David. Have you finished your studies in Vienna?"

"Yes," Lewis interjected. "Edith and I are so joyful that he has come home."

Alexander walked over to David and patted him on the back. "I am glad you have returned to your homeland," he said. "Nicholas insisted that he come with me on this voyage." Nicholas looked toward David with a reassuring nod.

"Nicholas, it's good to see you once again," David replied. The two young men smiled at each other.

Alexander turned toward his son and said, "Nicholas, why don't you and David talk? It has been many years since the two of you have spoken." The young men glanced at each other without saying a word. The Tsar knew about their correspondence.

The two fathers climbed the stairs that led to the office and sat down on the wooden chairs near Lewis's desk. Lewis walked over to his liquor cabinet and pulled out the bottle of vodka. He placed two cut crystal glasses, once belonging to his father, on the small oval table and poured a healthy amount of vodka in each glass. They lifted their glasses.

"To our meeting," said Alexander.

"To your health," replied Lewis.

There was a long silence which Lewis didn't know how to fill. The whole situation felt strange and Lewis did not want to make any missteps. To his relief, Alexander began the conversation.

"I hear from Nicholas that David did very well in his

engineering studies at the university. What are his plans for the future?"

Lewis hesitated for a few minutes before responding. "While in Vienna, David met a music student and they fell in love. He's hopeful they will marry next year. For now, he is helping us with the business and travelling as needed to sell our furs and violins. I know he dreams of being an engineer and working on the railroad one day. I pray his dream will come true."

The Tsar nodded thoughtfully. "Comrade, as you know, I have always promised Russia that I would begin construction of the Trans-Siberian Railway. My resolution has been written. I intend to send three expeditions to find paths for Zabailkalsky, Middle Siberia, and in the southern part of Ursati. I'm forming the Siberian Railway Construction Committee and will begin construction once the paths for rail travel in these regions are agreed upon."

Lewis looked very concerned. He did not know what the Tsar was implying. He hoped Alexander was not considering David to be part of any of these expeditions. Alexander must have picked up on Lewis's facial expression and decided to offer some reassurance.

"Do not worry, my friend. David will remain in Odessa. Maybe he can be in charge of the railroad one day," said the Tsar.

Lewis did not know how to respond. "I think this is just a dream for David," he replied after a pause.

"The future is uncertain, but I can see this in David's future," said the Tsar. "However, for right now, I have a request for you. I want you to make me a one-of-a-kind fur coat for my beloved wife. I want it to be made from the fur of the silver fox, and I want the Romanov Crest embroidered with jewels and inserted into the design. Lewis, you are the finest furrier I know. Can you do that for me?" he asked.

"Of course. It will be my honor and privilege," replied Lewis.

"When I receive word that the coat is ready, I'll have the jewels delivered to you. I'll command my guards to wait here until the jewels are embedded into the royal crest," said the Tsar. "My final request is for you to sew a message into the coat to my Minnie. No one but you can ever see this message," Alexander added forcefully. Then he handed Lewis a handwritten note.

"No one ever will," replied Lewis.

Lewis was relieved after he heard Alexander's request. He opened another bottle of vodka and simultaneously, the two men raised their glasses.

"To Russia and the royal family," Lewis exclaimed.

Downstairs, Nicholas and David were enjoying their own conversation, reminiscing and laughing. David was relieved to see that the past few turbulent years hadn't hardened his friend. Nicholas wanted to hear all about David's experiences in Vienna.

"Good to see you are back in Odessa. This is where you belong," Nicholas said, initiating the conversation.

"I'm glad to be back home," David replied. "Nicholas, is it true that a railway is going to be built connecting Russia and Siberia?"

"Yes, my friend, it is so. It will be one of the greatest accomplishments of this decade," Nicholas said proudly. "I'm very honored that my father has asked me to coordinate one of Russia's greatest feats. Are you interested in this endeavor?"

"Yes, very much so. As you know, I completed my studies in Vienna and received my Engineering Certificate. I'm hopeful that one day I'll be able to put my education to good use and work as an engineer on the railroad," David said proudly.

"David, you have always done what was right by your parents. It's no different than what is expected of me in my future," said Nicholas. "In that regard, I hope you will one day be able to follow your dreams. Now, tell me about the university in Vienna. As you know, I have visited Vienna many times, but I have never had a university experience. My education was always with private tutors. Tell me everything."

David locked the front door and placed a sign that said *Klozd* on it. Then the two young men walked to the back of the store and pulled up a couple of chairs in the corner. They chatted like old friends. They talked about the last three years, mostly about David's schooling, day trips, and working for a lawyer doing research and odd jobs. Then David told Nicholas all about Adela and his plans for marriage.

"David, I'm happy for you. I wish you a long life with many children," said Nicholas.

"Thank you, Nicholas. But enough about me. Tell me what is going on in your life," asked David.

Nicholas wanted to share his desire for Alix. He selected his words cautiously. "I think I have met the girl I want to marry," he said. "It was several years ago in 1884 when I was first captivated by Alix's beauty. At the request of my father, I attended the wedding of my uncle, the Grand Duke Sergi Alexandrovich to Princess Elisabeth of Hesse-Darmstad. Alix was a bridesmaid. She is the granddaughter of Queen Victoria," he continued. "When I first saw Alix walking down the aisle with a bouquet of white roses clutched in her hand, she took my breath away. She is three years my junior, but we quickly developed very strong feelings for each other."

David smiled. He patted Nicholas on the back and shook his hand. "I hope your dreams with Alix will all come true," he said, his voice flooded with emotion.

They continued to catch up about what had gone on since they had seen each other last, and shared what might lie ahead in the years to come. Their conversation went on for hours.

Then, very tentatively, Alexander walked back down the wooden stairs. "Nicholas, it's time to leave," he said. "David, take good care of your father and mother. It was good seeing you and being back here again."

"*Spasibo*," said David as he saluted, and the two men walked out. Lewis nodded at David with approval.

Lewis was honored that Alexander had selected him to create such a one-of-a-kind coat for the Tsarina. He would begin work on it immediately. It would be like no other coat he had ever made. He couldn't wait to share this news with Edith. She would begin the design this evening. When the coat was ready for the jewels to be embroidered into the crest, Lewis would send word to St. Petersburg that the package was ready for delivery.

Many months later, there was quite a buzz in Odessa that the grand railroad was going to be built across Siberia. The official announcement came a couple of months after the Tsar's last trip to Odessa when his resolution was first posted:

> *I have so many reports from the Siberian governors that now I can admit with sadness that our government did almost nothing to satisfy the needs of this rich but neglected region. It is time to correct this mistake. The construction of the Trans-Siberian Railway will begin soon and will be a great national event. It will be built by Russian people and with Russian materials. I have issued the order to start building the first continuous railway across all of Siberia. I want it to connect Siberian regions rich in natural resources with the rest of the Russian railway infrastructure. I will be using the funds from the Russian treasury. I want you to declare this as my will after my return from the countries of the East.*

When the news reached Odessa, everyone was amazed. Everyone except Lewis and David. They were expecting the announcement.

In the fall of 1887, David finally married his beautiful bride. The service was in the small synagogue in Odessa at the end of town, near the Jewish cemetery. The wedding was very traditional.

David wasn't nervous or even anxious as many grooms are.

He was excited, filled with joy, and bursting with love for his bride. The morning of the ceremony, Lewis called David into the back office and handed his son a small box.

"This is for you. I would like you to wear this when you recite your vows," said Lewis.

David opened the box, and inside was a beautiful kippah that David had never seen before.

"Your grandfather gave this to me before he died. He wanted you to wear it on your wedding day," said Lewis.

Respectfully, David lifted the kippah out of the box and placed it on his head. Neither man said another word. They both recognized the solemn moment of passage from one generation to another.

Adela wore a simple but elegant satin gown. The gown had full-length sleeves with satin-covered buttons from her elbow down to her wrist. The beaded train flowed softly behind her. Adela's mother carefully placed the veil on her daughter's head. She attached it to Adela's golden hair, which had been pulled up into a bun, and then gently lowered the veil to cover Adela's face. The beautiful laced veil, which had belonged to Adela's grandmother, was now being passed on to her. Adela would one day pass it on to her daughter.

White acacia flowers adorned the chuppah held high by four white satin-wrapped posts. All four sides were left open, welcoming everyone into David and Adela's life. Two goblets of wine had also been placed on a small, carved, wooden pedestal under the canopy as a symbol of joy.

The guests seated themselves on wooden benches. The women sat on one side of the temple and the men on the other. The rabbi stepped forward. The wedding service was about to begin.

David walked through a small side door. He felt neither fear nor anxiety. His face radiated only pride, desire, and love. His dark wavy hair had been trimmed around his ears at the nape of his neck. He wore black boots under his trousers, which increased his height by two inches. His bride was several inches taller than he was, and David wanted the two of them to look into each other's eyes, starting as equals in every way.

David took the traditional plain gold ring out of its satin pouch and placed it on the pedestal. The back doors opened. Adela took two steps forward and placed her hand in her father's. Lewis played the violin as Adela walked toward her groom. David's heart began to pound. He took a deep breath and calmed his excitement.

When the moment came for David to place the wedding ring on Adela's finger, he confidently declared, "Behold, you are betrothed unto me with this ring according to the law of Moses and Israel."

The rabbi placed a glass wrapped in plain white cloth on the floor. David lifted his right leg and forcefully lowered it, shattering the glass.

"*Mazel tov!*" everyone cheered.

Joyful music echoed through the halls of the temple as family and friends celebrated David and Adela's union. Two chairs wrapped in white ribbon were placed in the middle of the room and Adela sat on one, David on the other. As the music purred from the violins' strings, family and friends joined hands, forming a very large circle. Everyone danced around the bride and groom singing, "*Hava Nagila*, let us rejoice."

Four men lifted Adela's chair and several more lifted David's chair. A white, satin ribbon was wrapped around Adela's wrist connecting it to David's. The guests encircled the newlyweds, singing, dancing, and handing over rubles for the young couple to place in their wedding pouch.

"Speech! Speech," yelled the guests. David stood up and walked toward the center of the room.

"As most of you know, I am a man of few words," he began. "Today, so many words are flooding into my brain, it is hard to choose them properly. First, I want to thank my parents and Adela's parents for their love and support. We are truly blessed," he continued. "Thank you for joining us on this momentous occasion. I can think of nothing more important than carrying on our families' commitment to our faith, our family, and our love for one another. Rabbi, would you like to say a few words?"

The rabbi walked to the center of the room and began to speak.

"I have known the Kaufmann family since David's birth," said the rabbi. "More recently, I felt honored to meet and get to know the Goldman family. I have spent a good amount of time with David and Adela. Their love is obvious to all. Their faith is true and absolute. Today it is my honor to bless David and Adela as they enter into this union together. David and Adela, please come over and stand next to me."

The newlyweds held hands as they walked toward the rabbi. Everyone bowed when the rabbi began the prayer.

"Blessed art Thou, O Lord our God, King of the Universe, who hath created joy and gladness, bridegroom and bride, mirth and exultation, pleasure and delight, love, peace, and friendship."

The rest of the evening was a joyful blur. A lot of wine and vodka was passed around the banquet room. Everyone danced the night away, even the rabbi. The couple received many beautiful gifts. The last gift David opened came in a beautiful mahogany box engraved with the Romanov crest. He gently opened the lid. Inside was a sterling silver letter opener. The note said, "*Dolgaya Zhizn,* long life." It was a wedding gift from Nicholas.

Chapter 9

Nicholas
St. Petersburg, 1888

In the fall of 1888, the Romanovs embarked on a rail tour travelling through as many Russian cities as possible. Their goal was to provide a united front and portray a sense of confidence and prosperity for the entire country.

The tour went perfectly, and the family felt confident their Russian citizens supported and were fully vested in Alexander's reign. Unfortunately, while heading back to St. Petersburg, tragedy, once again, fell upon the family.

As the Romanovs were finishing their breakfast in their private dining car, the train derailed and plummeted down a steep hillside. Grinding metal shrieked and roared through the walls, floorboards, and ceilings. Loud detonations drowned out their screams. The family clapped their hands over their ears, preventing them from bursting. Alexander had heard that sound before. He was certain a bomb had just ripped through the train. The strong smell of burnt wood overpowered the dust and odor of the hot metal.

The runaway train rocked and twisted its way down the mountain. The Tsar and his family were thrown to the floor, somersaulting against the walls until the dining car came to an abrupt stop. The walls crashed underneath the roof. An eerie silence followed.

In the dim light, Alexander yelled, "Is anyone hurt?" He called out again. "Is anyone hurt?" One by one, voices began to call out. His wife and children were all safe.

Not wasting any time, the Tsar commanded, "We need to get out now. I'm going to push on the roof and I want everyone to climb out!"

The roof was now leaning on its side. With an extraordinary burst of strength, Alexander pushed his body against the metal roof, creating an opening from which they could escape. One by one, they climbed out through the mangled steel, and then huddled together in a daze on a grassy knoll.

After his family was safely outside the wreckage, Alexander went back inside the rail car. The only member of the royal family who was unaccounted for was their beloved dog, Kamchata. Alexander worked his way through the wreckage searching for his sidekick. His magnificent Akita lay still at the foot of the dining table, dead.

He carried Kamchata off the train and gently placed him underneath a large acacia tree. After he covered his loyal companion with his jacket, he walked up the hill to be with his family.

Several of the Royal Guards travelling with the Romanovs surrounded the family to protect them. While they waited, Alexander commandeered carriages and horses from Kharkov to take the family back to St. Petersburg.

The following day, every newspaper throughout the Empire and around the world printed vivid images of the twisted wreckage and reported the details of the crash. Numerous accounts described how the Tsar lifted the edge of the train's roof on his shoulders to allow his loved ones to flee the wreck. One of the Russian newspapers wrote, "God did not permit misfortune for Russia. The Tsar, Tsarina and Tsarevitch, and the rest of the children were preserved for the Motherland."

The Tsar expressed his relief and gratitude to his citizenry:

This day will never be erased from our memories. It was too terrible and too miraculous. Christ wished to prove to all Russia that He still makes miracles and saves from imminent death those who believe in Him.

Unbeknownst to Alexander, he sustained serious damage to his kidneys during the crash which haunted him for the rest of his life.

The train crash had a profound effect on Nicholas. After realizing how, in an instant, one's life could be snapped away, he began thinking about Alix. It had been five years since they had met and their mutual affection had certainly grown. But this near-death experience had emboldened Nicholas to hasten matters between them. He invited Alix to come to Russia so they could be together once again.

After receiving Nicholas's invitation to join him in St. Petersburg, Alix sent word that she was pleased to accept his invitation. She arrived in St. Petersburg in early December and stayed with the Romanovs for six enchanted weeks. With each passing day, the couple fell more deeply in love.

After Alix returned to Vienna, Nicholas felt a numbing sense of loss. He expressed his feelings in his diary.

"It is my dream to one day marry Alix. I have loved her for a long time, but more deeply and strongly since 1888, when she spent six weeks in St. Petersburg. I pray that my dream will come true and she will become my wife." Nicholas and Alix would wait another four years for that dream to come to fruition.

The horrible train crash did not hamper the Emperor and Empress's desire to travel. Two years after the crash, in 1890, the Romanovs journeyed to Egypt, India, Singapore, Bangkok, and Japan. While traveling through Otsu, Japan, history repeated itself again. The Tsar was the target of another failed assassination. This time the assassin's gun jammed and the bullet never discharged.

The Empress pleaded with her husband. "I'm afraid I am going to lose you. I need you. Russia needs you. I can't live without you. I want to go home."

Alexander held his wife lovingly in his arms. He had never seen his wife like this. It worried him. He kissed her cheek and stroked her face. "I will take you home," he told her.

Alexander kept his fears silent. Concern for the safety of his family was his number one priority. He closed his eyes, masked his tears, and pressed on.

Chapter 10

Nicholas and Alix
St. Petersburg, 1894

In the spring of 1894, Nicholas decided that he was finally ready to propose to Alix. Nervously, he prepared to express his intentions to his father, waiting to broach the subject until the two of them were alone in the residence. Late one evening, Nicholas came into the library where Alexander was reading.

"Father, I have something very important to discuss with you," Nicholas began hesitantly.

Alexander looked up. "Yes, Nicholas. What is it?"

"I want to ask for your permission to propose marriage to Alix." The Tsar beamed. He put down his book, stood up, and patted Nicholas on the back.

"Nicholas! I'm delighted! Delighted! And of course I give you my permission and my blessing." He smiled at his son with satisfaction.

"You've made a wonderful choice. Alix will be a loving wife and an excellent mother. She's a very good match for you, and I know she will always help you through the difficult times. Most importantly, I am certain she will stand by your side through all of life's challenges and adventures."

Nicholas felt overwhelmed with relief. "Father, I'm so grateful for your love and support." The Tsar put his arm around his son's shoulders and kissed Nicholas's head. For a few moments, the two men stood in silence. It was a touching moment for both of them.

"When do you intend to propose?" Alexander finally asked.

"When I go to Coburg for Alix's brother's wedding," Nicholas replied, and the Tsar nodded with affection.

With his father's permission, Nicholas travelled to Coburg with his most trusted Cossacks and a small Russian delegation. While in his stateroom, Nicholas rehearsed what he would say when he asked Alix to marry him.

After arriving at Ehrenburg Palace, Nicholas summoned one of his Royal Guards. He handed him a letter in a sealed envelope.

"I want you to deliver this handwritten note to Alix and wait for her response," he said.

The Royal Guard nodded, placed the letter inside his coat, and set off. After receiving confirmation that Alix would indeed meet him the following morning, the Royal Guard returned to the palace. That evening Nicholas was too excited to sleep.

Shortly after his morning breakfast meal of biscuits, sausage, and mint tea, Nicholas made his way to the chateau where Alix was residing. The sky was a deep, iridescent blue and the spring air was soft and calm. It was a magnificent day for a proposal of marriage.

Alix had been expecting the Royal Guards. But when she was summoned outside, she was surprised to see a luxurious red carpet spread in front of a magnificent white and gold carriage. At first glance, Alix did not see Nicholas, who was seated in the back corner of the carriage. She hesitated for a moment and then Nicholas stepped out. The two of them greeted each other with a kiss on each other's cheek. Nicholas reached out his right hand as they both walked up the carriage steps. Alix leaned into Nicholas, and the two kissed with a sense of urgency.

The Royal Guard grabbed the reins and steered the royal carriage out of town. The clap from the horse's hoofs slowed and then came to a standstill. They had arrived at their destination. The Royal Guard opened the carriage door as the couple stepped down from their coach. The soft breeze felt welcoming. Nicholas and Alix held hands, unable to take their eyes off one another. Nicholas's heart was pounding with joy.

Nicholas asked two of his Royal Guards to set up a picnic blanket under a beautiful shady tree that provided a canopy from the glow of the sun. A feast of meats, cheeses, fruits, nuts, and tea was placed on elegant china plates. The Royal Guards were dismissed, but continued to keep a close and protective eye on the couple.

When the Royal Guards were far enough away to ensure privacy, Nicholas reached out for Alix, and they held each other with warmth and love. Finally, Nicholas pulled away ever so slightly.

"Alix. I have been in love with you for years, and I know you feel the same. I think we could be very happy with many children in our future and a long magnificent life together. Will you marry me?"

Alix took his hand. "Yes," she whispered. "Yes, my beloved." They kissed until their lips were raw. Then they embraced and fell asleep under the branches of the majestic oak tree.

In the autumn of 1894, five months after Alix accepted Nicholas's proposal, Alexander III faced his own death. Not from an assassin's bullet, but from the kidney injury he had sustained six years earlier when he had lifted the metal roof on the train to free his family.

Alexander knew that he had not adequately prepared Nicholas for the responsibilities that would soon be bestowed upon him. He had always thought that he had many years to prepare Nicholas for the role he would inherit, but time had run out. Now Alexander had to trust in the Lord to guide Nicholas through the days, months, and years ahead. Alexander knew there was one thing he could do to help Nicholas prepare for this untimely transition. Accordingly, he asked Nicholas to summon Alix to the imperial palace at Livadia.

When Alix arrived, Alexander insisted on receiving her in his official uniform. His devoted wife, Maria, helped him prepare for this very important greeting, steadying him as he sat down in his favorite armchair.

"Tell Alix to come in," he said. "I'm ready." Maria kissed her husband and walked out through the connecting foyer.

"It's good to see you, Alix," she told the young woman. "My husband would like to talk to you."

Alix tiptoed down the hall to the opened door and the Tsar signaled for her to sit in the chair directly across from him. He began speaking slowly and deliberately.

"My dear Alix. I have witnessed your love and devotion toward my son. I have seen his love for you. I have seen firsthand how your gentleness and warmth settles and calms Nicholas with the burdens and challenges he endures. Your role as Tsarina will be to encourage, support, and guide Nicholas through the difficult times, and celebrate the joyous ones. Time is running out for me to bless you and my son as he recites his loyalty and oath of marriage to you. So, before my breath leaves my body, I give you and Nicholas my consent and bless your marriage."

On November 1, 1894, at 2:15 p.m., Alexander III died in Maria's arms. He was forty-nine years old. His son Nicholas, now twenty-six, became the Tsar of Russia.

Maria was heartbroken and devastated. She didn't know how she would be able to live without her husband. She sought comfort from her mother, Queen Louise of Denmark, by expressing her grief and emotions in a letter:

I begin writing this letter alongside my deeply beloved Sasha, now everything is over! My life is broken forever, for how can I imagine living without he who was everything to me? I hoped that God would not allow this, that He would take pity, hearing all those millions of prayers addressed to Him for the life of my angel, Sasha. But no! It is impossible to describe the pain with which my heart is overflowing.

Thank God, in the final days he let me do everything for him, as he could no longer do anything himself and did not want to let the chambermaid help him. Every evening he thanked me touchingly for my help. He was always patient and never complained. Only I saw how sad and unhappy he was, poor thing, when he looked at me with eyes full of sorrow. At 6:30, he was allowed to get up, and with great difficulty, was moved into a comfortable armchair and taken to the hall where he remained until the end. The whole family went in to see him. He kissed everyone, and even at such a moment remembered that it was Ella's birthday. He congratulated her and demanded ebullience.

Father Yanyshev was still not there, and apparently sensing the end approaching, Sasha asked several times if he would be coming. When Yanyshev finally arrived, Sasha said with a heavy breath, "I'm so tired." He himself read two prayers after Yanyshev, taking communion with joy and tranquility. After communion, everyone left, leaving us alone with the children and Alix, who was so nice and shared everything with us as if she had always been one of us. He asked for the priest from Kronstadt, who I think you have heard of, to come and pray for him. This was a particularly poignant moment, demonstrating the wonderfully meek soul of my angel, Sasha. The priest quietly prayed, placing both hands on his head and kissing it. Every time he stopped, Sasha said, "Again, it is better that way." Sasha told him the most wonderful things, that the Lord had heard his (the priest's) prayers because he was so good and his faith so strong that he was close to our Lord, and finally said, "You are a holy man." Until the last minute, he remained fully conscious. He spoke with us until quietly and without any struggle, he fell asleep in my arms forever.

Alexander's priest consecrated Nicholas later that evening. Alexander's reign was short-lived, and when he died, he left his work unfinished and an heir unprepared to rule.

The whole world was stunned and saddened when the news of the Tsar's death reached them. But the Kaufmann family had no tears left.

Twelve days earlier, before Lewis' fiftieth birthday, the doctor had told the family that his death was imminent. Edith sat on the wooden chair in their bedroom. She held her husband's hand. Lewis's breath was shallow. He whispered, "I love you." Edith gently moistened his lips. David sat on the edge of the bed and stroked his father's head.

"David, don't look so sad. I have had a good life," Lewis said to his son. "We have been more fortunate than most. Never forget who we are and what we believe." Lewis was gasping now for air.

David's eyes filled with tears. "Father, do not worry. I will take care of everything. Just rest." David leaned down and kissed his father's head. Lewis's eyes fluttered as he took his last breath.

Edith Kaufmann mourned the death of her beloved husband Lewis. David, now twenty-seven years old, grieved the loss of his father. David buried his father three days later in the local Jewish cemetery on the outskirts of the city near where he and Adela were married.

Two women grieved the death of their husbands. Two sons grieved the death of their fathers. Two sons took over their father's position in life. Edith died of a broken heart two years later. She was buried next to the love of her life.

Chapter 11

Nicholas and Alix
St. Petersburg, 1894-1901

After burying his father and trying to comfort his bereaved and heartbroken mother, Nicholas, unprepared, overwhelmed, and grief-stricken, received fierce criticism for the numerous tasks and details left unattended.

Concerned about the enormous pressure her son was experiencing, Maria suggested that the date of Nicholas and Alix's marriage be pushed forward. She believed that Alix could successfully guide her son through this difficult transition and Nicholas agreed. Just the thought of having Alix by his side calmed him and gave him the strength he needed to carry on. Twenty-five days after Alexander's death, Nicholas and Alix were married. There was no reception.

The newly married royals moved into the palace at Tsarskoye Selo, just outside St. Petersburg. It was the same palace where Nicholas had taken his first breath. Several months later, Alix found out that they were expecting their first child and informed Nicholas he was going to be a father. When Nicholas told his mother, she wept for joy.

"Nicky, this is a blessing from God, when someone dies, a baby is born," she said. "And I know that your father's soul will be part of this child."

Their first child, a daughter, was born in November 1895. She was named Olga, meaning holy. Nicholas held his newborn daughter and kissed her forehead.

"You have your grandfather's eyes," he whispered into Olga's ear.

"Nicky, tell the nurse to bring your mother in to see her

granddaughter," Alix said.

A short time later, Maria walked into the sitting room adjacent to the royal bedroom. She stared at the baby in rapt silence. Maria whispered at last, "I wish your grandfather were here. You have your grandfather's eyes."

"Mother, I believe Father is watching over us," Nicholas told her.

"I know he is," was Maria's response.

Now that the baby was born, Alix knew that the time had come for all Russians to acknowledge her husband as the Tsar of Russia.

"Nicky, it is time for your coronation," she told him decisively. "You are a Romanov and we need to celebrate. Talk to your advisers and have them arrange a festival, a large one. The people need this. The country needs this. We need this."

The coronation was held on May 14, 1896, in Uspenski Cathedral, located within the Kremlin. The celebration for the people of Russia was held four days later at Khodynka Field at the artillery training center just outside Moscow. Nicholas's advisers had selected the historic site because it was regarded as the sacred center of the Russian Empire. The advisors hoped that this event would shore up Russian support for Nicholas who was not as popular as his father or his grandfather. Unfortunately, Nicholas's advisers made a fatal blunder and tragedy for the Romanovs struck once again.

The advisers failed to take into account the massive crowds of over one hundred thousand men, women and children who came to eat free food, drink free beer, and have a good time. More importantly, they also failed to recognize that the prior military training ground, with its uneven and undulating terrain, would create obstacles for the massive crowds.

As is human nature, when free food and drinks were offered, thousands of Russians charged forward making sure they got their fair share. What was meant to be a joyous and celebratory time turned into a full-fledged nightmare.

People ran, pushed, shoved, and trampled over whoever got in their way. Approximately fourteen hundred men, women, and children died, and another thirteen hundred were seriously injured. Instead of the event being one of celebration, the devastating tragedy was looked upon as a bad omen for things to come for the Romanovs.

Over the next five years, Nicholas performed his duties as competently as he could, but he was not a natural ruler. He was happiest as a husband and father, enjoying himself with Alix and his growing family. His second daughter, Tatiana, was born in 1897. Two years later, his daughter Maria was born. The fourth daughter, Anastasia, was born three years later in 1902.

After Anastasia's birth, Nicholas was anxious and overwhelmed. He began to isolate himself more and more from the affairs of Russia. Alix prayed that with the passage of time, he would be better able to find a balance between his public life and private life. When she didn't see that happening, Alix decided that she would put her own plan into action and hoped that it would cheer him up.

Alix knew all about the longstanding relationship between the Romanovs and the Kaufmann family, especially the warm friendship between her husband and David. So she decided that a visit to Odessa to see his old friend would provide just the break her husband needed. Casually, she brought up the subject one evening.

"Nicky, I am in desperate need of a new fur coat. I remember your mother telling me about a wonderful family in Odessa who always made her the most spectacular fur coats. Your father had one made for your mother for her fortieth birthday."

"Yes," Nicholas answered. "The Kaufmanns. That is correct, Alix. It was a magnificent coat. The father died around the same time as Papa, and his son, David, runs the business now."

"Nicky, I'd like you to commission David to make a custom

fur coat for me and maybe he can make something for each of the girls as well. I want it to be made from the pelts of the silver fox. And to make sure that the order is carried out to our satisfaction, I think you should go to Odessa and oversee everything yourself."

Nicholas smiled. He knew his loving wife well and understood why she had made this sudden request. Alix was aware of the enormous toll the last six years had taken on him, and perhaps her plan was a good one.

"I think it would be good for you to go to Odessa and see David," Alix said firmly.

"I will think very hard about what you are saying," Nicholas replied.

Alix, determined to convince her husband, continued her plea. "Nicky, you know for thousands of years the silver fox was thought to be a very lucky symbol."

"I have heard that more than once. Alix, you are right. We could certainly use a little luck," Nicholas said half-heartedly.

The symbolism did not escape Nicholas. He hoped that going to the beautiful seaport town and visiting his old friend might indeed breathe new life into his heart, put a gallop back into his step, and give him the courage to continue on.

It didn't take long for Nicholas to prepare for his journey to Odessa. For the first time in a very long time, he found himself excited, even gleeful. He tried to remember how long it had been since he had last seen David.

He thought about his father and his grandfather. He thought about their simplicity. He thought about their kindness, loyalty, and leadership. He grieved in private.

Travelling had always soothed Nicholas. He travelled with his most trusted Cossack and felt well protected. As the train pulled into the beautiful seaport town, Nicholas felt a sense of calm. Yes, Alix was right. This trip would give him a new perspective and a renewed sense of hope.

Chapter 12

David and Adela
Odessa, 1888–1902

Less than a year after their marriage, David and Adela welcomed their first child, a daughter they named Bella. She was the spitting image of her mother with an oval face and glistening green eyes. She was a happy baby and very well nourished. She slept well after sucking the milk from her mother's breasts. David, mesmerized by his little girl, stared at her for hours until Adela, laughing, had to push him away.

When Bella was eleven months old, Adela made an announcement. She smiled at her husband and said, "I have something to tell you my dear. I'm with child again. I have a good feeling this baby is going to be a boy." David stared at her. Tears of joy filled his eyes.

"David, what's wrong? I thought you'd be so happy hearing this news!" Adela asked, surprised.

"I'm overwhelmed, absolutely overwhelmed! Adela," he replied. "I can't believe our good fortune! Can you feel him moving inside you?"

"Yes," said Adela. "Now put your head on my stomach and talk to your son. He will be in your arms very soon. She was correct. Their son was born on September 18, 1889.

From the beginning, there was something remarkable about this child. He was strong, stubborn, and determined. He was impatient and feisty, the complete opposite of his sister. When David held Jacob in his arms, his heart burst with happiness. When he looked into his son's eyes, David saw tremendous success in his future. But he also sensed horrific tragedy. David's hands actually began trembling with that thought.

"David, your hands are shaking." Adela said with concern. "Is something wrong?"

"No, my love, my hands are trembling with pride and love. Look what we have created, a daughter and a son. My whole body is trembling with joy."

On July 12, 1892, their third child, Samuel, was born, and two years later, on June 30, 1894, their fourth child, Carl, completed the family.

Eight years had now passed since David and Adela had become husband and wife. During that time, life in Odessa had changed a great deal. Many Jews were leaving to make America their new home. For the first time in his life, David realized his children might not grow old in his homeland and his grandchildren might not be Russian.

David worried desperately about the future. He didn't want to leave his country, but he knew that starting soon, his family and the families of so many others would be in harm's way. The Jews had become a convenient scapegoat in Russian society and the violence was escalating.

Townspeople marched through the streets chanting, "Jews must leave." Local Jewish businesses were vandalized, and thousands of families needed to make the very difficult decision to stay in Russia or leave the country they loved.

Then, on an unusually chilly summer day in 1902, Nicholas walked into David's shop just like his father Alexander had done thirty-five years earlier. David was stunned, even a little alarmed at first. There had been so many changes throughout Russia over the last ten years, and unexpected visits from anyone associated with the Romanovs came with concern and worry. More and more Jewish families were harassed and threatened. Some were harmed, and children no longer roamed freely through the streets of Odessa. Fear had crept into every corner of Jewish life.

As the Tsar walked into the Kaufmann's mercantile store, David saluted Nicholas with great caution. Nicholas spoke first;

his voice was warm and vibrant. David began to relax slightly.

"How have you been my good friend?" Nicholas asked. "It's been too many years since we were together, far too many. When I last saw you, both of our fathers were still alive," he continued. "What a tremendous loss we've both suffered. I can't believe they're gone. They died too soon. They were both remarkable Russians and wonderful men."

"Yes, the last eight years have been very hard. But we must never forget what they gave us. It is our turn to do the same for our children," replied David.

For a brief moment, David reflected back to that day in 1886 when Alexander had come into the Kaufmann's Mercantile store with Nicholas. David, almost nineteen at the time, had recently returned from Vienna. He remembered the discussion he had with Nicholas and how they had talked about the Trans-Siberian Railway. The enormity of the project and the prestige and growth it offered Russia had enthralled both young men. David had to admit he was a little bit jealous that Nicholas, and not he, would be working on the project. David had always felt that working with the railroad was supposed to be his destiny.

Just as he was about to share that memory with Nicholas, Adela came through the door with a kettle of hot lemon tea and some *sushka*. Her mouth fell open and she stood still, the kettle steaming out of its spout.

"Mrs. Kaufmann, it is very good to see you again. You must be very proud of your family," Nicholas said softly.

"*Da*," Adela nodded, and went back into the small kitchen as quickly as she could. She sat down and prayed this visit was one of friendship. She was afraid to move.

After she left, Nicholas began speaking again. "David, as some things change, some things stay the same."

"That's true," replied David, not at all sure where this conversation was going.

"Do you remember the day when our two fathers were

standing right where we are now, talking about the Trans-Siberian Railroad?"

"Yes, of course I do. We had a wonderful discussion, one I will never forget."

Nicholas smiled. "David, there is something I need to talk to you about. Do you still have some vodka up in your father's old office?"

"Of course."

"Then can we go upstairs and sample it?"

"It will be my honor," David replied.

Before ascending the stairs, the Tsar scanned the inside of the shop. It looked almost exactly as he remembered it. "Is that Jacob?" he asked, turning toward the boy.

"Yes," replied David. "He will turn thirteen this year."

Nicholas walked over to the boy. "Jacob, my father was a friend of your grandfather," he said. "I have come to this town and this shop many times before you were born. Your father and I have known each other for many years."

Jacob was taken by surprise and he did not know how to respond. "My father grieved when the Tsar passed," he said after a pause. David nodded with pleasure at his son's response.

"And my family grieved for your family when your grandfather Lewis passed," Nicholas replied.

"Thank you. We all miss him and my grandmother very much," said Jacob.

Nicholas turned toward David and said, "Let's go upstairs and toast to our children's long life and good health."

The two men walked up the wooden stairs to an office that hadn't changed much over the years. Very quickly, the reason for the meeting became clear. Nicholas and David spoke for several hours, and much was discussed. David was overwhelmed, excited, fearful, and appreciative. So much was about to change.

When the Tsar was ready to leave, David raised his right arm and placed it inside his jacket over his heart. He saluted the Tsar.

"*Spasibo, moy drug.* Thank you, my friend," he said with much gratitude. "I will send word when I have completed the fur coats for the Tsarina and your daughters."

Nicholas nodded his head and David walked back into his store. He looked at Jacob and said, "Nicholas is a good man."

Shortly thereafter, the Tsar put David in charge of the railway station, the steam-driven carriages, and the funicular at the end of town. David's dream had finally come true.

Now that David's career had taken this unexpected turn, his most pressing priority was to try and sell the family business. It had to be done soon, before this window of opportunity closed. He wondered whether Anthony Locante was still interested in purchasing it. Anthony had floated the idea to David two years ago, but David had no reason to sell at the time.

Anthony was Italian and his wife was Russian Orthodox. The Locante family had lived in Odessa for at least ten years. They were a respectable family and Anthony had no reservations about buying the store from a Jew. He paid David a small but fair sum under the circumstances, and in 1902, the Kaufmann mercantile store was renamed Locante's Exchange. Shortly after the sale, the Tsar doubled the taxes on all Jewish businesses.

Three months later, an entourage of Royal Guards came to Odessa. They walked into the railway station holding two crates, one large and one small. Inside the large crate was a silver fox which paced back and forth within the four corners of his chamber. Attached to the fox's collar was a beautiful gem-studded leash. In the small crate was a metal box engraved with the Romanov crest. A note was attached:

"It is important that the people of Odessa know you are representing the Tsar. The silver fox will keep you safe." The Romanov crest was stamped next to the Tsar's signature.

Every night when David left the train depot, he walked through the streets of Odessa, collecting the receipts of the day and putting the currency in his metal box. The box was strapped over his left shoulder. In his right arm, he held the gem-studded leash and walked through the streets with the silver fox leading the way. It was a responsibility David was proud to claim. Very unexpectedly, his dream of working with the railroad had come to fruition. But it was more than that. It was also a gift of protection and security, at least for now.

David loved his new post in life. It was challenging and fascinating. He knew that he was a lucky man. He was finally an engineer in charge of all of Odessa's transportation. It was more than anything he could have ever dreamed of.

Many of the townspeople found this appointment questionable, and they became suspicious of this unlikely position for someone of the Jewish faith. Others thought the government appointment would be good for Odessa, and that it might help them through the difficult times that everyone knew were still to come.

Chapter 13

Cecilia and Mary
Odessa, 1890–1898

Cecilia Jacobsky and David Kaufmann had known each other since childhood. Cecilia's father, Joseph, was a grain merchant, and a friend of David's father. It was common to see the two men strolling together after leaving the synagogue before dusk on the Sabbath. Both families often broke bread together after the fast during Yom Kipper.

Everyone in town had long speculated that the Kaufmann family and the Jacobsky family would arrange a marriage between David and Cecilia, but Cecilia's marriage had been pre-arranged before her birth. She was always going to be the wife of Myron Leis, also from a family of grain merchants.

Cecilia was petite and very pretty with golden blonde hair resting on her shoulders. Her smile was infectious and warm. When Cecilia turned seventeen, she and Myron married. They made a very handsome couple, although Myron paled in comparison to Cecilia's natural beauty. After a lavish wedding, the couple moved into the Leis's two-story home close to the sea-port. From the upstairs sitting room, one could see a framed view of the Black Sea, the fishing boats, and the wooden barrels that would soon be filled with ice cream. It was a large comfortable home with several bedrooms which the couple planned to fill up with many children.

On July 30, 1890, their daughter Mary was born. Mary did not have her mother's beauty or her father's stature. She was a little butterball with a round chunky face and small stubby fingers. She was content, playful, and loving. Her smile beamed happiness and joy. From the beginning, Mary was daddy's little girl, and her father was the center of her world. Whenever father and daughter left the house, Myron held her in his arms. As she grew older, father and daughter would be seen holding hands, walking through town.

The first seven years of Mary's life were perfect. She grew into a beautiful little girl. She was busy and content. She loved the water and loved to swim with her Papa in the Black Sea. Mary also loved to help her mother sew beautiful kippahs for the temple.

But tragedy struck the Jacobsky family on a warm summer day in 1898. In the early morning hours, just as the sun was rising, Myron, who was standing with his back up against one of the grain storage bins, was crushed between the bin and the cargo that was being unloaded off the dock. To this day, it is still unclear how the accident happened. It was never discussed or explained. The funeral was held three days later. Mary was barely eight years old when she sat alongside her father's pine casket.

Although Cecilia had some help from relatives and the Jewish community, she struggled financially. When Adela and David heard about their friend's plight, they asked Cecilia if she would like to work for them in the store. Cecilia gratefully accepted their offer and started working for the Kaufmanns as a dressmaker and seamstress.

Mary was nine when her mother began working. When she wasn't in school, she would spend her days at the Kaufmann's mercantile store. After finishing her studies, Mary would sit in the corner of the store with her sketchpad and draw her own dress designs. Sketching was the one thing that anesthetized her pain.

As Mary transitioned from childhood to womanhood, she often talked hopefully of the loving marriage she one day would have. Cecilia would listen in silence, deliberately choosing not to tell Mary the truth—that her marriage to David Kaufmann's son Jacob had been arranged since the day of her birth.

At the time, it had seemed like a faultless plan. But as the children grew to adulthood, with neither Mary nor Jacob suspecting the truth, both mothers had growing concerns about the unsuitability of the match. The differences between Jacob and Mary were becoming increasingly profound. Jacob was energetic, adventurous and outgoing. He was impatient with people who could not keep up with him. Physically, he was lean, muscular, very fit, and handsome. Mary, by sharp contrast, was quiet, reserved, and timid, and her body was unshapely and overweight.

Adela comforted herself with the hope that over time, Jacob and Mary would learn to grow together, taking each other's best qualities and creating a quilt of woven threads and patterns which would unite them as one. But in her heart, she was doubtful that this was ever going to happen.

When the Kaufmann's sold their mercantile store to Anthony Locante, he graciously agreed to have Cecilia and Mary, now thirteen, work for him. Cecilia continued designing and fabricating her beautiful dresses and coats while Mary's job was to sew fur on the collars and cuffs. In time, Mary soon began creating some of her own designs.

Chapter 14

Nicholas
St. Petersburg, 1904

Two major events occurred in 1904. The first was the much-anticipated completion of the Trans-Siberian Railroad. The second long-awaited announcement was that the Empress had given birth to a male child, the next heir to the throne. The royal couple named their son Alexi. This was a celebratory time for the royal family, and there was much enthusiasm and hope throughout Russia.

In a rush of his newfound optimism, Nicholas decided that this was the time to expand his empire. Looking to the Far East, he saw potential in Port Arthur, off the coast of Japan. This angered the Japanese who had recently been pressured to relinquish some of their land when Russia built the Trans-Siberian Railroad through part of Manchuria. Now with the threat of yet another acquisition by Russia, Japan felt further provoked.

In hope that they could come to some compromise, Japan sent diplomats to Russia on two separate occasions to negotiate an accord. Each time, however, Nicholas refused to meet with them and ordered that the diplomats be sent home.

Finally, the Japanese ran out of patience. With no other viable options, they decided they would take control of the situation by launching a surprise attack on Russian warships. The Japanese fleet sank two of Russia's ships and blockaded the harbor at Port Arthur. Japan drew first blood. The Russo-Japanese War had officially begun.

The thought of Japan declaring war against Russia was never in Nicholas's calculations. Tragically, it was a shortsighted misstep, which caused the deaths of over eighty thousand Russian soldiers. Nicholas felt betrayed and disgraced but would never admit that he had been outfoxed. Eventually, the Tsar was forced to surrender to Japan.

Disgraced and humiliated by the event, Nicholas spiraled into a deep state of depression. He told Alix that he felt as if he was in the middle of an avalanche, being buried alive, and barely able to breathe. But Nicholas's problems didn't stop there. The Russian working class was angry, frustrated, and determined to take control over what they felt was an intolerable situation. In St. Petersburg, workers secretly gathered in back rooms planning several protests and numerous labor strikes. The strikes, along with no available work, caused many Russian families to go hungry, and some died from starvation.

Nicholas's troubles continued to multiply. A few days prior to the infamous "Bloody Sunday," the socialist labor leader Father George Gapon informed the government that he intended to lead a procession to the Tsar's Winter Palace where he would then hand a workers' petition to the Tsar. Hearing this and on the advice of his generals, Nicholas and his family left the palace before the workers arrived.

On Sunday, January 22, 1905, an estimated 120,000 workers led by Gapon locked arms and marched peacefully through the streets of St. Petersburg singing the imperial anthem, "God Save the Tsar." As the workers walked through the city, infantry solders blocked their path. Without warning, the soldiers opened fire on the crowd. Hundreds of protesters were killed and others seriously wounded. The unprovoked massacre became the catalyst for more strikes and uprisings. The 1905 Russian Revolution had officially begun.

Outside Russia, the future British Labour Prime Minister, Ramsay MacDonald, attacked the Tsar, calling him a "blood-stained creature and a common murderer."

After hearing this, Nicholas expressed his thoughts in his diary:

In St. Petersburg there were serious disturbances due to the desire of workers to get to the Winter Palace. The troops had to shoot. In different places of the city, there were many dead and wounded. Lord, how painful and bad.

Gapon escaped the carnage. He retreated to his secret refuge and days later issued the following letter to the Tsar:

Nicholas Romanov, formerly Tsar and at present, is the soul murderer of the Russian Empire. The innocent blood of the workers and their wives and children lies forever between you and the Russian people. May all the blood which must be spilled, fall upon you and your hangman. I call upon all the socialist parties of Russia to come to an immediate agreement among them and bring an armed uprising against tsarism.

Instantly, it seemed terror had spread throughout the Russian Empire. The unrest escalated and once again riots led to many more deaths. When Russians weren't blaming the Tsar, they were blaming the Jews. The tide was coming in with forceful and angry waves of hatred and despair.

Nine months later, there was another anti-Jewish riot in Odessa and thousands were killed. Although it was miles away from the center of town, David was deeply worried. This was no longer the Odessa he knew so well. And what would the changes in this dire new world mean for him and his family?

Chapter 15

David
Odessa, 1905

Toward the end of 1905, the riots in Odessa escalated. Railway workers, industrial workers, shopkeepers and craftsmen united and organized a protest march from the seaport to the famous steps. David felt torn. He wanted to join the protest in support of his friends and neighbors, but he was also concerned about his job security. As it turned out, he did not need to waste any time worrying; his decision was made for him.

Shortly after the sun came up on a brisk clear day, a large group of railway workers and local shopkeepers joined hands and stopped in front of the Kaufmann home. Some were men who had broken bread and drunk wine with David and Adela on the Sabbath. Others were at the bris of David's sons, Jacob, Samuel, and Carl. Now these same men were at David's doorstep, angry and full of hate and fear. They were all standing in solidarity, waiting for David to join them.

David saw the faces of his fellow railway workers strained with grief and fear. He saw shopkeepers with sadness in their eyes. In that moment, he understood that his friendship with Nicholas was no longer a gift; it was a curse. David walked out of his house, locked arms with his fellow Russians, and marched in solidarity.

For the next few months, David continued his duties managing transportation for the Tsar. He did not vary or alter his routine in any way. He walked through the streets at night with his silver fox and metal box, collecting the receipts for the day. He completed his daily reports and at the end of each week, he turned over all the receipts and fees to the Tsar's deputy of transportation. He worked even harder than usual with the hope that things would eventually calm down. But if it didn't, he knew what he had to do. He would leave and take his family to America.

Chapter 16

Jacob
Odessa, 1906–1908

A year later, on a snowy day in December, an envelope marked *Personal and Confidential* was delivered to David at the train depot. The note, which was handwritten, read: "My grandfather and father would have wanted me to instruct you to put your affairs in order. It is time, comrade. God speed."

As instructed, David destroyed the note. He did not tell anyone, not even Adela. David understood this was the last gesture of friendship between the Romanovs and the Kaufmanns.

For a few minutes, David just stood there, frozen by the note and the knowledge of what it all meant. Then, restlessly he left the depot and began to walk. For hours, David walked through his beautiful town, his cherished Odessa.

The town had changed much over the last forty years. Even the beautiful branches and blossoms from the acacia trees had changed. The branches had thinned and the scent of the flowers seemed to have morphed into something foul, something rotten. The fragrance of his childhood had disappeared.

The wooden barrels of wine and ice cream were rarely filled now. Instead, the barrels had been broken up by the citizens to use for fuel for cooking large pots of soup and baking loaves of bread. Laughter, even from the children, was muted, and the men walked the streets of Odessa with heavy and slow footsteps.

David wandered along the cobblestone streets for hours, without purpose, as he tried to capture a snapshot in his memory of the only home he had ever known. Odessa was his entire world. Finally, utterly exhausted, he went back home. The time had come to journey to America.

During the last ten years, many of the Kaufmann clan had already immigrated to Chicago and New York where they were thriving. The Goldman side of the family had, over the years, paid the passage for many family members. But every émigré had to start over. The transition was difficult, whether you were a doctor, a lawyer, a rabbi, or worked in the trades. Each person shared an unbridled determination to succeed, but there were many serious and legitimate concerns to consider. The journey itself was dangerous and difficult, and in many cases men, women, and children died before they reached America's shores.

Then, on a blistering cold fall day in late October 1907, while sitting across from the warm dancing fire in the living room hearth, David turned to Adela and began to speak.

"Adela, the time has come for Jacob and Samuel to immigrate to America." Adela started to tear up. David wiped her tears. "I am going to write to your Uncle Benjamin. He will be able to take our sons in until we can reunite."

"Do not cry my love," David continued. "This is just another chapter in our life. We both know this is what needs to be done. Our children will be safe in America. We will reunite with them very soon, I promise. I'm going to tell Jacob and Samuel they will be leaving for Vienna. They will have time to visit with your family before their journey begins. Before they leave Odessa, I am going to take them to the cemetery to say goodbye to their grandparents."

Adela reached out to hold David's hand. He lifted her hands and gently kissed them. Tears trickled down her face as she said, "My love, can't we wait until all the family can travel together? I trust you, but I am very afraid something will go wrong. What happens if the boys get sick on the ship? Who will be there for them?"

"I wish we could all go to America at the same time, but that isn't possible," David replied. "I have spoken with our children, and they understand that it will be better if just a few us leave at a time. Trust me. This is what we need to do. We need to keep them safe."

In her heart, Adela knew David was right. It was more dangerous to stay in Odessa than starting a new life in America. She prayed they were making the right choice.

The first thing David did was to compose a letter to Adela's Uncle Benjamin who had emigrated ten years earlier. He lived in Chicago where he had opened a small tailor shop on the South Side. Over the years, he had expanded his business into several clothing stores. Word had it that his business was thriving.

David decided he would write Benjamin and ask him whether he would be able to take in Jacob and Samuel until the rest of the family could be reunited. As he sat down at his desk to write the letter, the finality of what he was doing hit him and his fingers quivered:

Dear Benjamin,

Adela and I hope you and your family are in good health and your life in America has been prosperous. Last year you sent word that when the time was right, you would help our family immigrate to America. What a generous and unselfish gift you have offered us. The time has come for us to begin this very difficult transition.

Leaving my homeland, my country, is the most difficult thing I have ever had to do. We are arranging passage for Jacob and Samuel. Once the arrangements have been completed, word will be sent to you. My sons will come with enough money to carry them through until the rest of the family arrives in our new land. You have my word that I will repay you for all expenses incurred for my sons' room and board. As you know, it is too risky to send the money ahead of time because thieves pilfer through the mail.

Sincerely, David

The Kaufmann household turned upside down with frenetic activity. Adela mended and washed her sons' clothes. Jacob and Samuel packed one suitcase each and squabbled over every inch of the steamer trunk they shared. They packed their prayer books in readiness of attending their new synagogue in America. Samuel wept for his small library left behind; Jacob was upset to have to leave his weights and boxing gear.

David tried to pass his days as if nothing was changing, but that was impossible. He stalked the streets in misery, making his daily rounds, feet and heart leaden with fear. David knew how fortunate his family was. He knew many people who had used their life savings to purchase a one-way ticket to a destination they had only heard about. They boarded a steamship with little more than the clothes on their backs and dreams in their head. David knew his boys would find work in Chicago. They had many relatives who had blazed the trail and doors would open for them.

Adela wept as she prepared meat, dried fruits, baked breads and cakes for the journey, and the boys stuffed the food into their knapsacks.

It was now time to say goodbye. After a short visit with their grandparents in Vienna, Jacob and Samuel travelled to Latvia where they would depart from Libau, the main port of emigration from Russia. They had their prepaid cabin class tickets and their government documents locked in a leather satchel. The brothers presented their official travel documents. They were steps from boarding the ship and gawked at the magnificent vessel that would become their home for the next several weeks.

They would be sailing on the *Smolensk*, a name familiar to both young men. They had studied about the *Smolensk* in school. The ship was named after the city that was used as a key fortress in 1812 to defend the Russian capital.

Jacob and Samuel stared at the massive ship. Jacob gave a low whistle. "Can you believe we're actually going to cross the ocean tomorrow?"

"And sail to America," Samuel added, his voice equally awed. The two boys shook their heads in sorrow, in excitement, and in wonder.

As it turned out, the two brothers, who loved being on the water, were ill prepared for the rough seas they encountered during their journey. On the first two nights, waves thrashed over the ship's gunnels and the giant ship bucked and rolled with the ferocity of Poseidon. Their mother had warned them to eat sparingly until their stomachs got used to the motion, but even with that warning, they were both up all night vomiting.

Their small cabin was less than adequate. The wood floor was marred with deep scratches. A small porthole provided the only light. Jacob immediately claimed the top bunk, leaving his younger brother sleeping on the lower, claustrophobic one.

The brothers decided to keep to themselves and not socialize with the other passengers, but as they roamed the ship, they ended up overhearing and absorbing some extraordinary stories.

One they would never forget involved a woman who, after arriving on Ellis Island, was certified by a medical doctor to be of "low intelligence" because she couldn't put together a jigsaw puzzle the doctors gave her. The woman's response was, "If you give me some chicken and some dough, I will make a delicious soup and bake you the best bread you have ever had." The officers looked at the woman, not knowing what to say. They let her pass through immigration and America became her new home.

Many years later, she went back to the port with a pot of chicken soup and a baked challah topped with sesame seeds. She gave it to the first immigration officer she came upon and said with a smile, "This was a promise I made many years ago to the immigration officer who stamped my papers when I first arrived in America. I hope you enjoy the soup and bread."

Another story which did not end as well was about a father who was a tailor and his son who was a student. The two men were not allowed to enter together. The immigration officer told the father that if he would be willing to go back to Russia, they would let his son into America. The father, who would have given his life for his child, said he would return to Russia. The son very reluctantly complied, but was heard to say, "One shall be taken and the other must go back to die." The son never saw or heard from his father again.

As each day slipped by, bringing America ever nearer, the excitement of the passengers increased to a palpable energy. When the announcement came that they would arrive in New York Harbor the next morning, everyone clapped, yelled, and cried. Jacob and Samuel stayed up all night. It was too exciting to sleep.

At first light, the brothers shaved in a communal bathroom, washed with soap and water, and dressed in special clothes they had set aside for this day. With shoes shined, they stepped out of their stateroom. Suitcases in hand, together they dragged the small steamer trunk toward the shores of America.

When they got on deck, they could see the skyline of New York City rising in the distance. And there, out of the depths of the sea, the Statue of Liberty stood tall and majestic. After fourteen days, the *Smolensk* pulled into New York Harbor. As they passed the statue, Jacob asked, "Have you ever seen a more beautiful woman?"

Samuel shook his head back and forth. Emotion overcame him and he could not speak.

"I feel as if she is wrapping her arms around us and will keep both of us safe," Jacob continued. "She has taken my breath away."

Jacob and Samuel Kaufmann arrived in New York on November 30, 1907, on a chilly, blustering day. Cirrus clouds formed delicate filaments of white bands across the dim gray sky.

The brothers put on heavy winter coats, wrapped wool mufflers around their necks, shoved their hands into brown leather gloves, and walked off the ship.

After all the questions had been answered satisfactorily, the official approved the brothers for entry and stamped their papers officially as Jacob Kaufman and Samuel Kaufman. Jacob and Samuel turned toward the massive blue exit doors. Once again, they showed their stamped papers. And finally, before entering their new world, the brothers looked up and read the written inscription on the wall.

Give me your tired, your poor, your huddled masses yearning to breathe free, the wretched refuse of your teeming shore. Send these, the homeless, tempest-tossed to me; I lift my lamp beside the golden door. This country's greatness and true genius lies in its diversity.

Outside, the sunlight filtered through the clouds, lighting up rows of imposing buildings. It was one of the most beautiful sights they had ever seen. Jacob and Samuel had arrived! They were in America!

Jacob looked at his brother and said, "My name is Jack Kaufman and I live in America."

With a tremulous voice, Samuel said, "My name is Sam Kaufman and this is my new home."

Chapter 17

Jack
Brighton Beach, 1907

For years, Jack had dreamed about what it would be like to live in America. Now those dreams, opportunities, and experiences were within his grasp.

The excitement Jack felt trickled through his whole body. His heart pounded with a mixture of joy, anticipation, and terror. His hands shook slightly as his knees buckled underneath him. He straightened up, took a deep breath, regained his composure, and scanned his surroundings.

The noises, the smells, and the chaotic pace of people searching for loved ones at the pier poignantly reminded Jack of what he had left behind in Odessa. But then his mind opened itself to the endless possibilities and opportunities in this new and exciting country. He put his arm around Sam's shoulder, and they began walking through the streets of New York.

They stopped every few minutes, just to take in all the sights. Jack wanted to remember this day forever. He surveyed the faces of all the different people around him and tried to guess what part of the world they came from. He recognized many Russian faces, émigrés from his old country.

Then Jack turned his attention to the man-made attractions of the city. He marveled at the buildings and the skyline they created with their architecture and rooftops. He walked through the wide streets. He memorized some of the street names: Broad Street, Wall Street, Exchange Place, and Fifth Avenue. He didn't know quite why he did that; all he knew was that he wanted this moment to be deeply imbedded in his memory. He closed his eyes, took a deep breath, and smelled the scents of his surroundings. New York did not smell anything like Odessa.

He could almost feel the luscious scents from the acacia blossoms, once so deeply ingrained in his pores, now disappearing from his memory. The smells around him now were a mixture of leather, dirt, grime, and sweat. Masking those smells, though, were the most scrumptious whiffs of a variety of international foods and spices. Ardently, he inhaled the bouquet of new and vibrant fragrances. Even the ice cream smelled deliciously different from the ice cream in the wooden barrels back home. Jack took a deep breath. It all seemed completely unreal. But one thing was certain—he loved New York.

Jack shivered from the cold, or perhaps it was sheer excitement. The sky turned silver, and shadows drifted west across the horizon. It looked like bad weather might be rolling in. He found himself wondering whether the raindrops would taste the same as in Odessa. He laughed at himself for even having such a silly notion, and felt, for a moment, that being in New York had turned him back into a carefree young boy again.

"Jack, do you know where we are going?" asked Sam, suddenly. Jack was shocked back to reality and a sense of responsibility.

"Of course I do."

Jack looked down at the instructions his uncle had provided him. Then the two brothers turned toward the Brooklyn Bridge. As they walked through the streets, scores of people, sometimes shoulder to shoulder, pushed and shoved themselves toward their destinations.

It wasn't until the boys were nearly at their destination that they realized it was Shabbat, the day of rest, celebration, and prayer. With all the chaos, it had completely slipped Jack's mind until he saw a group of men walking into a nearby synagogue. The two brothers stepped quietly inside and joined the congregation, leaving their suitcases and steamer trunk in the back corner of the temple.

The prayers felt especially meaningful on this Saturday morning. Jack thanked God for their successful voyage. He prayed for his family's safety and a speedy voyage to this new and remarkable land.

Two hours later, Jack whispered, "Sam, we should get going." They quietly walked out.

As they approached the Brooklyn Bridge, Sam eagerly asked, "Can we go on the steam-driven cable cars?"

"Why? Is there something wrong with your legs?" Jack replied.

Sam responded with a blank stare until Jack said, "Just joking. Let's hop on."

The ride was exciting, but all too short. After they disembarked, Jack approached a well-dressed man, standing nearby.

"Excuse me, sir," he began politely. "We have just arrived from Odessa and are in need of directions to this boardinghouse." He showed the address to the stranger. "My uncle has made arrangements for my brother and me to stay here for a week before we meet our family in Chicago." Jack paused while the man read the address.

Then he remembered his manners. "My name is Jack Kaufman, and this is my brother Sam."

The man smiled. "Well Jack and Sam, welcome to New York. My name is Joe." Joe scanned the page of directions. "This is your lucky day. I know your boardinghouse well. In fact, I live very close to it. Would you like to walk there with me?"

"That's very kind of you," Jack replied.

"We would like that," Sam added.

As the three men walked through the streets of Brooklyn, Joe told the two brothers a little bit about Brighton Beach. He also told them about his great grandfather, who emigrated from Ireland in 1850.

"My great grandfather went from nearly starving to becoming

a successful businessman right here in Brooklyn," Joe explained. "He started working at the Quinebaug Mill and then opened up his own linen business. New York is a great place to live. Make sure before you leave New York that you spend some time at the boardwalk in Brighton Beach. It has been open for almost two years now and is a mile long. You boys should go on some of the rides, especially the steel roller coaster. They call it The Chase Through the Clouds. There is also a scenic railway and a carousel."

"Sounds great," Sam blurted out.

"You probably would also enjoy the "Great Far East Show," Joe added. "As I remember, it has camels and Russian Cossacks."

Sam made a wry face. "That sounds like a great time, but I think I've seen my share of Russian Cossacks to last a lifetime."

Jack grinned at Sam. Boardwalks! Carousels! Railways! What a place America was. Jack's head was spinning with wonder and intrigue. He had to pinch himself again and again to make sure this was really happening. But at the same time, he felt a little guilty. He knew his father would not approve of any of it. Finally, they came to a two-story brick building.

"Well, this is the place," Joe told them. "Enjoy yourself this week. It was a pleasure meeting the two of you. Good luck."

They shook hands and Joe continued walking. The brothers watched him disappear. Before mounting the stairs to their first home in America, Jack took a deep breath and then rang the doorbell.

"Who's there?" asked a man in a thick Russian accent.

Jack shouted at the closed door, "Jack and Sam Kaufman. We have just arrived from Odessa. I have a note for you from my father, David Kaufmann."

The door was flung open and a large, bearded man with a cynical smile greeted the boys. "I was expecting you. What took you so long?" Boris asked. "Come in. Come in. Your room is upstairs. Follow me." They walked upstairs and Boris opened the door to the room the brothers would share for the next seven days.

"The water closet is down the hall. There is a small sink and double bed in your room, and I put two wooden chairs in there for you," Boris told the boys. "The Brighton Beach Baths are a few doors down the street. You can get a steam and soak for five cents. Speaking of money, how long are you staying?" he asked.

"We would like to stay for seven nights. I have the money right here," Jack answered.

Jack opened the inside pocket in his vest and put the bills in Boris's hand. Then Jack and Sam walked into the room, closed the door, and collapsed on top of the double bed.

The brick boardinghouse was adequate. There were a couple of chairs in the living room and a wooden table in the kitchen. In some ways it looked a little like the kitchen they had in Odessa. The table was marred and the floors were scratched, squeaking with every step. Everyone went their own way and there was no interaction.

Over the next six days, the brother's walked on the board-walk, ate hot dogs from the "dog wagons" and went on as many rides as they could. They decided to skip the "Great Far East Show. "

On day seven, suitcases in hand, Jack and Sam re-crossed the Brooklyn Bridge into Manhattan, dragging their small steamer trunk. They spent their last day exploring and sampling some of New York's kosher hotdogs, salted pretzels, pastrami, and chestnuts. They both decided they preferred the food from the "dog wagons" because it reminded them of their homeland.

As the week ended, they were ready to embark on the next leg of their journey. They would settle down and start their new life, although Jack couldn't imagine his life in Chicago would be as exciting as the week he had just spent in New York.

Finally, it was time to head toward Grand Central Terminal and board the Pennsylvania Special, the train that ran from New

York City to Chicago via Philadelphia. Jack purchased two one-way tickets and the brothers climbed up the steel steps into one of the cars.

"Let's put our bags up on the racks. But first, take out the food we bought from the wagons. I'll take the window seat," Jack exclaimed. They settled in and Jack stared through the small window.

"All aboard who's coming aboard," hollered the engineer.

The train slowly pulled out of the station and quickly picked up speed. The landscape changed as they moved farther and farther from New York City. It began to rain.

Unexpectedly, Jack started to feel a little homesick. He missed his father, his mother, Bella, and his brother Carl. But then he closed his eyes and thought about all the possibilities and experiences that were yet to come.

PART TWO

Chicago

Jack and Mary

Chapter 18

Jack and Sam
Chicago, 1907–1912

The train squealed and shrieked to a grinding halt as it pulled into the depot in Chicago. Jack and Sam could hardly control their excitement. The Kaufman boys, with luggage in hand, pushed toward the door. They were the first to jump off the train.

Their final destination was Evanston. They quickly bought their last round of tickets, and waited with great impatience for the commuter train to arrive. To distract themselves, they focused on the World Series banners and posters plastered on the station walls. Some were peeling away from the stucco and others had been marked up with celebratory notes. Jack heard all about the recent World Series during their week in Brighton Beach and was excited about going to his first game.

"Evanston Special leaving in ten minutes on track four," hollered the engineer.

Jack put his arm around his brother's shoulder. "This is it, Sam. We are going to our new home."

During the short train ride, Jack found his thoughts still lingering on the baseball posters he had seen in the train station. He vowed that he would go to as many games as he could when the season opened in 1908. Maybe he could even play the game himself one day? He was fit and strong and had the body of an athlete. After all, he had trained for the sport of boxing in Odessa. He had dedicated many years, training in the gym almost every day. He'd fought in as many boxing bouts as possible and usually emerged victorious.

"Baseball couldn't be harder than boxing," he whispered to

himself. When he settled into their new home, he'd start lifting weights again and eat raw eggs every day. That was the key to a long life.

As he settled into his seat, he found a newspaper clipping about the Chicago World Series and began reading the article:

The year 1907 is all about the Chicago Cubs. The Cubs played the first three of the five games at the West Side Grounds in Chicago and the remaining two games at Bennett Park in Detroit. This year, Detroit added their young rising star, Ty Cobb, to their roster. But even Cobb could not save the day for the Tigers. Game one was brutal and hard fought. It ended in a 3–3 tie after twelve innings. The next four games were a sweep. The Cubs shut out Detroit in game five to win the World Series.

Sam nodded off. The last three weeks had finally caught up with him. But then into his reverie came the conductor's voice. "Evanston! Evanston! Next stop, Evanston! We will be arriving in about fifteen minutes." They were going to their new home at last.

The brothers gathered their belongings as the train slowed to a grinding halt. Jack waited until the train pulled out, then looked at Sam and said, "We've gone halfway around the world and our adventure has just begun." They picked up their suitcases and started walking to their new home.

Jack pulled out the map to his uncle's house and began to study the directions his uncle had sent him.

"It looks like we aren't too far away. I say we walk so we can see a little of Evanston," suggested Jack, a hint of melancholy in his voice. "We have a couple of hours left before the sun goes down."

Jack's mind began to wander as they walked through the streets of their new home. Oddly, the one thing he was fixated on was going to the next World Series. If it were in Chicago, he would definitely go.

In contrast to the hustle and bustle while in New York, Jack sensed calm as he and Sam walked the streets of their new city. Evanston seemed much more cordial then New York. There was no pushing or shoving. People greeted friends and relatives while hugging and kissing. It was welcoming and already felt like home. His mind wandered as he was walking.

"Jack, Jack!" yelled Sam. "What are you doing? You almost walked right into that hole."

"Sorry, Sam. I guess I was just thinking about something," he replied, shaking his head to clear the ridiculous thoughts.

"Stop your thinking and let's get to our uncle's house," Sam replied.

Jack looked at the note again and continued following the detailed directions to the Goldman home.

Suddenly, he stopped and asked, "Can you smell it?"

Sam nearly bumped into his brother. "Smell what?"

Jack grinned. "The lake. I can smell Lake Michigan. The smell is different from the Black Sea. Let's take a quick detour and walk toward the water. We're only a few minutes away!"

"No, Jack. We can do that tomorrow. Let's get to our uncle's house," Sam said firmly.

They followed the numbers posted on the doors until they finally reached 3792 Lake Drive. They were home! And a lovely home it was.

The outside walls of the house were gray and tan with light red stones set in the facade, Chicago's version of the brownstones they saw in New York. Two vertical windows flanked each side of the wooden entry door. A black cast-iron doorknocker in the shape of a closed fist was centered perfectly in the middle of the door. The home soared two stories to a dormered roof, and rows of red brick placed horizontally below the roofline traced a decorative pattern.

Jack put his suitcase onto the porch landing. Drawing a

slightly shaky breath, he lifted the black cast-iron handle and knocked as loudly as he could.

"Who's there?" asked a deep voice.

"Jack and Sam Kaufman."

Benjamin opened the door. He was a large man, six feet tall, with a solid muscular frame and a commanding presence. When he saw the boys, he gave a delighted chuckle.

"And here I was expecting Jacob and Samuel."

All three laughed and embraced.

"Welcome, boys. Welcome home," Benjamin said warmly.

As they went inside, their Aunt Sophie came racing out of the kitchen to greet the boys. In contrast to her husband, she was barely five feet tall with curly blonde hair, pale blue eyes, and a kind face.

"Oh my, you have grown so much," she exclaimed. "You are now men. No longer boys getting into mischief. Come here. You must be so hungry. Come into the kitchen."

Jack and Sam didn't need to be asked twice and sat down at the kitchen table.

The kitchen reminded them of their own kitchen back in Odessa, although this one was much bigger and newer. A large window over the sink had a view of a yard with mature trees, now dormant until spring.

"How are your mother and father doing?" asked Sophie eagerly.

"Very well, though I know that leaving Odessa will be very difficult for them both," replied Jack.

Sophie nodded. "Your parents are strong people. They will get through this transition." She paused, then added with a smile, "And how are my Bella and Carl doing?"

"Bella is excited to come to America. I'm not sure that Carl will leave with them. He has his heart set on becoming a musician and wants to study in Vienna," Jack informed her.

"Well, I can't wait to see them," replied Sophie. "Now let's eat so I can give you the grand tour and show you your room. Then you can freshen up and rest a bit. You will have plenty of time to get acquainted with our beautiful city."

Sophie placed two bowls of chicken soup in front of Jack and Sam. They both slurped up every drop. Then their aunt placed plates of brisket, potatoes, and applesauce on the table. The boys gobbled down every last bite.

The house was impressive. In addition to the kitchen, the first floor included a large library, a sitting room, a formal dining room, and a small utility room. Upstairs, there were three bedrooms and a bath. The basement had been turned into two rooms with a water closet and a small sink. Jack and Sam would share one of the basement bedrooms. Sophie said they could also use the second room, which contained a large writing desk, for their studies.

"It's perfect," Sam beamed. "Thank you, Auntie."

Before the boys left Russia, David had given Jack a letter to give to his uncle upon their arrival. When Jack began unpacking, he pulled the envelope out, and even though he knew it by heart, he read it over one last time.

Dear Benjamin,

I have so much gratitude for you and your wife Sophie that it is difficult to put into words how much I thank you for what you have offered to do for my family. I have instructed Jacob to repay you for all monies you have spent helping us make this journey. We are very hopeful that we will arrive in your country before Passover next year. You are saving us from what we know, and what we do not yet know, will happen in our homeland.

Sincerely,

David

After unpacking, Jack went upstairs to give his uncle the letter. Benjamin read it over twice. David had insisted before they left that Jack continue his schooling. His education at the Trud School in Odessa, which was the pride of southern Russian Jewish education, was praised throughout the Russian Empire. Now Jack wanted to go to Northwestern to continue his studies. He had heard Northwestern was an excellent university with a highly acclaimed business program, and happily wasn't too far from where his aunt and uncle lived.

Once the boys had time to settle into their new surroundings, their uncle decided they would also begin working part-time at one of his department stores while they attended school. That way, they would have more flexibility and be able to put their education first. Benjamin believed that "opportunity only knocks but once," so he wanted his nephews to seize every opportunity presented to them.

For the next six months, Jack followed his routine. First thing in the morning, he ate six raw eggs. He would complete his chores around the house and then go to work at Goldman's Department Store. In the late afternoon and early evening, he took business classes at Northwestern.

Since he didn't have time to go to the gymnasium, in his spare time he lifted bricks or took a run along Lake Michigan. As he ran, he reminisced about his past and dreamed about his future.

The 1908 baseball season was in full swing. Even a song about baseball had been written, titled, "Take Me Out to the Ball Game." No matter where you went, someone was singing it. The song was becoming baseball's unofficial theme song. Jack heard it at his very first Cubs game. It was one of the most exciting nights of his life. He loved the feeling of being part of a large, cheering crowd, and he vowed that baseball would be an important part of his life forever.

The 1908 World Series evolved into a rematch of the 1907 Fall Classic. The first game was played in Detroit. The Cubs trailed 6–5 as they came to bat in the ninth inning. The Tigers' knuckleballer, "Kickapoo" Eddie Summers, had been pitching well in relief up to that point. But the Cubs came back, stringing together six straight hits and five runs against Summers for a 10–6 victory.

The next game took place in Chicago. In game two, the Cubs scored six runs in the eighth inning to win 6-1. The win took just ninety minutes. Jack attended the West Side Park that day. He was sitting way out in the bleachers. He promised himself that when he had a son, he would teach him how to play baseball and take him to the games.

The Tigers were confident that they would get enough runs on the scoreboard to win game three in their hometown. Their up-and-coming star, Ty Cobb, went 4 for 5 with a double and two RBIs and the Tigers won 8–3. The last two games were played in Chicago. The Cubs shut the Tigers out in both.

The fans went ballistic. People danced and celebrated in the streets. Storefronts hung banners celebrating the World Series victory. Confetti flew from front stoops and rooftops. Everyone in Chicago had instantaneously become a fan of the game.

As the months went on, Jack nurtured yet another dream. The Ford Model T was being mass-produced on assembly lines and selling for $850. The automobile was a life-changing event in Chicago and around the country. Jack loved this car. He promised himself that when he became successful, he would buy a new Ford every year. All things considered, being a young man living in America was the most exciting thing in the world.

The winter of 1908 was a joyful time. David, Adela, and Bella finally immigrated to America and joined Jack and Sam. Carl, who wanted to follow in his mother's footsteps, went to the University of Vienna to study music.

When the family reunited, they moved into their own apartment in Evanston. Benjamin asked David to be a furrier at one of the Goldman Department Stores and David gratefully accepted the position. Concerned about David's limited English,

Benjamin assigned a Russian employee from Minsk who spoke Yiddish to be David's assistant.

Out of respect, the family spoke only Russian when David was around. They honored the fact that David would forever grieve the loss of his homeland. America was where he now lived, but it would never be his home. He did what he needed to do for his family's safety and his children's future, but he did not come to America for a new nationality. He was Russian, and that would never change.

In 1910, the Kaufman family moved out of Evanston and rented a two-story house in the South Side of Chicago. That same year, the Chicago White Sox also found their new home. The new ballpark was built on a former city dump that Charles Comiskey bought in 1909 to replace the old wooden South Side Park. Jack, as an avid baseball fan, went to a few White Sox games, mostly because of the proximity of the park to his house. He had become a Cubs fan after attending his first baseball game, but the White Sox quickly won him over and became his American baseball team.

Over the next five years, Jack completed his schooling and then took a job in the trades. His earnings helped provide a steady income for the family, and he hoped his savings would be used one day to buy the family home.

Life was good for Jack, as good as he had dreamed. In fact, if only he had an American girlfriend, everything would be perfect. One like all his friends had, fun, free, and sexy. Jack knew that simply wasn't going to happen. His choice for a wife had been arranged before he was even born. That was what was expected. It was tradition. It was the custom. It was the way things were done. But until his marriage was consummated with Mary, Jack decided that he would test the waters and have some fun. A lot of fun!

Jack found American women exciting, interesting, stunning, and absolutely hypnotic. He liked free-spirited sexy women who just wanted to have a good time. He was careful not to allow himself to get emotionally involved, but his physical attraction to them was a completely different issue.

Many of Jack's "companions" were experienced women who more than satisfied his physical needs and desires. The sex was not ordinary. It was euphoric, exciting, and exhilarating. His body responded in ways he did not know were even possible.

Jack wanted a marriage like his parents, who were still deeply in love. But he also knew that would never happen with Mary. She was old world and would never change. He would honor his commitment and wed Mary, accepting that his life with her would be routine and mundane. Jack was under no illusion. He knew what his father expected him to do.

Chapter 19

Jack and Mary
Chicago, 1914

As the ship pulled into New York Harbor, Mary and her mother, Cecilia, anxiously waited on the boat's oak-planked lower deck. They inched their way to the outside rail, scanning with awe their first sight of America. Crowds of men, women, and children huddled together on the dock yelling and cheering in a combination of different languages and dialects. Mary's emotions were mixed with joyful excitement to absolute fear.

Jack and Adela had travelled from Chicago to New York and were now waiting to greet the disembarking pair. In spite of Jack's reservations about marrying Mary, he was curious to see what she looked like. He closed his eyes for a moment and remembered so many memories from his childhood.

Jack remembered the beautiful violins and the fur coats his father and grandfather made from the pelts of the silver fox. He remembered doing his schoolwork in the corner of the shop. And then he remembered Mary's kind gentleness.

The ship's anchor fastened into the rocky shoreline as the rope lines were secured. Finally, the gangplank was lowered and families huddled together as they walked down the final bridge, from sea to land, a bridge from their old life to the new.

Jack and Adela scanned the arrivals, looking for Mary and Cecilia. Adela saw Cecilia first. Jubilantly, she exclaimed, "That's them! They're on the walkway!"

At the same time, Mary spotted Jacob. It had been seven years since she had seen him. She blushed to realize that the tall man waving at her from the dock was as handsome as she remembered.

For Jack's part, he saw that Mary had filled out and was actually very pretty. Not a beauty like some of the American women he was accustomed to seeing in Chicago, but definitely attractive. He hoped that she would soon love her new country as much as he did.

Jack brought with him papers from the rabbi at the synagogue, documenting the upcoming marriage and providing corroboration of Jack's employment. These certificates would help Mary through the immigration process should any questions come up about her short stay in New York City.

Jack decided to stay in New York himself for a couple of days. He gave Mary some time to visit with her Aunt Dora and made sure that she and her mother, Cecilia, were settled into the apartment in Brighton Beach.

Jack then checked into his room which was nearby, and walked to the Brighton Beach Baths, and took a steam.

While in the baths, reality suddenly hit him, and Jack felt overwhelmed by a pervasive sense of doom. Of course, he had always known that he and Mary would eventually marry; he had grown up with that reality. But now, it was no longer a vague event that would happen far in the future. Mary was only a few blocks away, and the marriage was only a few days away.

Jack gave way to momentary panic. He didn't want to marry her. He didn't want the old ways and Russian traditions. He had been in America almost seven years and was an American now with new and brash American dreams. He wanted a woman who would share those dreams. But now that he had actually met her, he knew without any doubt that Mary was not that woman.

Jack sighed. Glumly, he made himself relax into the hot steam. He knew there was no escaping. All his dreams and desires, they added up to nothing. He would never have the courage or the cruelty to disrespect his father's wishes. He knew that he would be marrying Mary on the appointed day, and that he would have to make the best of it. Mary would be his wife.

He got dressed and took a long walk on the beach, watching the waves crash on the sand. He calmed his nerves and returned to the boardinghouse, drank a glass of bourbon, and fell asleep.

While in Brighton Beach, Jack took Mary to the boardwalk, and they both rode the carousel and ate candied corn. They took long walks and built a large castle in the sand. Every evening, Jack would go to Dora's apartment and have dinner with the family. He was starting to feel comfortable with Mary and could sense that the feeling was reciprocated. Brighton Beach felt familiar and safe to her, as there were Russian Jews everywhere. The beachside community was even referred to as "Little Odessa."

Since Mary spoke very little English, the newly united couple spoke to each other in Yiddish. Mary showed Jack some of her sketches and designs, and Jack was impressed with her artistic talent. Jack and Mary were courteous, respectful, and pleasant to each other. But in spite of Mary's hopes and Jack's best efforts, it was painfully clear that there was no romantic connection.

Five days later, on a misty New York day, Adela, Jack, and Mary boarded the train back to Chicago.

As they pulled into the depot, the couple saw a delicate rainbow arching over the sky above them. The colors reminded them of the rainbows over the Black Sea. Jack looked at Mary and said, "When you see a rainbow, you have to close your eyes and make a wish."

Mary's wish was that she and Jack would one day share the same type of love her mother had with her father. But in her heart, she didn't think that was even possible. Jack's wish was that one day he would become a famous movie director and his story would be printed in the *Chicago Tribune.*

A week after arriving in Chicago, on Wednesday, November 4, 1914, Jack David Kaufman and Mary Leis were married in a traditional Jewish ceremony at Temple Beth Shalom. David and

Adela were present, as were Jack's brothers, Sam and Carl, and his sister, Bella.

Adela designed the chuppah for her son and daughter-in-law. The chuppah is symbolic of the home the new couple will build together and also represents the groom walking his bride into their new life. Adela's chuppah was made from light blue and white cloth with a Star of David embroidered in dark blue thread. It was especially beautiful and meaningful, and David was proud of Adela's work.

As Mary stood under the chuppah reciting her wedding vows, nothing seemed quite real to her. She found herself longing for her mother. Cecilia hadn't been well enough to make the train journey from New York. Mary pretended her mother was standing next to her now, watching the ceremony with happy tears. She knew her mother would have told her how beautiful she looked and that everything would work out. But her sadness turned to joy when she thought about the children she would one day bring into this world.

Jack and Mary were standing directly beneath the Star of David when the rabbi began the service. David and Adela, sitting in the front row of the congregation, were holding hands and smiling with joy. They prayed God would bless them with many grandchildren and the couple would have a long and blissful life together.

The rabbi recited the religious marital blessings and the blessing over the wine. After Jack and Mary recited their prayers, they both sipped wine from the same sterling silver cup that was used by David and Adela at their wedding.

Sam was given the honor of holding the wedding ring. Right on cue, he stepped forward and handed his brother the simple gold ring. Jack took the ring in his hand and looked into Mary's eyes.

Jack recited, "Behold, you are betrothed unto me with this ring, according to the Law of Moses and Israel." Then Jack took

Mary's hand into his and placed the ring on her forefinger.

They were now man and wife.

The rabbi gently rolled open the ketubah and recited the words beautifully written in the marriage contract. It described Jack's duties and responsibilities to his new wife. Jack was to provide Mary with food, shelter, and clothing. He was to be attentive and supportive of all her emotional needs. The Hebrew words were beautifully scrolled in ink and intertwined amidst lovely decorative artwork. Jack was going to have it framed so they could hang it in their home. It was his wedding gift to Mary.

The rabbi recited the seven blessings over the second cup of wine. Jack and Mary joined in the blessings. Then the rabbi placed a glass on the floor and Jack shattered it with the sole of his right shoe. "Mazal Tov! Congratulations."

Now as husband and wife, Jack and Mary would share their first meal as a married couple and consummate their union at the Morrison Hotel. As they left the synagogue, Bella handed Mary a bouquet of yellow and white flowers. It was a thoughtful gesture. It reminded Mary of the flowers from the acacia trees in their homeland.

Mary fought to keep from weeping. Odessa was the only home she had ever known. Russian and Yiddish were the only languages she spoke. She was now in a strange land marrying a man who bore little resemblance to the boy she remembered. But she kept her fears tucked away and prayed her father was looking down on her.

As the newlyweds exited the synagogue, the sunlight broke through the clouds that had threatened rain all day. Was this a good sign of things to come? Mary prayed that it was.

The newly married couple moved into the basement apartment in Jack's family's home. Although the two transom windows offered very little light, the space was comfortable. Jack bought a small table and two chairs. He put fresh flowers in a porcelain vase and placed it in the center of the table. The wooden dining chairs had cushions with painted flowers on the seat. The brand new dark blue sofa was a gift from his father and mother.

In the bedroom there was a double bed and a wooden dresser with a hand-carved mirror centered on the wall above. A small icebox in the apartment held hard boiled eggs, beet borsht, and bread and butter. All their cooking would be done in the kitchen upstairs.

The first twelve months of married life flew by, and Jack and Mary celebrated their one-year anniversary by going to a lovely restaurant that specialized in Russian cuisine. Both Jack and Mary felt that on the whole, the marriage was working. Jack was attentive and a very good provider. He worked hard and was building a reputation as a competent motion picture projectionist.

While Jack was at work, Mary studied English, but she continued to speak Yiddish when Jack wasn't home. She wanted to obey her husband, but hoped that one day she would be able to follow her dream of becoming a famous American dress designer. Whenever she had a free moment, she would sketch designs of dresses, but hid the sketches from Jack because she didn't think he would approve of her ambition.

Then, on October 12, 1915, a warm fall day, Mary and Jack welcomed their first child. Their son, Myron David Kaufman, had dark hair and pale skin. When Mary looked into Myron's eyes, she saw Jack's eyes. When Mary held Myron's long fingers, she felt her husband's strength. But when she smelled her son's flowery scent, she thought about Odessa, and tears trickled down her face.

Mary looked at her baby boy and couldn't believe she now had a son, a husband, and a home. But underlying her content, her anxieties were still present. Would this happiness last? Would she ever become the American wife Jack wanted?

She decided she wouldn't think about the future. She wouldn't even allow herself to think about her past. She would simply hold on to her son and never let him go.

World War I had begun in Europe on July 28, 1915, when the Austro-Hungarians declared war on Serbia and then invaded the country. Russia mobilized in support of Serbia. Germany quickly invaded Belgium and Luxembourg and advanced toward France. The United Kingdom declared war on Germany.

Mary was filled with unease for friends and family back home, but was grateful she was living in America. She knew that if they were still in Russia, her husband would have been called to the front lines and probably killed. But as things stood, she knew her family would be safe in America.

On June 5, 1917, Jack, Samuel, and Carl registered for the draft, but they were never called up for active duty. World War I ended in a victory for the Allies on November 11, 1918. This war had been the deadliest war in history, with nine million soldiers and seven million civilians killed. Again, Mary mourned the victims and felt great gratitude that her own loved ones had been spared.

Jack worried about his Russian comrades who lost their lives while fighting for their homeland. He shared a sense of relief that he and his brothers were spared, but also a sense of sorrow for the men who had lost their lives.

Chapter 20

Jack
Chicago, 1916–1918

The whole city of Chicago seemed to have been taken over by theater mania. Becoming a movie mogul was the new dream of countless families, especially ones who were Jewish. Father-and-son duos and brother-and-brother duos sprang up all over, each one vying to be the most prominent contenders of them all.

The current high-fliers were Morris and Sam Katz, Jack Kirsch, and his brothers-in-law Charles Cooper and Carl Laemmle. But in 1916, a new team soared above them all. When Sam Katz and A.J. Balaban combined their experience, expertise, and money, they quickly acquired control over a large percentage of the theaters in Chicago. The two tycoons dominated the industry for years. You couldn't go anywhere in the city without seeing the Balaban & Katz logo, which they proudly displayed.

Other Jewish theater owners were also making their mark. Julius, Adolph, Leonard, Milton, and Herbert, better known as Groucho, Harpo, Chico, Gummo, and Zeppo, would become one of the most famous entertainment families of their time. The Marx Brothers conquered every aspect of the entertainment business from vaudeville to the silver screen. They were pioneers and trailblazers.

Jack saw his first movie, Chaplin's *One A.M.*, at the Logan Theatre in 1916. Although it was only twenty-seven minutes long, Jack knew beyond any doubt that he wanted to be part of the motion picture business. He wanted to be an owner and not a projectionist. In the meantime, he would be up in the booth working behind the scenes learning everything he could.

Jack found the movie business exciting, risky, profitable, and fast-paced. He was mesmerized with the creativity, the glitz, the glamour and especially the power. He saw tremendous opportunity. His heart pounded with excitement and glee every morning when he woke and every evening as he drifted off to sleep. He wanted it all!

The motion picture industry was one sector where being Jewish was an advantage, not a detriment. Attitudes toward the Jews had been changing, and with the fast growth and increasing Jewish theater ownership, the future looked promising.

Jack continued to pay close attention to the comings and goings of the men who were spearheading the industry. He was determined to work his way through the industry's maze and absorb every piece, every detail, and every bit of minutiae he could. His quest for success and power was insatiable.

In 1916, while Jack was working in one of Balaban's theaters, A.J. Balaban himself walked into the theater with a gorgeous blonde wrapped around his arm. Jack looked up and gasped. She was the most beautiful woman he had ever seen. He felt his skin tingle and his heart pound. A.J. noticed Jack's stare and walked up to him.

"What's your name, son?"

"Jack Kaufman," Jack replied, embarrassed.

"I couldn't help but notice that you were staring at my fiancé," A.J. said with some amusement. "I don't remember seeing you before. Where are you from?"

"I live on the South Side."

"I asked where you were from," A.J. said more pointedly.

"My family is from Odessa," Jack told him.

A.J. nodded. "And when did you come to America?"

"In 1907." Jack cleared his throat. "I'm so sorry Mr. Balaban. I didn't realize I was staring. Please forgive me."

A.J. smiled. "Nothing to forgive you for. She is one beautiful woman. I'm a very lucky man. By the way, did you know that my parents were Russian Jews?" he added unexpectedly.

"I believe I had heard that sir."

A.J. looked at him shrewdly.

"Jack Kaufman, there is something about you that reminds me of myself. Keep up the good work," he said. "Hard work leads to opportunity and opportunity leads to success. You can be a projectionist in my theaters any time you want." Then he asked, "Are you a member of the Local 110?"

"Yes, sir! There is just a small group of us right now, but I'm trying to recruit more of the men to join." As soon as Jack said it, he could have kicked himself. Balaban probably didn't like unions.

A.J. made no response. Instead, he asked, "What is your ultimate ambition, Kaufman? What do you want to do with your life?"

"I want to own my own theater one day."

"Is that so? That's a good goal," A.J. exclaimed. "When you think you have mastered the business side of the movie industry, let me know. Maybe I can be of some assistance."

"Thank you very much, sir. I will do that," Jack responded, dazed.

"See you around, Jack. It was a pleasure meeting you." Then A.J. Balaban slapped Jack on his back and handed him his business card.

Shortly after his encounter with Balaban, Jack started getting a lot of work as a projectionist. He wondered whether this had something to do with his meeting with Balaban, and hoped it did.

Jack loved his job, every aspect of it. He loved being in the booth. He loved the feel and the smell of the film. He respected and understood all the sounds the reel made while projecting images on the screen below.

Morning and evening, when Jack passed by the theatre, he felt excited whenever he saw the lit up marquee. Dreaming about owning his own theater never failed to send chills up his spine. He would own his own theater one day! He knew it in his heart and in his soul.

And of course, he had Balaban's card safe in his top drawer. He would hold on to it until it would become his golden ticket to achieving his dream.

In 1917, there were already one hundred theaters in Chicago and this number was continuing to grow. Owning theaters was becoming big business. With the industry's growth, more and more men were needed to work in the trades as electricians, projectionists, and carpenters.

The Local 110 chapter of the International Alliance of Theatrical Stage Employees in Chicago was now almost a year old. Their mission was to support its members and establish fair wages throughout the industry. The Local 110 was budding like a newly planted seedling, but growth was slow. It was time to germinate the union with new blood and new enthusiasm.

Jack liked the whole concept of the union, but what he was most excited about was the camaraderie it provided. He strongly believed that workers needed to stick together and come together with one voice. He knew how powerful that solidarity could be. Jack took the lead and started to talk to his fellow projectionists about becoming members in the Local 110 chapter. His fervor was contagious, and before he knew it, word started spreading.

At first, there were fifteen men who met in the evenings in someone's living room, basement or backyard. They talked about their jobs, their pay, and their future. Jack began to lead the discussions and encouraged everyone to set forth their ideas. His positivity and enthusiasm quickly garnered him a great deal of respect. He was knowledgeable, pragmatic, and charismatic. But most importantly, Jack always came up with achievable and sensible solutions.

The men enjoyed going to the homes of their fellow workers

for their ad hoc meetings. They all especially liked the bonds being established and the trust that flowed from that connection. The movie business was fast-paced, exciting, glamorous, and powerful. What Jack could not have imagined at the time, was that his union affiliation would one day change him and his family's life forever.

Chapter 21

Nicholas II
St. Petersburg, 1913–1918

Halfway around the world, the Romanov dynasty celebrated three hundred years of tsars. In honor of the celebrations, the Russian jeweler, Peter Carl Fabergé, handcrafted the Romanov Tercentenary egg. The egg was made out of gold, silver, rose-cut diamonds, and rock crystal. It represented the Romanov dynasty from 1613-1913.

The one-of-a-kind egg was hand-painted with double-headed majestic eagles in minuscule and intricate color patterns. The eagles framed each crown of eighteen past and present tsars. Among the rulers were Michael Romanov (1613–1645), Peter the Great (1682–1725), Catherine the Great (1762–1796), and Nicholas II. The egg was specifically made for Nicholas to present to his beloved wife on Easter Sunday.

That same year, Nicholas, with his wife Alexandra, made the decision to go on a pilgrimage retracing the path Michael Romanov had travelled on his way to St. Petersburg three hundred years earlier. The tercentenary celebrations were extravagant and well attended by the masses in spite of Nicholas's unpopularity since the 1905 Russian Revolution. It seemed that public opinion was slowly turning in favor of the Romanovs. But that sea change would not last.

Slowly and insidiously, attitudes toward the Romanovs began to reverse themselves once more. It wasn't noticeable at first, but as time passed during the early years of World War I, so did the support for the Russian monarchy.

With Nicholas away at the front from 1915 to 1916, authority in St. Petersburg began to collapse. The capital was left in the hands of strikers and disgruntled soldiers as the Russian government failed to ensure supplies for their comrades and food for their citizens at home. Mounting hardships created massive riots and even more unrest. The Tsar's cabinet begged Nicholas to return to St. Petersburg and restore order. Nicholas refused, and instead continued to stay away at staff headquarters, leaving organizers, dissidents, and other opposition groups to plot another revolution.

Five hundred miles from St. Petersburg, Nicholas was wrongly informed by his Minister of the Interior that the situation at home was under control, and ordered that firm steps be taken against the demonstrators. Unfortunately, history repeated itself again with grave consequences.

By early 1917, Russia was on the verge of total collapse. The army had taken fifteen million men from rural farms to fight for Russia. As a result, food prices soared. The severe winter dealt the railways, now overburdened by emergency shipments of coal and supplies, the final blow for the Russian people.

On Sunday, March 11, 1917, despite huge posters ordering the people to keep off the streets, massive crowds gathered in the capital. The police fired upon the crowds, killing Russian men, women, and children. Order broke down completely. A provisional government was put in place to try and restore the peace. Members of the government issued a demand for Nicholas to abdicate. Faced with this demand, and with his family now firmly in the hands of the provisional government, Nicholas had no choice but to comply.

On March 15, 1917, Nicholas II abdicated the throne in favor of his son, Tsarevitch Alexei. After consulting with Alexei's doctors, the Tsar and Tsarina determined that their son, who suffered from hemophilia, would not live long if he was separated from his family. So, Nicholas drew up a new manifesto naming his brother, Grand Duke Michael Alexandrovich, as the next Emperor of all Russia. His manifesto read:

In the days of the great struggle against the foreign enemies, who for nearly three hundred years have tried to enslave our motherland, the Lord God has been pleased to send down on Russia a new heavy trial. Internal popular disturbances threaten to have a disastrous effect on the future conduct of this persistent war. The destiny of Russia, the honor of our heroic army, the welfare of the people, and the whole future of our dear motherland demands that the war should be brought to a victorious conclusion whatever the cost.

In agreement with the Imperial Duma, we have thought it well to renounce the throne of the Russian Empire and to lay down the supreme power. As we do not wish to part from our beloved son, we transmit the succession to our brother, the Grand Duke Michael Alexandrovich, and give him our blessing to mount the throne of the Russian Empire. May the Lord God help Russia.

The Russian people never saw or heard this statement. Grand Duke Michael refused to accept the throne. The announcement of the Tsar's abdication was received with delight, relief, fear, anger, and confusion. Three centuries of Romanov rule came to an end.

Chapter 22

David
Chicago, 1917

Jack hadn't thought about Odessa for quite some time, but on Monday, March 19, 1917, he felt very emotional when he saw the headlines in the morning edition of the *Chicago Tribune*. "Tsar of Russia Forced to Abdicate the Throne"

David, whose grasp of English was still very limited, was only able to read the headline. "Jack, read me what this says," he demanded.

As Jack read the article in a combination of English and Yiddish, David's hands began to tremble. His face turned white. He put his hands over his eyes and shook his head.

"They are going to kill Nicholas," David whispered brokenly. "I hope they don't kill the children too."

"Father, they won't kill Nicholas," Jack asserted with confidence. "I'm sure Nicholas, his family, and his whole entourage will leave St. Petersburg and move into one of their palaces. You know how much the Romanovs love to travel. That is probably what they are doing right now." David just closed his eyes and shook his head.

David's health had been failing for several years. But since hearing about Nicholas's abdication, he seemed to have lost his desire to live. He became fixated on the Romanovs and their unlikely survival. With each passing day, David became more overwhelmed and disheartened. He was worn out and void of all joy, each day slipping further and further into his past. He wanted to go home to his beloved Odessa.

It was a difficult time for the Kaufman family. There was little anyone could do to help David through this transition. Adela stayed by David's side, willing her husband not to die. Then on Wednesday, December 3, 1917, on an unusually warm winter day, David Lewis Kaufman took his last breath. His passing was peaceful. He died in Adela's arms with Jack, Sam, Carl, and Bella all at his bedside. He was fifty years old.

Adela was overcome with grief. She had met David almost thirty-two years before and now she didn't know how she would survive without him. She withdrew into her past memories, no longer listening to music, working in the garden, or cooking the family meals. She no longer used her sewing machine and she stopped strolling through the neighborhood. Jack sympathized completely. He felt as if he lost a part of his own heart and a large part of his past. The responsibility for taking care of his mother now fell to him. A role he willingly accepted.

Seven months had passed since David's death, and Jack missed his father more than he thought was possible. Visits to the cemetery gave him some solace. When Jack brought flowers and placed them on his father's grave, it was the only time he allowed himself to cry.

Jack waited for the tombstone to be completed so it could be unveiled. He had talked to Saul Weiss several times and was frustrated the tombstone still wasn't ready. On July 18, 1918, the call finally came.

"I would like to speak with Jack Kaufman," a voice said.

"You are speaking to him," replied Jack.

"This is Saul Weiss at Waldheim Jewish Cemetery. We are ready to set your father's tombstone for the unveiling, but somehow the photograph you gave us has disappeared."

Jack closed his eyes in irritation. He had instinctively disliked Weiss from the moment they met.

"Well, Saul, it couldn't have just walked away, could it?" he said, his annoyance obvious. "I don't have to go to work today, so I can deliver another picture of my father to you later this afternoon. Is the tombstone in the same place? Or did you lose that too?" Weiss ignored the sarcasm.

"Yes, the tombstone is set in place. We can insert the photograph without any problem."

"Well let's hope so. I wouldn't want my father to appear in your dreams, Weiss," Jack added sarcastically, and hung up the phone. To distract himself from his bad mood, he decided to walk over to the nearby newsstand and buy a copy of the *Chicago Tribune*. As he approached, the headline on the Thursday Edition of the newspaper shouted in bold black print:

"The End of a Dynasty. Tsar Nicolas II and his Wife and Five Children were Brutally Assassinated Yesterday, July 17, 1918."

Jack stumbled through the article.

In the early hours of July 17, 1918, the Romanov family was awakened at 2:00 a.m. They were told to dress, and then led down into a half-basement room at the back of the Ipatiev House. The guards told them they needed to be moved because anti-Bolshevik forces were approaching, and the house might be fired upon.

Nicholas, Alexandra, their five children, three of their servants, and their family physician were led to the basement. The soldiers drew their revolvers and pointed their weapons directly toward Nicholas's head. In unison, the Bolsheviks stepped closer and closer until both victim and murderer were looking into each other's eyes. Then the soldiers began discharging their weapons. The loud popping sound, smells and smoke penetrated the small concrete block walls where their captives were imprisoned. Nicholas was the first to die. As he lay in his own blood that identified the exact spot where the Tsar took his final breath, his family stood motionless. Not a single whimper, groan, or gasp was made. They stood still, and then, as if their movements had been rehearsed, they held hands and closed their eyes.

Alexi was the next to die. The Tsarina, Anastasia, Tatiana, Olga and Maria miraculously survived as the first hail of deadly bullets bounced off their torsos. Alexandra and her four girls were wearing over 1.3 kilograms of diamonds and precious gems that had been sewn into their clothing and into their fur coats. The armor provided them a short reprieve. Stunned that their first attempt to kill the women was in vain, the executioners stabbed them with bayonets. Then, for good measure, they shot them at close range in the head.

For the first time in seven months, Jack was grateful his father wasn't there to read the article.

"Everything all right Mr. Jack?" Jefferson, the owner of the news stand asked, sounding concerned. It took awhile for Jack to answer.

"Not really, Jefferson. My father knew the Tsar and his family when we lived in Odessa." He took another look at the headline. "What a tragic way to die." Jack shrugged.

"For me, Mr. Jack, I just want to die in my sleep. But with all these murders here in Chicago and bullets flying left and right, you never know what can happen."

Jack tried to make light of what Jefferson was saying. "That's where my boxing skills will come in handy," he replied.

"I hope you don't need all that bobbing and weaving one day," Jefferson said.

"I hope not too," Jack responded.

As Jack walked home, he reflected on all the stories his father had told him about his grandfather Lewis and Tsar Alexander. He also remembered the stories about David's tremendous friendship with Nicholas. And now both men, each only fifty years old, were dead. It was very strange, coincidental, and heartbreaking.

Chapter 23

Lenore
Chicago, 1919

After his father's death, Jack buried himself in his work, spending a lot of his time as the Local 110 union organizer. No one could comfort him for his loss. Mary tried, but Jack withdrew from her, choosing to be alone more and more as the weeks passed. Only Myron, their two-year-old son, nicknamed Mike, seemed to bring him joy.

Seeing how happy Jack was when he was with their son, Mary hoped another child would make things better. She also hoped Jack might start to sing again. She missed hearing his beautiful voice singing "Take Me Out to the Ball Game," when he was trying to lull Mike to sleep. Mary would sometimes sing the song herself to Mike when Jack was at work, but it wasn't the same. She had yet to go to a baseball game, and to figure out what was so exciting about hitting a ball with a stick and running around a square of dirt.

Almost two years after David's death, on September 11, 1919, Mary gave birth to a baby girl. They named her Lenore after Jack's grandfather, Lewis. When Mary looked into her daughter's eyes, she saw her own reflection. She felt gentleness in Lenore's soul and calmness in her daughter's sprit. She now had two children she could pour her love into. She whispered to her daughter, "I will never let you go."

When Jack walked into the hospital room, Mary was asleep holding his daughter. He stared down at the tiny infant and whispered, "Lenore, I will always be there for you. I promise I will always take care of you and love you. You and your brother are the two most important people in my life. I will never let you go." Then without waking either mother or daughter, he left.

Chapter 24

Jack
Chicago, 1919

On January 16, 1919, an historic event changed the entire nation, and Chicago in particular. The United States Senate approved and ratified the Eighteenth Amendment, The National Prohibition Act, in spite of President Woodrow Wilson's veto. The act established the "legal" definition of intoxicating liquors and laid out the penalties for its production.

By the terms of the amendment, the country would go dry on January 17, 1920. Prohibition was now the law of the land. However, as things turned out, the amendment actually had the complete opposite effect. Instead of reducing liquor consumption, it increased its use multifold, and further stimulated rampant crime. The underworld now had a free pass not only for corruption, but also for murder. The only thing that had any worth for the mob was supply and demand, and the booze-consuming public conspired to keep the liquor flowing.

In Chicago, the Mafia, crooked cops, and corrupt politicians quickly infiltrated the unions. If bribery didn't work, brutal beatings did. At first, the mob's efforts to penetrate the Projectionists Union were subtle and insidious. Only three years old, the Local 110 was fertile ground for a takeover, and there were many opportunities for extortion, power, and greed. Recognizing the union's vulnerability, the mob quickly established a firm grasp in the Projectionists Union. Behind it all were Al Capone and Tommy Maloy.

Corruption and greed weren't just limited to the movie business. The Mafia also infiltrated the game of baseball. In 1919, baseball would witness the worst scandal in the history of the game.

The owner of the Chicago White Sox, Charles Comiskey, was a shrewd businessman. He didn't care if he was liked or if he was hated. He was a power player and money was his only reward.

If you wanted to play baseball for the Sox, and most players did, then there was absolutely no negotiating. Part of Comiskey's very restrictive contract involved his players being prohibited from playing on any other professional team without his permission. The catch was that Comiskey automatically refused permission, so the clause was a farce. His players were tied to him as long as he chose. Since the players had no negotiating power, Comiskey was able to keep salaries ridiculously low. Everyone knew that if players didn't fall in line, their careers were over.

The mob knew that the baseball players needed more money to take care of their families. They also knew that the players were vulnerable and were fair prey. It was a perfect storm.

It did not take long for some of the White Sox players to be approached and then enticed by the Mafia. Ultimately, a meeting was set up on September 21, 1919, at the Ansonia Hotel in New York City. A sizeable group of players came to that meeting thinking they would collectively find a way to "fix" their situation. Unfortunately, that meeting ultimately led to the end of the careers for eight ballplayers.

"Shoeless" Joe Jackson, who earned his nickname by once playing in stockings when his baseball shoes weren't yet broken in, was a great ballplayer. He had a career .356 batting average, one of the highest ever. However, that did not save him from being one of the players banished from the sport because of his involvement for "fixing" the 1919 World Series.

Jackson was reportedly promised twenty thousand dollars to throw the game. He claimed that he received only five thousand, hoping that receiving less than what he was promised would exonerate him. It was a very painful lesson for Jackson and for seven other Sox players.

The Chicago White Sox lost the series to the Cincinnati Reds that year. The eight White Sox players were accused of intentionally losing the games in exchange for money from gamblers. They went to trial and were acquitted in the eyes of the law but not in the eyes of the public. The players received a lifetime ban from baseball and were forbidden from being inducted into the Baseball Hall of Fame.

Jack was saddened and shaken by the scandal. He loved the game. He loved being at the ballpark. He loved what had become America's favorite pastime. But, Jack knew that whenever there were large sums of money to be made, there would always be someone to try and take it.

He thought about his own union and about his fellow workers. He was very worried about the corruption that was brewing just below the surface and feared that it would end up percolating to the top. And then what would he do?

Chapter 25

Tommy Maloy
Chicago, 1920

During the last four years, the Local 110 had become an ever-increasing priority in Jack's life. The bonds and trust that were developing between the men in the union were naturally evolving into a genuine fraternity. Many of the men began to share stories of their family's aspirations and hardships. They also discussed their future, and the challenges they faced to better their lives and the lives of their children.

Jack and his fellow union workers were deeply concerned about the corruption and crime seeping through the perimeter of their lives. With each passing week, it became more obvious that certain thugs, working in the trades, were infiltrating the Local 110, and were now positioning themselves to take control of the union. One of those mobsters was Tommy Maloy.

Labor racketeer Thomas "Tommy" Maloy had moved up in the gangster world very quickly. His association with the mob started just before World War I when he worked as a chauffeur to the labor boss, Maurice "Mossy" Enright.

Enright emigrated from Ireland in 1887 and started his career as a plumber's apprentice. In 1911, he joined the Local 520 of the United Association of Steamfitters, and quickly became much in demand as a muscle man. He was strong, mean, and killed without remorse. If a skull needed to be cracked, it was Mossy, "The Enforcer," who was willing to crush it.

When a bitter and violent dispute erupted with another local plumbers union over the right to work on some buildings under construction in the Loop, things turned deadly. Mossy's target was Vincent Altman, the enforcer for the rival plumbers union. Altman ended up dead, and Mossy walked away adding another notch to the barrel of his gun.

Mossy had a fatal lapse of judgment that day, which would ultimately catch up to him. When he ran from the scene, Mossy was carrying his overcoat over his left arm. A courageous onlooker, seeing him fleeing down the street, grabbed the coat and yanked it out of Mossy's hand. Mossy's identification was in one of the pockets.

Mossy was arrested, prosecuted and convicted. He began serving a life sentence at Joliet Penitentiary for Altman's murder. But Mossy still had his connections. In 1913, the Governor of Illinois, Edward Dunne, gave Enright a complete pardon. These pardons, given over the years by various corrupt Chicago politicians, soon became a recurring theme.

When Enright got his "get out of jail card," he wasted no time. Within weeks after walking through the locked gates at Joliet, he put his plan into action to seize control of the First Ward Street Sweepers Union, known as the "White Wings." But in order to do this, Mossy had to eliminate the gangster Mike Carrozzo, then president of the White Wings.

With two of his henchmen by his side, Mossy walked up to Dago Mike, aimed, fired, and missed! Not a single bullet even grazed Dago Mike or either of his two bodyguards. Instantly, the tables had turned. Enright's botched attempt now made him a marked man.

On February 4, 1920, Mossy left his office in the Loop at 5:30 p.m. He drove his Grey Ghost sedan to his favorite saloon, and after having a few drinks, left the bar. Driving home, he failed to look in his rear view mirror. If he had, he would have seen that he was being tailed by another infamous automobile, a rare Chalmers seven-passenger touring sedan. It was a perfect gangster's car because the plate glass side windows could easily be removed. The car had been advertised as "A sedan to take care of any condition you might encounter while touring in and around town."

Mossy pulled up in front of his house, still unaware that anyone was following him. The Chalmers pulled up next to Mossy's car. Two shots were fired from a sawed-off shotgun and Mossy Enright's blood was splattered across the front seat. James Vinci confessed to the murder and was convicted, but after two key witnesses mysteriously disappeared, Vinci was exonerated.

Tommy Maloy, who had been Mossy's chauffer, coincidently quit his job seven days before Enright was murdered. With Enright out of the picture, his followers now jockeyed to fill the void.

Maloy thought briefly about stepping into Enright's position, but his sights were never on the Steamfitters or the Plumbers Union; his sights were on the prestigious and big–money Motion Picture Projectionists Union.

Maloy, himself a projectionist, was a member of the Local 110. He felt he had paid his dues and was ready for his own takeover. He saw that the current president, Jack Miller, was in a vulnerable position. Maloy decided that the time was ripe to put his plan into motion. It was a plan he had been orchestrating for years.

When Miller took over the Local 110, his immediate goal was to grow the union membership and make as much money as he could in the shortest possible period of time. His ultimate goal was to purchase a string of movie theaters and become a bona fide movie mogul.

The tactics Miller used to expand the union were pretty straightforward. You either joined the Local 110 or you never worked again in any theater in Chicago or elsewhere. Threats, force, and violence were weapons of choice, and he used them masterfully.

In a short period of time, Miller was able to bring a very large number of operators into the Local 110, and his revenue increased exponentially. What Jack Miller did not anticipate was that someone else was hanging around on the sidelines, waiting to replace him.

Maloy did not have to invent a clever plan to take Miller out. The tactics used to acquire sole control of the Local 110 had been proven effective many times before. All Maloy needed to do was copy the same tactics his predecessors had used. He would dangle the carrot and lead Miller right down the deadly path of no return.

Maloy knew that Miller wanted to buy a chain of movie theaters, so Maloy offered Miller a sweet deal. He would pay Miller for his ownership interest in the union, which would give Miller the seed money he needed to buy his first theater. In exchange, Miller gave his promise to support Maloy in the upcoming election.

Miller agreed, gave up his ownership, and waited for Maloy's money, but it never came. A hitman came instead. The single bullet went right through Miller's right eyeball and out the back of his head. The murderer was never identified.

With Miller's ownership interest safely transferred, there was one last obstacle remaining in Maloy's path, a man named Jack Williams, who was running unopposed for the position of business agent.

Williams had been a member in the Local 110 since its inception in 1916 and was well liked. Maloy knew he couldn't take any chances in the upcoming election. He had to get the membership behind him and to do that, he needed to come up with something dramatic that would show the members that he was tough, tougher than Williams could ever be.

To set the scene, Tommy made up a dramatic and graphic story. At an opportune time, when most of the members were in the local meeting hall, Maloy casually began. speaking.

"Hey guys, did you hear what happened the other day while I was up in the booth?"

"No, what happened?" several men asked.

Maloy continued. "Well, it was after midnight, after a long day screening a film. I had just poured myself some whiskey and these four hoods with knives climbed into my booth. The sons-of-bitches wanted to kill me. It was four against one. I guess they thought with four of them, their odds were pretty good. But guess what? They were wrong. I beat the shit out of the first two. Then I head-butted the second two with each other's thick dumb skulls. Then I grabbed two at a time, dragged them down the stairs, and threw them into the back alley. The first two numbskulls were just coming around when I got back to them, so I dumped them on top of their buddies. I pointed my gun, told them to start running for their lives, and started to count to ten. I should have killed them, but I guess I'm just a sweetheart. Anyway, I fired off a few shots and yelled out, 'If you mess with Tommy Maloy again, or any of my fellow projectionists, trust me, you will get what you deserve.' I bet those wimps peed in their pants."

The men roared with laughter. That was music to Maloy's ears. The story was ninety percent fabricated, of course, but the message was clear.

Maloy's story spread like wildfire. But that still wasn't good enough for Tommy. He felt he needed to make his point even more clearly. So, late one night, he had some of his goons grab Williams, brutally beat him up, and then throw him out on the street for everyone to see.

Jack, of course, had heard all about Enright's murder and Williams's beating. He didn't give a damn about Maloy or his bullshit story, but also knew he could not ignore the fact that Maloy was dangerous.

When the voting began, Jack cast his vote for Williams, but to no avail. Maloy won the election by a large majority and became head of the Motion Picture Projectionists Union in 1920. His official title was business manager, but his unofficial title was thug and murderer.

Jack didn't need to stick around until the votes were counted. He knew the mob had just established a firm stronghold in the Local 110, which came as no surprise. It was the reality of the world they all lived in. He decided that his only recourse was to try and stay outside the fray and fly below the radar as long as he could.

It was a difficult goal to accomplish. Maloy's reign of terror would last for the next fifteen years.

Chapter 26

Jack and Mary
Chicago, 1921–1923

Mary knew she and Jack were growing apart. Overnight it seemed, it had grown from a large crack into a cavernous trough, one that would be very difficult to fill. She feared they had reached a point of no return in their marriage. Mary wanted her husband to want her, and she was determined to do what she could to keep her marriage from falling apart. She hoped there was still time to turn things around.

She sighed as she washed the breakfast dishes. It was a hot morning, and she told herself that it was the heat that was making her feel so depressed and lethargic. But she knew better.

Her glance fell on Jack as he sat reading the morning paper. His whole attitude looked stiff and unwelcoming. She bit her lip.

"Jack," she said brightly. "Would you like a little more coffee?"

For an answer, he only grunted, and pushed his cup forward.

Mary returned to the sink. It all felt so hopeless. She tried so hard to please Jack. But the truth could no longer be avoided. The gap between the two of them was increasing every day. And the worst part was that she sill loved him and still wanted him to want her. Tears filled her eyes as drops of sadness trickled onto the dishes in the sink. Jack put the newspaper down.

"Mary," Jack said abruptly. "I'm going over to Johnny Butler's today. We have some union business to discuss and I'm taking Mike with me. Johnny's son is a friend of Mike's. We won't be home for dinner."

Mary despised the desperation that crept into her voice.

"What time are you coming home?"

Jack threw down his paper. "What difference does it make?" he snapped. "We'll get home when we get home. Time to go, Mike," he called out to his son.

"Can I bring my baseball cards, Dad? John Junior and I want to trade some players. I need a shortstop and he needs a catcher."

"Sure, hurry up. I'll meet you outside."

Jack drove the Ford Model T Touring car out of the carport and waited for Mike to emerge from the house. His black sedan was a beauty equipped with an L-head, four cylinder cast-iron engine with an electric start and 22.5 horsepower. After some serious negotiations, Jack had gotten the car for a mere $390. It was perfect for his family because it had three doors and room for five people.

Mike jumped in the front seat next to his father. "Dad, can I sit on your lap and hold the wheel?" he asked eagerly.

"Not this time, buddy." Mike nodded. He knew not to ask a second time.

The ride to Johnny's house took about twenty minutes. Johnny lived with his wife, Megan, and his two boys. Megan was a looker with light red hair, legs like a flamingo, and bright green eyes. Jack never could understand how Johnny was able to get her to marry him.

By the time Jack pulled up in front of the house and shut the engine off, Mike was already out of the car and running up to the front door. Johnny was standing waiting for them.

"Hey, Kaufman. Hi Mike." He nodded. "John Jr. is upstairs waiting for you." As Mike charged up the stairs, the two men looked after him and then made their own way into the house.

"Let's go into the library, Jack. What you drinking, Kaufman?" Johnny asked.

"Got some Irish whiskey?"

The two men shared work stories for a while. Then Jack came

to the real reason for his visit.

"Johnny, I remember you telling me that one of your brothers got a divorce." Jack sighed and awkwardly scratched his chin. "You know that my marriage was arranged. I didn't have any say about my future. My father and Mary's father entered into an agreement when my family was in Odessa." He shook his head. "I've tried to hold up my part of the bargain, but I just can't."

Johnny frowned and held up his hand. "Let me stop you right there. As your friend, I am telling you, don't go down that road. Patrick started the process and then he had to back off. The judge was going to take his kids away from him. Honestly, Jack, my advice for you is to wait until the kids get older. Try and work it out with Mary. If you can't work it out, then get yourself a mistress."

Jack nodded thoughtfully in response.

"Now let's smoke ourselves some cigars," Johnny said, deliberately changing the subject.

Adela walked into the kitchen and poured herself a cup of tea. She glanced over and saw Mary sitting at the table, head bowed. She knew things hadn't been going well for her daughter-in-law lately, but was reluctant to intrude. Still, seeing Mary sitting there now, looking so miserable, she felt she had to say something.

"Mary, why don't you go into town?" she suggested brightly. "Maybe get your hair done and buy a new outfit. I'll watch Lenore. Wait here, I want to give you something." She hurried into her bedroom and pulled out some cash from under the mattress.

"This is for you."

Mary was very touched by the gesture. She squeezed her mother-in-law's hand. "Thank you. This is very kind," she whispered.

Mary went upstairs to get her purse and freshen up. When

she looked into the mirror, she saw a much older version of herself. A version she barely recognized. She sighed and then walked the ten blocks to Goldman's Department Store.

As she was walking, Mary unexpectedly thought about her father. He had died so long ago but she still missed him. She missed holding his hand and skipping alongside him as they walked the streets of Odessa. She missed his tender hugs and boisterous laughs. She wondered what advice he would give her now. She wiped away her tears, straightened her spine, and walked into the store.

After the two men finished their cigars, Johnny said abruptly, "Jack, have you thought about taking out Maloy?"

Jack was astonished. "What the hell are you talking about?"

Johnny laughed. "Calm down, Jack. I only mean, have you ever thought about running for president of the union? You're a natural, and if anyone could do it, it would be you."

Jack grimaced. "Thanks, but that would be a death sentence. I need way more tread on my tires before I would even consider that. And do me a favor. Don't repeat this conversation to anyone. In fact, let's pretend this whole evening never happened!"

"Sure, Jack," Johnny replied. "But one day we'll have to have this talk again." The men returned to the library. Johnny plucked the bottle off his desk and tipped it toward Jack.

"No thanks, Johnny. I should be getting Mike home. Why don't we go upstairs and see how the boys are getting on?"

The two boys were playing with some baseball cards when Jack came into the room. Mike looked up eagerly.

"Mike, it's time to leave," said Jack.

"But Dad! John Jr. asked me to spend the night! Can I stay over?"

Jack hesitated. "I don't think so, Mike. It would be a big imposition."

"Oh, let him stay," Johnny said easily. "I can drive him home tomorrow before church."

Jack shrugged and agreed. He liked the idea of Mike having a little independence. He was somewhat reluctant, but when Johnny offered to drive Mike home in the morning, he agreed. He was happy Mike was branching out and feeling more and more confident. He wanted Mike to feel a sense of independence. He was worried that being surrounded by women all the time might make his son a little soft. Jack wanted to make sure his son would be able to stand on his own two feet.

"All right. Mike, make sure you do what you are told. Don't let me hear that you got into no good. Behave yourself," he said. Playfully, he tousled Mike's hair, and then Jack pulled Mike in for a bear hug.

When Jack got home, he found no one there. Mary had left a note: "Jack. Your mom has Lee and I am going to the store. I will be home later. Mary."

Jack was pleased he had the house to himself. He went to the sideboard cabinet, pulled out a bottle of whisky, poured himself a drink, and walked out back. Then he lit a cigarette and enjoyed the quiet on his back porch. He thought about the conversation he had with Johnny, and couldn't shake off what Johnny had asked him to consider.

Jack was resting on top of the bed when he heard Mary come home. He wondered whether he should pretend to be asleep, but before he could decide, Mary swayed into the room. She looked different, absolutely beautiful in fact. She was wearing a silk blouse and a soft flowing skirt that he had never seen before. Her shiny hair rested softly on her shoulders. Jack sat up, startled.

"Mary, what did you do to your hair? I like it. And is that a new blouse?"

"Yes. It's silk. Do you want to touch it?" Mary asked with a smile.

"Come here, let me take a closer look."

Mary sat down on the edge of the double bed. Jack quickly

undid the buttons on her blouse and then he unhooked her brassiere. Jack cupped the soft mounds of her large breasts and kissed her neck. As Mary's hand loosened Jack's belt buckle, she slipped her hand over his underwear. She began massaging him and found that he was already hard with anticipation.

Their lovemaking was passionate, and when they finished, Jack rolled over and looked at his wife. She was glowing.

Over the next six months, Mary and Jack appeared happier than they had been in a very long time. Mary was now five months pregnant with their third child and Jack was excited and attentive. For the first time in a long time, Mary felt secure about her future.

Inspired by the thought of his burgeoning family, Jack turned his attention to a long-time dream of his: On May 4, 1922, he applied and petitioned for United States naturalization.

To his immeasurable disappointment, his petition was denied. He was just shy of meeting the required fifteen years of residency. Jack was undaunted and vowed that he would apply again as soon as the law permitted. He wanted nothing more than to shed his Russian identity forever. He wanted to do something important. He wanted to be well known, and he wanted his children to always be proud of him.

To achieve these ends, Jack began working even harder. He loved being a projectionist, but never let go of the dream that it would lead to bigger and better things.

That one day the Kaufman name would be in lights on a theater marquee. That was his American dream and he would make it happen. Just as he would make sure the next time he applied for citizenship it would be granted.

Mary was now eight months pregnant. Mike was almost seven years old, and Lenore was turning four. Jack worked day and night. He was getting more active and more involved in the union. He was a natural leader and the other members all appreciated this. When the men had a problem with job assignments or working conditions, the first person they went to was Kaufman. Jack's unofficial title was union organizer.

The membership was increasing. This meant more money for Maloy, so Jack's position was secure, at least for now. Jack understood that becoming a prominent figure in the union wasn't necessarily a good thing. It was really better if you didn't stand out and blended in with the other men. As he had told Johnny all those months ago, anything else would be a death sentence. Still, he had never forgotten Johnny's suggestion that he oppose Maloy as union leader. It was something he was thinking about more and more. And he knew that the other men were thinking about it too. Several of them had come up to him on the sly and asked him to run. Jack had only smiled, shrugged, and said, "Maybe someday." Truth be told, he was looking forward to that "someday" more than he would admit. For right now though, he needed to be patient. He would keep his head down and wait for the next election.

When Jack wasn't working, he concentrated on being a family man. He spent many afternoons with Mike, taking him to the boxing gym and the ballpark. And at night, he would read to Lenore and sing songs they heard on the radio. Lenore and Mike were thriving and appeared happy.

His relationship with Mary was also going well, and he was hopeful that their marriage had turned a corner. Mary seemed to be thinking less and less about Odessa these days and accepted America as her new home. Her English improved and she had begun sketching again. When Jack saw her designs, he surprised her with her own sewing machine and Mary hugged him, saying it was the best gift she had ever received.

And now a new baby was about to join the family. Jack Kaufman told himself he was a very lucky man.

The morning of August 16, Mary cried out, "Jack, hurry, I need to go to the hospital. This baby is ready to be born." Jack drove to Mount Sinai Hospital in record speed.

Francine Edith Kaufman entered the world the following day on August 17, 1922. Their family was now complete. After meeting his little girl, Jack went back home to get some sleep. When Jack walked through the front door of his house, his mother was standing inside waiting for the news.

"It's a girl, Mom. She is beautiful," Jack told her with a smile. "She looks just like you." Then he heard footsteps running down the hall.

"Daddy, where's my new brother?" Mike demanded.

"I want a sister!" Lenore wailed.

Jack wrapped his arms around his children. "You both have a new sister."

"Your mother and sister both need some sleep first. They will be home in a couple of days."

"What is her name, Daddy?" asked Lenore.

Jack savored the words. "Francine Edith Kaufman."

The following day, Jack took Mike to the hospital to visit Mary and see his new sister. When Jack opened the door to Mary's room, he could see Mary was nursing Francine. He left Mike in the hallway and walked toward Mary's bed. Mary didn't know Jack was in the room. She was totally focused on her precious daughter, totally consumed with their child.

Jack walked closer to the bed. He stared down at the two of them, feeling a tremendous rush of protectiveness. Not only for his delicate little girl, but also for his tired looking wife who held her so gently. Jack was under no illusion that his marriage would ever be easy. But time had definitely softened him, and he vowed to try harder and continue to make things work for his family.

In that moment, Mary looked up and saw Jack and Mike in the hall and smiled. "Mike," she said, "Come meet your little sister."

Shyly, Mike came into the room and approached the bed. He leaned down and whispered into Francine's tiny ear, "Francine,

I'm your brother, and I will always protect you."

Jack and Mike stayed for a few minutes more. Jack could see that Mary was getting tired.

"We'll let you get some rest now," he told her. "I'll come back again tomorrow." He whispered, "Francine Edith Kaufman, welcome to the world."

Mary watched them go. Her gaze returned to her new little daughter. She placed Francine back in her basket and stared at her for what seemed to be hours. Her daughter looked so content. Mary stroked Francine's fingers. They were long, slender, and graceful. She thought her daughter had the hands of an artist. Then Mary looked at Francine's legs. She saw the legs of a dancer. When she listened to the sweet sounds her new daughter constantly made, she heard the melody of a singer.

There was also a sense of fragility about this child, juxtaposed with unusual strength and a strong spirit. She sensed that there would be hard times in Francine's future. She prayed that her intuition was wrong.

As Jack drove home, thoughts and questions rushed into his head at lightning speed. "Was Francine brought into this world to bring happiness and joy back into the Kaufman home? Could he become the husband Mary wanted?" Only time would tell. In that moment, Jack promised he would try harder.

When Francine was a year old, Jack came home one day with an exciting announcement. He had found the family's dream house, the house where they would all live together forever.

Everyone was so excited by the news that Jack loaded the entire family into his brand new 1923 Ford and drove them to their new home. The house was a gracious red brick, two-story bungalow in Chicago's South Side. As they pulled up to the house, fresh glistening snow covered the ground.

"It's beautiful!" Mary gasped.

The children ran into the backyard and began to play. They had a snowball fight, which made them all giggle so much that their stomachs ached.

"Mike, I think this yard is big enough for a baseball dia-mond," Jack observed. "Would you like me to build you one in the spring?"

Mike shrieked with joy. "Can I help you build it?"

Jack felt his eyes growing unexpectedly moist. "You bet."

Life in the new home soon fell into a pleasant, comfortable rhythm. The house was large, with three bedrooms upstairs and a "mother-in-law" suite downstairs for Adela, Bella and her young son, Norman.

White shiplap covered the walls in the front sitting room and in the large kitchen. The rest of the walls were painted a pale yellow. Peg and groove wooden floors were spread throughout, and there was a large swing hanging from the front porch. Large magnolia trees shaded the property. The scent reminded Jack and Mary of the fragrant blossoms of the acacia trees. It already felt like home.

Jack bought new furniture for the sitting room and a large oak table so the whole family could sit together for their meals. Lenore and Francine were now sharing a room and Mike had the small bedroom all to himself. This home truly represented Jack's success and he felt as if he was, indeed, living the Ameri-can dream. He still dreamed that one day he would own his own movie theater and the marquee would have the Kaufman name in lights.

Mary loved the house and was so very hopeful that things were changing for the better. She believed that Francine was the missing piece in their life's puzzle. She also believed that this new bundle of joy was the glue that would keep her marriage together. She vowed that she would try harder to be the Amer-ican wife Jack wanted.

Jack made good on his promise to his son. The following spring, Jack threw out the first pitch, and pretended that he was announcing the game:

"Ladies and Gentlemen, let's play ball! Now, batting lead-off is Mike Kaufman, the famous slugger for the Chicago White Sox!" And with a flourish, Jack tossed the ball to Mike, who then ran around the bases Jack had carved out of the grass.

This quickly became a Sunday tradition for the whole family. While Jack and Mike played ball, Lenore would sit on the back porch with her primers. She was only five, but was already reading some of Mike's schoolbooks.

Francine was still too little to play in the yard when Jack and Mike were playing ball, but she loved to run the bases with her brother. Her long legs made her a fast little runner. Sports, however, would never be her passion. Francine loved to sing and dance with her Papa. As she got a little older, she would memorize the words and melody of every song she could get hold of, singing them all day long, then inventing steps to the rhythm of the music. Francine was a loving, energetic little girl, a precious gem. Lenore loved her sister.

Life was falling into a comfortable rhythm. Mike became the protective big brother and Jack was a doting, loving father. It was a happy life, and Jack felt very blessed. All that was needed now was to have the Kaufman name blazing in lights on a theater marquee. Jack new that day would happen, and then he would truly be living his American dream.

Chapter 27

Capone
Chicago, 1923

Alphonse Gabriel Capone was born on January 17, 1899, in Brooklyn, New York. He lived with his mother, father, and eight siblings. Being the fourth of nine children, he was expected to take care of his younger siblings, a task he despised. From an early age, he was a troubled youth filled with intense anger. At age fourteen, he was expelled from parochial school for hitting a female teacher in the face. He worked odd jobs, including working in a candy store and a bowling alley. At age nineteen, Capone married Mae Josephine Coughlin.

Capone's first gang association was with the small-time Bowery Boys. But he quickly moved up and became part of the Brooklyn Rippers, and then the more powerful Five Points Gang. When Capone was in Five Points, he worked for the racketeer Frankie Yale. Yale tended bar in a Coney Island dance hall and also in a saloon called the Harvard Inn. Capone was the club's bouncer.

Frank Galluccio, another gangster and a good friend of Frankie Yale's, came to the Harvard Inn one infamous Friday evening. Capone was working the front entrance, patting down the customers before they entered. As Galluccio and his sister began to walk into the club, Capone stopped them. Eyeing the unattractive woman, he blurted out, "Galluccio, is she the best you can do?"

In one swift move, Galluccio pulled out his Soviet NR 43 combat knife, and in a blink of an eye, slashed Capone's face. Frankie Yale saw what was going on and wedged his body between Capone and Galluccio.

"What the hell are you two doing?" Yale shouted. "You are on my turf now." Then looking directly into Capone's eyes, he demanded, "You apologize to Galluccio's sister right now! We don't talk like that to ladies."

Capone looked murderous, but for the first time in his life, he did what someone else told him to do. Under his breath he murmured, "I will never make another apology again!"

He walked through the saloon toward the kitchen, his hand pressed firmly on his cheek where the blood was gushing out of a deep, large gash. Grabbing a dish towel, he then walked out into the back alley. That incident ultimately led to Capone's infamous nickname, "Scarface," a name Capone detested.

Frankie Yale knew that his friend would be a dead man if Al stayed in New York much longer. Capone had already killed a rival gang member and a "kill-on-site" order for a scar-faced man was now circulating through town. For now, Capone was laying low until Yale could get him out of town. Finally, Yale managed to hook Capone up with Johnny Torrio, who in turned introduced him to Big Jim Colosimo. Shortly after that encounter, Capone was spirited out of Brooklyn to Chicago.

In 1923, Capone set down stakes and purchased a small house at 7244 South Prairie Avenue in the Park Manor neighborhood on the city's South Side. His first job was as a bouncer for a brothel, a job he was good at. He enjoyed beating up anyone and everyone who looked at him the wrong way. He also enjoyed the variety of women at his disposal.

In a short amount of time, Capone settled into his "inherited" territory and began expanding his bootleg operations at warp speed. His actions were flagrant, open, and obvious, and violence became his trademark.

No one got in Capone's way, not even the police, and especially not the elected officials. The Mayor of Chicago, William Hale Thompson, and the city's police department, passively ratified their arrangement with Capone. By paying everyone off, Capone became untouchable.

Colosimo had immigrated to the city in 1895 when he was seventeen years old. He was Italian Mafioso who got his start in Chicago as a pickpocket, and then went on to build the legendary "Chicago Outfit." Colosimo organized a coalition of thugs, pimps, and extortionists who turned Chicago into a *"Criminale Paradiso."*

Colosimo's downfall came when Johnny Torrio wanted Big Jim to expand into bootlegging. Colosimo, who had made a fortune in prostitution and illegal alcohol sales in his restaurants, didn't want to risk attention from the Feds by expanding into a full-blown bootlegging operation.

Johnny Torrio, on the other hand, saw bootlegging as a great opportunity. He set up a meeting with the leaders of the New York Mafia to discuss the matter. After the meeting, the leaders agreed to make Torrio the head of the Chicago Outfit. But there was one condition. Johnny had to wait to take over until Big Jim was dead.

On May 11, 1921, Torrio met Big Jim in the foyer of one of Colosimo's restaurants under the pretext that a bootleg shipment had just been delivered. When Colosimo arrived and saw that nothing had been delivered, he realized he had been set up, and ran for the front door. But it was too late. A gunman hiding in the coatroom shot Big Jim in the back. The bullet exited through his heart. He died instantaneously. The gunman looked a lot like Frankie Vale, but no one was ever prosecuted for the murder.

The city of Chicago gave Big Jim a lavish funeral. There were fifty-three pallbearers, including congressmen and judges, and more than one thousand members of the Democratic Party. To no one's surprise, Johnny Torrio took over Colosimo's empire.

After Big Jim's death, Torrio, now better known as Papa Johnny, brought Capone into his inner circle. Torrio had known

Capone back in New York in the days when he was in the Five Points Gang. Torrio made Capone *"un'offerta che non poteva rifutare"*. . . an offer that he could not refuse. Capone became Torrio's bodyguard and assistant. In return, Johnny taught Capone everything he needed to know about the underworld of crime and murder.

Johnny Torrio was now the new head of the Chicago Outfit, which illegally supplied booze throughout the city. He had political protection through the infamous *Unione Siciliana,* but protection is never 100 percent foolproof.

On January 24, 1925, while Torrio was parking his car outside his apartment, Hymie Weiss, Vincent Drucci, and Bugs Moran set their sights on him. In perfect precision, a spray of bullets fired through the car's glass windows. Bullets were lodged in Johnny's jaw, lungs, groin, legs, and stomach, but the kill-shot bullet to Johnny's head jammed in the gun's barrel. When the three men saw that Johnny was still alive, they kicked him repeatedly and then left him to bleed to death.

Miraculously, after numerous surgeries, Johnny Torrio survived. Capone ordered a group of trusted men to guard his friend around the clock. After a long and difficult recovery, Torrio was persuaded to retire. He moved back to Italy with his wife. On his way out, he gave control of the Outfit to his assistant, Alphonse Gabriel "Al" Capone.

As the new boss of Torrio's organization, Capone took control of all of Torrio's illegal breweries and the massive transportation networks which reached Canada and beyond. Capone also inherited all the political and law enforcement protection he needed. Now with this protection, Capone was able to use even more violence to increase his revenue. Refusal to purchase liquor from Capone often resulted in the brewery, restaurant, or store in question being blown up, another of Capone's signature moves.

Over the next five years, Capone's name began appearing in

the sports pages in the Chicago newspapers where he was self-described as a boxing promoter. He was also frequently seen at the White Sox games.

It was at a Sox game that Jack Kaufman first saw him. It wasn't hard to recognize Capone. He wore custom suits and large costly jewelry draped around his neck. He always smoked a cigar and had a different female companion on his arm every night.

You always knew when Capone was in the stands because the fans and spectators sent out loud enthusiastic cheers. Capone was seen by some as a modern-day Robin Hood because of the numerous donations he made to various charities around the South Side of Chicago. That image would not last, and his new title would soon become Public Enemy, No. 1.

Chapter 28

Barney Ross
Chicago, 1923

In 1923, Jack started going to Kid Howard's gym on the South Side of town. He met many émigrés from Eastern Europe and Russia at the gym. Many were top-rated boxers. One of the most promising of these men was Barney Ross, whose given name was Dov-Ber Rosofsky. Ross was an émigré from Russia. His father, a rabbi, owned a small vegetable shop in Chicago's Maxwell Street neighborhood. When Barney was fourteen, his father was murdered while trying to stop a robbery. The tragedy broke the family apart and Ross started fending for himself in the ghetto.

Before Rosofsky changed his name to Barney Ross, he was a street fighter, thief, and money runner for Al Capone. During this time, he met Jacob Rubenstein, another wayward Jewish ghetto kid. Rubenstein had a passion for boxing and saw Ross's potential. The two teamed up, and soon Ross turned all his efforts to the ring and began training with Rubenstein.

Everyone knew that Ross had the goods. He had chutzpah. He was quick, fearless, and hungry. His explosive jab was usually followed by a mean uppercut. His hard counter-punches, delivered with rough arrogance, gave him an edge against his opponents.

Ross rose quickly in the ranks and became Chicago's Inter-city Golden Gloves Champion. Al Capone soon became a regular at Ross's fights, and so did Jack Kaufman.

At Ross's first paid fight, on September 1, 1929, Jack was sitting in the stands. When he came home that evening he was euphoric. Jack knew he had just witnessed boxing history being made that night and was proud to have been a part of it.

Chapter 29

Maloy
Chicago 1923–1925

Capone was not too worried about Maloy. As far as Capone was concerned, Maloy was a one-man operation, a small fish in a big pond. Nevertheless, Capone didn't like to take chances, so the two gangsters created an alliance. Capone gave Maloy a license to run the Local 110, and Maloy put Capone and his men on a fictitious payroll. In exchange, it was understood that as long as Capone got his license fees, he would leave Maloy alone.

Maloy ruled the union with an iron fist. Those who dared to stand in Maloy's way tended to find themselves covered in blood, gunned down on the streets, or mutilated in their homes. This was the sign of the times. Extortion, bribes, beatings, and murder became the new normal. It was par for the course for the average Chicagoan to hear that a neighbor, a worker, or a family member had been killed. Families were shattered, children were orphaned, and there was no end in sight.

Union headquarters dominated the corner of Harrison and Wabash in 1923. Maloy's office for the Local 110 was on the second floor. Con Shea of the Teamsters and Steve Kelliher of the Janitors Union had their offices on the first floor.

Having all three unions in the same building offered numerous opportunities for the three union leaders to increase their revenue by as many illegal means as possible. Maloy, Shea, and Kelliher got together to run a gambling racket in the sub-basement under their offices. What better way to utilize the unused space?

The initial agreement between the three men was that they

would share the profits equally. But that agreement didn't last very long, and soon Maloy and Kelliher got into a nasty fight over their cuts. When Maloy decided that he had had enough of Kelliher, he orchestrated a power shift in the union and put his plan into action.

First, Maloy hired an up-and-coming goon named Danny McCarthy. Once McCarthy was in his employ, Maloy invited McCarthy and Kelliher to join him for a drink at Tierney's, a bar on Calumet and Twenty-fifth Street. Tierney's was conveniently located next to one of the theaters Maloy controlled.

The three men took a private booth in the back of the bar. A heavy red velvet drape hung from the ceiling and separated their booth from the rest of the patrons. As soon as they took their seats and ordered a round of drinks, McCarthy initiated a heated argument with Kelliher. In a matter of seconds, the argument escalated into a full brawl. Kelliher threw his glass of scotch toward McCarthy. McCarthy drew his gun. One shot to the head and Kelliher was dead.

McCarthy ran out the back door right into a pair of policemen. He was arrested and thrown in jail. He pleaded self-defense. A dozen of Maloy's most trusted goons swore that McCarthy was simply trying to protect himself. Danny McCarthy beat the rap and was acquitted of all charges.

In 1925, Maloy schemed to raise the cash in his till. He issued work permits to non-union members and then closed the union to any new members. When the members found out what had happened, they were furious and decided to retaliate. Jack Kaufman, Johnny Butler, and Billy Murphy called for a secret meeting, recruiting a small contingent of men to meet at Jack's house. Mike and Lenore were in school, and Jack told Mary and Adela to take Francine into the city for the day.

When the men showed up, angry and disgruntled, Jack quickly began the meeting. "Settle down, guys. We have a lot to discuss. We've been dealing with this asshole for the last three

years, and I know we've had it up to here with him. But we all
have mouths to feed and we love our jobs. So we've got to be
smart about this and come up with a plan."

"I got a plan, let's kill the son of a bitch!" yelled Frankie. The
group cheered in response. Jack ignored the outburst.

"As I see it," Jack continued calmly, "a lock-out would be in-
effective. Maloy would just issue more work permits and the
day workers would fill all of our positions. None of us want that.
It also sets a very dangerous precedent. The other option would
be to organize a united front with, ideally, all our members, but
at least with a large majority. We make our demands at Thursday's meeting. If that fails, then the next move would be to block
the day workers from entering the theaters. That might lead to
some blood being spilled, but it would get the message across.
And if that fails, the last option would be . . ." Jack stopped before saying what everyone else was thinking. "Eliminate
Maloy!"

The men all looked at one another, suddenly very nervous.
They knew that eliminating Maloy meant that their own lives,
and their families lives, would be put in jeopardy. In spite of
their deep concerns and fears, they agreed to Jack's plan. They
would take things a step at a time.

First, they would organize a protest at the next union meeting. The men planned to meet at St. Mary's Church. Once everyone arrived, they would walk from the church to the union
meeting hall. Then they would line up single file and sit down.
Jack would be the last one to go inside. Next, Jack would walk
right up to Maloy and calmly confront him with the strategy that
they all had worked out.

But when the meeting actually took place, the men couldn't
contain themselves. As soon as they opened the doors, everyone
stormed the union hall. To their horror, they discovered that
Maloy was prepared for the attack. Someone in the group was a
turncoat.

"Men, start firing!" ordered Maloy.

Maloy's men opened fire. Their machine guns were initially aimed toward the ceiling. Maloy hoped to scare the union workers into submission. But if that didn't work, he had ordered his goons to take a few of the union men out. But not Kaufman! He wanted Jack to see his men laying lifeless in a pool of blood. Maloy made that very clear.

The earsplitting spray of bullets penetrated the shiplap on the ceiling, and the echo bounced loudly off the floorboards. The walls shook. Chunks of plaster and wood fell like winter hail. The floorboards vibrated. Some of the men took cover, while others stood shocked and motionless.

Jack didn't budge. He was standing next to Maloy, the safest place he could be. When the gunfire finally stopped, Jack raised his hand and gestured for his men to leave the hall. Everyone got up and walked out. A couple of them had been injured from debris, but no one was dead.

Jack glared at Maloy and said, "You can't kill all of us, Tommy."

"But I can kill some of you. And you will be first in line, Kaufman."

"As long as I take you with me," Jack rejoined. Lightly, he added, "Tommy, are we done with the foreplay? Let's talk. I think we can work this out without shutting down all the theaters. That is what you want, isn't it, Tommy?" It was a bold move, considering the fact that the barrel of a gun was pointed right at Jack's chest.

Maloy was dangerous, but he also respected strength. Jack knew this was a game of cat and mouse and miraculously the ploy worked. The two men walked down the hall to a small office. Jack spoke first.

"Tommy, let's cut to the chase. Take it or leave it. My men are prepared to strike. You and I both know what that would do to your revenue, and my men know what it will do to their ability to provide for their families."

"Cut the crap, Jack. What do you want?" Maloy demanded.

"Monthly dues frozen at three dollars for the next two years," said Jack. "Permit workers don't work more than seven days a month. Fifteen percent of their paycheck is paid back to the union creating a widow's fund. We want a death benefit of $500."

Jack knew that Maloy would probably use the fifteen percent as a straight kickback, but he saw this as a way of making inroads for his men in the future. The bigger sticking point was that Maloy's day workers were making $175 a week. That amounted to a large cut for Maloy if he agreed to the proposed terms.

Maloy stood up and started heading for the door. He spun around and said, "Kaufman, ten percent and ten days a month for day workers. No death benefit. What do you think this is, day camp?"

A deal was made, but both men knew it wouldn't last for long. A showdown would be coming. It was only a matter of time.

Chapter 30

Francine
Chicago, 1927

On Wednesday, August 17, Francine turned five years old. Jack took the day off to celebrate his daughter's birthday. The kids were out of school for the summer break, and the four of them planned on going to their favorite spot along Lake Michigan for a swim and a picnic lunch. A light refreshing breeze whispered through the air as puffy white clouds wandered eastward. It was a perfect day for a birthday celebration.

Mary was not accompanying them. She didn't enjoy going to the lake or driving in automobiles. She made three cheese sandwiches for the children, and a salami and onion sandwich for Jack. Mary was planning on staying home to prepare Francine's birthday dinner.

The children jumped into the car according to their pecking order. Jack placed the picnic basket and thermos of lemonade on the floor, turned on the radio he had recently installed, and they all set off, singing along to the blasting music. They clapped and laughed, savoring every moment of the trip to the lake.

After arriving at their special spot, the kids ripped off their clothes, revealing bathing suits underneath.

"Last one in is a rotten egg!" yelled Jack. He watched affectionately as his children raced into the lake.

Mike was always the first one in. Francine ran after her brother, giggling as the frosty water tickled her toes. Lenore approached more methodically, carefully assessing her surroundings. The water was chilly but refreshing, and the family laughed and splashed uproariously. Finally Jack called out,

"Time for lunch. Everyone out."

Splashing out of the lake, the children hurried into dry clothes before settling down on the picnic blanket. Jack had spread the blanket under a beautiful tree. They grabbed their cheese sandwiches, and Jack took his salami and onion sandwich. They gobbled them down in record time.

"Papa, put me on your shoulders so I can see if it's still there!" Francine yelled out. This was a ritual between the two of them. Jack lifted Francine up high above his head.

"I see it, Papa, I see it!" Francine squealed with delight.

"What do you see, Francine?" Jack chuckled.

"I see Canada!"

"What else do you see?"

"I see high mountains with white snow all over!"

"Do you see a big balloon tied to a tree?" asked Jack.

"I do! I do!" hollered Francine.

"That is your birthday balloon." Right on cue, Mike cut the balloon loose and handed it to his sister.

"Now make a wish," Jack said. Francine closed her eyes and held her breath. She wished for the new doll that was on display in the window of Krause's Department Store.

Jack opened the car's small trunk and pulled out a wrapped package. He handed his daughter her gift, and the whole family started singing, "Happy Birthday to You."

Slowly and meticulously, Francine unwrapped the beautiful, flowered paper from the box, making sure not to tear it. When all the wrapping was off, she jumped up with pure delight.

Hugging her father, she yelled out, "Papa, this is the doll I wished for! How did you know I wanted it?"

Jack smiled. "A little birdie told me. I love you, Francine Edith Kaufman, and don't you ever forget that." Jack turned to Mike and Lenore and added, "I love you guys too, and don't you ever forget that either."

The afternoon cooled as the breeze picked up. Whitecaps

sparkled across the surface of the water and sailboats dotted the horizon, sails puffing in the wind. They packed up the blanket and picnic basket and got back into the car. Jack took the long way home. Francine clutched her doll on her lap, rocking her new baby to sleep. After a few minutes, she placed her head on her sister's shoulder and dozed off.

While her family was at the lake, Mary had also been busy. First, she walked to the Jewish butcher shop to buy chicken thighs, chicken wings, and ground turkey. She also bought freshly-made gefilte fish, Jack and Mike's favorite. Next, she stopped at the local grocer's where she bought all the ingredients she needed for her famous Russian cream. It was her mother's signature dish in Odessa, and Mary wanted to continue the tradition.

She spent the remainder of the day making her irresistible chicken fricassee with meatballs, one of Francine's favorite dishes. Adela also contributed to the festivities, baking Francine a chocolate fudge birthday cake decorated with lavender roses, Francine's favorite flower.

Next, she decorated the backyard with streamers and balloons. Finally, she placed the birthday presents on a round metal table under the sugar maple tree.

After dinner, everyone gathered outside for dessert. Adela's fudge cake was delicious, as were the massive scoops of chocolate ice cream and Mary's Russian cream.

Francine opened her remaining presents very carefully, pulling the tape from the wrapping and making sure she didn't tear the beautiful papers. She planned to keep the paper and decorate her room with it, a tradition she had started with her Papa several years before.

Everyone began singing, "Ain't she sweet, see her coming down the street," and then Jack bowed to his daughter, asking, "Do you want to dance?"

"Yes, Papa," Francine whispered. She placed her feet on her

father's gleaming black leather shoes and they glided over the wooden planks on the back deck. No ballroom floor had ever been more magical.

"Papa, spin me around," begged Francine.

Jack twirled his little daughter in his arms.

"Again Papa, again."

The dance repeated itself over and over until both of them were exhausted. It was a glorious day, one that Francine would remember for the rest of her life.

Chapter 31

Jack
Chicago, 1927

On September 22, 1927, Jack David Kaufman became a citizen of the United States. To celebrate the milestone, he bought himself a cashmere suit, and a red, white, and blue silk tie.

The whole family attended the naturalization ceremony. Mary, their three children, Adela, Bella and her son Norman sat in the viewing gallery as Jack proudly placed his right hand over his heart. He recited:

I, Jacob David Kaufman, hereby declare, on oath, that I absolutely and entirely renounce and abjure all allegiance and fidelity to any foreign prince, potentate, state, or sovereignty, of whom or which I have heretofore been a subject or citizen; that I will support and defend the Constitution and laws of the United States of America against all enemies, foreign and domestic; that I will bear true faith and allegiance to the same; that I will perform noncombatant service in the Armed Forces of the United States when required by the law; that I will perform work of national importance under civilian direction when required by the law; and that I take this obligation freely, without any mental reservation or purpose of evasion; so help me God.

After the swearing-in ceremony, the whole family climbed into Jack's new 1927 Ford Model T and went out to dinner at Caruso's, an Italian restaurant in Hyde Park. Carlo, the owner of the restaurant, had been told the cause for the celebration, so not only were drinks on the house, Carlo also picked up the tab for dinner. Jack was now a citizen! The other diners were also made aware of Jack's new status and chanted, USA! USA! It was a wonderful, memorable evening.

At the headquarters of the Local 110, the tension and friction between Maloy and the members of the union was akin to a ticking time bomb. No one could guess how long this hostile environment would last, but everyone knew that a massive explosion was inevitable.

Jack's role had evolved into being a full-time mediator. All concerns and grievances now went through him, and he organized frequent ad hoc meetings at his house. His job, at least for now, was just to keep everyone calm and employed.

The members wanted change and were pushing hard for Jack to run against Maloy at the next election. His children were thriving, and he did not want to do anything to complicate their lives. Jack also knew that if elected, he would be spending more time with his men and less time with his kids.

Mike, at twelve, was almost as tall as his father. He had also inherited Jack's good looks, charm, love for automobiles, and everything mechanical. He loved to build and fix things. He dressed like his dad, so Jack made sure Mike always had at least two new suits at the beginning of each year. The only problem was that Mike was growing out of his clothes as fast as they were bought. That didn't bother Jack in the slightest. He believed that if you looked affluent, your status would be elevated and doors which would otherwise be closed, would open. At his father's insistence, Mike also worked part-time at the A&P. Jack wanted Mike to understand how difficult it was to earn a buck.

Lenore, now eight years old, was their little genius. Every morning, she would read the newspaper before going to school. She read books a twelve-year-old would struggle with and was the star student in her classroom. Lenore skipped a grade, became the teacher's assistant, and began tutoring some of her fellow classmates with reading and writing. She was already talking about going to Northwestern University, just like her Papa did. She wanted to study literature and hoped that one day she would teach at a prestigious college for women.

Francine, now five years old, was always happy and playful. She loved to help her mother in the kitchen, but her passion was singing and dancing. She would always make up her own dance moves and pretend she was gliding on a ballroom floor. Francine had a beautiful voice for such a young child. When the music played, Jack would sometimes lift Francine into his arms and then the two of them would sing and dance together.

Mary and Jack tried to resurrect their marriage. But you can't build on something that you never had. She and Jack were never in love and there was never any passion in their relationship. Love was not a word they used to describe their marriage. Their marriage settled into one of duty and responsibility and she foresaw tough times ahead.

Mary, who had never known anyone who was divorced, was now meeting many Russian women whose husbands had left their foreign-born wives and replaced them with American wives. She hoped that she and Jack would stay together for the children's sake, at least until Francine graduated from high school. Mary didn't see her marriage lasting until death do us part.

The movie business continued to boom. On October 6, 1927, a momentous film event took place in New York City at Warner Brothers' flagship theater. The first feature film with sound, *The Jazz Singer*, starring Al Jolson, was released. The date of the release was no coincidence. It was chosen to coincide with Yom Kippur, the Jewish holiday around which much of the movie's plot revolved.

The Jazz Singer was about a young man, Jakie Rabinowitz, who rebelled against Jewish tradition and refused to follow in his father's footsteps as a cantor in the local synagogue. Instead, he changed his name to Jack Robin and followed his dream of pursuing a career singing popular jazz songs.

In the movie, when Jakie's father became gravely ill, he was faced with a difficult choice. Does he, should he, can he, put his religion above his own ambitions? Ultimately, Jackie cancelled his own performance so he could sing in his father's place. The doors of the temple were left wide open, and Jakie's father was able to hear his son sing the Kol Nidrei prayer.

The musical was a blockbuster, even with a production cost for Warner Brothers of $422,000. The film also pioneered an innovative sound system and a new type of sound production which presented multifaceted challenges for the projectionist up in the booth.

After premiering in New York City, *The Jazz Singer* premiered in Chicago at the Piccadilly Theater. Jack was the head projectionist at the Piccadilly, in charge of integrating the new sound system. He studied the format and procedures that the union provided to the membership and was confident the first showing of *The Jazz Singer* would go on without a hitch.

Each of Jolson's musical numbers was mounted on a separate reel with an accompanying sound disc. Even though the film was only eighty-nine minutes long, there were fifteen reels and fifteen discs to manage. Jack had to be able to thread the film and cue up the Vitaphone records quickly. He was well aware that any failure, the smallest stumble or hesitation, would result in public and financial humiliation for him and the theater owner. *The Jazz Singer* proved that feature-length "talkies" were big business and now the future for motion pictures.

The entire family came to the premiere. Jack's brothers Samuel and Carl, his sister Bella, Adela, Mary, and Mike, sat in the mezzanine. The subject matter of the film was especially meaningful, and knowing that Jack was the projectionist made the evening a proud moment for the family.

In December, Thomas Edward Maloy threw one of his famously lavish parties. The invitation was addressed to Mr. Jack

Kaufman. The card was trimmed in gold ink and the handwriting was similar to the script associated with the Declaration of Independence. It read:

> *The honor of your presence is requested*
> *Sunday, December 11th at 7:00 p.m.*
> *at the Maloy residence*
> *6806 Chappel Avenue*
> *for cocktails and hors d'oeuvres*
> *Formal attire requested*
> *Thomas Edward Maloy and Effie Maloy*

On Sunday, December 11, as Jack drove down Maloy's long circular driveway, a parking attendant requested his car keys. Jack was apprehensive about letting one of Maloy's goons take his car, but tossed the valet the keys and then walked up the steps to the front porch.

Jack was greeted at the door. Antonio, one of Maloy's most intimidating goons asked, "Are you carrying a weapon?" Antonio's pale, blue eyes were cold. Jack tried to make light of the situation. "Who wants to know?" Jack responded.

Antonio was not amused. "Don't play games, Jack. You're not on your turf now. This is the boss's home court."

Jack sighed in an exaggerated way. "No, Antonio, I'm not carrying a weapon."

The pale eyes did not waver. "I still need to pat you down."

Jack felt his face turning red, but he submitted to the humiliating search without comment, and then walked into the grand foyer of the house.

It was an impressive sight. The floors were black and gold marble. The walls were covered with artwork capturing picturesque scenes from an array of Italian cities and famous Italian landmarks: the Leaning Tower of Pisa, the Coliseum, and the Vatican. Butlers walked through the room with trays of hors d'oeuvres, caviar, and champagne.

Jack turned to one of the butlers and said coolly, "I don't drink champagne. I prefer some of Maloy's whiskey, the finest he's got."

The butler went over to Maloy and Tommy signaled for Jack to come join him. As Jack approached Maloy, he noticed a stunning woman out of the corner of his eye, standing near the bar. She had vivid, deep, green eyes and long auburn hair. In an instant, Jack decided she was the most beautiful woman he had ever seen.

Jack continued to walk over to where Maloy stood, but he really wanted to be walking toward the woman at the bar.

"Kaufman, I heard my champagne isn't good enough for you! My butler said you wanted whiskey. I thought you would be asking for vodka," Maloy sniped. Jack knew what Tommy was doing and he wasn't going to be led down that road.

"What's the matter, Tommy? Are you saving the good stuff for yourself? I thought you were more gracious than that. You don't share the big money booze with your fellow union *compagnos*?" Maloy nodded to the enormous man at his right posing as a butler and Jack was handed a tumbler of the best Kentucky bourbon money could buy.

The talk then turned generally to the growth of the motion picture industry since *The Jazz Singer*, and the additional money that would be generated. Jack was finding it hard to concentrate. All he could think about was the woman with the green eyes.

"Tommy," he said finally. "I see a couple of my men over by the bar and need to meet their wives. Good party," he added.

Maloy whispered into Jack's ear, "Next time bring a gun. You never know when you might need it." As Jack walked away, Maloy grinned and said to his goon, "This is going to be easy. I knew those green eyes would get him."

Jack walked toward the bar. The green-eyed beauty was still there. He felt his face flush and for once, his charm deserted him.

He could think of nothing to say. The woman smiled at him.

"Hey good-looking," she murmured. "What's your name?"

Jack was still speechless. He gaped at the woman and finally came up with the brilliant rejoinder, "What's yours?

She smiled, tilting her head to the left. "Theresa," she said softly.

Jack didn't know what to say next. He was completely and utterly captivated. Finally, he got hold of himself and managed to smile back.

"Glad to meet you, Theresa. Can I buy you a drink?"

She chuckled. "Of course, but I think the drinks are complementary. What's your name?"

"Jack."

"I'm glad to meet you, Jack. Do you have a last name by any chance?"

"Kaufman. Jack Kaufman."

They talked for close to an hour before Theresa said, "I hope we'll meet again, Jack Kaufman." And Jack knew that she meant it.

Chapter 32

Jack
Chicago, 1928

The Roaring Twenties, infamously labeled as the Lawless Decade, roared on. In 1928, the wealth of the nation had doubled over the past eight years and prosperity was at its all-time high. Wall Street was bursting at the seams with investments and huge profits.

Millions of women entered the white-collar job market as stenographers, secretaries, bank tellers, and managers, and for the first time, women had their own income. Also, thanks to the Nineteenth Amendment, women were finally allowed to vote in local and federal elections. It was a time of unprecedented freedoms. All moral codes had been tossed aside and sex was uninhibited, thanks to the use of the diaphragm.

Fashion was keeping pace with the times, making its own progressive and very risqué statement. Women hiked their skirts above their knees and cut off their long tresses. Short bobbed hair become the rage. The Charleston, the Black Bottom, and the Flea Hop were not only new dance crazes, they symbolized fun, freedom, and playfulness. Prohibition had become just a fantasy and a farce. Now drinking and smoking had become the norm for women.

One out of every five Americans owned a car. The Ford Model T was a staple for couples and families, while single men were competing to acquire the latest and most equipped models. Car radios were being installed on a daily basis.

Perhaps the most exciting discovery was in medicine with the invention of the iron lung. Doctors were using the ventilator for treating children with poliomyelitis, and this innovation would save thousands of children from the dreaded disease.

It was an exciting time all around, but Jack Kaufman had something more urgent to concentrate on. He was fixated on the red-haired, green-eyed woman he had met at Maloy's Christmas party. He knew she was destined to be part of his life. But he didn't even know her last name.

Five weeks after her green eyes cast a spell on him, Theresa walked into the projectionist booth at the Piccadilly Theater where Jack was screening *The Circus* staring Charlie Chaplin. The movie had just ended, and Jack was getting ready to put the reels back on the rack when he heard the door to the booth slam shut. He turned his head and there she was.

At first, Jack thought he was dreaming. He took a few steps toward her.

"Theresa, what are you doing here?" he asked in almost a whisper.

"I was hoping for a private showing of *The Circus*," she replied with a spellbinding smile. "I hear the projectionist is out of this world," she added in her sexiest voice.

Jack smiled as his heart pounded. He rose to his feet and locked the door. Theresa slowly started to undress. She took her time opening her blouse, licking her finger before touching each button. Then she took off her black lace brassiere. Her firm breasts were perfectly shaped. Jack could hardly breathe. Next, Theresa removed her garter belt and sheer silk nylons. She was not wearing underwear. Jack gasped with pleasure. He could not move.

Theresa unbuttoned Jack's shirt. Then she unbuckled his belt and pulled down his trousers. Taking Jack's hand, she guided him over to the small couch and soon Jack surrendered to her perfectly proportioned body. He had never experienced such rapture and ecstasy.

Afterward, they lay quietly on the couch in each other's arms. Jack was overwhelmed and humbled by sheer happiness. This was what he had always dreamed of having. A moment like this, feelings like this, and a woman like this. Now he had finally found her. All that was left was how to keep her in his life forever.

Chapter 33

Jack and Theresa
March 1928

Mark Twain once said: "It is hopeless for the occasional visitor to try to keep up with Chicago. She outgrows his prophecies faster than he can make them. She is always a novelty; for she is never the Chicago you saw when you passed through the last time."

Chicago had now become the second largest city in the country and its population increased every day. With that growth, Chicago had also become one of the most lawless and corrupt cities in the country.

Al Capone's bootleggers, gangsters, and hit men, ran the city and the unions. Tommy Maloy was too big to fail and too powerful to be taken down. Maloy believed that he was untouchable.

The members of the Local 110 had had enough. It was time to take Maloy out. Secret meetings occurred on a regular basis and Jack found himself in the middle of it all, which is where he wanted to be. The men continually pressured Jack to run against Maloy in the November election. Jack had resisted running up until now, but knew time was running out. He finally made his decision. He would run against Maloy. The only unanswered question was, at what cost?

His relationship with Theresa continued to be the best part of his life. It was no longer just about great sex. They found they could talk about anything. When Jack withdrew deep in thought, Theresa had a way of making him feel as if he could trust and confide in her.

Following one of their lovemaking marathons, Jack told Theresa he was thinking about running against Maloy in the next election. To his surprise, Theresa became agitated. She tried to talk him out of it, an edge to her voice.

"Jack. Why do you want to take that on? You don't need this in your life. We barely have time to be together now. If you run, we'll never have time to see each other." Jack was taken by surprise with the comment.

"Theresa, I thought you, of all people, would understand. I want to do this for us and our future."

"Jack, if you do this, we won't have a future," Theresa snapped.

Jack gasped. "What are you talking about? Do you know something you're not telling me?"

Theresa began to weep. "I only know that I would not be able to survive if something happens to you. I'm begging you to change your mind. I will not stand by and watch you commit suicide."

"Nothing is going to happen to me. I promise," Jack said firmly. "I can take care of myself. Everything will be fine. Trust me."

Their discussion morphed into a full-blown argument. Theresa begged Jack not to go up against Maloy but refused to give any reason. Jack grew angry, saying that his decision had been made. Finally, it got to the point where Theresa ordered Jack out of her apartment saying she never wanted to see him again.

"What the hell is going on?" he demanded, but she only pointed to the door and told him to get out.

Jack left. He wandered the streets for a while, utterly dazed. He had never experienced this type of rejection and pain before. It was as if Theresa had destroyed a part of his very being.

He rewound their final conversation over and over in his mind. Something did not add up. It just didn't make any sense. Theresa knew his running against Maloy was inevitable. So why was she suddenly behaving like this?

After Jack left, Theresa threw herself down onto the bed and wept. How she wished she could have told him the truth, but it was impossible. She couldn't stand to see the pain and disappointment in his eyes. She couldn't stand to tell him that she was a fraud. A spy! And that she was being paid to lead Jack to his doom.

Theresa had been on Maloy's payroll for a long time. It had first begun when she was only sixteen when her brother had been beaten beyond recognition for selling one of Maloy's liquor orders to a higher bidder. To save her brother's life, Theresa agreed to deal with Maloy. Whenever he wanted to keep a close watch on somebody, Theresa would seduce the victim, get whatever information Maloy wanted, and report back to him. It had worked time and time again. Now the latest victim was Kaufman.

There was just one difference between this assignment and all the others. Theresa had fallen in love with Jack.

Jack continued to process the night's events. Something wasn't right. He felt it in his gut. He couldn't stomach going home to Mary so he turned the car around and drove out to the lake. He parked his car and strolled, perplexed and baffled, along the water's edge. After several hours, he went back to his car and fell asleep. As the sun rose, he drove home.

It had been almost four weeks since Jack and Theresa had last spoken. And then one evening, while Jack was in his office at the Piccadilly, he thought he saw her silhouette. It took a second or two before he was sure it was actually Theresa. He could not catch his breath.

Theresa stepped into the office and closed the door. Jack stood up and moved toward her. Theresa's body stiffened as she moved away from him. Jack froze, confused.

Theresa's voice was level and very calm. "Jack, I have been offered a part in a musical in New York and I'm leaving today."

Jack swallowed. "How long do you think you will be gone?"

"At least six months, maybe a year," replied Theresa.

Jack could not bear the thought.

"Can I come to New York and visit you?" he asked. "I would love to show you Brighton Beach and all the places I went to when I first arrived from Odessa."

Theresa's voice was shaking. "I don't know, Jack. I don't think that would be a good idea. Please don't do anything unless I contact you first."

"Theresa!" Jack began.

"Don't say anything, Jack. Please. Not now." Then Theresa turned around and walked out the door.

Thanks to the influence of her friend Marilyn, the on-and-off mistress of the theater producer Florenz Ziegfeld, Theresa had landed the role of lead dancer in the Broadway musical *Rosalie*. The story told the tale of a princess from a faraway land who comes to America and falls in love with a West Point lieutenant.

Theresa was doing six shows a week and at first it was a great distraction, taking her mind off Jack. But as the weeks and months crept by, she couldn't mask the ache in her heart. She missed Jack immeasurably. But her decision remained absolute. For his sake, she had to stay away.

It had been three months since Theresa left Chicago, and with each passing day, Jack's heart ached more and more. He knew beyond any question that she was the only woman he would ever love. But he also knew what he had to do with regard to the union. Jack had made his decision; he would run against Maloy at the next election. And if he won, he would have to think of some way to keep Theresa in his life.

Jack thought about visiting Theresa but he couldn't leave Chicago. Things had heated up at home and at work. The tension in the union was combustible and his relationship with Mary, difficult at best, was deteriorating by the week. The two of them argued about everything. They found themselves yelling at each other all the time. Jack usually slept on the couch in the living room and some nights he didn't even come home.

In late July, a dispute erupted between the theater owners and the Musicians Union. The musicians wanted more money and more work as well as the usual assurances and guarantees, and a new contract. This conflict had percolated for months and it finally came to a full boil in mid-August.

It was unlikely that the demands being made by the musicians were going to be agreed upon by the theater owners without serious compromise. Jack wanted to stay out of this fight but his men voted unanimously to join their striking brethren. They wanted Jack to be part of the solution. If several of the other trade unions joined in, hundreds of theaters would be shut down for a long time and many families would endure great hardships.

Jack agreed to do what he could. He knew Jimmy Petrillo, the head of the Musicians Union, and suggested the two of them meet. Jack wanted to see what issues the musicians were willing to compromise on. That way he could determine whether the Local 110 really needed to get involved.

Petrillo agreed to a meeting the following Monday at the Shoreland Hotel in Hyde Park. He would bring a small contingent of men from his union and Jack agreed to do the same. Petrillo had heard about the tension between Maloy and Jack and he believed that things would be a lot better for everybody if Jack, and not Maloy, was in charge of the 110. But he also knew the only way that would happen would be if Maloy took a bullet through his heart.

The Shoreland Hotel, which had been open for two years, was a popular and well-known establishment. Many prestigious and high-profile events took place at the hotel including a massive banquet held in Amelia Earhart's honor after she returned from her transatlantic flight.

The Shoreland also gained the reputation as the hotel where you could conduct meetings safe from any prying eyes. It was

Capone's hotel of choice. Capone conducted his "business" on the third floor of the hotel in soundproof rooms he personally handpicked. The security in this area was tight, with an elite shadow staff servicing those meetings. The staff was made up of Chicago cops who were either on the take, on Capone's payroll, or both.

Petrillo set up the meeting with Maloy, Jack, and leadership from several of the other trades. Petrillo, Maloy, and Jack met in the lobby. Maloy was still fuming that Petrillo wanted Kaufman at the meeting. The three men walked downstairs to a meeting room which was designated for union representatives. It was directly underneath the lobby. Soundproof panels had been installed on the ceiling.

The leadership from several of the other trade unions were already seated around a large U-shaped table. The meeting lasted for eight hours and in that time, some progress was made. A general consensus had been reached. Now they had to see whether leadership could resolve those remaining issues. In the meantime, the men could not return to work.

The motion picture theater owners were running out of time and the men agreed to one final stab at negotiations. But there was one condition. They did not want Maloy to do their bidding. Instead, they wanted someone from the union that the men trusted, who would protect their interests. The men wanted Jack to be part of the remaining negotiations and represent the rank and file. Maloy was livid.

As the negotiations continued, Maloy and Jack tried to present a united front, but everyone knew that is was just a façade. Miraculously, however, on September 6, all the remaining issues were resolved. The strike was over. As Jack and Johnny started to pack up and go home, Petrillo pulled Jack aside. "Jack, do you have a few minutes to discuss one more thing?"

"Sure, Jimmy," Jack said cautiously. Then he added, "Can Johnny join us? He's family."

Jimmy nodded. "Let's wait until everyone is gone though. Do you want a drink?"

"I'll have Scotch," Jack responded. "Johnny?"

"Whatever Jimmy's having, but make mine a double."

Jack knew what Petrillo wanted to talk about. He wanted him to run against Maloy for business manager of the union. He thought it was important to have Johnny there as a witness to anything that would be said.

After all the other men left, Jack faced Jimmy and Johnny. "I want you two to know that I've made up my mind. I'm running against the son of a bitch at the next election."

The two men nodded, satisfied but anxious.

"You'll need a lot of protection, Jack," Johnny said.

Seeing their long faces, Jack laughed. "Don't worry. I probably won't win. And if I don't, then he won't kill me."

Jimmy shook his head. "You will win, Jack. And it's not only you we're concerned about. It's your wife and kids. They're going to need protection as well. You really need to think about this."

Jack shrugged. "There's nothing more to think about. I'll have a whole union of guys to protect me."

The following day, an article about the end of the strike appeared on the front page of the *Chicago Daily Tribune*.

"Strike Averted for Moviegoers"

Thomas Maloy, business agent for the projectionists, Jack Kaufman, union organizer, and George Browne, head of the stagehand's organization, delivered their ultimatums early this evening to Jack Miller, President of the Motion Picture Association. The apparent end of the tense situation came suddenly, after it was believed a strike would close all the motion picture houses for a very long time.

Jack didn't need to read the rest of the article. He put the newspaper down, poured himself another cup of coffee, and wondered what was going to happen next.

Chapter 34

Jack and Maloy
Chicago, 1928

The air was both calming and crisp without any humidity, a rarity for September 9th in Chicago. The breezes that rustled through the leaves brought life into the surrounding foliage. Fall was sneaking through the clouds.

Mary didn't notice the beautiful surroundings as she left to visit her mother and her Aunt Dora in Brighton Beach. She planned on staying in New York for at least three weeks. The visit would be good for her. She needed some time away from the stifling situation she found herself in.

Jack insisted on driving Mary to the train station, not as a loving gesture, but because he wanted to make sure she boarded the train. The drive was unbearable. Neither looked at each other or uttered a word. When Mary said goodbye, each knew what the other was thinking. How much longer could this sham continue?

Jack didn't have to work this Saturday and told the children he was taking them on an outing.

"Where are we going, Papa?" Francine asked.

"It's a surprise, princess."

"Give me a hint, Papa!"

Jack chuckled. "It has sawdust on the floor, sweet-smelling popcorn, and silly men with floppy shoes and big red noses."

Francine, who had never been to a circus, looked very confused.

"We're going to Grant Park," Jack added. That was the truth. The Ringling Brothers and Barnum & Bailey Circus had set up right in the middle of the park. Francine looked more confused than ever.

"No more questions, Francine. Let's finish our breakfast."

Just then, Lenore and Mike walked into the kitchen and Francine announced importantly, "Papa is taking us to see silly men with big red noses."

Lenore and Mike, who were in on the surprise, exchanged amused grins. Francine gushed with excitement and soon all three kids were giggling.

Jack watched them with a smile. It had been a long time since he had heard the sounds of happiness. The four of them were going to be spending the day together and Jack felt certain it was going to be a glorious day indeed.

He rinsed off the breakfast dishes, poured himself another cup of coffee, and sat down to read the morning paper. Suddenly, there came a loud knock on the front door.

"Who's there?" Jack called out.

"Police. Open up."

Suspicious, Jack went to the door. There were two men in police uniforms standing on his front porch, but no squad car parked out front. He thought about asking to see their identification, but decided to hear them out first.

"What do you want, officers?" he asked.

"You need to come with us, Mr. Kaufman," the taller of the two men said. "There was a situation at the Local 110 last night. A fire broke out."

"What time was the fire?" Jack demanded. "Was anyone hurt? Why wasn't I called?"

"Come with us, sir," the second policeman said. "All your questions will be answered in due time."

"First, I need to tell my son to watch his sisters." Jack stepped back from the door. He didn't have a good feeling about this. His gun was locked up in a cabinet in the basement but he didn't want to move away from the door. He couldn't do anything with the children in the house.

He yelled out to Mike. "Mike, I have to run a quick errand. Take your sisters to your grandmother. I'll be home soon."

As Jack and the two officers walked down the front steps, a black sedan pulled up alongside the curb. The back seat driver's door swung open and a man stepped out of the car. Jack recognized him. He was one of Maloy's henchman.

"What the . . ."

Before Jack could finish his sentence he was pushed inside the sedan. His hands were cuffed behind his back and tape was put over his mouth. The car door slammed shut. Jack was able to twist his head to the left and look back toward the house. He could see Mike staring out the front window. The sedan sped away.

A few minutes later, one of the officer's ripped off the tape.

"You son of a bitch," Jack hissed. "What do you want?"

The thugs didn't answer. Jack recognized the route the car was taking and knew where he was going. They were headed toward Maloy's office. Jack tried to calm his racing pulse. He tried not to think about what might be awaiting him. Instead, he concentrated his rage on who might have ratted on him. It had to be someone from the meeting at the Shoreland Hotel. As soon as he got out of this situation, he would find out. Oh yes, he would find out, and would get even with the dirty bastard. He cursed himself for falling into the trap. How could he have been such a sucker? Now he had to keep cool and stay calm.

When Mike saw his father being spirited away, he did not waste any time. He took his sisters downstairs to his grandmother's apartment, and then called his best friend Alvin. Alvin's father, Leon, was a judge. Jack and Leon were good friends and Mike hoped the judge would know what to do.

The phone rang eight times before Judge Adelman lifted the receiver. He heard Mike's voice but could not make out what the boy was trying to say. Mike was stuttering.

"Calm down, son, just tell me what's wrong. I'll help you."

"They took my father!" Mike gasped." Two cops took my father. They put him in a black sedan, handcuffed him, and put tape over his mouth." The panic in Mike's voice grew. "They took him. They took him! They took my dad!"

"Where are your sisters?" Leon asked, trying to keep his voice calm.

"With Grandma."

"Good." Leon took a breath. "Mike, your father is going to be fine. You know how strong your dad is. I promise you I'll find your dad and bring him home. I'm going to make a few calls now and then I'll come over to your house. In the meantime, you need to stay with your sisters. Will you do that for me?" Leon pleaded.

"Yes, I promise."

The first call Leon made was to one of his oldest friends, Leroy Gilbert. Leroy was the Chief of Police for South Chicago Heights for the last six months. He was a straight shooter and as honest as they came, which was rare during these times. Leroy would be able to find out whether the police were involved, and if so, why. Leon's hunch was that this was more likely a mob-related abduction. Leroy told Leon to call him back in an hour. He hoped by then to have more information.

Leon then got in his car and headed toward Spaulding Avenue to pick up Jack's three kids. He planned to bring them back to his house where he could protect them. He also wanted them to be with him if it turned out that something had happened to Jack. He had a sick feeling in his gut that he might never see his friend again.

After Leon got back home with the kids, he called Leroy. "Any news?"

Leroy sighed. "It's not the police, Leon." Both men knew what that meant. There was a long silence. "I don't think your friend is coming home," Leroy said finally.

The black sedan pulled into the underground garage of

Maloy's building. Everyone stepped out. The cuffs were taken off and Jack rubbed his wrists to get the circulation going again. He was feeling a little calmer. During the ride, he had time to calculate a plan. He thought he knew what this was all about. Tommy wanted to get some assurances that Jack would not run against him in the upcoming election. Jack was ready for this. On some level, he had been expecting this hour of reckoning for a long time.

The four men walked up the wooden steps which led to a metal door. The door opened and Jack walked in. Maloy was seated at his desk.

"Kaufman, glad you could make it. Sit down!"

Jack reluctantly sat down and everyone else left the room. Jack spoke first. He wanted to control the conversation.

"You son of a bitch. Are you proud of yourself for coming to my home and trying to terrorize my family? After all these years you really think this prank of yours is going to intimidate me? We both know what this is about, Tommy. You want me out of your way. But you also need me because without me, you would have a revolt inside the union and things would be uncovered. You can't risk that, can you Tommy?"

Maloy frowned. "Shut up, Jack. You're in my office now. Show a little respect. Do you want a drink?"

"No, Maloy, it might be laced with arsenic," Jack shot back.

Maloy scoffed. "If I wanted to kill you, Jack, you would have been dead a long time ago." He paused. "And you're correct, I brought you here because I want us to come to an understanding! If we do, your sweet little girls and your look-alike son will have their father at their next birthday."

Jack felt the blood rush to his head. He jumped out of the chair and suddenly found himself being grabbed from behind. One of Tommy's hit men had come through a concealed door in the wood paneling. The mirror on the wall must have been a two-way. Jack broke free, turned around, and kicked the man in his balls. The man fell hard onto the floor, knocked out cold. A full-on brawl erupted.

More men ran out of the secret entrance and jumped on Jack. Jack got a few solid punches in, but was grabbed from behind. A sharp piercing pain reverberated through his right kidney and Jack grimaced. He twisted his body, trying to pull his attackers down. Rancid sweat filled the air. The assailant leapt aside, then twirled back toward Jack, a metal truncheon gleaming dully as it connected with Jack's knee. Jack dropped to the floor, groaning with every blow.

Maloy fired a round of bullets, signaling to his men to stop the beating. Then he swaggered over to Jack and pointed a sawed-off shotgun at his head.

"Those were warning shots, Jack," Maloy said casually. "See how easy it would be to make your wife a widow and your children fatherless."

Shakily, Jack hoisted himself to his feet.

"What do you want, Tommy?" he asked flatly. "What the hell do you want?"

"I want your loyalty," Maloy demanded. There was dead silence.

When Jack got home, the house was empty. Frantic, he ran upstairs and passed right by the note Leon had left for him on the hall table. Then he rushed downstairs and found his mother and sister sitting in the living room, their faces an ashen grey. When he walked through the door, they leapt to embrace him.

"Jack! Jack! You're alive. Thank you, God! Thank you, for answering our prayers," Adela wailed.

"God had nothing to do with this," Jack said tersely. "Where are my children?"

"They're with Leon. They're fine. Leon left you a note. It should be in the foyer."

Jack raced over to grab the note. It read: "The kids are home with me. We'll wait for you to come and get them. See you soon. Leon"

Jack headed for the door. "I'm going to Leon's to get the kids." Adela put a restraining hand on his arm.

"Your shirt is ripped and you need to wash the blood off your face first. You don't want to scare the children," she told him.

Jack didn't respond. His mother was right. He washed up and changed his clothes. As he got dressed, he came to a decision. He would not jeopardize his family's safety. He would not run against Maloy, but Maloy would never get his loyalty.

Jack called Leon, who told him to come right over. When Jack arrived at Leon's house, the children were waiting. He hugged the three kids and reassured them that everything was fine.

Leon looked at him meaningfully and then said to his wife, "Abbey, can you stay with the kids while Jack and I go into the study for a little talk?"

"Of course."

Leon got right to the point. "Jack, you need an affidavit summarizing what happened today. I'll witness it and lock it in my safe. If something ever happens to you and Maloy is behind it, I want us to be able to nail that bastard." Leon looked into Jack's eyes and Jack knew his friend was right.

Jack told Leon all the details of his kidnapping. Leon wrote everything down in the affidavit.

"Jack, read it over, and if everything is accurate, sign it." said Leon.

Jack nodded. He took a deep breath and calmed the quiver in his hands as he began to read the document Leon had prepared.

I, Jacob (Jack) Kaufman, hereby declare:
I am of sound mind and sound body and am writing the following
affidavit under my own accord, free will, and without any influence
by any person. I was born on September 18, 1889, in Odessa, Rus-
sia. I immigrated to the United States of America in 1907. I married

Mary Leis, also from Odessa, Russia, on November 4, 1914. We have three minor children, Myron, Lenore, and Francine Kaufman. On September 22, 1927, I became a citizen of the United States. I am currently employed through the Motion Picture and Projectionists Local 110 union as a projectionist and union organizer.

On September 9, 1928, I was taken from my home by two police imposters under the pretext that there was a fire at union headquarters. I was shoved into a black sedan, handcuffed, blindfolded, and had tape placed over my mouth. I was taken to Tommy Maloy's office where I was threatened, intimidated, beaten, and warned not to challenge Maloy's re-election efforts as president and business manager of the Local 110.

I declare under penalty of perjury that the above statement is true and correct.

Signed: Jacob (Jack) Kaufman
Witnessed by: Judge Leon Adelman

When Jack finished reading, he said, his tone expressionless, "That's what happened!"

The abduction changed Jack. More and more he began to withdraw into himself. His shoulders drooped and his mouth tightened into a sullen frown. He found himself reflecting more on his past and less on his future. He thought more about his grandparents' enduring love and passion for each other. Then he thought about how he had been cheated out of that love through an arranged marriage. It was always the same for him. Everything he ever wanted—love, passion, even his own movie marquee, was held just beyond reach. Now he had this situation with Maloy. He was conflicted, but his decision was made. He would not run against Maloy in the next election. But he vowed, clenching his fists, that this was not over. It was not over by a long shot.

Six weeks had passed since Mary left for New York. She returned to Chicago two days before Mike's Bar Mitzvah at Temple Beth Shalom on Saturday. It was, she thought ironically, the same synagogue where Jack and Mary had gotten married.

The two of them watched proudly, united for a moment, as their thirteen-year-old son stood at the pulpit wearing a navy blue suit, his white, starched shirt adorned with a gray, striped tie. His brimless white, cloth cap with the Star of David was on his head.

Mike's voice was confident and clear. "Before I begin, I want to thank all of you for coming today and participating in my Bar Mitzvah. My Torah reading is about peace," he began. "Each generation is challenged to pursue peace. Some meet that challenge better than others. If peace eludes us, we must ask if it is because of circumstances beyond our control, or because our attitudes interfere with its realization. We work for peace when we believe it is an ideal. We gain strength with peace by joining with others. To those who claim that peace is not possible, I say, people who believe in nothing, change nothing for the better. We must risk believing in peace and work for the future. My hope for all of us is to find peace in our lives."

Jack found himself profoundly moved by his son's words.

The rabbi and the congregation read from their prayer books. Jack was called up to the pulpit to read a passage from the Torah as were Mike's uncles, Sam and Carl. Leon was also given the honor to recite a prayer. When the service was over, everyone clapped and yelled, *"Mazel tov!* Congratulations!"

The family hosted a scrumptious lunch in the adjacent banquet room featuring corned beef, egg salad, chopped liver, and an assortment of vegetables. For dessert, there were platters of fruit, cookies, and cakes. Wine was poured freely, and everyone had a wonderful time.

After the guests left, Jack asked Leon to take a picture of him and the children. Francine and Lenore wanted Mary in the picture too, and Jack reluctantly agreed. Through the lens of the camera, Leon could see the picture clearly. He saw pride in Jack's eyes when he looked at Mike. He saw love in his friend's eyes when he looked at Francine and Lenore. But he saw a blank stare when Jack looked at Mary. Mary shared the same stare.

Leon knew that look. He had seen it in his courtroom countless times when he ruled that a marriage was now dissolved. Leon was worried about Jack's family. He was worried about his best friend and he saw hard times ahead. He knew Jack was strong enough to weather the storm, and hoped Mike, Lee and Fran would get through this transition unscathed.

After the Bar Mitzvah, tensions in the union seemed to increase by the week. The hostility and hatred between Jack and Maloy was combustible. Jack would stay on the straight and narrow for now, but there was no way he would stay in the shadows for long. He would make his move when opportunity knocked. Jack promised himself the bastard would not get away with anything more. He hoped Maloy's days were numbered.

On a stormy winter day in November, as Jack was walking out the front door, he noticed a festive-looking envelope on the table in the front foyer. It was addressed to him. He picked it up, thinking it might be an early holiday card. Then he recognized the archaic script. What did Maloy want this time?

> *Thomas Edward Maloy and his wife Effie Preston Maloy*
> *cordially request your presence*
> *Sunday, December 16th, at 7:00 p.m.*
> *at the Maloy residence, 6806 South Chappel Avenue.*
> *Black tie and formal attire requested*

Fury rose into Jack's throat at the sheer chutzpah of the gesture. As he turned to toss it away, he noticed another envelope that must have fallen onto the floor. It was also addressed to him. As he picked it up, his heart began to race. He knew the handwriting all too well. It was from Theresa.

"Dear Jack, I'm coming home. I miss you. I need to see you. Sending Love."

For the next two weeks, he tried not to be too hopeful or full of any expectations. But as each day passed, Jack became more and more anxious. Finally, Jack received the note he had been waiting for.

"I will be in Chicago the first week in December. I promise I will never leave you again. Love T."

When Theresa got off the train, she went straight to the Piccadilly, hoping Jack would be there. Jack was up in the editing room and saw her silhouette. He was breathless. His heart pounded. He and Theresa looked into each other's eyes and picked up right where they left off. The following week, with Theresa hooked onto Jack's arm, the couple walked into Maloy's home for the holiday party.

Chapter 35

Jack
Chicago, 1929

Jack opened the front door and yelled out his usual greeting, "Papa's home!" Francine was usually the first one to great him but today it was Mary.

"Jack," she said coldly. "Two men were here today and wanted to talk to you. They said it was important. They left this card and asked you to contact them immediately." She frowned. "What is this about, Jack? Is this about one of your gangster friends?"

Jack sighed. "Mary, I don't know what it's about. And don't use that tone. I'm doing my best to take care of you, my mother, and my children, but obviously nothing is good enough for you!"

Jack grabbed the card, turned around and walked back outside. The card read:

U. S. Department of Justice
Federal Bureau of Investigation
Field Office Chicago Division
2111 W. Roosevelt Road
Chicago, Illinois
Special Agent Rivas White

Jack stared at it for a minute. He had never heard of Rivas White. He read the card again. It looked official with the embossed FBI logo, but after his experience with Maloy, he wasn't convinced. It could still be a setup.

He didn't want to go back in the house. Mary would just

pepper him about the card. He also didn't want to wait for Mr. White to come back, so he decided he would go to him. That was the only way he could be sure Agent White was really who he said he was.

But first he needed to talk to Leon. He was well connected with the Feds. Jack went back into the house and called Leon.

"Leon. I need to run something by you. It might be important. When would be a good time for us to talk?"

"Right now is good. Come on over."

"See you within the hour."

Before Jack left, he went into his son's room. Mike was on his bed sorting through his collection of baseball cards.

"Mike, I need to go to Leon's house. Tell your mother I might not be coming home tonight."

"Okay, Dad." Mike was used to his father not coming home.

The next morning, Leon pulled up in front of the Federal Building and found a mob of people gathered around the corner newsstand. He parked the car and the two of them went over to see what all the commotion was about. Jack glanced over the heads of the crowd and saw the headline in the Chicago Tribune. It was in bold print:

"February 14, 1929: "St. Valentine's Day Massacre"

Jack picked up the newspaper and he and Leon began reading.

"On this frigid morning, in an unheated brick garage at 2122 N. Clark St., seven men were lined up against a whitewashed wall and pumped with 90 bullets from submachine guns, shotguns, and a revolver. It was the most infamous of all gangland slayings in America, and it savagely achieved its purpose — the elimination of the last challenge to Al Capone for the mantle of crime boss in Chicago.

By 1929, Capone's only real threat was George "Bugs" Moran who headed his own gang and what was left of Dion O'Banion's band of bootleggers. Moran had long despised Capone, mockingly referring to him as, "The Beast." At about 10:30 a.m., four men burst into the SMC Cartage Company garage that Moran used for his illegal business. Two of the men were dressed as police officers. The quartet presumably announced a raid and ordered the seven men inside the garage to line up against the wall. Then they opened fire. Witnesses, alerted by the rat-a-tat staccato of submachine guns watched as the gunmen sped off in a black Cadillac touring car that looked like the kind police used, complete with siren and rifle rack.
    The victims killed outright or left dying in the garage included Frank "Hock" Gusenberg, Moran's enforcer, and his brother Peter "Goosey" Gusenberg. Four of the victims were Moran's gangsters. The seventh dead man was Dr. Reinhardt Schwimmer, an optician who cavorted with criminals for thrills. Missing that morning was Capone's prize: Moran, who slept in."

Jack and Leon looked at each other. "Shit. Leon, maybe we shouldn't go upstairs," Jack stated.

Leon shook his head. "This is exactly why we should, Jack. Trust me. We have to get this bastard before he gets you. You have no other choice."

They walked into the Federal Building. Leon flashed his State Bar Card and told the guard they were there to see Rivas White. He showed White's card, and a few minutes later they were issued a pass and escorted up to Rivas's office.

Four hours later, Jack and Leon walked out. Jack had never before considered collaborating with the Feds, knowing it could be suicide. But Rivas had proven to be a sensible man, sensitive to the nuances of Jack's situation. He revealed that the FBI already had an investigation into Capone and was planning to investigate Maloy. Leon thought this was positive news but Jack wasn't convinced.

Leon noticed the vacant look in Jack's eyes.

"Jack, we've got to talk about this."

"There is nothing to talk about Leon," Jack said abruptly. "I changed my mind. I can't do it. I don't trust the Feds. Even they can't nail Capone."

Leon sighed. "Let's not talk about this now, Jack. We just need to step back and break it all down. Let's go back to my house, have a drink, and explore your options."

Over the next several months, the Federal investigation merged with the State Attorney General's office, with the Attorney General now taking the lead. Two Assistant State Attorneys, Charles E. Lounsbury and Charles Bellows, were in charge of the investigation.

Leon became the intermediary contact between the Attorney General's office and Jack. Jack had finally agreed to a meeting with Bellows. They were going to arrange a meeting in an apartment, the Attorney General's office he used in Hyde Park. The details were being worked out.

Before Jack knew it, the children's summer break was almost over and the kids had to go back to school. Because of the suffocating summer heat, Jack decided that they would take one more drive out to the lake in his brand new 1929 Ford Model A.

"Hey girls, what do you say we go to the lake this afternoon to cool off? Lenore, can you help Francine get ready? And maybe make us some sandwiches?"

"Of course, Papa," Lenore beamed.

"Francine, let's you and me get some towels and our picnic blanket." Both girls giggled with anticipation. They loved going to the lake with their father.

"What about Mike?" Francine asked.

"He has to work today. We'll pick him up on our way home, so stop asking questions and get a move on." Fifteen minutes later, everyone was ready to go.

"Papa, can we listen to the radio on the drive?" asked Francine.

"Of course, my little princess." Then, as if he had just thought of it, he added, "How about we ask Theresa to join us?" Jack knew the girls would agree. They liked Theresa. She was fun and always baked special treats.

"Do you think Theresa will braid my hair?" asked Francine. Jack smiled. "I'm sure she will."

It was a typical humid Chicago summer day. The temperature had risen into the low nineties and the heat was atrocious, sticky, and wet. Jack was hoping that when they got closer to the lake they'd find a little breeze.

Theresa was waiting in the entryway with a small picnic basket in her hand. She was wearing a yellow sundress and a large-brimmed straw hat.

"You look gorgeous, Theresa," said Jack. "Today is going to be a great day." They embraced and the foursome headed out to the lake.

The windows in the car were down and the radio was blasting. Lenore, Francine, and Theresa sang along with the lyrics. Before they knew it, they could feel the breeze wafting across the lake. They had arrived. Jack found his favorite parking space near a patch of grass. They grabbed the towels, picnic blanket, and food. Theresa had a thermos of lemonade and had baked the girls their favorite chocolate chip cookies. After lunch, Jack turned to his daughters.

"Girls, why don't you play hide-and-seek while Theresa and I take a little walk? Then we can all go swimming."

Once they were away from the girls, Theresa said, "I can tell you've got something on your mind, Jack. Is it Maloy?"

"Yes. But I can't talk about it right now. All I can tell you is that I'm hopeful Maloy won't be around much longer."

"Jack!" Theresa's voice was quivering. Jack put his fingers over her lips.

"Everything will be alright. I promise. The Feds are going to nail his ass." With Jack's response, Theresa knew that her worst fears were coming true. Jack was now officially part of the investigation.

"Please be careful," she whispered. "I don't know what I would do if I lost you." Jack pulled Theresa close to him. They kissed with a desperate sense of urgency and walked back to the girls without saying another word.

"Let's go swimming," hollered Jack. He and his daughters ran to the shoreline and jumped into the lake.

Theresa sat down under the tree, fighting tears. What had she done? What had she done? And what would Jack do if he ever found out that she had been Tommy's mole this entire time?

The girls had a wonderful time at the lake. It was a day they would always remember. They liked Theresa, not only because she was a lot of fun, but also because their Papa was so happy when he was with her. This was a good day. It was a great day. Reluctantly, as the sun began to set, they all got back into Jack's Model A and headed for home.

"After we drop Theresa off, let's surprise Mike and swing by the A&P," Jack said.

"Papa, can we have a chocolate egg cream soda at the lunch counter?" Francine asked hopefully.

Jack laughed. "As long as you don't tell your mother."

The drive home was wonderful. Lenore and Francine sang along with all the songs on the car radio. When "Happy Days are Here Again" blasted through the dashboard, Jack and his girls sang as loud as they could. Even Theresa joined in.

They dropped Theresa off at her apartment and drove to the A&P where Mike, now fourteen, had been working as a checker all summer. He was saving his money for a car, even though he was pretty sure his father was going to buy him one when he went to college. Mike was already planning to follow in his father's footsteps and enroll at Northwestern.

While Jack parked the car, the girls ran into the A&P with big hugs for their embarrassed brother. Jack joined them and they all sat down to enjoy their chocolate egg creams while Mike finished his shift.

Driving home, Jack could not stop thinking about Theresa. Her scent was still in the seat beside him. He closed his eyes and imagined his future with her. When they got to the house, the kids ran inside, but Jack lingered in the car for a few minutes. Then he sighed and went into the house. As he walked up to the front door, he smelled the scrumptious aroma oozing under the threshold. The familiar smells of the Shabbat dinner whiffed through the air.

Seven weeks later, on Thursday, October 24, the financial world exploded. Significantly and ominously, five days later, the stock market plummeted, losing thirty billion dollars in just one week. It was the worst economic crash in history.

The morning of October 29, Jack went out to his front porch, picked up the newspaper and stared at the headline.

"Greatest Crash in Wall Street History
Billions Lost as Stocks Crash"

With the crash, the Roaring Twenties came to a screeching halt. Job security was no longer part of anyone's dialogue. Now everyone's reality was faced with uncertainty for their future and the future of their children. Massive unemployment, food lines, and soup kitchens provided a means for survival. No one knew what this all meant or how long it would take for everyone to recover.

Jack was one of the few lucky ones. He had never been a gambler, and when it came to money, he was both frugal and cautious. For years, he hadn't even trusted his money to sit in the bank. Instead, most of his money was still in a metal box in the basement under the floorboards. No one knew it was there—no one except him.

Chapter 36

Jack and Mary
Chicago, 1930

Times were tough. Businesses closed and thousands of people lost their jobs following the crash. No one had extra money to go to the movies, so the theaters didn't need as many projectionists. Jack still worked, but his hours had been cut back. For the first time in years, he worried about his family's financial future.

Several men Jack knew from the trades needed to move out of their homes because they couldn't afford to keep them anymore. Some families moved out of the area and out of the state to live with relatives. A recurring story about desperate people jumping off buildings to their death appeared in the *Chicago Tribune*. Those poor souls had lost all their money in the crash and just couldn't bear the thought of having to start over.

The crisis had severe repercussions for Jack and Mary's marriage. They no longer talked to each other. Instead, they yelled, screamed, and shouted terrible insults. It was terrifying for Francine, Lenore, and Mike to witness their parents throwing things at each other and to see the trash filled with broken glass or shattered dishes.

Jack never came home for dinner anymore, but he did try and make an appearance in the evening before the girls went to bed, spending time reading to Francine and doing crossword puzzles with Lenore.

Mary spent a lot of time in bed. She was having increasing pain in her stomach and experiencing intense daily headaches. She thought about going to New York again to visit with her mother and her aunt as she knew they would help her regain her strength. She floated the idea to Adela, and asked Adela if she would talk to Jack.

When Jack came home that night, Adela was waiting for him at the door.

"I need to talk to you in private. Let's go."

Later that night, Jack walked into the bedroom. Mary was in her chair knitting a sweater, and Jack sat down on the ottoman.

"My mother said you spoke to her," he began without a pre-amble. "She told me that you were thinking about going to New York to visit your mother. I think that's a very good idea."

Mary nodded, grateful that Jack had no objection. She was afraid to speak, knowing it would only turn into an ugly brawl.

"I'll get you a train ticket and you can leave on Tuesday," Jack went on. "I think the trip will be good for your nerves." Then he hesitated for a moment. "I think that when you're in New York, you should see a doctor, one who specializes in your condition."

Mary heard the condescension in his voice and shook with rage. Her nerves! Her condition! Mary could feel the blood rush-ing to her head, but she made herself respond calmly.

"Jack, it is not my nerves that are the problem. It is . . ." she stopped herself before saying, 'It's you. It's all you!' Instead, she replied, "It is my stomach."

"Then see a doctor for that," Jack replied stiffly and stalked out of the room.

A few minutes later, Mary heard the car engine roar away. She mumbled under her breath, "Does he really think I don't know he is going to be with his whore?"

Mary sat on the bed, trying to stay calm. She couldn't remem-ber when she had felt this helpless or unsure. Was going to New York really the best idea? Yes, the trips always did her good, but at what cost? She thought of her children. She knew Jack was constantly trying to turn them against her. Always taking the kids out for outings and giving them treats behind her back.

Making stinging little comments that made her look old-fash-ioned or stupid. If she left, he would have them all to himself. Who knew what he might say about her then? Who knew what ways he would find to lower their esteem for her in everybody's eyes?

Mary believed that Jack wanted all three of their children to turn against her. The thought of losing the love of her children struck Mary as an unbearable blow. She was afraid it had al-ready happened with Mike. Mike had been his father's boy from the beginning, but she was damned if she was going to lose her girls as well. Abruptly, she stood up and went into her daugh-ter's room.

The girls were in bed and looked surprised as Mary came in. She smiled uncertainly at them and sat down on the edge of Lenore's bed.

Come here Francine, and sit on my lap. Lenore, come sit next to me. You both know how much I love you, don't you?"

"Of course, Mama," both girls said in unison.

Mary continued, "I need to go to New York to see a doctor for my stomach. He is going to make me all better so I can come home and take care of you. I'm going to be fine, I promise. While I am gone, I want you to . . ."

She trailed off. What could she say? I want you to still love me? I want you to ignore anything bad your father might say about me? I want you to have faith in me?

Mary could say none of this. She finally settled on, "I want you to promise me you will be good girls. Will you do that?"

Lenore answered for both of them. "Of course, Mama."

Mary hugged both of them and went back to her room. She closed the door and cried into her pillow until she fell into an exhausted sleep.

On Tuesday, April 15, Mary boarded the train to New York. It was a tearful goodbye, painful for both Mary and her girls. During the weeks and months that followed, Jack made sure the children were kept busy with school and outings. He moved back into the bedroom and spent much more time at home. But as far as his marriage was concerned, he knew what he needed to do.

At the end of May, Jack went into the city to meet with the lawyer Leon had recommended. Five weeks later, Jack's lawyer filed a "Bill for Divorce" in the Circuit Court of Cook County that stated:

> *Mary Kaufman, wholly disregarding her marriage vows and obligations toward your orator, engaged in repeated cruelty toward your orator in that she is a woman of great austerity of temper, and very frequently, during the past five years, indulged in violent sallies of passion, and used toward your orator very abusive language without any provocation whatever, and frequently refused to prepare your orator's meals and perform such other household duties as it was incumbent upon her to perform; and on numerous occasions, during the time mentioned, has used personal violence toward your orator which he did not feel disposed to resent or even defend himself against on account of her sex; and particularly your orator charges that on or about December 16, 1929, the said Mary Kaufman, without any provocation whatever, threw sticks and chairs and other things of a similar nature at your orator; and again, on or about April 14, 1930, the said Mary Kaufman again attacked your orator in their house and severely bruised him, including personal violence upon the body of your orator. On April 15, 1930, said Mary Kaufman willfully deserted and abandoned herself from your orator and said children.*

That evening, Jack sat the kids down at the dining room table. "I have something to tell you. Your mother has decided to stay in New York."

There was a long silence. "When will she come home?" Lenore finally asked her father in a small voice.

"I don't know," Jack replied.

Lenore could feel her blood rushing to her head. Numb and disconnected, she went into her bedroom and buried herself in her books.

Francine remained quiet as she bent her head down. She stared at the floor, motionless, holding back her tears.

Mike was furious. "I will never forgive her for doing this. I'll never speak to her again!"

Francine began to cry. Jack picked her up into his arms. "Everything is going to be fine, my little princess. I promise."

The weeks went by. Francine, confused and frightened, seemed to miss Mary more and more. She wrote notes to her mother, constantly asking her when she was coming home. What the girls did not know was that as soon as Mary became aware of the divorce proceedings, she had in fact returned to Chicago. She'd hired her own attorney and was fighting Jack for custody of her children.

Mary's attorney filed her answer to Jack's claims. Her response included the following statement:

During the month of April 1930, while this defendant was ill, the said complainant and his mother requested that she visit her mother in New York, which might be beneficial to her health. And that while she was visiting her mother, said complainant filed his bill for divorce and falsely made an affidavit that this defendant was residing out of the state and could not be found. And falsely with intent to deceive the court made an affidavit as to her last known place of residence, while at the time he knew where she was visiting, and had the exact address of this defendant, and endeavored to impose upon the court and deprive this defendant of her rights in the premises, and obtain a divorce upon service by publication.

This defendant further states that upon the day that the said bill of complaint was filed in this cause, this defendant was in the city of Chicago, and the complainant knew of her presence here, as this defendant was at their home and the complainant, to wit, on the 21st day of June, 1930, forced this defendant from their home and refused to permit her to see and visit with her children. That said time this defendant was in need of medical attention, suffering from a tumor and her condition remains the same. At present, she is required to undergo an operation and is without funds to do so.

The divorce battle raged on. One court hearing after another was either taken off the calendar or continued to another date. Days merged into weeks and weeks merged into months without Mary seeing her children. On August 17, Francine turned eight years old, Lenore turned eleven on September 11, and Mike celebrated his fifteenth birthday on October 12. The holidays came and went and there was still no resolution.

These were difficult times for all families, businesses and unions. The Local 110 was in disarray, with the men fighting for any work they could get. The pecking order for job assignments was becoming a dog fight. No one was spared.

Jack saw what was happening and wanted Maloy to reduce or suspend the dues for the men who couldn't afford to stay in the union. Instead, Malloy's solution was to increase the dues so there would be fewer workers for fewer jobs. As a result, the men who needed the work the most also became casualties of the times.

Tragically, a couple of Jack's men who could not bear the situation any longer, shot themselves in the head. It was common for a priest or rabbi to lead the men in prayer for one of their fallen brothers, and Jack made condolence calls on a regular basis. Death and despair abounded.

Homes and businesses were boarded up, and there were long lines all over Chicago where people would wait all day to get a bowl of soup and a loaf of bread. Everyone was saying this was only temporary and things would get better, but things just seemed to get worse.

With 1931 looming just beyond the horizon, Jack made three major decisions which would change his life and the life of his family forever. He would run for president of the Local 110, he would continue cooperating with the State Attorney General's office regarding their investigation of Tommy Maloy, and he would ask Theresa to be his wife.

Chapter 37

Jack and Mary
Chicago, 1931

On January 23, 1931, the judge ruled that Mary must be allowed to be with her children. Eight months and nineteen days after her nightmare began, Mary was finally granted custody of all three kids. However, the battle didn't stop there; it only intensified.

Jack disobeyed the judge's order and he also refused to appear in court. Mary requested assistance and the judge ordered the Bureau of Public Welfare to help Mary obtain custody of Francine and Lenore.

Several weeks later, after reviewing the recommendations from the Bureau of Public Welfare, Judge Daniel P. Trude announced his ruling in open court. Both Mary and Jack stood at opposing tables alongside their attorneys. Mike was sitting in the gallery behind his father. The girls were not present. Before announcing his ruling, Judge Trude asked Mike to approach the bench.

"Young man, I have been told by your father's attorney that you would like to address the court. Is that true?"

"Yes, Your Honor," Mike mumbled.

The judge looked at Mike keenly.

"Mike, would you come into my chambers so we can talk privately? Your father and your mother have both agreed that I can talk to you."

Mike looked at his father, who nodded.

The clerk called for a recess and the bailiff escorted Mike into the judge's chambers. Thirty minutes later, Mike walked back into the courtroom and took his seat. He did not look at either of his parents.

"All rise," said the bailiff.

Judge Trude took the bench and began to speak. "This is a very sad case and my ruling in this matter has been one of the more difficult decisions of my career. Mr. Kaufman, I know you must love your children, but it appears to me that your hatred for their mother is greater than your love for the three of them. I have been on the bench for twenty-five years, and whenever I have to make these types of decisions, it breaks my heart. But I am doing what I believe is in the best interest for your children."

"As for the two minor girls, Lenore, age eleven, and Francine, age eight, I hereby order they be placed in the care, custody, and control of the Ruth Club, located at 5356 Drexel Avenue, Chicago, Illinois, during the pendency of these proceedings, or until a further order of this court."

"As for your son, Myron Kaufman, who is fifteen, I have put much weight into his wishes. Myron wants to live with you. It is so ordered that Jacob (Jack) Kaufman have care and custody of Myron Kaufman until further order of this court. I further order that Myron Kaufman visit with his mother, Mary Kaufman, on Sunday afternoons of every week."

"Jacob Kaufman is hereby ordered to pay the cost thereto. It is also ordered that all relatives and friends of the parties are hereby restrained and enjoined from visiting Lenore and Francine. That only Jacob Kaufman, Mary Kaufman, and Myron Kaufman shall have the right to visit the children, and the parties are restrained and enjoined from taking the children for visits to any of their relatives until further order of this court."

"It is hereby ordered that the Department of Welfare remove the minor children, Lenore and Francine. The minor children shall remain in the custody of the Department of Welfare until said time that the minors can be taken to the Ruth Club. Mrs. Gross will be coordinating those arrangements."

"It is further ordered that Jack Kaufman be restrained and

enjoined from meeting, visiting, or accompanying one Theresa King, at, to, or from, any place or places at any time until further order of this court."

"It is further ordered that Jack Kaufman pay Mary Kaufman the sum of seventy-three dollars for past orders. From this point forward an amount of twelve dollars, on the first day of each and every week, shall be paid for alimony, support, and maintenance, effective on February 11, 1931. These payments will continue until further order of this court."

Jack didn't move. He could hardly breathe. His face was turning red and his eyes welled up with tears. Mary seemed to have difficulty comprehending the magnitude of the decision. For the first time, maybe ever, Jack and Mary were thinking the same thing: What have we done?

Then the judge added, "Mr. Kaufman, I want to make clear the procedure that you will follow. Two police officers will escort you and your attorney to your home. Mrs. Gross, a social worker from the Department of Welfare, will meet you there. You will be permitted to go into your house and explain to your daughters that they will be going with Mrs. Gross, who will make sure that they get settled into the Ruth Club. You will also explain to your daughters that the Ruth Club is a special school where they will be with other girls and that they will be able to stay together and share a room. You are to assure them that you, their mother, and their brother Myron, will be able to visit them. If you, the children's grandmother, or their aunt does anything to obstruct the order of this court, you will be taken into custody and I will immediately revoke any and all visitation privileges. Do you understand everything I am saying, Mr. Kaufman?"

Jack's attorney didn't wait for Jack to respond. "Yes, Your Honor. Mr. Kaufman understands the court's order."

"I want to hear from your client," the judge responded.

"Yes. I understand," Jack replied in a broken whisper.

"Mrs. Kaufman, I have instructed Mrs. Gross to allow you to

visit your daughters as soon as she determines that the girls have settled into their new environment. Hopefully, that will be within the week. The remaining issues brought before this court will be addressed by me in due time."

"Mrs. Kaufman, do you understand the terms of my order?" Her attorney nodded to Mary, and she replied, "Yes."

Jack then walked out of the courtroom, his face ashen.

"How could this have happened? How could this have happened?" Jack mumbled over and over again.

Jack and Mike got into the car. Neither one said a word. Finally, Mike spoke.

"Dad, isn't there something we can do? We can't let them just take Francine and Lenore."

Jack did not reply. He parked the car and walked up the stairs. Mrs. Gross was already waiting on the front porch. All three of them walked inside. The girls were with their grandmother, waiting in the living room.

Francine ran up to her father and jumped into his arms. A tear trickled down Jack's face. He didn't want to let go.

"Who's that?" Francine asked, nodding suspiciously at Mrs. Gross.

"This is Mrs. Gross. She is a very nice lady and is here to help us." Lenore's eyes grew wide with suspicion. "Let's sit in the living room," Jack said quickly. "I have something very important I need to talk to you about."

Francine curled up next to her father. Lenore sat next to Mike. Jack tried to calm his nerves before speaking.

"You know how much I love all of you."

"We love you too, Papa." Francine said eagerly.

"And you know I will always be there for you. But for right now we have to make some changes." Lenore closed her eyes. She knew bad news was coming.

With a crackle in his voice, Jack continued speaking. "Sometimes when Mama and Daddy live in different houses, a judge needs to decide where the children will live. Today, the judge decided that for a very short time, you and your sister are going to live at the Ruth Club. It's a beautiful house. You will have your own room. There are other girls there your age that will be your friends. And I promise I will visit you every day until I can bring you home."

"Is Mike going to be with us?" Lenore asked.

Jack tried to smile. "No, this special house is just for girls. Now, let's go up to your room and pack some clothes."

Lenore did not say a word. She could hardly breathe. She wouldn't look at her father. She knew her family was breaking apart. She understood what divorce meant. She angrily marched up to the bedroom she shared with her sister, pulled out her overnight bag, and began throwing her clothes into the suitcase.

Jack held Francine's hand and helped her pick out clothes and some of her favorite stuffed animals. Mrs. Gross offered to help, but Jack didn't want her anywhere near his girls. She stayed in the living room.

When it came time for the girls to leave, there was an awful scene. Jack couldn't stand it. He ran from their room as tears poured down his face, his whole body shaking with sobs.

Things didn't go as planned. The room at the Ruth Club, which was supposed to be held for the girls, wasn't available. The only other option was for the girls to be taken to Juvenile Hall until a room opened up.

Lenore was numb and Francine was crying as they were processed into the system. Lenore was fingerprinted first. A black stain remained on her thumb. Francine went next. She thought this was some kind of game and said, "Look, my finger is just like yours." Lenore did not say a word. She knew this was not a game.

Lenore and Francine were placed into a holding cell ten feet long by ten feet wide. In the cell, there were two small iron cots, a stainless steel toilet, and a small sink. A small window over the sink was notched into the cinder block walls. At night, the rolling floor-to-ceiling-gate was locked.

Lenore took care of her little sister. She told her stories to distract her. She wiped Francine's tears and cleaned up the vomit after she threw up. It was seventy-two hours of pure hell before Mrs. Gross came back. She took the girls out of Juvenile Hall and drove them to the Ruth Club. Those three days would haunt the two sisters for the rest of their lives.

When Mrs. Gross pulled up in front of the large three-story house, she told Lenore and Francine that this is where they would be living until they could go home. Neither one of them said anything. Their faces were blank. Their bodies were still. Their heartbeats were racing.

A woman with golden, blonde hair, green eyes, and a sparkling smile, greeted the girls as they walked through the front door.

"My name is Sarah. Which one of you is Lenore?" she asked.

Lenore raised her hand, ever the dutiful student. "Please call me Lee."

"That must mean you are Francine." Copying her sister's response, Francine said, "Please call me Fran."

"I'm going to be here with you until you can go back home." She smiled and then said, "I bet you're hungry!" Both girls shook their heads, indicating they did not want to eat. "Then let's go look at your room. Follow me."

Mrs. Gross said goodbye and Fran and Lee followed Sarah up the stairs.

"Here it is. Let's take a look," said Sarah brightly.

The room was cheerful in colors of yellow, pale blue, and mint green. There was a handmade satin quilt on the double bed and soft and fluffy pillows leaned against the carved headboard. A white wood dresser would hold their clothes. The girls' suitcases stood at the foot of the bed. Jack had delivered them earlier in the day.

"How long do we have to stay here?" Fran asked bluntly.

"I don't know. It's up to the judge. But it should not be very long," came Sarah's subdued response.

But one week turned into two, then three and then four. Four weeks turned into eight weeks. And before they knew it, the girls had been at the Ruth Club for three months with no end in sight. The divorce proceedings were still being litigated.

Finally, on May 14, the case was put back on the court's trial calendar.

Jack was hoping he would be able to bring his girls home before the Fourth of July. He rented a room close to the Ruth Club so he could see the girls as much as possible during the week. Mary, now working as a seamstress in downtown Chicago, tried to visit her daughters on the weekends.

At first the girls, feeling abandoned and betrayed by their mother, did not want to see Mary. The counselors at the Ruth Club helped the girls understand how much their mother loved them. They explained that their mother was doing everything she could to bring them home. In time, the brief visits evolved into pleasurable picnic lunches at Coleman Park, right down the street.

Eventually, Jack got permission to take the girls on outings. Sometimes they went to the movies. Other times they would take a drive down to the lake. If Mike wasn't working, he would join them, and those were the times everyone cherished the most.

It was Monday, June 15. Jack had been planning to take his daughters out to dinner for their usual Monday night pizza and ice cream, but something came up. Jack had been offered work at the Lincoln Theater at 3132 South State Street. He called the Ruth Club and asked Sarah to tell the girls that he had to work, but would stop by the following day.

When Jack arrived at the theater, he ran into Crawford Johnson. Johnson was one of the black operators, and he and Johnson always had gotten along. Jack seemed glad to see him.

"Mr. Kaufman, rumor has it you just got your new automobile. You know I sell car radios. I can make you a good deal," Johnson told him.

"I don't know, Johnson, I don't think I have time right now. I'll have to think about it," Jack replied.

"How about I meet up with you on Wednesday at the union office? I have to pay my dues anyway. Then I can take you over to my nephew's garage," Johnson persisted.

"Where is the garage?" asked Jack.

"It's very close, right on Princeton. My nephew David Greer owns it. He can install the radio whenever you have the time. I can get you a good deal," Johnson said with an assuring grin.

"I know that garage. It's behind the white house, right?"

"Yes," replied Johnson.

"I can meet you at the Local around one o'clock," Jack replied.

"That sounds good, Mr. Kaufman. I will see you on Wednesday."

On Tuesday, as promised, Jack went to the Ruth Club and took his girls out for spaghetti and meatballs at a nearby Italian restaurant. Usually on Tuesday nights they had someone at the piano playing songs. Tonight there was a woman singing show tunes. Most of the patrons joined in and sang the familiar lyrics. Jack and the girls had a great time belting out their favorite tunes.

When Jack dropped Lee and Fran at the Ruth Club, he told them he had to work the next two days and he might not be able to stop by until Friday.

Tears trickled from Fran's eyes. Lee gripped her sister's hand tighter. "Dad, when can we go home?" she whispered.

Jack bit his lip. "Very soon, very soon. I promise, and you know I always keep my promises."

He put his arms around them and held them tightly.

"You are the best little girls in the whole wide world. You're my little princesses. And we will all be together again, very soon."

On Wednesday, Jack went to the union office and picked up his work schedule. He was surprised to see that once again, he was assigned to work at the Piccadilly Theater. Maloy's hoods usually got that venue, but Jack wasn't complaining. The pay was good and he loved working the Piccadilly.

He met up with Crawford as planned, and the two men went to the Princeton Garage where David Greer, a former operator, was waiting. Greer said he would install the radio Saturday night after Jack got off work. They agreed on a price and the men shook hands.

On Friday, June 19, Jack pulled up to the Ruth Club in his brand new Ford. He walked up the front steps and knocked on the door.

Sarah greeted Jack with a smile.

"Hello, Mr. Kaufman. I hear there is a special outing planned for Fran and Lee today. They are both very excited."

"Not as excited as I am," Jack told her. "First, we're going to the lake, and then we're having dinner at a Chinese restaurant. I also promised the girls chocolate ice cream on the way home. I'll bring them back by seven-thirty"

"The girls are upstairs. I'll get them and make sure they have what they need. Please wait for them in the sitting room," replied Sarah.

Five minutes later, Fran and Lee ran down the stairs. When Fran saw her father, she jumped into his arms. Jack took Lee's hand and the three of them went to the car parked alongside the curb.

Lee gasped, "Is that your new car?"

"It sure is," Jack told her proudly. "Pile in girls, we are going for a ride."

"Can we turn on the radio really loud so we can sing,"

asked Fran.

Jack shook his head. "Today, we're going to sing without the radio. It's being installed tomorrow." He began singing, "Happy Days Are Here Again," and his daughters chimed in.

Six glorious hours later, Jack brought two very happy but tired little girls back to the Ruth Club. Breaking all the rules, Sarah let Jack take his daughters up to their room and tuck them in for the night.

After leaving the Ruth Club, Jack went to the A&P.

Mike was finishing up behind the counter, and when he saw his dad, he broke into a grin.

"Ready to go?" Jack asked.

"You bet. I'm starving."

They went to the Jewish delicatessen down the street and sat down in a corner booth. Liz, their favorite waitress, walked up to them, smiling.

"Hello, boys. Your usual, Jack?"

"Just a cup of coffee tonight. I've already eaten with my girls. I'm just here to keep this kid company."

Liz turned to Mike. "Corned beef sandwich with Russian dressing?"

Mike smiled and nodded. "Can you add some potato salad and a cream soda?"

"You got it, kid," Liz said.

When she had left, Mike leaned toward his father. "Dad, did you see Fran and Lee today?" Mike asked.

"Yes, I did. We had a great afternoon. They're doing fine. I'm going to go see them on Sunday," Jack said.

"Did they ask about me?" Mike inquired.

"Of course they asked about you. They can't wait to see you." Mike smiled.

"When are they coming home, Dad?"

Jack sighed. "I don't know, son, but I hope soon." There was an unhappy pause, and Mike made an effort to change the conversation.

"Well, what about Theresa. Did she say yes? Did she like the ring you bought her?"

"I haven't asked her yet, Mike. I want to make sure the girls come home first and we are all together again."

After Mike gobbled down his dinner, they went home. Instead of turning as usual toward his bedroom, Mike hesitated.

"Do you want to play a game of Gin Rummy? I'm feeling lucky tonight."

"Sure, with one condition," Jack stated. "If you lose, you pay up. Deal?"

"Deal," replied Mike. He knew his father would never take his money. After a couple of hours and a few dollars poorer, Jack called it a night.

"I'm getting the radio put in the car tomorrow night. I should be at the Princeton Garage around seven. Do you want to meet me there?"

"Sure, Dad."

"I'm leaving early in the morning, so I'll say goodnight now. Love you, Mike."

"Love you too, Dad."

Chapter 38

Jack
Chicago, June 20, 1931

Jack got up early and drove to Theresa's apartment. He knew he was violating the court order but he needed to talk to her. Things between them had been rocky lately. At their last meeting, he had hinted that Maloy wouldn't be in charge of the union much longer. When Theresa questioned him on how he knew that, he confessed he had been working with the State Attorney General for almost a year. He explained that they were gathering enough evidence against Maloy to go before the grand jury, and that his own testimony was going to put Maloy away for a very long time.

Theresa had listened in cold silence. Then she asked if she should start digging his grave now, or if he wanted his son to do it later. At that, Jack stormed out of her apartment. They had hardly spoken since, but he was going to try and patch things up.

Jack knocked on the door. "Who is it?" asked Theresa.

"Who do you think it is?" Jack replied, trying to sound light-hearted.

Theresa opened the door. It was early in the morning and she was wearing the black negligee Jack had bought for her. He looked into her eyes and knew she had forgiven him. She took his hand and led him to the bedroom. Jack wrapped his arms around her as they walked over to the bed. After making love, they lay in each other's arms, gently stroking each other's body. Jack knew that the moment had arrived.

Theresa, I'm in love with you. I see my future with you. My children adore you." Jack raised himself up on one elbow and looked into her eyes. "Please be patient. Just say that you'll marry me, and I promise everything will work out."

Theresa put her hand up to his lips to silence him.

"Jack, I love you too, but I would never be able to live with myself if something happened to you. You scare me when you say you're working with the Feds. I know Tommy well, Jack, maybe too well. And he'll never let you or a grand jury take him down. He will eliminate you a thousand times over before he'd let that happen."

Jack suddenly looked puzzled, and Theresa realized she had said too much. Jack got up without saying another word, took a shower, and got dressed. When he came back into the living room, Theresa was waiting for him.

"I'll be working at the Piccadilly Theater tonight, but how about a late dinner tomorrow night? We have a lot to talk about," said Jack.

He seemed his usual self and Theresa was relieved. "Of course," she said.

Jack left and started to head toward the theater. As he drove, he couldn't seem to shake off the uneasy feeling inside him. Theresa had never before referred to Maloy by his first name, and until today she never admitted she knew Tommy very well. Something was definitely wrong.

He let his mind go back to the first time he met Theresa, every detail replaying starkly in his mind. And then he gripped the steering wheel and groaned aloud.

"What a fool I've been. Meeting her wasn't fate. It wasn't a coincidence. It was a set-up, right from the beginning, I have been played for a sucker. Theresa has never loved *me*. She's Tommy's girl."

He wrapped his fingers around the ring he had bought her; it was warm in his pocket. He pulled it out and held it up to the light. He wanted to throw it out the window and run over it, obliterate it, the way she had obliterated him.

Then through gritted teeth he mumbled, "How could I have been such a fool? You aren't going to get away with this Maloy. This isn't over! This isn't over!"

Jack arrived at the theater around eleven. He wished he could cancel, but he was now the lead projectionist and he needed the money. His divorce lawyer was bleeding him dry. As the hours passed, Jack grew more and more upset by his conversation with Theresa. His mind kept drifting away from his work, and he found himself so deep in thought that he almost forgot to change the reel during the movie. What began to worry him most was what he had told Theresa about going to appear before the Grand Jury. Jack had a sick feeling deep in his gut. Telling her had been a big mistake. He prayed he was wrong. He had to be wrong.

The State Attorney General's investigation had slowly been coming to a head. Jack had been instrumental in providing them with the names of operators who were willing to testify about their own experiences with Maloy. All of these men were victims of, or witnesses to, beatings, kidnappings, and murder.

Jack was going to be the State's last witness. As Attorney Bellows put it, Jack would be the last nail in Tommy Malloy's coffin. The grand jury had been in session now for almost five weeks and Jack was going to testify Tuesday morning.

After work, Jack drove straight to 2525 Princeton Avenue to have his car radio installed. He pulled up alongside the small, white house, looking to see if Mike was already there. He wasn't. He thought that maybe Mike was already in the garage. Jack drove his car slowly down the long driveway. The garage door was open. He drove into the work bay where Johnny Greer was waiting for him.

"Hey Kaufman, thought you were going to be a no-show." Jack smiled briefly.

"How long do you think this is going to take? My son is meeting me here, and I don't want him to have to hang around too long."

"Maybe an hour. Not much longer," replied Greer.

Greer started to install the radio. Jack was standing just outside the garage door scanning the street to see if he could spot Mike.

Then Greer yelled out, "Kaufman, can you hand me the pliers on my workbench?"

Jack walked over to the workbench and picked up a needle-nose. He walked back to where Greer was standing, but didn't see him. Jack stepped up on the running board. That was when he saw Mike crossing the street out of the corner of his eye.

"Dad!" yelled Mike.

At the same time, Jack saw a silhouette of a young man walking toward him. He didn't know where he came from. He was wearing a white linen shirt and white flannel trousers. There was something disturbing about him. He looked familiar. Jack knew he had seen him before. Then he remembered. He was the kid who parked his car at Maloy's party.

With a single fluid motion, the man put his hand in his pocket, pulled out a revolver, pointed the gun at Jack, and pulled the trigger. Five successive, deafening, sonic booms were heard several blocks away.

Jack slowly lifted his hand over his chest. He stumbled off the running board and fell down on both knees. He tried to get up. He needed to get to Mike. When he found he couldn't stand, he started to crawl out of the garage toward his son. The ground was wet with his blood. The world was turning dark around him. He was still conscious but could not move. "Mike, run!" he whispered.

A woman floated into his vision. She took her sweater off, folded it into a makeshift pillow, and gently placed it under Jack's head. She whispered, "Hold on, don't die. Please don't die."

High-pitched wailing sounds from the invalid coach startled

Jack as the woman disappeared into thin air.

Mike, paralyzed by the sight of his father, was grabbed from behind and thrown into the back seat of a black sedan. He was blindfolded and his wrists tied together. Mike was numb with fear. His only thought was his father and how he needed to get back to him.

The car travelled for a long time, but in which direction, Mike couldn't tell. He tried to stay calm. When the car finally stopped, two men dragged Mike out of the car. Then they pushed him down seven concrete steps into a damp, dark basement.

Alone and blindfolded, his wrists still bound, Mike didn't move. He could barely breathe. It was eerily silent.

He yelled out as loudly as he could, "I need to see my father." But there was still only silence. He yelled out again, trying to mask the panic in his voice, "God damn it, take this blindfold off. I'm begging you, let me see my father." But there was still no answer. The minutes ticked by.

Mike stood up. He rubbed his face against the wall to loosen the blindfold. The blindfold slipped down to the bridge of his nose. He squinted in the dim light and saw he was below ground. There was a small window that he thought he could probably climb through.

Mike worked the ropes on his wrists until his skin was chafed and raw. Finally, he managed to free one hand. He ran toward the window, but relief soon turned into frustration as he realized it was too high to reach. His heart was pounding.

He scanned the room. There was no other means of escape except the door, which of course would be locked. He tried the handle as a last resort. To his amazement, it turned. His heart thudding, he crept up alongside the rail until he was at street level. Then he ran like hell.

After Jack was hit, a neighbor hearing the gunshots called the police. In short order, a squad car and invalid coach arrived at the Princeton Garage. Jack was loaded onto a stretcher and taken to the Little Company of Mary Hospital. Three bullets had been fired into his chest and two bullets into his abdomen. His white shirt, now stained with dark, red blood, made a somber contrast with the dark, red blood pumping life out of him onto the gurney.

Floating in and out of consciousness, he was wheeled into the emergency room. A doctor asked him if he wanted his family notified, and Jack whispered, "Call Charles Bellows."

The police officer standing alongside the gurney said, "I know Bellows. I can make the call."

Bellows rushed to the hospital and paced the small waiting room anxiously until Jack came out of surgery.

"When can I talk to him?"

The attending surgeon said, "I'm sorry, Mr. Kaufman won't be in any condition to talk for at least four hours."

"But he's a key witness in a grand jury investigation. We're going to court on Tuesday and we need to know who shot him!"

Jack probably wasn't going to survive, so the doctor granted permission. Bellows asked that everyone leave the room so he could speak with Jack in private. The doctor posted a nurse just outside the door and requested that the door remain ajar. Bellows moved a chair up to the edge of the bed. He leaned in close.

"Who did this to you, Jack?" he whispered. "Tell me who did this and I will get the son of a bitch."

Jack didn't respond. He was floating in and out of consciousness. Bellows repeated the question again. Finally, Jack mumbled a name.

Immediately, Prosecutor Bellows requested that an "arrest on sight" order be issued for Tommy Maloy as well as his henchmen, Ralph O'Hara, Danny Stanton, Martin McCoy, Jack Quinn, and Eddie Donovan.

Mike ran until he was exhausted and couldn't run anymore. He slumped against a building and tried to figure out where he was. If he could just get to a phone, he could call Leon, who would know what to do. Mike saw a bar about a block away. The sign was lit up with the name 'Duke's Bar and Grill.' He stumbled in and asked to use the phone. The bartender could see the distress and fear on the boy's face.

"Come with me, son, there is a phone in my office," he said soothingly. Mike followed him into the office.

"Is there anything I can do to help?" he asked. Mike, already dialing the phone, didn't answer. The bartender walked out of the office but kept the door ajar so he could listen to the call.

Leon, preparing for an upcoming court hearing on Monday, had not yet gone to bed. When his phone rang, he was surprised at being called so late and alarmed when he realized who the caller was.

"Judge," came Mike's quavering voice.

"Mike, what's wrong?"

"I need help. They shot my Dad. They shot him. Five times. I don't even know if he's dead."

Leon tried to stay calm. "Tell me where you are, son. I'm coming to get you."

"In Duke's bar."

"I'll be right there."

Leon hung up the phone. He knew where the bar was. He also knew he probably would never see his best friend again.

Chapter 39

Mike
Chicago, June 21, 1931

As Leon approached, he could see Mike's whole body was shaking.

"Judge!" Mike cried out. "You've got to help me find my dad. We have to go right away!"

Leon shook his head. Mike had already been abducted once, and he couldn't risk his safety a second time.

Mike covered his eyes. Dread traveled though his entire being as tears flowed down his face. He pleaded with Leon to let him try and find his father. Leon was concerned that searching for Jack would put both of them in danger. He insisted they go back to his house and try and figure out where Jack had been taken.

Leon knew the Princeton Garage was fairly close to the Little Company of Mary Hospital. If Jack was still alive, there was a good chance he would have been taken there. The first call Leon made was to the hospital.

"Little Company of Mary Hospital, this is Sister Charlotte speaking. Can I help you?"

Leon took a careful breath. "I hope so. This is Judge Leon Adelman. I'm with the family of Jack Kaufman. I was informed that Mr. Kaufman was probably brought to your hospital by ambulance. Can you confirm that for me?" Leon continued. "He was shot several hours ago. I'm here with his son, Myron," explained Leon.

The Sister sounded flustered. "Judge, my shift just started and I don't have my list of the new admissions. May I call you back?"

"Of course." Leon gave her his phone number and hung up the phone.

He and Mike stared at each other in silence as the grandfather clock in the hall ticked away the minutes. Mike flinched at each click. The wait for Sister Charlotte's call was the longest of both of their lives.

"Leon, what's going on?" Abbey called down from the second floor landing.

"I'll be right up, Abbey," replied Leon. "Mike, I'll be right back."

Leon told Abbey the little he knew. "Oh my God. Not Jack. This city is a war zone! When will you find out if Jack is still alive?"

"Abbey, I'm waiting for the hospital to call me back," Leon stated and clambered back down the stairs. The phone started ringing. Mike ran from the office to pick it up but Leon was already holding the receiver in his hand. It was Sister Charlotte.

"Is this Judge Adelman?" asked the woman.

"Yes." Leon managed to keep his voice even.

"Judge Adelman, I can confirm that Mr. Kaufman has been admitted to the hospital. But I cannot provide any information about his condition. Any information about Mr. Kaufman has to be released by State Attorney Charles Bellows."

Leon frowned. "I understand. Can you please tell Mr. Bellows to call me on my house phone? He knows the number."

"Of course, Judge," replied Sister Charlotte. "I will also pray for your friend."

"Thank you, Sister. He is going to need all of our prayers." Leon hung up the phone, lowered himself to the bottom step, and began to cry.

"What is it? My dad is dead isn't he? Tell me! Tell me the truth!"

Leon pulled Mike down onto the stair beside him. "Your father is in the hospital and we're waiting for news."

Just after midnight, the phone rang again. It was Bellows.

"Judge Adelman, this is Charles Bellows. I'm so sorry to tell you that Jack Kaufman died shortly before midnight."

Leon closed his eyes, too drained and too shocked to say a word.

The judge sucked in a sharp breath. "No! No! It can't be. He's got a young family. He's . . ." Leon stopped speaking when Mike appeared in the hallway.

"I'm so sorry, Judge," Bellows went on. "Jack was a brave man. There aren't very many guys in Chicago who would have been willing to go up against the Maloys and Capones in this city. There will need to be an autopsy to remove the bullets for their evidentiary value," Bellows added.

"I understand," Leon replied. "I will advise the family and will make arrangements for Jack to be transported to the mortuary after the autopsy. Do you know who did this?" Leon asked.

"I can't discuss that right now," Bellows said cautiously. "But you can call me on Monday. I'll be in my office all day."

"Thank you, Charles."

"Judge, I think it's obvious who ordered the hit," added Bellows. "Oh, and one more thing. I was given Mr. Kaufman's wallet. Who would you like me to pass it along to?"

"You can give it to me and I will make sure it gets to the children."

Leon sat down on a chair next to the phone. Abbey sat next to her husband, taking his hand. There was nothing either one of them could say.

"Is my father dead?" Mike whispered.

"Yes, Mike." Abbey took Mike's hand and drew him into their circle of grief, holding the two men until their sobs slackened.

Leon did not sleep that night. As dawn came, he heard the slap of the Sunday edition of the *Chicago Tribune* landing on the front stoop. He went outside, picked it up and stared at the headline.

"Movie Operator Shot to Death in Mystery Attack
Prosecutors Hunt for Motive"

A youthful gunman, immaculately clad in white flannel trousers and other summery attire, walked into the garage at 2525 Princeton Avenue at seven o'clock last night and shot Jack Kaufman, 41 years old, five times, inflicting fatal wounds. Kaufman died at midnight. Kaufman, a movie picture operator, was scheduled with other members of the Movie Picture Operators Union to be subpoenaed before the grand jury investigation on rackets. Notified of the shooting, Assistant State Attorney Charles Bellows went to the Little Company of Mary Hospital where physicians tried for four hours to save Kaufman. Bellows, with Assistant State Attorney General Charles Lounsbury, has been investigating the Operators Union.

At 6 o'clock last evening, Kaufman left the Piccadilly Theater in Hyde Park and drove to the Princeton Avenue garage to have a radio installed in his car. John Greer, a Negro attendant, started installing the radio. A few minutes later, the flannel-clad gunman entered the garage.

Kaufman, his foot on the running board of his car, turned around. No words were spoken. The visitor yanked a revolver from his pocket and fired five shots at close range. The movie operator collapsed with three bullets in his chest and two bullets in his stomach. The gunman ran from the garage to a maroon-colored sedan containing two other men.

After several hours of inquiry, at the request of Prosecutor Bellows, a police order was sent out to "arrest on sight," Tommy Maloy. Danny Stanton, along with four other men, was also questioned in connection with the killing.

Crawford Johnson owns the garage where Kaufman was shot. Johnson, it was said, tried for two weeks to sell Kaufman an automobile radio and succeeded finally in making an appointment for the installation for last night. It is unclear whether Johnson played a role in the shooting.

Dropping the paper, Leon closed his eyes and muttered, "Those poor little girls, those poor little girls."

Leon began making calls. His first call was to Jack's brothers, Sam and Carl. They were at the Spaulding house with Adela and Bella. They were huddled near the phone, waiting for Leon's call. Sam picked up the receiver, and before Leon could say anything, Sam said, "My brother is dead, isn't he?"

"Yes," Leon confirmed.

Leon decided to wait until Mike woke up to talk to him about what needed to be done. After talking with the family, Leon called the Ruth Club. Sarah answered the phone.

"This is Leon Edelman."

"Hello Judge," she replied. There was a moment of silence. Then Leon said, "Jack is dead."

"I am so sorry to hear this horrible news. What can I do to help?" Sarah asked.

"I'll come over later today with their brother and we will talk to the girls."

Leon had no idea what he was going to say to Fran and Lee.

Chapter 40

Mike
Chicago, June 22, 1931

Mike tiptoed down the stairs and opened the front door. He wasn't allowed out of the house and he did not want to wake up the judge, who was sleeping on the sofa. He scanned the street. He didn't see any unfamiliar cars and darted out to pick up the morning paper from the small patch of grass adjacent to the walkway. Back inside, he unfolded the newspaper. There it was, another article about his father. Tears rolling down his face, he read:

"Chicago Daily Tribune Final Edition
Cops Seek Union Czar in Slaying of Film Operator"

Thomas Maloy, business agent of the Motion Picture Operators Union, is wanted for questioning concerning the Saturday night murder of Jack Kaufman, a veteran of the union who had opposed Maloy's rule.

Kaufman, it was learned, was to have been a witness before the grand jury tomorrow. He was prepared to aid the prosecutors, who have been presenting evidence against the union leader to the jury for two weeks, seeking an indictment of its leaders on conspiracy charges.

Mike couldn't continue reading the rest of the article. He folded the newspaper and placed it into the shoebox along with the other articles he had collected about his father. He had to get out of the house. He didn't know what to do or where to go but he couldn't sit around and do nothing. He slipped out the front door and wandered in the neighborhood for hours. Finally, he found himself in front of the diner he and his dad frequented. Those were the moments Mike thought that he would miss the most.

When Mike sat down in the corner booth, he noticed Liz, the waitress, staring at him. Her red-rimmed eyes said she'd been crying. She disappeared into the kitchen. A few minutes later, she brought over a corned beef sandwich with Russian dressing and a chocolate egg cream. She took off her apron and slid into the booth.

"Can I sit with you for awhile?" she asked softly.

"Sure Liz. Thanks." He stared at her for a moment, then burst out, "What am I going to do now?" Mike began to weep.

"You are going to make your father proud," came Liz's instant answer. The dam cracked and Mike's worries, fears and grief poured out.

"Liz, Lee and Fran won't even talk about the killing. Fran is in a trance. She's only eight years old. And Lee is in total denial. Her mind is wandering away somewhere. I don't know how to help them." He shook his head, frustrated. "How will they ever recover from this? And how will I? Liz, I just want to die, too."

Liz sighed. "Mike, you're the man of the house now. You need to pull yourself together so that you can help get your sisters out of that Ruth Club. The three of you need to be together and you will get through this." Mike nodded, but was then hit by another wave of despair.

"He had five bullets in his chest and stomach. Five bullets! Those bastards are all cowards and they need to rot in jail!"

Liz didn't reply, but she suspected that the hit men were more than likely out there on the streets, waiting for the next kill order.

"Mike, I'll be right back." A few minutes later, Liz came back with a cup of warm milk and honey. "This should calm your nerves," Liz said.

"Liz, I can't go home tonight. Can I stay here at the restaurant?"

Mike asked.

"I have a better idea. Why don't you come to my house? I have a spare bedroom and you can get some sleep. We can talk in the morning. Just let the judge know where you are going," Liz replied.

"Thanks, Liz. You are a really good friend." Mike looked down in grief and despair.

Chapter 41

Francine
Chicago, June 24, 1931

It was the hottest heat wave Chicago had experienced in the last hundred years. Buckets of raindrops were falling from the sky, and it seemed to Fran as if the raindrops were tears from heaven. She felt so lonely. Mike hadn't visited her and Lee since that horrible Sunday afternoon when he came to the Ruth Club with Judge Adelman. That was when he told Lee and Fran that their Papa had been in an accident and had died. As tears trickled down Mike's cheeks, he said, "Papa made me promise we will stay strong. He told me that he would always be with us. He said when we need him, we only have to look up at the clouds and know that he is watching over us."

For the first time ever, Lee and Fran did not want to believe their brother. They refused to believe that their Papa was really gone. Fran said over and over again, "I can't believe I will never see Papa again. He promised he would always take care of us. This is all just a bad dream!" Lee looked down as her teardrops dripped onto the floor. Mike stayed with his sisters for several hours trying to comfort them, trying to make them understand.

Sarah knocked on the door and Mike let her into the room. She told Mike that their mother was coming to pick up the girls so that they could say goodbye to their father. Mike did not want to be there when his mother came. He kissed his sisters goodbye and told them he would see them at the cemetery. Sarah stayed with Lee and Fran while waiting for Mary to arrive.

Finally, Mary opened the bedroom door. She held out her arms to her girls and Fran and Lee ran into them, sobbing.

"I promise both of you that we will all be living together very soon," Mary assured them. "You won't have to stay at the Ruth Club much longer, I swear."

But Lee was confused. The two girls had been at the Ruth Club for over three months now, and the last time Jack visited, he told the girls that they needed to remain there until he could take them home. But now their Papa was dead. So did that mean they would have to stay at the Ruth Club forever?

Frustrated and frightened, Lee turned to her mother. "I don't believe anything you say anymore!"

Mary's eyes were red and blotchy from crying. The girls had never seen their mother cry before. Fran wrapped her arms around Mary's waist and Mary kissed Fran's head. Then grudgingly, Lee kissed her mother. Mary whispered, "Don't worry, my darlings. I love you and will always take care of both of you."

From the downstairs foyer came the sound of voices. One of them sounded very familiar. Lee and Fran held their breath and prayed it was their father's voice. The girls ran out of the room and flew excitedly down the stairs. They slowed, sick with disappointment, when they saw, waiting at the bottom of the stairwell, their uncles, Carl and Sam, and their Aunt Bella.

Uncle Carl held his arms out and stroked Fran's head while Sam tried to comfort Lee. Mary and Bella stared at each other with hate in their eyes.

Then Bella announced coldly, "Your mother needs to go home. Right now! I will help you wash up and get dressed. I'm going to take both of you to say goodbye to your father."

Mary tried to smile. "I will see both of you very soon. I promise we'll be together again." Mary kissed her daughters and left.

The girls felt exhausted. They could hardly lift their arms when their aunt tried to help them undress. Bella wanted Fran to wear the dark blue suit that she made for Lee and had been handed down to Fran. Fran rebelled. She hated that suit. She wanted to wear the pretty pinstriped dress her father bought her.

Finally, her aunt told Fran she could wear the dress if she put a shawl over her shoulders to cover her arms. Bella pinned a lace doily on Fran's head and one on Lee's head. As they got inside the car, the girls could see Mary was standing under a tree across the street from the Ruth Club, crying.

It was a long car ride through an unfamiliar part of town. But as they finally approached the black wrought iron gate of the cemetery, Lee and Fran remembered being there once before.

One spring morning, their Papa had taken them to visit their Grandpa David's grave. There was a photograph of David on a marker which rose up from the ground. Jack touched the picture, then kissed his two fingers and touched the picture a second time. The girls did the same. Before they all walked away, Jack left a rock on the gravesite. He told his girls that if they left a rock, their Grandpa would know they were here.

The car drove through the large gates and pulled alongside a curb. As they got out of the car, Fran and Lee noticed several policemen lined up along the walkway. There were also a lot of men in black suits. Mike came to greet them and the girls asked him why strangers were at their Papa's funeral. Mike told them that their father was a very important man.

Mike held Fran and Lee's hands and led them to the white chairs near a mound of dirt. Fran was looking down at the ground and suddenly she saw her father's polished black wing-tip shoes. She looked up startled, confused, and full of hope, but then realized it was Mike walking in her Papa's shoes.

Lee and Fran sat down next to their grandmother. Lee was crying. Fran was told that it was time to say goodbye. She blurted out, "I will never say goodbye! I know I will see my Papa again. I know I will." Her Uncle Carl picked her up and Fran cried in his arms.

Six men carried Jack's pine box from the black car to the gravesite. The Jewish Star of David was carved into the top of the burial box. Mike, Carl, and Sam carried one side of the box.

Leon, Bellows, and Weiss carried the other side. A police officer walked in front and another policeman walked behind Jack's coffin which had been draped with the American flag. The flag was folded by two police officers. One of them handed the flag to Adela. Adela then handed the flag to Mike.

The rain had stopped but the ground was still wet and muddy. The rabbi recited the prayers in Hebrew and Fran put her hands over her ears to block out the sound. She wanted to stop breathing so she could die too.

Four men lowered the coffin into the ground and Sam handed the shovel to Adela. She took dirt from the ground and put it on the shovel, then threw the dirt into the grave.

Fran felt a tug on her arm. It was her Uncle Sam.

"Francine, please follow me." Fran did so, and Sam handed Francine the shovel.

"What are you doing?" she stammered. She turned her head because she couldn't bear to see dirt being thrown on her father's box. Mike took the shovel from her and put more dirt in the grave. Then he handed the shovel to Fran, but she wouldn't take it.

"We have to do this for Papa," Mike told her.

"No! Please don't make me do this!" Fran wailed.

Lee came over and put her hand on top of Fran's. The girls picked up the shovel together and threw the dirt into the grave. Then the rabbi pinned a black ribbon on Mike, Lee, and Fran. He made a small tear in the ribbon and said, "This ancient Jewish custom is symbolic of the tears that are in the mourners' hearts. When a parent dies, it is torn on the left side closest to the heart." Then everyone recited:

From the moment I wake 'til I fall asleep, all that I do is remember him.

In the blowing of the wind and in the chill of winter, I remember him.

In the opening of buds and in the rebirth of spring, I remember him.

When I look above and see the images of the clouds, I remember him.

On every day, and in every way, I know that he is with me and I remember him.

When the service was over, Sam picked up Fran and carried her in his arms. As they were walking away, Fran saw Theresa standing on the hillside looking down towards the gravesite. Then she disappeared.

Sam drove the girls back to the house. Lee and Fran hadn't been home for over three months and they had both dreamed of this moment and planned for it. But now everything was so different. As they pulled up in front of their house, Lee said sadly, "Nothing will ever be the same again." Fran was silent. She bowed her head and clenched her fist. Anger and fear ran through her being.

A pitcher of water had been placed outside the house for everyone to wash his or her hands. When the girls walked into the house, it looked different. All the mirrors were covered and the house felt cold and empty. Their aunt told them that in the Jewish religion, when someone goes to heaven, we don't look at ourselves in mirrors, because we only want to think about the person who is no longer with us.

"I just want my Papa!" Francine cried and she ran to her room. She put her shawl under her pillow, closed her eyes, and dreamed. She remembered the story her father told her about the Russian princess. Her name was Anastasia and she wore a beautiful fur coat made from the pelts of the silver fox. The princess had long, brown, curly hair, and her skin was white as the snow of winter. As she walked in the palace gardens, she picked beautiful lavender roses and yellow acacia blossoms. Then she would put them in her satin pouch and disappear into a rainbow made out of flowers.

The door opened and a figure came into the room. Fran thought for a moment that it was her father. Mike kissed Fran on her forehead and sat down on the edge of her bed. "*Ikh libe ir meyn shenyn printsesin*. I love you my beautiful princess."

"I love you too, Papa," Fran said, half-asleep. "I dreamt about the princess." Mike stayed quiet.

"Papa, will I be an angel in heaven one day?"

"Yes. We will all be in heaven waiting for you in the most beautiful cloud in the sky," Mike said as he cradled Fran in his arms.

When the last mourner left, Leon took the girls back to the Ruth Club. Mike didn't want his sisters to leave but Leon said that he had to comply with the judge's order.

A week later, on June 30, Mary filed a petition advising the court of Jack's death and asking for full custody of her daughters.

It read:

"Your petitioner respectfully represents that she is the defendant in this matter, and that pursuant to an order of court, two children of your petitioner, namely Lenore Kaufman and Francine Kaufman, have been temporarily placed in the care of the Ruth Club, 54th and Drexel Boulevard, in the city of Chicago.

Your petitioner further represents that on the 20th day of June, A.D. 1931, the complainant, Jacob D. Kaufman, departed this life, and that the said complainant had paid for the support and maintenance of these two children at the Ruth Club.

Your petitioner further represents that she has been appointed administrator of the estate of Jacob D. Kaufman, deceased, and that the said Jacob D. Kaufman, deceased, is unable under the present circumstances to take care of the children herein above set forth, and that there is no other person other than your petitioner who is able to devote the proper care and attention for the support of these children.

WHEREFORE, petitioner requests that she be granted custody of these two children, Lenore and Francine, and that an order be entered herein commanding the Ruth Club to turn over the two children, Lenore and Francine, to the custody of your petitioner. Signed: Mary Kaufman"

Chapter 42

Mary
Chicago, August 1931

Two months later, on Friday, August 14, Mary was back in the courtroom.

"All rise!"

Mary stood next to her attorney as the judge took the bench.

"Mrs. Kaufman, I know this has been a very difficult time for you and your daughters. Unfortunately, sometimes these proceedings take longer than we expect. I have reviewed your petition and I am hereby granting you custody of Lenore and Francine. Since this is Friday, you will need to wait until Monday to pick up your daughters. In the meantime, my clerk will advise the Ruth Club that you are allowed to take your daughters home. Is there anything you would like to say?"

Mary began to sob. "Your Honor, thank you. I am very grateful my daughters will be coming home." Mary bowed her head and tried to hide her tears of gratitude.

"Mrs. Kaufman, I wish you and your children a happy life." He stood up, grabbed his gavel and pounded on the desk. "Court is adjourned."

Mary's attorney turned to her. She saw that he too had tears in his eyes.

"Mary, it's finally over. I'm sorry this took so long to resolve. Take care of your girls." Mary turned, walked toward the back door of the courtroom, and headed home.

Mary had three days to prepare for her daughters' homecoming. She was overwhelmed, but excited. For the first time in her life, she was in control of her future and vowed to make a good life for her and her girls. She prayed this horrific custody battle would not scar her daughters forever.

Certainly, she needed to leave Chicago with Lee and Fran as soon a possible. Other than that, Mary wanted to be with her mother. She wanted her girls to swim in the ocean and stroll along Brighton Beach. She wanted calm, not chaos. And she never wanted to step into a courtroom again.

Over the next three days, Mary readied the small apartment for her daughters' homecoming. She bought out much of the Jewish butcher shop. When she returned home, she began cooking Lee and Fran's favorite foods.

Expertly, she cleaned and salted the chicken and plopped it gently into the pot of boiling water. Then she molded the matzo mix into perfect round balls and added them into the broth. Next came the noodle kugel and potato latkes. On Sunday, she would cook the brisket. Her girls loved her brisket. For dessert, she would make her Russian cream and a chocolate birthday cake for Fran who was turning nine years old. She would also have to go to the store and buy her daughter a birthday present. She'd get a little something for Lee too.

Mary laughed aloud. Her head was spinning. She was giddy. Her skin was tingling. She felt alive!

Chapter 43

Leon
Chicago, August 14, 1931

As a professional courtesy, Judge Trude called Leon to tell him he had granted Mary guardianship and custody of Lenore and Francine and that he had also told Mary she could pick up her girls on Monday morning.

Leon hung up the phone with a tremendous sense of relief. He went into his office and opened his bottom drawer. He pulled out Jack's wallet, holding it reverently for a moment, and then extracted from its interior a business card with a handwritten note on the back. The note read: *"I am ready to sell you an interest in the Central Park Theater. I will be in Chicago the first week in August. We can go over the terms in person. A. J. Balaban."*

Leon read over the note countless times, and each time he did, he was swept away by the tragic irony of it. If Jack had only lived, he would have finally achieved his dream of owning a movie theater.

He sat motionless at his desk, staring at the card. It was time to pass the wallet along to Mike, and Leon couldn't make up his mind what to do. Should he give Mike the card, or tear it up? With an effort, Leon leaned forward, ripped the card in two, and threw it away. Now it was time to concentrate on Lee and Fran.

When Leon heard the good news that Mary had been granted custody of Fran and Lee, he asked Adela to pack up the girls' belongings from the house and include an assortment of photographs of Jack and the family. He told Adela he would stop by on Sunday, and hoped she would be able to complete the task. Since Jack's funeral, Adela had been in a near catatonic state of grief. She was exhausted and decided she would not fight Mary for custody. Leon predicted she would never recover from Jack's murder. Next, Leon called the Ruth Club and asked Sarah to call him when Mary arrived.

On Monday morning, August 17, 1931, Mary came to take her girls home. She made Francine her favorite chocolate cake and brought paper plates and paper cups that said, 'Happy Birthday.' It was Fran's ninth birthday. Sarah staged a little party with the other girls.

Mrs. Gross gave Fran a beautiful handmade sweater. She also gave several books to Lee. For the first time in a long while, both girls were hopeful they would laugh again. After the party, Leon picked up Mary and the girls. Then he drove them to Mary's apartment to begin their new life.

The apartment in downtown Chicago was very small. Lee and Fran slept together in the twin bed and Mary slept on the couch in the living room. Since it was only temporary, nobody minded.

Before leaving Chicago, Mary took the girls to Waldheim Cemetery to visit Jack's grave. Lee and Fran each wrote a letter and placed it at the base of their father's headstone. Then they placed two lavender roses on Jack's grave. It had been his favorite flower.

The next few years brought many changes. Mary and the girls moved to Brighton Beach and lived with Mary's mother, Cecilia. It was a happy, quiet time, just what Mary had so craved for her family.

Mike refused to leave Chicago and temporarily moved into the Spaulding house with Adela, Bella and her son Norman. Adela slept in one bedroom, Bella slept in another, and Norman slept in the third bedroom. Bella made Mike sleep on an army cot in the kitchen.

Eventually, Mike moved in with his Uncle Carl and his cousins, David and Paul. His relationship with his mother had deteriorated to the point that when Mary made the move to New

York, she didn't even tell her son what she had done.

Mike, unable to find his sisters, panicked and reached out to Leon, who hired a private investigator to find out their whereabouts. When Mike found out that Mary had taken his sisters to New York and they were now living in Brighton Beach, he was furious. He vowed that he would never see or talk to his mother again and would never forgive her.

The following year, Adela died of a broken heart. She was buried in Waldheim Cemetery. After her mother's death, Bella moved into a small apartment. She died three years later on April 28, 1935. She was buried near Jack's grave.

PART THREE

New York

Lee, Mike, Mary and Fran

Chapter 44

Fran
Brighton Beach, 1935–1944

Brighton Beach, also known as "Little Odessa," was a large community comprised of Russian Jews and émigrés, primarily from Odessa, Kiev, and Minsk. For those who spoke only Russian or Yiddish, there was no language barrier. One could still communicate in their native tongue with ease. Unlike in Chicago, Mary felt safe in Brighton Beach.

During the tumultuous years of her marriage, her trips to Brighton Beach always gave Mary refuge from the emotional rollercoaster she rode on in Chicago. It also provided her with a sense of belonging and acceptance.

Once Mary moved permanently to Brighton Beach, there was a significant change in her. It was almost as if she was going back to the land of her birth. She began smiling more and even laughing. She also started sketching again and began designing American-looking dresses. Fran, who had inherited her mother's artistic talents, also started drawing. She found that drawing gave her a sense of peace. And Lee's safe haven, as always, was immersing herself in her books.

Although much had changed outwardly in the four years since Jack's murder, Fran was still haunted by what had happened to her father. She fantasized constantly about getting justice for him. She wanted to know his shooter was caught, and she wanted Maloy gunned down the same way his thugs gunned down her father. Fran could feel how her hatred and pain was slowly eating away at her, but she did not know how to stop it.

Lee encouraged Fran to start reading more, and that seemed

to help. Fran could enter into a make-believe world of adventure and beauty which numbed her grief. Once a week she would still go to the corner newsstand and buy a copy of the *Chicago Tribune*.

Fran convinced herself that reading the *Tribune* gave her some type of connection to her father's family. But there was a darker reason. What she was really hoping to see, in black and white print, was that her father's murderer was dead. When Lee figured out what Fran was doing, she made her sister stop reading the paper. Lee said they couldn't live in the past and that they all needed to move on. Reluctantly, Fran agreed.

Then on Wednesday, February 5, when Fran got home from school, there it was. Even though they no longer subscribed to the newspaper, a copy of it had been wedged between the bottom of the screen and the front door. Fran bent down, brushed off the snowflakes which dusted the newspaper, and placed it on the round dinette table. She made herself a cup of hot chocolate and began reading the story on the front page.

"Chicago Union Head Slain in Gang War
Gunmen Send Ten Slugs into Head of T. E. Maloy,
Movie Projectionists Union Leader
Police Fear General Outbreak of Killings after Daylight Murder on the Lakefront"

Chicago, Feb 4—Two blasts from a sawed-off shotgun fired by one of two assassins in broad daylight on one of the city's most thickly traveled motor highways today ended the turbulent career of Thomas E. Maloy, business agent and "Czar" of the Chicago Motion Picture Projectionists Union.

While hundreds of automobiles sped in both directions, a volley of bullets from a pistol and shotgun shattered the window glass of the car and slugs struck Maloy in the back of the head.

The dead man, whose union rule of twenty years was marked by beatings, bombings, and murder, was shot in his limousine shortly after 1:00 p.m. as two unidentified men drove up alongside the car on the outer drive across from the World's Fair buildings.

Maloy, age 45, died instantly. His fingers slipped from the steering wheel and his car veered to the left side of the road as he slumped against the door. His companion, Emmet Quinn, a dentist, who is also a steward in the union, pressed the foot brake and stopped the car.

The killers sped north on the drive and were out of sight before passing motorists could organize a pursuit. An autopsy at the county morgue showed that ten of the shotgun slugs had entered Maloy's head. Several others had grazed and furrowed his right ear.

"I drove to Maloy's home, then he took the wheel," said Dr. Quinn. "At Twenty-fourth Street we were traveling about 35 miles an hour. I had noticed two men with their coat collars turned up riding in a Ford behind us. They drove pretty close to us and Tom swerved the car a little to let them pass. I saw him look at the men, but he paid no further attention to them. Then I heard the crash of glass. I thought it was an accident. The next I knew, Maloy had slumped against the door on his side. The other car sped on ahead. I saw one of the two men holding a shotgun. I pressed my foot on the brake. The car stopped after sliding about 50 yards."

"I shook Tom and asked, 'Are you alright?' He didn't answer me, and I saw he was dead. Some of his blood was splattered over me."

The killing, which was reminiscent of gang slayings in the heyday of Capone's underworld rule, caused police to fear a new war of extermination among racketeers after a period of comparative peace. As a result, detective squads went through the city tonight rounding up the remnants of the old Capone gang in their search for Maloy's killers.

Fran put the newspaper down and walked into her bedroom. She looked over to the picture on her nightstand and told her father that justice had finally been done. When Lee came home, Fran silently handed her sister the paper. Lee frowned.

"I thought you promised you wouldn't stop at the newsstand anymore."

"I didn't," Fran told her. "The newspaper was sitting on the front porch."

The girls looked at each other.

"It was Papa," Fran finally whispered.

Over the next few weeks, Fran often stopped at the newsstand. She wanted to see if there were other articles about Maloy's death. On February 10, the *Chicago Daily Tribune* headline in bold print read:

"Slain "Czar" of Union Buried"

Fran cut out the many articles and put them in a shoebox in her closet. From time to time she would pull them out and reassure herself that Maloy was really dead. Fran hoped that reading the articles would temper her anger and lessen her hatred. But it never did.

Years later, Mike told Fran that he had actually gone to Maloy's funeral. When Fran asked him why, he said, "I had to make sure the bastard was really dead." He added that he stayed at the gravesite until everyone else left, and that he had "done something!" Fran knew her brother, and she never asked what the "something" had been.

Mike had grown up to be a strong and self-sufficient man, someone Jack would have been proud of. After high school, he enrolled at Northwestern University to study business, just as his father had. In his senior year, however, he had a pretty bad accident, falling off his bike and breaking his arm in several places. Since he couldn't afford to pay both the doctor and his school tuition, Mike paid the doctor and dropped out of college.

Leon offered to pay the medical bills but Mike was too proud. He insisted it was his responsibility now. His friend Alvin begged him to let his father help, but Mike stubbornly refused. He decided on a career in sales and succeeded brilliantly in his chosen profession.

Lee graduated as class valedictorian from Abraham Lincoln High School in June 1936, three months before she turned seventeen. She could have gotten into any college she wanted but decided to go to secretarial school instead. When she completed her courses, she began working full time; the family needed her income.

On October 12, 1936, Mike turned twenty-one. As a birthday present to himself, he went to New York to visit his sisters. Lee and Fran met him at the train station the day before Lee turned eighteen. The three of them went into the city for Lee's birthday dinner and had a wonderful evening. Over the next two weeks, they went to the beach, the boardwalk, and the movies. They played tourist in Manhattan and spent as much time as they could together.

A few days before Mike was scheduled to go back to Chicago, he bought a ticket to the Polo Grounds to watch Barney Ross fight Ceferino Garcia. Mike had been following Ross's bouts since the first time he saw him at Kid Howard's boxing gym in Chicago.

The last time Mike saw Barney Ross fight was when Jack took him to Ross's first professional fight in 1929. It was at Chicago Stadium and Barney Ross won the match against Al DeRose. After the fight, Jack and Mike went into the locker room with Ross's trainer and manager. Mike got to meet Ross and congratulated him on his win. Ross signed Mike's ticket, which was something Mike held in his wallet for years.

When it was time for Mike to leave, it was very hard to say goodbye. The girls always felt so safe when Mike was around. He was their rock, best friend, and closest confidant. Mike always made his sisters feel special and beautiful and did everything he could to protect them. But he still blamed Mary for Jack's death and vowed he would never talk to his mother again.

Early in 1938, Lee met the love of her life. She was having dinner with friends at a restaurant in New York City where there were singing waiters. When Sidney, one of the waiters, walked over to Lee's table and started serenading her during her meal, it was love at first sight. Sidney was eight years older than Lee and that did not make Mary happy, but the couple was steadfastly in love. Two years later they were married.

Fran followed in her sister's footsteps and went to Abraham Lincoln High. Over those four years she kept very busy working at the five-and-dime store as a clerk in her spare time. She wanted to save enough money for singing and dancing lessons even though she knew a career on the stage was only a pipe dream.

She continued to be a very good artist, sketching a variety of clothes any chance she got. During her infrequent spare time, she would test out her drawing skills by sketching dresses. Drawing came naturally to Fran, but she feared her hopes of being a professional dress designer would never be fulfilled.

One day, while sitting in her social studies class, Fran's teacher was handed a note from the school principal. After class she gave Fran the note, which read, "Please come to the principal's office after school today." Fran panicked. Going to the principal's office was never a good thing. Fran walked into the office and handed the note to the clerk behind the counter. The clerk picked up the phone and then escorted Fran into Mrs. Stein's office.

"Please sit down, Francine." Anxiously, Fran took a seat.

Mrs. Stein cleared her throat. "I just wanted to say that I know all about your family situation," she said. "I was wondering if there is anything I could do to help. I heard that you've been working at the five-and-dime and it occurred to me that we might be able to offer you a better job in the school office. Would you like to work there? Susan has offered to mentor you. I understand you are a very quick learner."

Fran was speechless with amazement. At last, she stammered, "Yes, of course. That would be wonderful. Thank you so much."

As it turned out, Susan became almost a surrogate mother to Fran. It was very comforting for Fran to talk to someone so worldly and kind. Susan's friendship helped Fran work through her anger and her sadness.

When Fran received her weekly paycheck, she gave Mary most of her earnings, but she was still able to save a little. Her goal was to save up enough money to go to Radio City Music Hall to see Sonja Henie.

Mike wrote often and called the girls every week. He never forgot their birthdays or the holidays, and sent money as frequently as he could. Even though they didn't live in the same city, Mike was always there for his sisters.

The World's Fair came to New York and opened on May 30, 1939. Mike decided to surprise the girls and he came to New York to take them to the fair.

It was a glorious adventure. The theme of the fair was, "The World of Tomorrow." And this concept of "the future" resonated with Mike, Lee, and Fran. They had survived the last eight years since their father's murder and it was now time to create their own paths in life.

They visited so many exhibits they lost count. Fran especially enjoyed being on the water bugs and bumper cars on the small man-made lake. Each of them had their own boat and tried to crash into each other. They laughed so hard their stomachs hurt. It had been a long time since they had laughed together and it felt great.

Mike stayed in New York for two weeks. They went to the theater in Manhattan. They went to the top of the Empire State Building where they could see the World's Fair through the windows from the top floor. It was breathtaking to look down and scan the city from the top of the world.

They also ate at several Jewish delicatessens. The girls were charmed to see that Mike still ordered his usual corned beef on rye with Russian dressing and a chocolate egg cream soda.

Mike insisted on buying clothes and makeup for his sisters, items Lee and Fran never had the money to buy. He made sure his two sisters had everything they needed before he went back to Chicago.

Fran couldn't bear to see her brother leave. When she saw Mike put his suitcase on the bed, she slammed it shut and begged him to stay. Mike put his arm around Fran's shoulder, holding her and stroking her hair. It was as if time had stopped and Fran was eight years old again. Mike intuitively knew when Fran slipped back to those dark, desperate, and painful years. Before leaving, he promised that he would try to see her and Lee more often. He left the next morning before his sisters woke up.

When Fran woke, she found, at the foot of her bed, a beautiful note from her brother along with a professional-quality sketchpad with a set of charcoal pencils. There were also three tickets to Sonya Henie's ice-skating show, one for Fran, one for Lee, and reluctantly, one for Mary. When Mary saw that Mike had purchased a ticket for her, she was speechless. It was the best gift she had ever received. Mary was filled with hope and promise that their relationship could possibly be mended.

During Fran's last year of high school she became more confident and began to be proficient in sports, especially tennis. She also started dating on a fairly regular basis. Since money was still scarce, she designed her own clothes and took sewing classes so that she could create her own outfits. Often, when Fran needed something to wear, she would borrow her sister's clothes and alter them to form-fit her slimmer, taller figure.

Like Lee before her, Fran chose to date boys much older than herself. Some of her boyfriends were already in college, and those dates were usually spent in their fraternity houses. She also dated a Russian boy from the neighborhood. Boris sang Russian songs to Fran, music to Mary's ears but not to Fran's. Boris was charming and very attentive, but Fran knew she wanted to marry an American man, someone who was born in Brooklyn.

Then in September of 1939, unfathomable events in Europe were set in motion. Germany invaded Poland on September 1st, igniting the beginning of World War II. Two days later, Great Britain and France declared war on Hitler's Nazi state. Australia, New Zealand, Canada, and South Africa also joined the war. Russia, now led by Joseph Stalin, in a pre-planned agreement with Hitler, invaded Poland from the east.

Everyone followed the news with watchful eyes. Although they were halfway around the world, most Americans believed that it would be difficult for the United States to sit idly by.

Lee and Fran were totally focused on their brother and what the war might mean for him. They both knew that they would never survive if anything happened to Mike. Every night they prayed desperately that this war would be over soon.

Chapter 45

Francine and Milton
New York, 1940–1943

Fran had always been amused by New Year's Eve celebrations. She never grasped how a ball dropping in Times Square could somehow provide hope and a sense of new beginnings as the calendar rolled over by one day. Yet, this had been a revered tradition in New York City for over thirty years.

This New Year Eve, Fran's girlfriend Shirley Jacobs invited her to tag along on a blind double date. Shirley had arranged to meet a guy named Jerry and at the last minute, Jerry had asked if he could bring along his cousin Milton. Fran and Shirley would have dinner with the fellows at a steak house in Brooklyn and if things went well, they would spend the rest of the evening at a dance club, bringing in the New Year.

Fran, never one for blind dates, double or otherwise, had serious reservations about the evening, but Shirley reminded her that she owed her a favor, so Fran agreed to go.

The plan was to meet the guys at Jack's Steak House near Brooklyn College. When Fran heard the name of the restaurant, she felt a small chill running up her back; she couldn't help but wonder if her father was somehow behind this evening.

As they walked into the restaurant, the man at the reception desk smiled. "Are you ladies meeting two fellows here on a blind date?"

A little sheepishly, Shirley and Fran nodded.

"They're sitting in the corner booth. Would you like me to walk you over there?"

"Yes, thank you," they replied in unison.

The dimly-lit, crowded dining room was packed with

patrons and filled with noise. Fran and Shirley approached the corner booth but the guys had their backs toward them. All Fran could see was that one of them had carrot-red hair. She whispered to Shirley, "I hope the redhead is yours. I dated a redhead once and he was a jerk. You know, Shirley, I'm beginning to think this whole thing was a terrible idea!" Shirley just rolled her eyes and pushed Fran forward.

The girls finally arrived at the booth where the guys were seated. The man with the brown hair and glasses said, "Hello ladies. I'm Jerry, and this is my cousin Milton."

Then Milton chimed in, "Which one of you is Shirley?"

"That would be me," Shirley said. She looked disappointed and so did Milton.

Milton turned toward Jerry and made a small gesture. Jerry nodded and then Milton turned to Fran and said, "Then you must be my date. I would like to buy you dinner, but I first need to know your name."

Fran could feel her face turning red. Red-haired or not, Milton had the most gorgeous green eyes she had ever seen.

"I'm Fran," she whispered. Milton got up to make room for her to slide into the booth next to him. He smiled and said, "And I'm Milt."

Fran felt the connection between them immediately. She had never experienced anything like it. They had chemistry, so much so, that they couldn't take their eyes off each other. It was magical. They couldn't stop talking, barely taking time to sip their wine. The waiter arrived with their entrees—veal immersed in lemon and caper sauce for Fran and ribeye steak and a baked potato for Milt, but neither had much appetite. Milt ordered a bottle of champagne but they barely touched it.

They talked about their pasts. Milt told Fran he had gone to Abraham Lincoln High School and was a catcher on the baseball team. He told her his passion was baseball. He had been going to see the Brooklyn Dodgers since he was five years old, and he promised to take Fran to a game as soon as the season opened. Fran exclaimed, "I went to Lincoln also!"

Fran couldn't help remembering her father and the small baseball diamond in the backyard of the house on Spaulding Avenue, and it seemed like another sign that he was watching over her tonight.

The two of them talked eagerly. Fran learned that Milt's father, Isadore, was from Hungary, and that his mother, Sadie, was born in Russia, although she claimed she was from Britain. Milt was the middle child, between Ruth the eldest and Rita the youngest. He also had a younger brother Danny who died at age four during heart surgery. Milt said he still missed him.

Fran was less open about her past. She told Milt about Mike and Lee, but didn't feel like mentioning anything about her life in Chicago.

The conversation turned to their jobs, and Milt told Fran his family was in the newspaper business. His father and uncles managed the *Daily Post*, and Milt would deliver the paper to the corner newsstands in the early morning hours. He told Fran that before he started his route, he would read the paper cover to cover.

These days, most of the news focused on Adolf Hitler and the worsening situation in Europe, but neither Fran nor Milt wanted to talk about the war overseas. They wanted to concentrate on each other.

After dinner, the four of them went dancing. Milt was a terrific dancer, expertly steering Fran through some swing dances, the jitterbug, and even the rumba. But Fran liked the slow dances the most, the ones where he held her close.

When the clock struck twelve, she and Milt kissed. In that moment, Fran knew he was "The One."

As Shirley and Fran were walking to the subway, Shirley turned towards Fran with a twinkle in her eye. "Still hate New Year's Eve?"

Fran and Milt soon became a couple. Since Fran had just turned eighteen, Milt didn't pressure her romantically which she secretly regretted a little. It was an easy, warm and happy relationship, and they were both very much in love.

The only shadow over their happiness, growing larger every day, was the war. Milt followed it very closely. He was convinced the United States was going to join the Allies' fight against Hitler sooner rather than later and he wanted to enlist.

When he discussed this with his father, Isadore talked to a family friend, a colonel in the Army National Guard who arranged for Milt to enlist in his division. Milt's basic training was going to be in Mobile, Alabama. He didn't have to report until January 3, 1941, so Fran and Milt were able to have another New Year's Eve together.

The couple went back to Jack's Steak House for dinner and danced until three in the morning. It was a very emotional evening. Fran looked into Milt's beautiful, green eyes and said, "Milt, I want to spend tonight with you."

"Fran, I want that too. But there are too many things that could go wrong when I'm shipped out," he replied. "I know in my heart that I will be coming home to you. But there is a chance something might happen to me. When I come back, we will get married! I'm sure of that."

This was a jolting and sobering moment for Fran. Up until now, she hadn't even contemplated that Milt could be killed. Fran bowed her head, trying to keep the tears from flowing. They held each other with love and a heavy heart.

Milt was stationed in Alabama for nine months. His army brothers started calling him "Red" from the first day of boot camp. When he wasn't in the field training, he wrote to Fran several times a week, and Fran did the same. They had hoped Milt would be able to come home for visits, but that never happened. The letters were their only connection.

When Milt completed his basic training, he became part of

the Army Quartermaster Corps, and once his special training was over, Fran knew he would be shipped out. From then on, the future was a complete blank. The only thing that was certain in their lives was that she and Milt loved each other.

At 7:48 a.m. on December 7, 1941, the Imperial Japanese Navy Air Service attacked the naval base at Pearl Harbor, Hawaii. The first wave of 183 Japanese planes had been sighted just north of Oahu, the main targets being battleships and aircraft carriers. The second wave of attacks targeted Ford Island, Wheeler Field, and Barber's point. The third wave of fighter planes dropped a total of 353 bombs, ensuring all the sites were completely destroyed.

Ninety minutes after the destruction began, the wave of attacks went silent. The bombers reversed course and headed back to Japan. Over five thousand soldiers, airmen, marines, and civilians were seriously wounded or killed. Eighteen ships were run aground or sunk.

The news and images from the attack on Pearl Harbor blasted all over the headlines.

The *New York Times* December 7 headline read:

Japan Wars on U.S. and Britain;

Makes Sudden Attack on Hawaii;

Heavy Fighting at Sea Reported"

The following day, the headline in the *New York Times* read:

"U.S. Declares War; Pacific Battle Widens"

When President Roosevelt delivered his famous "Infamy" speech to Congress, everyone turned on the radio and listened intently:

My fellow Americans. Yesterday, December 7, 1941, a date which will live in infamy, the United States of America was suddenly and deliberately attacked by naval and air forces of the Empire of Japan. The attack yesterday on the Hawaiian Islands has caused severe damage to our navy and military. Many American lives have been lost. American ships have been reported torpedoed on the high seas between San Francisco and Honolulu. Americans will remember the character of the onslaught against us.

The men and women who had already enlisted in the military were immediately deployed. Those who hadn't already enlisted were signing up at recruiting offices all over town. Everyone was concerned and frightened.

Fran was walking through the hall when the phone began ringing. She ran to pick up the receiver, almost knocking it off the small side table in her haste.

"Hello?" she said anxiously.

"Fran, it's me," said Milt. She could tell immediately that something was wrong.

"Are you okay?" she asked

There was a pause. "I'm fine," he replied. "I just needed to hear your voice. I'm shipping out later tonight." Though this is what she had been expecting, Fran fought not to break into sobs.

"Where are they sending you?" she asked, sounding concerned.

"I can't say," he replied. "Just remember our conversation about where you wanted to go on our honeymoon," he added very emotionally. "And remember, I love you. I'll write as soon as I can."

The phone went dead. Numbly, Fran put the phone down, tears gathering on her cheeks. She reflected for a moment and then understood, with horror, what Milt had been trying to tell her. Hawaii was the place she had chosen for their honeymoon.

"Oh, God," she prayed, "Please don't let Milt be sent to Hawaii. Not to the most dangerous place on Earth."

Fran began to retch with fear. It had taken her ten years to feel safe; it had taken her ten years to trust again. And now she was petrified that someone else she loved would be taken from her in an instant.

Now that the United States was officially at war, life seemed to change overnight. Terrifying headlines blurted out the latest news from Europe, the Pacific, and Africa. The "Killed-in-Action" lists devastated families on a daily basis. But at last, things began to settle down, and an alternate version of life, a sadder, tentative, more anxious one, became the new normal.

For Fran, life was about surviving emotionally. She took care of her mother and her grandmother as best she could, and kept her sanity by writing incessantly to Milt and Mike. Mike was now in the army, 'somewhere in the South Pacific.' He assured Fran he was safe, working as a cook in the canteen. But Fran knew her brother all too well, and wasn't sure she believed him. She dreamed of the day the two men in her life would come home and they would all be a family again.

Fran plunged into working. She completed her coursework at secretarial school in record time and her first job out of school was as an assistant at the Stock Exchange. It was an easy commute by the J train, which pulled right into the Broad Street station.

Entering the financial district was like stepping into another world. The pace was insane; everyone was incessantly shouting orders and making trades. The heightened sense of urgency continued to intensify as the hours passed. It was exhilarating and in a strange and consuming way, the chaos helped blur out the war for Fran.

After a couple of months, the work became too intense and Fran quit. She began to work instead as a model for a fur coat manufacturer. She assumed she got the job because she told the owner, who interviewed her, that her grandfather had been a furrier in Odessa and had made fur coats for Tsar Nicholas II. But a few days into the job, Fran discovered the real reason she had been hired; it was because she was very well endowed. Her boss assumed she wouldn't object to his male clients stroking the fur over her large breasts as she modeled his products.

But he soon discovered his mistake when Fran slapped one of his clients in the face. Fran then tore the coat off, announced that she was quitting, and walked out the door.

Fran found another job as a legal secretary in Manhattan. Her employer, Mr. Weiss, an attorney, ran a general practice. He did a little of everything and took most clients who came through the door. He had two sons in Europe, officers in the navy, and understood Fran's worry about Milt. Fran and Mr. Weiss became great friends. They gave each other moral support and encouragement while waiting for the war to end and their loved ones to return home.

The world situation was becoming even graver. The dismal and horrifying news reported each day cast a shadow over everyone. The United States was now in a full-blown war on two fronts. There was fighting in the Pacific and in Europe. Everyone knew somebody who had lost a loved one in the war.

Fran wanted to help in the war effort so she volunteered at the local Red Cross in her spare time. Another woman in her forties volunteered on the same days Fran did. Her name was Doris. Her husband, John, was somewhere in Europe.

When the war began, Doris had moved back into her parents' house with her two young sons so that if the unthinkable happened, they could be together. Fran and Doris became close friends and Fran was often invited to join Doris and her family for dinner. After dinner, when the boys went to their room, the adults would play a competitive game of Gin Rummy. It was a good way to think about something other than the war.

Days turned into weeks and weeks into months. Fran lived for Milt's letters but they were frustratingly sporadic. Sometimes weeks would pass without getting a letter, and then she would get a dozen letters in one week. Other times it could be a month without any word at all. The letters were usually short and nondescript, and always censored. Fran had no idea where Milt was, although he did try and give her the weather report from time to time, which gave her some clues. One thing was constant. In each letter, Milt always told Fran he loved her and asked her to wait for him to come home.

The year 1942 was coming to an end. This was going to be the second year Milt and Fran hadn't gotten to spend New Year's Eve together. Fran prayed that 1943 would be the year this dreadful war would be over. So many young men returned in body bags. Many more came home disfigured, missing an arm or leg, or both. Fran couldn't bear the thought that something like that could happen to Milt.

Finally, on a Friday evening in March, Fran received the letter she had been praying for:

My Dear Fran,
I have been waiting for the day when I could tell you that I am re-turning home. I am not coming home to Brooklyn right away, but my unit is being transferred to California. I'm working on getting leave to come home to Brooklyn as soon as possible. You remember me mentioning that my Irish Colonel and I have become friends. I'm not sure why he befriended a Jewish redhead from Brooklyn, but I'm grateful that he did. He is going to try and arrange a short furlough so I can come home to you. I will let you know when I will be arriving. It probably will be at least a month or two, but I couldn't wait to tell you. I know you are waiting for me. I will be there soon.
Love Milt.

Five weeks passed, and another letter arrived.

Dear Fran,
I'm stateside and I'm coming home to Brooklyn in a couple of weeks. As soon as I have my train ticket, I will give you a call. I hope you can meet me at the train station. I have important news to tell you. You are the one I want to see when I get off the train. You are the

one I want to spend the rest of my life with. I hope you still feel the same way. Please write and let me know if you will be there when I arrive. Love, Milt.

Fran pulled out a piece of stationary and wrote, "Dear Milt, I will be waiting for you with open arms. Love, Fran."

Milt got a two-week furlough and came home on September 10. He decided to surprise Fran. That afternoon, when Fran came home from work, she found Milt sitting in the living room talking to her mother and waiting for her. Fran ran into Milt's arms and kissed him passionately. Mary walked discreetly into the kitchen.

"I have plans for us. I was hoping to take you out to dinner," Milt told her. "Do you want to freshen up?"

"No, I'm ready, let's go." She squeezed his arm.

"Mom, we're going out. I'll be home late," Fran called out.

She and Milt walked out of the apartment hand in hand. Before they got to the stairwell, they began hugging and kissing each other until their lips felt raw.

"How long will you be here?" Fran asked finally.

"We have two weeks."

"Then let's make the most of it," Fran whispered.

Milt took Fran back to Jack's Steak House. He had reserved the booth in the corner, the booth where they had first met. He ordered two glasses of champagne. When the drinks were poured and the waiter left, Milt pulled a small box out of his pocket. Trembling, Fran opened it and found a lovely pearl ring inside.

"Will you marry me, Francine Edith Kaufman?" Milt asked softly.

"Yes. Yes!"

Milt put the ring on her finger. At the adjoining tables, people began to clap. The waiter, beaming, came up to the couple and said the champagne was on the house. The owner of the restaurant hurried over to the table to congratulate them and told them the meal was also on the house. He then shook Milt's hand and said, "Thank you, soldier."

Milt leaned closer to Fran and put his hands over hers. "Fran, can you come back with me to Marysville? We can stay in one of the apartments for married soldiers. The colonel has already made the arrangements for us. Can you be ready to leave in two weeks?"

"Of course I can," Fran told him. "Nothing is more important than starting our life together. I'll give notice tomorrow."

The first thing Monday morning, Fran bolted out of the house, hopped on the subway, and went into Manhattan. When she walked into the office, Mr. Weiss was sitting at his desk reading the newspaper.

"Francine, I wasn't expecting you this early." Then he noticed the ring on her left hand. "Francine, are you engaged?"

"I am. Milt surprised me last night and proposed at the restaurant where we first met," she told him excitedly. "He's on leave for another twelve days and we are getting married this week. I'm so happy! I'm going to California where he is stationed." She took a breath.

"Mr. Weiss, I have really enjoyed working for you. I don't know what the future holds for me, but I do know that I need to be with Milt. I hope you understand."

"Of course!" Mr. Weiss told her. "I wish the very best for you."

"Thank you so much, Mr. Weiss."

Then he added, "Francine, can you wait a few minutes? There is something I need to do."

Mr. Weiss went into his office for a moment and came out holding an envelope. "Find a beautiful wedding gown," he told Fran. Inside the envelope was three hundred dollars.

Fran gasped. "Mr. Weiss, I can't accept this."

"It's a thank you to your soldier for his service to this

country, and a thank you for being the best assistant I ever had."
There were tears in Fran's eyes when she hugged Mr. Weiss
farewell.

The wedding was set for Sunday, September 19. Fran rented
a beautiful satin wedding gown with a sweetheart neckline and
long lace sleeves. Her beaded veil floated down the back of her
gown. Mary made her daughter a corsage with white and sterling silver roses connecting the rosebuds with lace. Fran felt like
a princess and Mary was delighted her daughter would have a
wonderful man by her side.

As Fran looked at herself in the floor-to-ceiling mirror in the
bathroom of the small synagogue, she thought she saw her father; she thought she heard his voice telling her the story about
the beautiful Russian princess who loved to pick flowers and
put them in a satin pouch. Fran smiled, tears in her eyes. She felt
her father's presence all around her. Her Papa was keeping his
promise. He would be by her side when she walked down the
aisle to wed her beloved Milton.

Lee was Fran's maid of honor. Since all of Milt's cousins were
overseas, Milt's best man was his father. When the piano keys
began playing, "Here Comes the Bride," Lee straightened Fran's
veil and whispered into her ear, "Papa is standing right next to
you." Lee opened the double doors to the synagogue and Fran
walked down the aisle toward Milt, who was attired in full dress
uniform. Milt held out his hand and Fran put her hand in his.

They stood under the traditional canopy. Milt draped his Bar
Mitzvah tallis over his uniform. Fran didn't remember anything
the rabbi said, but she did remember when Milt put the gold
ring on her finger and said, "Behold you are consecrated to me
with this ring according to the laws of Moses and Israel."

The glass wrapped in plain cloth was placed on the floor.
Milt stepped on it, breaking it into a thousand pieces. He looked
into Fran's eyes and she looked into his. They kissed. Everyone
clapped and yelled, "*Mazel tov.*"

The reception room adjacent to the synagogue overflowed with food. Mary's Russian cream was placed in individual glass bowls and champagne and wine were on full display. Mary and Milt's mother, Sadie, hovered over the food, making sure everything was perfectly placed on the tables. Lee and Sidney brought their daughter Joni, who had just turned one. All of Milt's immediate family, his sisters Ruth and Rita, his aunts and uncles, and most of his female cousins, also came.

Sadie and Izzie had hired a piano player for the reception. They played "*Hava Nagila*," let us rejoice, and that is what they did. Then everyone joined hands and formed a large circle. In the middle of the circle were the traditional two wooden chairs. Milt sat on one and Fran sat on the other. They each held a corner of a white handkerchief connecting the couple. Several men lifted their chairs up in the air. Milt and Fran held on for dear life while their guests clapped and sang the words to the Hebrew song.

It was a magical night. When all the guests had gone, Fran and Milt went directly to the St. George Hotel in Brooklyn to finally spend their first night as a married couple.

Majestic white and gold marble floors glistened throughout the hotel and the front desk was made out of beautifully carved mahogany. The concierge welcomed Milt and Fran and handed over the room key. The bellboy, holding their small valise, accompanied them to their room. Milt thanked him, gave him a tip, and closed the door.

First, Milt gently removed Fran's veil. Then he took off her corsage and started to unbutton her gown, kissing the back of her neck. He ripped off his clothes, leaving only his underwear on. Slowly, he removed Fran's brassiere, garter belt, and nylons. Then he lifted Fran onto the bed and they made love. It was a night neither one of them would ever forget.

For the next two days, the couple stayed at Milt's parents' home, and then it was time to board the train to California. Izzie,

Sadie, and Mary came to the train station to see the couple off. Mary knitted Fran and Milt a beautiful blanket and Sadie baked chocolate chip rugelach and a challah. She also prepared an assortment of dried fruits and meats for her son and daughter-in-law.

Fran and Milt boarded the train and were grateful for their new blanket. The train was packed. There were quite a few men in uniform as well as families with babies and young children. Fran and Milt longed to curl up and make love, but that wasn't going to happen. The trip seemed endless. By the time they reached California, they vowed they would never travel on a train again.

When they arrived in Marysville, the Colonel had a driver pick them up and take them to the Uriz Hotel. There, they were greeted by all of Milt's army buddies and their wives who had planned a party in honor of the wedding. There was a lot of drinking, something Fran was not accustomed to, and she spent the rest of the night vomiting. Getting drunk was another thing she vowed never to do again.

Being an army wife offered a new beginning for Fran. It provided her with a large extended family of women who shared a similar reality and similar fears for their husbands' safety. They all kept the conversation light, never talking about their anxieties, but should the worst happen, each knew that she would have the total support of the others.

The women were also very caring and helpful on a more practical level. Fran had never set up a home before and her cooking skills were all but non-existent. The other wives were wonderful, teaching her culinary tricks, bringing her care packages, and sharing their meals.

Fran started volunteering for the Red Cross in Marysville, visiting injured soldiers and comforting them during their recoveries. Every time she left the hospital, she said the same prayer, "Please, God, keep Milt safe. I can't go through this again."

A year after she had arrived in Marysville, Milt's unit received orders that they were shipping out. The military buzz was that they were heading to Marseilles, France. All the wives in his unit went to the train station to say goodbye. Everyone prayed their husbands would return in one piece.

Milt and Fran held each other close until the conductor yelled out the final, "All aboard." The unit was headed first to Fort Dix in New Jersey, and then to somewhere in Europe.

With Milt gone, Fran decided to return to Brooklyn. Before leaving California, she sent a letter to Mr. Weiss asking if he knew anyone who needed a legal secretary. A few weeks later, she received a postcard from Mr. Weiss with a picture of the Statute of Liberty on one side and a short response on the other side. It said, "Can you start working on Monday morning?" Fran was relieved and very touched.

After Milt left, Fran closed up their small apartment and took the train back home. She moved in with her mother and grandmother and tried not to think about what her future might look like if Milt didn't make it back.

It was hard coming home and hearing about all the men who never made it home. Some of the many names were boys she had gone to school with. Every time Fran would meet someone from the neighborhood or a classmate from Lincoln High, the first thing that was said was, "Have you heard what happened to . . . ?" Most of the names were just a vague memory of boys she never really knew. But one name was inescapable.

Fran lost contact with Boris after they stopped dating. She had forgotten Boris had joined the navy. What she didn't know was that Boris was on the *USS Arizona*. When Fran heard that Boris had died in the attack at Pearl Harbor, she thought about his family and what they must be going through. She wondered whether he had left a widow or a child. Fran decided she would try to contact the family and offer her heartfelt condolences. The reality of war had become personal. It was now in her backyard.

Fran forced herself to remain positive and believe that Milt would come home to her in one piece.

After settling back in with her mother and grandmother, Fran went into Manhattan to meet with Mr. Weiss. She found out that one of his sons had been badly injured and was now back in New York recovering from his wounds. His other son, a lieutenant who had served in the Philippines, was now stationed in San Diego, California. Mr. Weiss had framed pictures of them both in uniform, which he proudly displayed on his desk.

Fran soon settled into her old, comfortable relationship with Mr. Weiss, and thought that on the whole, she had much to be grateful for.

Chapter 46

Milt
Europe, 1945

The days turned into weeks and the weeks into months. Another year had come to an end and it was now 1945. There was hope in the air for the first time in years. The war was winding down. Men and women who served their country with pride, dignity and loyalty were coming home.

Milt was still in Europe. Fran was receiving some letters, but they were coming more and more infrequently. When she did receive his letters, Milt always ended with, "I will be home soon. I love you." Milt's unit was moving from base to base, resupplying everything the soldiers still needed until the base was deactivated. The end was near, but the date for Milt's return was uncertain.

Knowing his cause was lost, on April 30, Adolf Hitler committed suicide. That event rearranged the course of history throughout the world. Seven days later, Germany surrendered to the Western Allies. On May 8, Winston Churchill announced, "Victory in Europe has been achieved." The war in Europe was finally over. But in the Pacific, the war raged on against Japan. Fran prayed Milt would not be sent to the Pacific, but nothing was certain.

The letter she was waiting for finally came. It was dated May 30, 1945.

My Dear Fran,
I will be home soon. I don't know if it will be one month or six, but I will be returning to Fort Dix as soon as possible. We're in the home stretch and will start the next chapter of our life together. I

can hardly hold back my excitement knowing that you will be in
my arms soon. I love you.
Milt

P. S. I have a surprise for you. Do you reminder the beautiful pho-
tograph you gave me? I still have it in my wallet. Well, while in
Germany, I showed your picture to a POW that was under my
watch. He couldn't have been more than seventeen years old. He
was always drawing portraits. He saw your photo and drew your
portrait. I'll show it to you when I come home. I will probably have
to hand-carry it because the only thing he could use to draw on was
a piece of wood. I hope you like it. XXXOOO.

June turned into July. Every letter Fran received said the
same thing, "I will be home soon." Everyone was cautiously optimistic. But as one day turned into another, Fran became more
and more anxious. Soldiers were being reunited with their loved
ones and positive electricity floated through the air. Unfortunately, the war in the Pacific still raged on and Milt was still not
home.

Fran finally got word that Mike was back in Chicago. He had
contracted malaria while he was on patrol in the South Pacific.
When he was well enough to travel home, he was discharged
with military honors.

Then on August 6, a devastating but determinative event
changed everything. The United States dropped the first atomic
bomb on Hiroshima, killing more than seventy-five thousand
people. Three days later, on August 9, a second atomic bomb
was dropped on Nagasaki. Shock and horror stunned nations
and governments around the world. The world held its breath
and we all prayed the senseless killings would end.

Six days later, on August 14, 1945, Japan surrendered to the
Allies and agreed, in principle, to unconditional surrender. On
September 2, 1945, Japan formally surrendered and World War

II was over!

Confetti flowed through the streets of New York City as people tossed reams of shredded paper out of their windows and over balconies. Men, women, and children hugged and kissed one another. Thousands of people joyfully danced in the streets. Radios blasted the song, "Happy Days Are Here Again." Fran joined in and sang every chorus over and over again, praying Milt would be home soon. Her joy abounded when she received the letter she had been waiting for.

Dear Fran,

I'm coming home. I will be in New York sometime next month. You will be in my arms once again and I will never leave you. I love you and can't wait to begin our life together. Start looking for an apartment.

Milt

The letter was dated September 24. Milt arrived at Fort Dix three weeks later. On October 20, 1945, Milt was honorably discharged with numerous Distinguished Service Medals.

Around a week later, the knock on the door was loud and undeniable. "Fran, open up. I'm home. I'm home!"

Chapter 47

Francine and Milton
Brighton Beach, 1946–1955

Milt had been home for two months and Fran still hadn't found an apartment. With all the GI's returning home, apartments were not only unavailable, they were at a premium and unaffordable. Milt's aunt and uncle offered to let Fran and Milt stay in their converted basement until they could find a more permanent home.

They settled into their temporary home and before they knew it, the holidays were upon them and another year was fast approaching. This New Year's Eve celebration would be meaningful for everyone who returned home. For those families who had lost a loved one, it represented pain, suffering, and a path to try and move forward. Milt's first cousin, Irwin Levy, never made it home. He was a pilot in the Air Force and was shot down over Germany. Milt told Fran that if they had a son, he wanted to name him Irwin after his cousin.

Fran and Milt knew exactly what they wanted to do on this New Year's Eve. They were going back to Jack's Steak House and then checking into a hotel. Milt had already made all the arrangements and told Fran to pack a few things in a small bag.

"I hope you don't mind, but I asked Jerry and Shirley to join us for dinner," Milt said.

"That's perfect," Fran replied.

After dinner, the couples wished each other a Happy New Year and parted ways. "Where are we going?" asked Fran.

"It's a surprise." Milt hailed a cab and the two of them climbed into the back seat.

"Where to?" asked the driver.

"The Roosevelt Hotel," Milt replied. Fran's eyes lit up. Milt leaned in and whispered, "I love you."

The driver stopped in front of the historic hotel. The doorman opened the cab door and they stepped out.

"Will you be staying the night, sir?" he asked.

"Yes," answered Milt.

Fran started to say, "But we can't. It is so . . ." but Milt put his fingers on her lips and said, "Yes we can, and we are."

As they stepped through the ornately carved gold painted doors, they both were transported back in time. The hotel, which had opened in September 1924, created an ambiance of the grand old days of the Roaring Twenties. Guy Lombardo and his orchestra had been playing extraordinary music at the hotel since 1929. Lombardo instituted the tradition of playing "Auld Lang Syne" on New Year's Eve. That tradition, which spread across the country, was fitting for this New Year's. Everyone was celebrating the end of World War II.

The orchestra performed every genre of music from the past thirty years. It was celebratory, sentimental, energetic, and magical. Fran and Milt danced until their feet throbbed. At midnight, the pendulum from the nine-foot-tall grandfather clock, perched in the corner of the ballroom, bellowed out twelve perfectly pitched acoustic bells. Everyone hugged and kissed their loved ones and each other. The orchestra played "Auld Lang Syne" as everyone began singing the chorus.

Shortly after midnight, the blissful couple went to their room. They took a scented bubble bath in the claw-foot porcelain tub, wrapped themselves in plush, white bath towels, and sank onto the magnificent mahogany bed. The cotton sheets were a pale blue and felt like silk. When Milt and Fran put their heads on the feather pillows, they felt as if they were floating above the clouds. They made love and fell asleep in each other's arms.

In the morning, they enjoyed coffee and an assortment of pastries filled with cheese, jam, and chocolate. It was a perfect ending to their magical evening. With the New Year, Fran and Milt turned toward married life.

The couple's first apartment, a two-bedroom on Ocean Avenue near Brooklyn College, was charming and efficient. The location was perfect. The scratched hardwood floors showed a bit of character. The apartment was bright. A large window faced the front courtyard where children played. The kitchen was narrow, but large enough for a refrigerator, a stove and a tiny table. The porcelain kitchen sink was a good size. The two bedrooms were adequate and there was a tub in the bathroom. It was home!

Milt took two jobs. He worked at the *Daily Mirror* at night, and also worked part-time at the *Tribune,* delivering papers to corner newsstands. Fran continued working as a legal secretary. More than anything, Fran wanted to have a baby. After the first year with no success, Fran worried. Milt reassured her that there was nothing to worry about.

Milt was right. Two years later, on September 24, 1948, their daughter entered this world. Her eyes were blue, her cheeks were full, and her hair was golden blonde. Fran and Milt were mesmerized with the miracle they had created. They named their daughter Cheryl Penny after Fran's grandmother Cecilia and Milt's grandmother Penelope.

Fran felt her grandmother's presence in this tiny bundle of joy. She also felt her father's presence. She believed they were both looking down on her with love and happiness.

She stopped working to take care of their daughter. When Cheryl was two years old, their second child, a son they named Irwin Neal, completed their family. Irwin was named after Milt's cousin. When his Uncle Nat came to visit his nephew, he cradled Irwin in his arms and was overwhelmed with love and gratitude.

The Kaufman family was also growing. Lee and Sidney already had two daughters—Joni, six years old, and Rosalie, three years old. They lived in Southern California. Mike and Florence lived in Skokie, Illinois. They named their daughter Jacklyn after Mike's father. Cheryl and Jacklyn were born just two months apart.

Over the years, Mary's stomach problems worsened. By the time she was diagnosed, the cancer had spread and was inoperable. Her only hope was to undergo radiation treatments to try and shrink her tumors.

Around the same time, Milt's cousin Dexter, who lived in Los Angeles and owned a chain of clothing stores, offered Milt a job. The offer presented a good opportunity for the family. Milt traveled to California for a trial run. Fran wanted to make sure the job was going to work for them before making such a big move.

The timing was awful. Fran was left taking care of two small children and a dying mother. Four months later, she packed up the apartment. With the children and her very frail mother in tow, they boarded the train to California.

When Fran spoke to her brother, Mike suggested the four of them stop in Chicago on their way to the West Coast. Fran was really happy that Mike wanted to spend some time with their mother before she died.

The three cousins got along beautifully. It was heartwarming to watch them play together. As Mike and Fran watched the kids, they reflected back to the days when they lived in the house on Spaulding and didn't have a care in the world.

Before Fran left Chicago, Mike and Fran went to Jack's grave. Fran sat down on the grass at the foot of her father's tombstone and talked to her Papa for over an hour. They left pictures of Jack's five grandchildren. Fran said goodbye to her dad because she didn't know when she would ever come back.

PART FOUR

Los Angeles, California

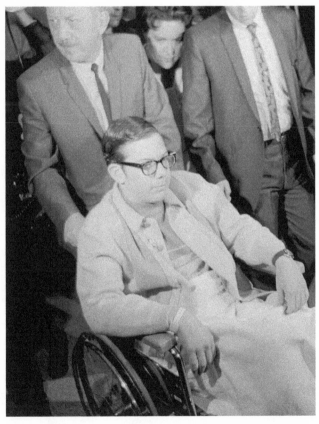

Irwin and Milt

Chapter 48

Francine
Los Angeles, 1955-1960

The apartment Fran and Milt moved into was on Kalzman Drive. The numerous stucco and brick buildings in the complex formed a small courtyard. There was a grassy area for families to congregate and for children to play. Fran loved the apartment and the sense of community it gave her. The compound was a melting pot for middle-class Americans of all faiths and ethnicities who came to the United States for a new start and a more prosperous life.

Fran and Milt's two-bedroom, one-bath furnished apartment came equipped with a refrigerator, a gas stove, and a red dinette table with four black chairs. A small frosted window tucked in the corner provided fresh air and light. The linoleum on the floor was pale beige and worn to the bone. There was a large closet in each bedroom and a small coat closet near the front door. In the bathroom, the small porcelain sink was adjacent to the tub. The bathtub was big enough for both kids to bathe and play with their floating toys.

The navy blue and red living room couch hailed from the pre-war era. It did not take long to unpack their sparse belongings and settle into their exciting new life.

The men, now fathers and husbands, had all fought during World War II. They still carried their battle wounds, some visible and some hidden deep in their psyches. As civilians, they joined the workforce as laborers, teachers, accountants, doctors, and businessmen. Their purpose now was to take care of their families and secure a better future for their children.

The trip across country had been very hard on Mary.

Fran saw, to her dismay, that her mother was weakening every day. She barely ate anymore and she could no longer get out of bed. Four weeks after they settled into the apartment, Mary was rushed to the hospital by ambulance. She died the next day with Lee and Fran by her side.

Mary's funeral was very small. Lee, Sidney, and the two girls were there, along with Milt's cousin Dexter and his family. Milt and Fran decided not to bring the children. They felt they were too young. As for Mike, Fran was glad that he and their mother had made their peace the last time they saw each other.

Mary was buried at Hillside Memorial Park.

The burial traditions were very familiar. The rabbi attached the morbid black mourners' ribbon onto Lee and Fran, which were placed over their hearts. Then he ripped the ribbon, making the symbolic tear. The casket was lowered and the rabbi handed Fran the shovel. Fran froze. Milt gently took her hand and whispered, "It's alright. I'll do it for you. You will never have to go through this again."

When they got back from the cemetery, Fran braced herself to go through the cardboard box that contained Mary's keepsakes. Mary had asked Fran and Lee not to open the box until after her death.

As Fran slowly opened the box, she saw the shawl she had worn at her father's funeral. She also found newspaper articles about her father's murder along with photographs of Jack, Mary, and Fran's grandmother, Cecilia.

Fran found a small sketchbook she had never seen before. She opened the book, expecting to see sketches of blouses and dresses. Instead, she found figures and scenes drawn on the worn and faded pages, carefully labeled and dated.

She stared at the drawings, amazed. Her mother had sketched a beautiful and detailed pictorial history of her youth in Odessa. There was a drawing of a mercantile store with a painted sign over the door that spelled out, "Kaufmann." There were also sketches of the Tsar standing in front of the mercantile, wearing a fur coat and holding a violin.

Mary had also sketched figures of men and women standing near a railroad station. One picture stood out. It depicted a man holding a leash that was attached to what looked like a fox. Fran suddenly remembered the story her father would tell her, Lee, and Mike, about their grandfather David walking the streets of Odessa with a silver fox.

The last sketch was a picture of a seaport, a dock, and a grain silo. In the foreground, there was a young girl with dark brown curly hair holding hands with a grown man. The two walked together down the cobblestone streets. Fran wondered whether that was a sketch of her grandmother Cecilia, and her grandfather Myron. Or perhaps, it was a picture of Mary as a child and her father who had died so young.

Next, Fran began reading the newspaper clippings. The articles were all about her father's murder. She soon became too emotional and shoved them into the box.

Fran replaced the lid and stared down at the shoebox. She understood the immensity of her mother's gift, her wanting to leave her daughters a piece of her own history.

As Fran gently placed the cardboard box in the closet, she found herself whispering, "Thank you, Mom, I love you. Rest in peace."

Chapter 49

Francine
Los Angeles, 1956

June had arrived and it was time for the one-year unveiling of Mary's headstone. The service was short, with Rabbi Cohen reciting the appropriate comforting prayers. As the family walked away from Mary's grave, Fran looked up to the grassy hillside near the mausoleum. She noticed a five-tier cascading waterfall that she hadn't seen the year before. As she got closer, she saw that there was a monument with a six-pillar structure surrounding an Italian marble sarcophagus. On the underside of the dome was a scene of Moses holding the Ten Commandments. Next to the grave was a bronze statue of Al Jolson down on one knee in his famous pose from *The Jazz Singer*.

Fran remembered Mike telling her many years ago when their father worked as a projectionist in Chicago, that Jack had screened *The Jazz Singer* when it first came out. Mike told her how impressed Jack had been. Fran found it ironic that her mother was buried so close to this legendary and celebrated man.

Life moved at top speed, filled with calm days, good friends, and an adorable new poodle they named Gimlet, after Fran's favorite drink. Cheryl and Irwin were thriving and doing well in school. For the first time in a very long time, Fran found herself not living in the past and looking forward to an amazing future.

For some time, Milt had been managing Dexter's clothing store in Santa Monica. Business was so good, that the family was able to move to a three-bedroom duplex with a beautiful yard. The grass, watered diligently by Milt every Sunday, was vivid green, and rose bushes adorned the white picket fence. Inside, textured white stucco walls and colorful tiled floors glistened. Fran loved those tiles. Each one, painted with a bouquet of yellow, red, and blue flowers, recreated an old-world feel and made for a bright and happy interior.

As content as Fran was with her own life, she was beginning to be very worried about the world outside her home, especially the political tensions between the Soviet Union and the United States. Nikita Khrushchev, the temperamental head of the Soviet Union, was making headlines every week. More recently, political friction was saturating the news on the airways on a daily basis. "A Cold War," it was called, but what did that mean? Fran began to fear the worst.

Chapter 50

Francine
Los Angeles, 1960–1963

The CIA escalated espionage missions in the skies over the Middle East and Russia. On May 1, 1960, the Soviets shot down and captured Francis Gary Powers, an American pilot flying a U-2 spy plane over Soviet airspace. The official statement from the White House was, "One of our planes had 'accidently' strayed off course."

Most people were skeptical of this account. But, as everyone was waiting for the next shoe to drop, fears about a war with Russia slowly faded. American attention now turned to the upcoming 1960 Presidential election. Nine candidates competed to be the thirty-fifth president.

Massachusetts-born John Fitzgerald Kennedy, the son of a wealthy and powerful Catholic family, was not only the youngest candidate at forty-three years old, but by far the most charismatic and the best looking.

In 1946, Kennedy threw his hat into the political ring and ran for the United States House of Representatives. He won, defeating ten other candidates. He then went on to beat his Republican opponent in the general election, taking 73 percent of the vote.

Kennedy served in the House for six years and then ran for the Senate against Republican Henry Cabot Lodge, who he defeated by seventy thousand votes. Now, with his glamorous wife Jackie by his side, running for President was a logical next step. Out of the eight other serious candidates, Lyndon Johnson, the Senate Majority Leader, seemed to be the one to beat.

The Democratic National Convention took place in Los Angeles on Monday, July 10, 1960. On the third day of the convention,

Kennedy won the party's nomination for President and Lyndon B. Johnson rounded the ticket as Vice-President. Milt and Fran, ardent Democrats, were glued gleefully to the television all night. Kennedy's acceptance speech was short and to the point.

It is with a deep sense of duty and high resolve I accept your nomination. I accept it with a full and grateful heart without reservation and with only one obligation, the obligation to devote every effort of body, mind, and spirit to lead our party back to victory and our nation back to greatness.

Two days later, John F. Kennedy addressed the nation. The last part of his speech was especially poignant and made a strong impression on Fran. Kennedy encouraged everyone to re-examine his or her own resolve and commitment when he asked:

Can a nation organized and governed such as ours endure? That is the real question. Have we the nerve and the will? Can we carry through an age where we will witness not only new breakthroughs in weapons of destruction, but also a race for mastery of the sky and the rain, the ocean and the tides, the far side of space, and the inside of men's minds?

Are we up to the task, are we equal to the challenge? Are we willing to match the Russian sacrifice of the present for the future, or must we sacrifice our future in order to enjoy the present? That is the question of the New Frontier. That is the choice our nation must make, a choice that lies not merely between two men or two parties, but between the public interest and private comfort, between national greatness and national decline, between the fresh air of progress and the stale, dank atmosphere of normalcy between determined dedication and creeping mediocrity. All of mankind waits upon our decision. A whole world looks to see what we will do. We cannot fail their trust. We cannot fail to try.

When his speech was over, Fran was exhilarated. The next morning, she showed up at the local Democratic headquarters and asked to volunteer. Working for the campaign was electrifying. Just thinking about all the synchronization required made her mind spin with excitement and wonder. She especially enjoyed meeting people from all walks of life who had come together for one singular purpose: to elect John Fitzgerald Kennedy as the next president.

Fortunately, the Los Angeles campaign was headquartered in the Biltmore Hotel, only a short bus ride from Fran's home. She went there often, and once, on a whim, took Irwin, who was now nine years old, with her. To her delight, Irwin really enjoyed the adventure. He spent the afternoon cheerfully stuffing envelopes, running errands, and generally helping out where he was needed.

On the bus drive home, Irwin asked his mother to tell him all about Kennedy and Fran was happy to oblige. She told Irwin everything she knew about John Kennedy and his family. It was hard to condense all the facts and information, so Fran tried to simplify the tale. She began to tell him the story.

"Kennedy's family came here from Ireland a long time ago. They lived in Massachusetts, which is not far from New York where you were born. Kennedy served in World War II just like your father and Uncle Mike did. John Kennedy was a very famous hero in the war and he saved the lives of a lot of sailors."

"How did he do that?" asked Irwin.

"It was when he was in the navy. Kennedy was in charge of a patrol boat that had torpedoes on it. It was a small boat and there were thirteen men on board. They were way out in the ocean past Hawaii. Their job was to patrol the seas and be on the lookout for enemy ships."

"But couldn't the enemy see them?" Irwin asked.

"No," Fran replied.

"Since Kennedy and his men were in such a small boat, they

were pretty much invisible. Anyway, it was very early in the morning and the sky was pitch black. *PT-109,* which was the name of Kennedy's boat, was on patrol in the South Pacific when a Japanese ship rammed it. Kennedy's boat was cut in half and all the men were thrown into the water. Kennedy knew he had to save his crew and find a safe place to take them until help could arrive."

"Did anyone die?" Irwin gasped.

"Yes. Two men were lost at sea. John Kennedy was a very good swimmer and one of his men was a famous boxer. His name was Barney Ross. Your grandfather and your Uncle Mike both knew Barney Ross and went to his boxing matches when we lived in Chicago."

Irwin gasped. "A famous boxer? Do you think Uncle Mike will tell me about him?"

Fran smiled. "I'm sure he will."

"So ,what did Mr. Kennedy and Barney Ross do? What happened next?"

"Kennedy saw a small island in the distance not far from the wreckage. He and Barney Ross took turns swimming, taking many trips back and forth to bring the crew to safety. Kennedy found a rotted-out canoe, pieces of candy, bits of crackers, and a small amount of drinking water which he rationed to his sailors. For the next five days, Kennedy and Barney Ross swam from island to island trying to find someone to help them.

On the sixth day, early in the morning while everyone was resting, eight islanders suddenly appeared through the thick palm trees. The men didn't know if the islanders were friendly, but luckily they were. They gave the men food and hid Kennedy and Ross in their canoe under a pile of large palm leaves. Then they took them to another island where they finally were able to make contact with a navy officer. John Kennedy and Barney Ross were both heroes."

"What happened after that?" Irwin asked.

"John Kennedy was in the hospital for a long time. When he was strong enough, he tried to go back and fight alongside his men, but his body was too injured. He was discharged from the navy and went back home to Massachusetts."

"I bet he didn't like that," Irwin commented.

"I bet he didn't," Fran replied. She looked up just in time to see that theirs was the next stop. "We're home," she said.

The Republican presidential nominee was Richard Nixon. And on September 26, 1960, he and John Kennedy began a series of groundbreaking debates.

Televising debates had never occurred in the history of presidential elections, and everyone was excited to watch. On the night of the first debate, Milt and Fran invited close friends to watch the event. Milt mixed up a batch of vodka gimlets and they ordered food from Chicken Delight.

The debate was riveting. The stark contrast between Kennedy and Nixon went beyond political ideology and campaign slogans. Nixon had a sinister look about him and his beady eyes and mannerisms made him appear insincere. In contrast, Kennedy exuded confidence, hope, and honesty.

While Nixon looked pale, tired, and sickly, Kennedy was tan, confident, and relaxed. When the debate was over, Milt switched off the television. Everyone agreed that Kennedy won the debate.

Two days before the election, on Sunday, November 6, the volunteers working out of the Biltmore were invited to a "get out and vote" rally. Fran brought Irwin with her. Hundreds, maybe thousands of volunteers were there. Sargent Shriver, who was married to John Kennedy's sister Eunice, and Robert Kennedy, John's brother and campaign manager, mingled through the crowd, thanking everyone for their hard work.

Robert Kennedy saw Fran in the crowd standing with her young son and he came over to them. He thanked Fran and showed her pictures of his own seven children, and encouraged

Irwin to pursue his dreams and continue to be active in the political process. Fran had never seen Irwin so enthusiastic before.
She was very grateful to Bobby for lighting a fire in her son's
heart and soul.

On November 8, when Irwin and Cheryl came home from
school, Fran took them with her into the voting booth. It was a
very solemn moment for all of them. After the polls closed,
everyone watched and waited as the returns trickled in. It wasn't
until early in the morning that the results were announced. John
Fitzgerald Kennedy had won.

On January 20, Fran and Milt hosted a small party. Friends
and fellow volunteers gathered in their small living room and
watched John Fitzgerald Kennedy give his inaugural address
from the eastern portico of the Capital.

The storm clouds were looming over D.C. and had been
dumping heavy snow onto the city streets, but miraculously
cleared up before the momentous event. Fran thought that was
a good omen. Chief Justice Earl Warren administered the oath
and John F. Kennedy gave an inspiring, hopeful, and brilliant
speech. The speech ended with:

> And so, my fellow Americans, ask not what your country can do
> for you, ask what you can do for your country. My fellow citizens
> of the world, ask not what America will do for you, but what to-
> gether we can do for the freedom of man.

Milt, Fran, and all their friends toasted to a future of renewed
hope, promise, and prosperity.

Chapter 51

Francine
Los Angeles, 1963

After the excitement of the election, life fell into a comfortable routine. Irwin graduated from Shenandoah Elementary. He wanted to go to John Burroughs Junior High where most of his friends were going.

Milt and Fran discussed their options and decided Irwin would do better if he didn't follow in his sister's footsteps. Fran needed to apply for an out-of-district transfer. She received notification that the school would be accepting a limited number of students and advised everyone to get in line early.

Milt and Fran got to the school at six o'clock in the morning, thinking they would be the first family in line. But, much to their dismay, there were already ten families ahead of them, camping out while waiting for the office to open. Milt wanted to leave, but Fran was insistent they stay. After five hours, they reached the front of the line. Three spots remained, and Irwin was accepted. Milt was not a happy camper. As they were walking back to the car, Milt said, "Irwin better work his ass off."

Irwin surprised everyone. He thrived at John Burroughs. In 1963, he became very interested in politics and current events and even got involved in student government.

November 22, 1963, began as just an ordinary Friday morning. Cheryl was rushing out the door to meet her friends at the corner bus stop. Milt left with Irwin, and dropped him off at school before heading to work.

After everyone left the house, Fran began her Friday morning cleaning routine. She usually had the radio on, but this morning, she decided to turn on her favorite soap opera, *Days of Our Lives*, while she was dusting and vacuuming. She turned on the TV and went into the kitchen to mop the floor.

A few minutes later, she heard a man's voice interrupting the scene. It was CBS news commentator Walter Cronkite.

From Dallas, Texas, the news flash is apparently official. President Kennedy died at 1:00 p.m., Central Standard time, 2:00 p.m. Eastern Standard time, some thirty-eight minutes ago. Vice President Johnson has left the hospital in Dallas, but we do not know to where he has been taken. Presumably, he will be taking the oath of office and become the thirty-sixth President of the United States.

Shakily, Fran walked into the living room and stared at the television screen in disbelief. She didn't know how long she had been standing there facing the screen, unable to move, when the phone rang and rang, until the obnoxious, repetitive sound jolted her back from her paralysis. She moved toward the receiver to pick up the phone. It was her friend Sally.

"Fran, are you watching television? Did you hear? Can you believe it?"

"No, I can't believe he's dead. It can't be true. How could someone do this? What kind of monster does something like this?" Fran replied.

"Do you think we should go to the school and pick up the boys?" Sally asked anxiously. Her son Mitch was in Irwin's grade and the boys were good friends.

"Sally, why don't you come here first and we can pick up the boys together. I don't want to sit here by myself," Fran confessed. She hung up the phone and a moment later, Milt called.

"Oh, Milt, I'm shaking all over. I just can't stop trembling. How evil does someone have to be to gun down someone's father?" Tactfully, Milt did not refer to Fran's slip of the tongue.

"Honey, we're all going to be fine," he said, trying to sooth her. "We'll all get through this. It is very sad. It's awful. But you're safe. The kids are safe. And I'll come home early."

"Thank you," Fran whispered.

Over the next couple of days, the details of the shooting and its deadly aftermath were replayed on television constantly. President Kennedy, hunching forward and slumping to his left. Jackie reaching toward one of the secret service agents who was trying to jump into the car as the motorcade sped away to the hospital.

Jackie stood next to Lyndon in her bloodstained, pink suit as Johnson was sworn in as the thirty-sixth President. Kennedy's casket was placed onto Air Force One for his final journey back to Washington.

Fran wanted to keep the children away from the television, but this was a time in history for all to remember. As they watched Jackie and her daughter Caroline kneel and pray at her father's casket, little John-John saluted. No one could hold back his or her tears.

Two days later, President Johnson spoke to the nation:

Mr. Speaker, Members of the House, Members of the Senate, my fellow Americans.

All I have I would have given gladly not to be standing here today. The greatest leader of our time has been struck down by the foulest deed of our time. Today, John Fitzgerald Kennedy lives on in the immortal words and works that he left behind. He lives on in the mind and memories of mankind. He lives on in the hearts of his countrymen. No words are sad enough to express our sense of loss. No words are strong enough to express our determination to continue the forward thrust that he began.

Johnson ended his speech with:

On the twentieth day of January in 1961, John F. Kennedy told his countrymen that our nation's work would not be finished in the first thousand days, nor in the life of this administration, nor even perhaps in our lifetime on this planet. John Kennedy said, 'Let us begin today.' Today in this moment of new resolve, I would say to all my fellow Americans, let us continue.

It was a powerful and a healing speech.

The capture of the assassin who killed Kennedy started seconds after the fatal shots were fired. An astute Dallas motorcycle policeman who was riding behind the presidential car, saw pigeons fly off the building of the Texas School Book Depository that was across the infamous grassy knoll.

Officer Baker turned, accelerated his motorcycle toward the entrance of the building, and began running up the stairs toward the roof. On the way up, he encountered the superintendent who informed him that an employee by the name of Oswald had come into the building earlier that morning. Baker called in a description of the potential suspect and continued his ascent toward the roof.

When Baker reached the sixth floor, he found boxes full of books which created a half-wall near an exterior window. A rifle with a telescopic scope lay hidden among the boxes. Now that the police had a description of the sniper, it was only a matter of time until he was caught.

The search intensified, and at 1:50 p.m., Oswald was found hiding in a Texas theatre. Oswald fired several shots at the arresting police officers, but was quickly overpowered. They handcuffed him, read him his rights, and threw the bastard into the squad car for transport back to the Dallas police station. Once again, everyone was glued to the television and Lee Harvey Oswald was the name everyone heard over and over again.

The expression, "Revenge is a dish best served cold," became more meaningful two days after President Kennedy's death. Jack Ruby, born Jacob Leon Rubenstein in the South Side of

Chicago in 1911, was a regular visitor to the Dallas Police Department. Ruby frequently brought donuts to the officers on official or unofficial business, and hosted them at his strip club on a regular basis. Besides the naked women who paraded through the club, Ruby always supplied free drinks to the men in blue.

On this occasion, when Jack Ruby walked into police headquarters on Sunday, November 24, at 11:21 a.m., Lee Harvey Oswald was being transferred from the city jail to the county jail. No one took a second look at the familiar Ruby.

Ruby moved quickly and decisively. Weaving through the maze of reporters and officials, he pulled out a .38 Colt Cobra from his pocket and shot Oswald in the stomach, killing him. The event was on live television with millions of people watching. The world was stunned.

Mike called Fran every Sunday morning at ten o'clock. The calls were usually short, but they kept brother and sister connected. Today, Mike sounded anxious.

"Fran. How are you doing? I mean, honestly?"

Fran began to weep. "It's horrible. I can't believe all this is happening.

Mike sighed. "I know. All I can think about is Dad."

"Me too."

Mike tried to sound more cheerful. "Well, I've got an interesting story for you. About a year before Dad was killed, Dad and I saw a boxer named Barney Ross. It was his first professional fight. Dad was very taken with him and they became friends."

"I vaguely remember that," Fran said.

Anyway, Ross had a good buddy who helped him train and was always around. His name was Jacob Rubenstein.

"That name sounds very familiar," Fran commented. "Jack Ruby?" Fran gasped.

"The same," Mike replied.

Fran suddenly felt a coldness come over her. With all the

craziness going on in the world, all the plots, the conspiracies, the deaths, it was probably better that nobody in the family admitted to any association with Jack Ruby.

"That's very interesting, Mike," Fran told her brother firmly. "And let's never mention it again."

"Fran, I'm sorry. I didn't mean to upset you. I just thought that you might find it pretty interesting."

"It is interesting," Fran replied. "I just don't want to ever talk about this again."

Mike quickly switched topics. "How are the Bar Mitzvah plans coming? Is Irwin doing well in Hebrew school?"

"Yes. Are you, Florence, and Jacklyn going to be able to come?"

"I will be there for sure. I'm not sure about bringing Florence and Jacklyn. It might be too expensive. But I'm coming," replied Mike.

"Great. I can't believe it's in a few months. It will be so good to see you."

"Got to go, Fran. Sorry if I upset you. You know I love you. Fran, you need to let it go," Mike said.

"I know," she responded. "Mike, I love you too. Talk soon."

The FBI left no lead unturned. Two weeks later, government agents tracked down Barney Ross, now sixty-three years old, and asked him about the connections he had with Ruby.

Several weeks later, Barney Ross testified before the Warren Commission as a character witness on Ruby's behalf. The honor code of loyalty from the hood was something that was to be taken very seriously!

Although Ross tried to put a positive spin on the facts, Ruby came across as an unstable man with a notorious short temper who frequently flew into rages and pummeled his victims into bloody messes.

Jack Ruby was convicted of Oswald's murder in 1964. Two years later, his death sentence was reversed to life in prison.

But Ruby's life sentence was moot, because on January 3, 1967, Jacob Leon Rubenstein died of cancer. Ironically, he died at Parkland Hospital in Dallas, the same hospital where President Kennedy was pronounced dead.

Barney Ross died of cancer on January 17, 1967, two weeks after the death of his childhood friend Jacob Rubenstein. Barney Ross will be remembered as an American hero. His boyhood friend will always be remembered as an assassin.

Chapter 52

Francine
Los Angeles, 1964–1967

Irwin was about to turn thirteen and Fran and Milt had an impressive Bar Mitzvah planned for him. Fran was looking forward to it enormously, especially because Mike was flying out for the occasion. He was coming two days early, so they would have plenty of time together before the festivities began.

Fran couldn't wait to see her brother. While Milt drove to the airport to pick Mike up, she put the finishing touches on dinner, ending with her mother's Russian cream and her own signature chocolate cake.

Finally, she heard familiar laughter echoing through the stairwell and ran to open the door. She felt like a little kid again. Mike looked wonderful, glowing, and strong. He wrapped Fran in a hug.

"Hi, Sis. It's so great to be here. How are you doing?"

"Great, now that you are here!" Fran beamed.

"So, when does the party start?" Mike asked.

"Right now!" Milt shouted. "What are you drinking?"

"Whatever you're pouring."

Fran gave her big brother another hug. "I wish you were staying longer, not just for four days."

Mike smiled at her. "Let's make every minute count!"

Irwin got home before Cheryl and was excited to see his uncle. Mike was equally excited to be with his nephew. When Cheryl came home an hour later, Mike went into Cheryl's room, and they chatted for almost two hours. Cheryl could talk to her uncle about anything and everything. They shared an unspoken bond.

Fran made a brisket with potato pancakes and applesauce for dinner. Afterwards, Milt took Mike to a nearby motel. Between the two-hour time difference and a couple of rounds of scotch, Mike was ready for bed.

The next few days were wonderful. Irwin and Cheryl adored having Mike visit. He was an attentive, caring uncle spending as much time with them as possible. He regaled Irwin, who was getting nervous about the upcoming celebration, with funny stories about his own Bar Mitzvah. And he had more long chats with Cheryl, listening to her teenage woes with patience and giving her excellent advice.

At last, it was Saturday, March 28, the day of the Bar Mitzvah. Fran had been planning everything for months, and she knew the day was going to be magical. Over a hundred people were coming to the event. A band had been hired as well as a magician to entertain the kids. Fran had splurged on everybody's clothes. Milt and Irwin had snappy new suits for the occasion. Cheryl was going to look like a princess in her pink suit for the service and her ivory satin and lace dress for the party.

The event was going to cost a fortune. They had been saving for three years, and it would take another year to pay it off. But Fran and Milt were proud that they were able to do this for Irwin. Once the Bar Mitzvah was over, they had to start planning for Cheryl's Sweet 16 party coming up in September. Fran mused that this was going to be a very expensive year, but completely worth it.

On Saturday morning, everyone got up bright and early, arriving at the temple at eight thirty. Milt and Mike sat on the dais. This was an honor given to the father and grandfather of the Bar Mitzvah boy. Since Fran's father and Milt's father had already died, Mike stepped into that role.

Irwin's Torah reading went well. His speech at the end of the service was thoughtful and moving. He talked about the importance of everyone being respectful, no matter what differences they might have. He also talked about the importance of paving your own path in life and following your dreams wherever they might lead. He thanked his parents and his sister. Irwin also thanked his uncle Mike for travelling from Chicago to be with him on his Bar Mitzvah day.

After the service, everyone went into the reception room for the breaking of the bread and sipping of the wine. Irwin recited the prayers for both. They ate fruit and pastries and went home to rest up before the evening celebration.

At five o'clock, they went back to the temple. The banquet room was decked out in a sports theme. The centerpieces, made out of Styrofoam, were in red, white, and blue, and balloons waved above the tables. The band played an array of both popular songs and nostalgic melodies. Hot dogs, burgers, fries, and soda were set up for the kids. The adults had ribeye steak, chicken, vegetables, and baked potatoes, along with a full bar. Cake and ice cream was served for dessert.

Lee and her girls, Joni and Rosie, came for the evening celebration. It was the first time in years that Mike, Lee, and Fran had all been together again. Seeing her handsome brother and lovely sister standing side by side, Fran found herself almost unbearably moved. Memories of the past they shared and the challenges they had survived together threatened to overcome her. It was a very special moment.

The last guests left a little after midnight. Fran, Milt, and Mike didn't want the evening to end so they all went to Cantor's Deli on Fairfax Boulevard.

Mike insisted on driving, which turned out to be a big mistake. When he turned onto Fairfax, he literally drove on the sidewalk, weaving around the lampposts. Fran and Milt were screaming as Mike pulled up right in front of the delicatessen with half the car on the road and the other half on the sidewalk. The car was inches away from the front glass door.

When the three of them got out of the car, they went into the restaurant and climbed into the largest booth they could find. They ordered breakfast and lots of coffee. Mike was not allowed to drive home!

Before Fran knew it, Monday morning had arrived, and Mike was going back to Chicago.

"I don't want to say goodbye," Fran told her brother.

"I know," Mike sighed. "I wish we lived in the same city. I hope you'll bring the kids to Chicago in July for Jacklyn's Sweet 16."

Milt and Fran looked at each other. "I don't think we'll be able to afford it," Fran confessed.

A couple of months later, an envelope arrived with three train tickets in it. The accompanying note from Mike read: "Pack your bags, you're going to Chicago!"

Fran, for a variety of reasons, had chosen not to tell the children how her father had died, but the truth finally came out on that visit to Chicago. Fran and the kids were invited to dinner at Flo and Mike's house, and Cheryl, as usual, ran upstairs to visit with her cousin Jacklyn. The two girls were in the bedroom, when suddenly Jacklyn pulled out a newspaper article from the desk drawer and held it out for Cheryl to read.

"I found this the other day," she said. "You might want to read it."

Curious, Cheryl picked up the paper. When she finished reading the article, her face was white. Jacklyn looked at her with concern, but Cheryl didn't speak. She threw the article on the bed, ran from the room, and found her mother in the kitchen.

"Why didn't you tell me?" she asked abruptly. "Why didn't you tell me that my grandfather was murdered?"

Mike saw Fran's eyes grow wide with terror and guilt, and he quickly took over. He took Cheryl's arm, led her into his office, and closed the door. Then he told her everything about those dark, painful days in 1931.

He explained why it was so difficult for him and his sisters to talk about their father's murder. Mike detailed how he witnessed the shooter and saw his father being gunned down. Then he shared his own story about his abduction, and the fact that to this day, he could still hear his father's voice yelling, "Mike, run!"

When Cheryl and Mike emerged from the office, it was clear that they had both been crying. Mike went outside for some air, and Cheryl walked toward her mother and wrapped her arms around her. "Mom, I'm so sorry. I didn't know how bad it really was."

The dam had finally cracked. The two of them cried until there were no more tears, and Fran promised Cheryl that when they got home, she would answer all her questions about her childhood. Fran knew the discussion would be difficult. But she also knew that her children had a right to know everything about their family history. This was a turning point for Fran. She felt as if she could finally let go of her pain.

When they got back home to California, Milt and Fran spoke with both Cheryl and Irwin about their grandfather's murder. In some ways, it was cathartic, but in other ways, it was excruciating. Fran was determined to let go of those dark days and release the pain still within her. She made a promise to herself that she would enjoy every single day of her life and never take anything for granted.

The next two years flew by. Cheryl was graduating high school with honors. She wanted to go to a four-year university, either UCLA or USC, which was where most of her friends were going. To her disappointment, Milt and Fran determined that they simply could not afford the cost. Cheryl ended up enrolling at LA Community College, finishing a two-year program in less than one year. She then went to work for a cardiologist in Inglewood.

Cheryl still lived at home, but there were definite tensions in the air. Fran knew her daughter was resentful because they had not saved up enough money for her education. Now she was craving independence. Fran suspected that very soon, Cheryl would either move into her own place or get married.

Fran's intuition was correct. At the beginning of 1967, Cheryl got engaged to a boy she had known for a couple of years. Marsh came from a good family and Cheryl seemed excited to start her life with him. Milt and Fran had their concerns because they were so young. They finally reconciled that this was what Cheryl wanted, so they began making wedding plans. Everyone was excited, even Milt.

The wedding was going to be held at the Ventura Club over Labor Day weekend. Cheryl's friends and cousins threw several bridal showers and she received almost everything she needed to complete her kitchen and bath. The kids were hopeful they would get enough cash to buy some furnishings.

Mike, Florence, and Jacklyn flew in from Chicago. Lee came with Joni and Rosie. The three cousins were Cheryl's bridesmaids. They were all hoping that being together would bring some happiness back into Lee's life. Sidney had died four years earlier, and his death had been hard on Lee and the girls. Lee was trying to rebuild their lives.

One hundred friends and family attended the wedding. The band played all the top hits. The Beatles song, "All You Need Is Love," played over and over again as champagne corks popped. A few of Marsh's friends shook the champagne bottles and sprayed as many people as they could. Then everyone in the room surrounded the couple with cheers and congratulatory wishes. At midnight, Cheryl tossed her bouquet and someone started throwing rice. The newlyweds had a plane to catch and whisked away, dragging strings of tin cans, to board their flight to Acapulco.

Chapter 53

Francine
Los Angeles, 1968

Nineteen sixty-eight was another election year and things were heating up in the political arena. It was now the middle of March and President Johnson still had not indicated whether he was going to seek another term. Everyone was on edge.

On Saturday, March 16, Robert F. Kennedy announced his candidacy for president. Irwin, Milt, and Fran sat around the television listening intently as Bobby made his announcement.

Fran was euphoric, remembering how kind Bobby had been to her and Irwin, and how he had shown her pictures of his own children. She felt almost as if he was part of her family! And now here he was, running for president.

Robert Kennedy's speech was inspirational and moving. He said he was running for the presidency not to oppose any man, but because he was convinced that the country was on a perilous course. Bobby wanted to end the bloodshed in Vietnam and close the gaps between black and white, rich and poor, and young and old. He believed he was the one who could make that happen.

The electricity and exhilaration that Bobby's speech generated gained him momentum for his campaign. Fran sensed a real movement underfoot. Bobby was determined to finish what his brother had started.

Fran decided she would help with the campaign as much as she could, even though she was now working at a demanding job in Beverly Hills as a legal secretary for the District Attorney. Irwin couldn't wait to volunteer. He'd caught the political bug from his mother and Fran was thrilled to see how enthusiastic he was about working for the campaign.

After Robert Kennedy made his announcement, the focus turned to President Johnson and whether he would commit to running for a second term. The last four plus years had taken a toll on him. Johnson was turning sixty in a few months and many believed another term of a discontented electorate and a divided Congress would be too much for him to endure. Rumor had it that Johnson feared the stress would kill him. He was convinced that he would die of a heart attack in his sixties just like his father, Samuel.

The following day, Johnson went on television and radio. In a very short speech, he announced that he would not seek or accept the nomination for another term as president.

Fran felt sorry for Johnson, having to take office after one of the most tragic and heinous assassinations in history. Johnson did what he could to step into Kennedy's shoes, but that was an unrealistic goal. Johnson's most impressive accomplishment was the passage of the Civil Rights Act in 1964. Unfortunately, his legacy will always be linked to the horror of Vietnam.

Now, Robert Kennedy was going to pick up the baton and finish what his brother Jack had started. Everyone was very hopeful that Bobby would win the presidency and there was excitement in the air.

Four days after Johnson's announcement, tragedy struck again. Another visionary leader, Dr. Martin Luther King Jr. was fatally shot in Memphis, Tennessee by James Earl Ray, an escaped convict. King was only thirty-nine.

Bobby Kennedy was a strong supporter of Dr. King and his work on civil rights. No one was surprised when Bobby recognized and honored Dr. King in an address to the nation shortly after the assassination. With controlled emotion, Bobby said:

What we need in the United States is not division; what we need in the United States is not hatred; what we need in the United States is not violence or lawlessness, but love and wisdom and compassion toward one another, and a feeling of justice toward those who still suffer within our country, whether they be white or they be black.

It was a beautiful speech and Fran felt more strongly than ever that Bobby Kennedy was the president this country needed.

Irwin, now seventeen, was the happiest Fran had ever seen her son. He was now working at Kennedy's headquarters on Wilshire Boulevard and was very excited about being part of Robert Kennedy's campaign. He had his own new car and the confidence and freedom it provided. He drove himself to campaign headquarters and was so busy there, that Fran and Milt hardly saw him anymore. He started eating dinner at Kennedy's headquarters and sometimes even slept there.

Bobby would often drop in to campaign headquarters for brief visits before flying around the state to speak at various venues. The first time Irwin saw Bobby at headquarters, he went up to him and told Bobby that he had met him many years earlier during his brother's campaign. He reminded Bobby that when they first met, Bobby had pulled out pictures of all of his children and showed them to him. Irwin didn't know whether Bobby remembered that, but Bobby said he did, and thanked Irwin for his loyalty and dedication to the Kennedys. Then Bobby added, "I've had a couple more kids since then, and another one is on the way."

Bobby Kennedy was not the only one with a new baby on the way. In May, Cheryl made the announcement that she was pregnant. Fran was delirious with excitement and she and Cheryl started going shopping for baby furniture and the layette. Cheryl registered at the Broadway Department Store where her Aunt Lee worked in cosmetics. After registering, they went to Lee's station and told her she was going to be a great aunt. Beaming with the news, Lee hugged and kissed both of them as customers looked on and clapped.

Cheryl wanted to keep the nursery neutral, filled with soothing colors. She decided on painting the walls a soft yellow. She then selected a three-piece, powder blue and white furniture set comprising of a crib, dressing table, and dresser. Cheryl was glad she selected it early, because it was made in Italy, and it was going to take a couple of months to arrive.

The baby was due at the beginning of October, so they still had plenty of time to get everything ready for this precious new arrival. As they were leaving the store, Cheryl told her mother that she had decided on a name. If the baby was a girl, she was going to name her Marni after her grandmother, Mary. Fran was deeply touched, and she knew how honored her mother would have felt.

Chaos reigned at Kennedy's campaign headquarters. Volunteers were tasked making phone calls, analyzing data, and canvassing neighborhoods. Campaign contributions were flowing in at record speed. The June 4th primary was just weeks away, and Irwin was working day and night.

On Friday, May 24, there was a huge benefit concert at the Los Angeles Memorial Sports Arena and Irwin was attending with a large group of friends. Some of the performers paying tribute to Bobby were Jack Lemmon, Shirley MacLaine, Gene Kelly, Sonny and Cher, Andy Williams, and the Byrds. The football player, Rosey Grier, was also going to be there.

More than fifteen thousand Kennedy campaign workers and supporters bought tickets, each costing $250. If you were a student, you could reserve a seat for five dollars. Milt and Fran wanted to go, but this was Irwin's moment, so they stayed home.

The event was televised and everyone was glued to the television. "Bobby for President" signs bobbed up and down through the crowds of loyal supporters. Fran and Milt searched to try and find Irwin. It was a futile exercise, but exhilarating to observe the combustive energy and enthusiasm roaring through the crowd. The event was a huge success and everyone felt more and more certain that Robert F. Kennedy was becoming unstoppable.

Four days later, on Tuesday, May 28, Bobby was going to speak in the Jewish Fairfax District. A podium and small stage were erected right in front of Canter's Delicatessen. The area between Third Street and Santa Monica Boulevard had been blocked off for the event. Bobby was going to speak at noon, and Irwin made arrangements for the three of them to sit with some of the campaign volunteers. They all wore campaign buttons and were fired up.

Bobby took the podium as huge cheers and chants echoed through the streets. When he began to speak, he put the entire audience under a spell with his warm smile and intoxicating Bostonian accent. Bobby believed in what he was saying, and he made everyone believe that victory was within his reach.

Over the next couple of weeks, Irwin finished the gift he had been working on for Bobby. He wanted to present it to Bobby after he won the California primary. It was a clear acrylic pillow. Irwin had designed it with the reverse image of Bobby's face painted on the inside. Once Irwin finished painting the portrait, he was going to seal the front and back plastic panels and then inflate it. He had been working on this project for at least a month and was close to finishing the portrait.

The campaign was now in the final stretch of the California primary. This was a must win for Bobby after losing the primary in Oregon to McCarthy. Irwin was spending eight to ten hours a day working on the campaign. He had found his passion. The pillow was done, and Irwin was planning on giving it to Bobby at the victory party.

On June 4, Irwin woke up bright and early. He wasn't going to school that day. He took a change of clothes with him, brand new blue slacks and blazer. He had been invited by the Kennedy family to come to the campaign suite at the Ambassador Hotel for the victory celebration.

As Irwin ran out the front door, he yelled, "Mom, Dad, make sure you vote early. And don't forget to look for me on television. I think I'm going to be standing near Rosey Grier. Don't wait up. I have no idea when I'll be home. This is going to be the best day of my life!" He bolted out the door, letting it slam behind him.

Fran and Milt were excited beyond words that Irwin was doing something he loved. They had never expected their son to get involved in politics. And they certainly never imagined that their seventeen-year-old-son would be presenting Robert Kennedy with an acyclic pillow that he had designed and made. Milt and Fran felt as if their hearts were going to burst from pride and joy.

As soon as Irwin left, Milt and Fran went to their polling station and cast their votes for Robert Kennedy. As the polls closed, voters turned on their television sets. Milt and Fran invited a few friends to come over for cocktails and dessert. They settled in for what they knew would be a glorious celebration.

Around ten o'clock, everyone went home, although the count was still coming in. Milt and Fran decided to stay up until they knew for sure that Robert Kennedy had won California. Things were looking good, but nothing had been officially called. Eventually, Milt took himself to bed and Fran dragged herself off the couch to follow.

As she was turning off the television, Fran heard it announced that Kennedy was the projected winner. Fran wanted to hear Bobby's victory speech, but her eyelids were getting very heavy and she went to bed. For some reason though, Fran couldn't sleep. She finally climbed out of bed and brewed herself a cup of chamomile tea.

While Fran was sipping her tea, the phone rang. At first she thought she hadn't turned off the stove and that the sound was the teapot whistle. But then she realized the ring was coming from the living room. Her heart stopped. Fran ran to the phone and saw Milt in the hallway. "Who the hell is calling us so late?"

Fran picked up the receiver. It was her friend Millie. "Fran, are you watching television?"

"No. What's wrong? What happened?"

"Milt," she yelled. "Turn on the TV."

Milt flicked the television on. A news announcer was saying somberly, "Robert Kennedy has been shot along with five others."

Fran felt as if she was going to pass out. Her knees shook and she dropped the phone.

Numbly, Milt picked up the receiver. "Hello?"

"Milt," Millie said, sounding desperate. "I just wanted to make sure you knew."

"Yes," Milt replied. "We just saw it on television. Kennedy has been shot."

There was a long, terrible pause.

"Milt, I'm afraid it is worse than that. There were others shot too." Millie could barely get the words out. "I think one of them may have been Irwin."

Milt struggled to keep his voice even. "Thank you, Millie." He hung up the phone.

Fran was staring at him. "What did she say?"

Quietly, Milt told her the news, and Fran began to scream. "No! Not my son! Not my son!"

As Milt tried to comfort her, the phone rang again. It was Cheryl. She had also heard the news and was coming right over.

Fran and Milt sat side by side on the sofa, waiting in silence.

Fran was crying, then she wailed, "No! Not my son! Oh my God, not my son! Please don't let him die. Don't let him die!"

Chapter 54

Irwin
Los Angeles, June 4, 1968

E arlier that day, Robert Kennedy was sitting on the couch in his fifth floor suite in the legendary Ambassador Hotel as the election results began to trickle in. It took hours until the final results were counted: Kennedy: 46 percent and McCarthy: 42 percent. Everyone was ready to jump out of his or her skin with exuberance. Bobby won California!

At the stroke of midnight, Bobby, with Ethel by his side, his boyish smile brimming with glee and relief, walked into the ballroom. With wit, humor, and enthusiasm, Bobby delivered his victory speech.

"My fellow Americans, I think we can end the divisions within the United States. What I think is quite clear, is that we can work together. We are a great country, a selfless and a compassionate country. Thank you all for your support and hard work. Now on to Chicago and let's win!"

Irwin listened to the roar of the crowds followed by boisterous cheers. The plan was for Bobby to walk through the ballroom, shaking hands and thanking his supporters. But seconds before Bobby's speech ended, two campaign aides surveyed the room and determined that there was no way Bobby and his entourage could navigate through the massive crowd. A decision was made. Bobby would leave the podium and go behind the gold curtains that led to an anteroom, and then to a narrow hallway connected to the kitchen pantry. A handful of staffers and a couple of reporters followed Bobby, who was in the lead.

When Irwin arrived at the hotel around six o'clock that evening, he was assigned to stand in front of the double doors that led to the kitchen pantry. When Bobby's speech ended, someone yelled out, "Irwin, follow us!" When Irwin got the signal, he wove himself into the procession line. Rosey Grier and Ethel followed the entourage near the back of the pack.

The group, with Bobby near the front of the line, proceeded through the double doors. Bobby looked back to find Ethel, then turned to shake the hand of a kitchen worker. Irwin was now about ten feet behind Bobby when he heard a popping noise and saw a small puff of smoke filtering up toward the pantry ceiling. At first, Irwin thought it was a firecracker, similar to the one that went off the day before, while Kennedy's motorcade drove through Chinatown. Within seconds, there was a series of more popping sounds. Staffers, standing behind Irwin, double-backed toward the doors. The orderly procession crumbled and people began to scream.

"Someone's shooting!"

"Take cover!"

"Look out!"

"There's a madman in here and he is trying to kill us all!"

"Get a doctor! Get a doctor! Bobby's been shot!"

"Get the son of a bitch!"

"Get the gun. Get the gun!"

Two security staffers instinctively grabbed the shooter's neck and tried to grapple the gun from his hand. They repeatedly pounded his fist against a stainless steel serving table as the revolver kept firing pop, pop, pop.

Two more security men shoved the shooter against another table. Rosey Grier came flying through the air, tackling and pinning the gunman to the ground. Rafer Johnson, the Olympic gold medalist and several other men jumped on the pile and were able to break the shooter's index finger, finally freeing the gun from his clutches. In an instant, someone's hands were around the gunman's throat. Then a scream, "Keep him alive! Don't kill him! We want him alive!"

The impact of the bullets propelled Bobby backward flat on his back. His eyelids fluttered, closed, and then opened, as if he was blinking into a sun-streaked sky. The first bullet went through Kennedy's skull and lodged into his brain. Another bullet pierced his armpit and lodged near the base of his neck. The third bullet smashed through his mastoid bone, angling into his brain.

Juan Romero, the seventeen-year-old kitchen busboy who had shaken Bobby's hand moments earlier, bent down and cradled Bobby's head. Bobby opened his eyes and asked, "Is everybody safe?" Romero whispered, "Yes. Everything is going to be okay."

Everyone clustered around, trying to help. Someone took off the senator's shoes and loosened his collar. Someone else pressed a rosary into his hands. Kennedy, aware of the precious beads, clutched them over his heart. His mouth began to move in silent prayer.

Ethel fought her way through the crowd. Someone kept shouting, "Make way, make way!"

As Ethel was hurrying toward her husband, she caught sight of a young boy lying on the ground, his body covered with blood. Impulsively, she stopped, knelt down, and gently kissed the top of his head. The young boy was Irwin.

Then straightening back up, Ethel made her way to Bobby's side.

Four other victims were sprawled out on the concrete kitchen floor. Paul Schrade, William Weisel, Elizabeth Evans, and Ira Goldstein had each taken a bullet from the assassin's revolver.

Police were surging through the ballroom, busting through the crowd toward the kitchen pantry. Ambulances were pulling alongside the hotel's vestibule. People were running outside as firefighters and paramedics rushed in toward the victims.

A swarm of police officers flew on top of the restrained shooter and pried him from the tight grip of his captors. The police cuffed him and ran downstairs past a mass of volunteers. Voices were yelling, "Kill him! Get the bastard! Lynch him, lynch him!" The shooter was thrown into a squad car and hauled away.

Central Receiving admitted Kennedy. When the emergency room physician saw Bobby's listless body and ashen face, he slapped Bobby's face, yelling in despair, "Bob, Bob." Another doctor massaged Kennedy's heart while Ethel held Bobby's hand. When the doctor got an audible heartbeat, he handed the stethoscope to Ethel so she could also hear her husband's beating heart. Kennedy needed more care than what was available at Central Receiving. Moments later, he was transferred by ambulance to Good Samaritan Hospital, four blocks away.

When Ted Kennedy got the call, he immediately boarded an Air Force jet and flew to Los Angeles. Jackie Kennedy, the Shrivers, the Lawfords, and the Smiths did the same. At the family's request, Vice President Herbert Humphrey flew in a renowned neurosurgeon from Boston to try and save Bobby's life.

The team of surgeons removed the bullet fragments and assessed the injuries to Bobby's brain, vital arteries, and cerebellum. They were not optimistic that he would survive. While in the recovery room, Ethel climbed onto an adjoining surgical table and lay down next to her husband.

The country and the world waited for updates and news. Minutes merged into hours, and hours into a new day. It was Thursday, June 6th. At Bobby's bedside, Ethel, Jackie, Ted, Pat, and the Smiths prayed.

Again, the course of history was changed.

Chapter 55

Fran
Los Angeles, June 5–8, 1968

Cheryl ran through the front door. "They've taken all the injured victims to Central Receiving!" she said urgently. "Dad, call them and see if Irwin is there!"

"I already did. They said they couldn't release any information."

Fran was wringing her hands. "He's there. I know he's there, Milt. I can't live through this again. I can't." Milt grabbed Fran and helped her down the stairs into the car.

Milt drove down Wilshire Boulevard, not stopping for a single red light. Fran couldn't speak. She tried to form some words, but her thoughts did not pass through her lips. Cheryl kept whispering in her mother's ear, "Mom, Irwin is fine. Irwin is fine. I just know it." Then she gently stroked her mother's cheek. The only movement Fran was able to make was to grab Cheryl's hand and bring it to her lips, gently kissing her soft fingers.

Fran knew they were getting close to the hospital when ambulance after ambulance whizzed by them. Police cars followed suit. Milt tailgated an ambulance as it pulled alongside the emergency room entrance. They flew out of the car, but the emergency bay had been barricaded, so they had to navigate through the hundreds of people who were standing hand-in-hand, waiting for news about Bobby's condition.

Adrenaline pushed them through the mass of onlookers. Fran felt like a zombie lurching, but a glimpse of Cheryl struggling through the crowds brought her back to reality. She stepped ahead to shield her daughter, struggling toward the main entrance, yelling, "Let us through. Let us through! My son was shot with Senator Kennedy. Please let us through."

A line of police officers blocked the doors. Milt talked to the officers and they let them into the lobby. Fran, Milt and Cheryl raced up to the front desk.

"My son, Irwin Stroll, was shot with Robert Kennedy," Fran said breathlessly. "We saw him on TV being carried out. We know all the victims were sent here. Please tell us where he is!" Milt and Fran shouted over the commotion.

The woman at the front desk did not have the names of the victims. She pointed in the direction of the emergency room entrance and the family hurried over, just as the double doors swung open.

Milt yelled out, "My son is here! He was shot with Robert Kennedy. His name is Irwin Stroll. Where is he? Is he alive?"

"You'll need to look for yourself," a panicky nurse said as she rushed by a gurney. "I can't help you."

The family split up. There were three different treatment areas, each draped with a gray hospital curtain. As they each passed a closed cubicle, they pulled back the curtain looking for Irwin. Milt kept doing this until he found his son. Irwin was alive, sitting in a wheelchair with his left leg propped up. His blue pants were soaked in blood. The left trouser leg had been ripped from his ankle to his groin, exposing the heavy bandages soaked in red, clotted blood. Milt urgently yelled out to Fran and Cheryl, "I found him! He's right here." Fran and Cheryl rushed to where Milt was standing.

Irwin stared blankly at the wall, his eyes hollow. Fran hugged him and pulled his chin up so he could look at her. His eyes were flickering.

"Milt, he's in shock."

"I'll find a doctor," Cheryl said, and ran out of the cubicle. She cornered a nurse and quickly explained the situation. The nurse told Cheryl to contact their own doctor and to get Irwin into one of the ambulances lined up outside. Fortunately, Milt had a very close friend who was a prominent cardiologist. Milt called him and was told to get Irwin to Midway Hospital. He said he would get an orthopedic surgeon there as soon as possible.

Milt walked outside to beg one of the ambulance drivers to take Irwin to Midway. There were at least twenty ambulances lined up, and Milt pleaded with each driver. The response was always the same. "We cannot release any ambulance until Senator Kennedy is transferred."

Finally, Milt went over to the ambulance that had just pulled into the lineup. He explained to the driver that his son had been shot with Kennedy and he needed to be taken to Midway Hospital for emergency surgery. At that moment, one of the emergency room nurses wheeled Irwin out and said, "This boy needs to be transferred to Midway." The paramedics put Irwin on a stretcher and lifted him into the ambulance. Milt, Fran, and Cheryl jumped in and the ambulance took off, sirens blasting.

When they arrived at the hospital, three FBI agents, already informed of the events, greeted them. Irwin was placed on a stretcher and taken away. The surgeon introduced himself and told the family he would come out to speak to them when he had more information.

A security guard escorted the family to a waiting room. A few minutes later, two FBI agents joined them. They told Milt that two other agents had gone into the operating room so they could retrieve the bullet from Irwin's leg. The bagged bullet was tagged and identified and handed over to the agent, who took it directly to FBI headquarters.

Fran lay collapsed in a chair in the waiting room. Cheryl's color had changed from rosy to pale gray. Holding her belly, she confessed she was experiencing some ominous cramping. She was afraid she might lose the baby.

Milt found a nurse to check Cheryl out. A kind, middle-aged redhead took Cheryl's blood pressure and then reassured Cheryl that the baby was fine. The nurse moved the family into a private waiting room with a couch so they could be more comfortable.

Irwin's surgery lasted for six hours. A hospital administrator and an FBI agent shared the waiting room with them as he received "unofficial" updates on Kennedy's condition. Nothing had really changed. Kennedy was still clinging to life.

It had been just over twenty-eight hours since the shooting. Irwin was asleep in his room and Fran, Milt, and Cheryl were by his bedside. The hospital administrator tapped on the door and signaled them to meet him in the hallway.

"Robert Kennedy died at 1:44 a.m. They have not released it yet to the public. I thought you would want to know."

Fran stood motionless, barely able to breathe. Then the dam finally burst. She cried until she was gasping for air. Milt and Cheryl's faces were also wet with tears. The FBI agent turned his face away from the family and slipped on his sunglasses; he was also crying.

The following morning, Milt called Mike. After getting the details, Mike insisted on flying to Los Angeles. Milt promised he would call him after Irwin was out of surgery. Milt knew that if he needed Mike, he would come in a heartbeat.

When the public was informed, the official statement read:

Senator Robert Francis Kennedy died at 1:44 a.m. today, June 6, 1968. With Senator Kennedy at the time of his death were his wife, Ethel, his sisters, Mrs. Patricia Lawford, Mr. and Mrs. Stephen Smith, and Mrs. John F. Kennedy. Robert Frances Kennedy was 42 years old.

Bobby's body was flown back to New York City where he lay in repose at St Patrick's Cathedral. The following day, on June 8th, mass was held, followed by his burial. Ted Kennedy eulogized his older brother:

My brother need not be idealized or enlarged in death beyond what he was in life. He will be remembered simply as a good and decent man who saw wrong and tried to right it, saw suffering and tried to heal it, saw war and tried to stop it. Those of us who loved him and who take him to rest today, pray that what he was to us and what he wished for others will someday come to pass for the entire world. As he said many times, in many parts of this nation, to those he touched and who sought to touch him: 'Some men see things as they are and say why. I dream things that never were and say why not.'

In Los Angeles, Sirhan Bishara Sirhan was charged with the murder of Robert Frances Kennedy. Two days later, Irwin was subpoenaed to testify before the grand jury about the shooting. Because he was a minor, Milt was permitted to accompany him with two FBI agents.

When Irwin and Milt arrived at the courthouse, a gaggle of reporters flashed their cameras, capturing Milt wheeling Irwin into the courtroom. Milt waited in the hall while Irwin testified and was dismissed. Then the two FBI agents transported Irwin back to the hospital.

The next day, a picture of Milt pushing Irwin in the wheelchair was published in the newspaper. Calls from family, friends, and the press flooded in for weeks. Overwhelmed, Fran felt as if she was functioning on automatic pilot, and Milt worried she was heading toward a nervous breakdown.

Irwin had a very nasty-looking scar from his knee down to his ankle. He lost quite a bit of muscle, but the doctors were hopeful that, because of his age, he would regain the strength in his leg in time. Milt and Fran were so grateful to all the doctors and nurses for the care Irwin received. Irwin was coming home!

Fran brought flowers and boxes of See's candy to give to the nurses and doctors. She attached a handwritten note on each box expressing gratitude for the wonderful care their son received.

Mike called every day. He could tell, just from hearing his

sister's voice, how she was coping. Fran assured Mike she was able to muster the strength necessary to care for her son. In a strange way, as Irwin was healing, so was Fran.

Chapter 56

Irwin
Los Angeles, 1969–1994

The six months after the shooting proved difficult for Irwin. His coworkers at the Democratic headquarters were supportive, visiting him almost every day. But even with the love and support, summer dragged for Irwin. He fell into a deep depression and refused to come out of his room. Fran did everything she could to prevent him from sinking into that dark hole she herself had experienced after her father's death.

Eventually, Irwin was out of the wheelchair and walking with a cane, slowly gaining more strength in his leg. The bullet caused a lot of damage to his muscles and arteries as it travelled from his ankle up to his knee. Physical therapy was helping with his recovery.

When he finished with his therapy, Irwin began making more of an effort to rejoin the human race. He decided to delay going to college for a year and was offered a job at an art and frame shop in Beverly Hills. He liked the work and especially enjoyed the shop's movie star clientele. In his spare time, he spent as much time as he could with his little niece, Marni, born four months after the shooting.

The Sirhan Sirhan trial started at the beginning of January 1969. It was difficult to ignore or block out, especially when Irwin was served with another subpoena to appear and testify as a witness for the People of the State of California.

On Friday, February 21st, Milt and Fran went with Irwin to the courthouse. As they climbed the concrete steps, they took a moment to look at the marble sculpture of the Scales of Lady Justice, perfectly balanced on both sides of her shoulders. Sitting on the very top of the sculpture was a watchful and inquisitive bald eagle.

Milt and Fran signed in at the reception desk. Two police officers escorted them into an empty courtroom. They waited for about an hour. At 10:00 a.m. the bailiff came in and escorted Milt and Fran into the gallery. Irwin was sitting next to the District Attorney.

Judge Ellis entered the room and took the bench. The judge was probably in his early sixties. He had gray streaks filtering through his meticulously groomed hair. Under his black robe, which was not zipped all the way up, Fran could see a blue striped tie with a perfect Windsor knot. Judge Ellis maintained a stern, no-nonsense glare as he gazed over his courtroom. Everyone was quiet.

The jurors entered and took their seats in the jury box. The court stenographer was seated adjacent to the witness stand. Her fingers were positioned over the chorded keyboard, ready to capture every spoken word.

Judge Ellis sat behind a raised, beautifully carved walnut desk. The front panel of the desk had carvings of the scales of justice. Under the panel was a carving in Latin, "*Actori incumbit onus probandi.* The burden of proof lies on the plaintiff."

The judge began to speak. "People versus Sirhan Sirhan. Let the record show the parties and counsel are present and the jury is in the jury box. You may begin your examination, Mr. Fitts."

"Your Honor, the people call Mr. Irwin Stroll."

Irwin stood up. The sheriff asked Irwin to take a seat in the witness stand. The clerk asked Irwin to raise his right hand.

"Mr. Stroll, do you solemnly swear the testimony you are about to give is the truth, the whole truth, and nothing but the truth, so help you God?"

"I do."

The prosecutor began his questioning. "Mr. Stroll, are you the victim alleged in Count III of this indictment, sir?"

"Yes, I am," Irwin, replied. The questioning continued.

"Directing your attention to the primary election in California on June 4, 1968, did you have occasion to go to the Ambassador Hotel that day?"

"Yes, I did."

"Mr. Stroll, can you summarize for me why you were at the hotel that evening?"

Irwin began to tell his story.

"I was a campaign volunteer for Robert Kennedy. I worked at the main headquarters on Wilshire Boulevard and I participated in many of the campaign events in California.

On June 4th, I arrived at the Ambassador Hotel at 6:00 p.m. I was assigned to stand in front of the doors leading to the kitchen pantry. My job that night was to prevent any unauthorized people from going beyond those doors. I stayed in front of the doors until the senator finished delivering his victory speech to the crowd.

I had been invited to go up to the senator's suite after his victory speech was over. I was told that I would be given a signal to follow the entourage when the senator left the podium, and that is what I did."

"Mr. Stroll, what happened next?" asked Mr. Fitts.

"When Bobby left the podium, Joe, one of the campaign workers, signaled me to follow him. We went behind the curtain to the anteroom and walked down a hallway leading to the kitchen. I was about ten to twelve feet behind Senator Kennedy when I heard a loud pop. The procession stopped. Then I heard five more pops. The line came to a full stop and I saw smoke rising toward the ceiling.

I felt like someone had kicked me in my left leg, between my knee and my ankle, and I fell to the floor. I looked toward my leg and saw that my left pant leg was soaked in blood. The next thing I remember is that I was carried out of the hotel, put in a taxicab, and taken to Central Receiving. I had surgery to remove the bullet from my leg later that morning."

"I have no further questions, Your Honor," stated Mr. Fitts.

"Anything further, gentlemen?" asked Judge Ellis.

"No, Your Honor," the attorneys said in unison.

"You may be excused, Mr. Stroll," said Judge Ellis.

Irwin did not move. He tilted his head down and closed his eyes. The courtroom was silent for several minutes. Then the judge spoke.

"Mr. Stroll, are you alright?"

After a few seconds, Irwin responded

"Yes, Your Honor."

"Take your time Mr. Stroll. I'm calling a ten-minute recess."

As the judge stood up, the bailiff said, "All rise."

Irwin stood up, stepped down from the witness box, and slowly walked toward the back of courtroom. His head was down. There were tears trickling down his face. He looked pale and broken.

Milt and Fran guarded Irwin from the onlookers as they walked to the car. No one said anything until they were safely in the car.

"I just want to go home," Irwin said. "I don't want to talk about it. This is something I'm going to have to learn to live with the rest of my life. Thanks for coming with me. I love you." They drove home in silence.

On April 17, 1969, Sirhan Sirhan pleaded guilty. Less than a week later, he was sentenced to death. His sentence was commuted three years later to life in prison after the California Supreme Court invalidated all pending death sentences imposed prior to 1972.

From that time to the present, Sirhan has been denied parole more than fifteen times. Over the years, even though Irwin wanted to lock those memories away, he appeared at several parole hearings and presented his witness statement, encouraging and pleading the parole board not to release this murderer.

Life went on with Irwin returning to work at the art store and gallery in Beverly Hills. Eventually, he got an apprenticeship with a well-known interior designer who had an A-list of clients ranging from actors and agents, to musicians and Olympic athletes. After a year, he was doing well enough to move into his own apartment.

In December of 1970, Cheryl gave birth to a baby boy, Bryan. The family was growing and they were all moving forward. They didn't talk about the assassination.

In January of 1974, Fran left her job at the district attorney's office. One of Irwin's clients was a family friend of the Getty's, and Fran was approached about the possibility of working as Jacqueline Getty's personal assistant.

Jackie's husband, George Getty, was the son of the oil billionaire John Paul Getty. He had died several years ago of a cerebral hemorrhage and Jackie never remarried. Fran was intrigued with the prospect of working for a billionaire and went to the Getty mansion to interview for the position.

Mrs. Getty and Fran hit it off right from the beginning. Jackie had obviously done a lot of research into her prospective employee. She knew all about Irwin's story and his connection to the Kennedy campaign, and was kind enough to inquire how Irwin was doing.

Fran got a tour of the house and the office she would be working in. Most of the work involved replying to correspondence and assisting staff in making arrangements for travel and accommodations. Jackie also said she might ask Fran to be a companion to her ten-year-old daughter when she travelled out of the country. Even though Jackie had security staff, she wanted to make sure her daughter had someone with her whom she was comfortable with. The pay was much more than Fran was making with the DA and she accepted the position instantly. Jackie was very generous, and Fran loved working for her.

The months turned into years. Irwin became one of the most

sought-out interior designers in Los Angeles. He was published in numerous design magazines, including *Architectural Digest* and *Designer's West*. His confidence was infectious, and his joy in what he was doing was palpable.

After all he had gone through, Milt, Fran, and Cheryl were very grateful to see that Irwin was so happy and so respected.

Fran's heart burst with pride and happiness.

Chapter 57

Irwin
Los Angeles, 1986

"Mom, I am going to beat this. I have the most renowned infectious disease doctor at UCLA. He's working directly with doctors in Boston and around the world to find a cure. Mom, I feel fine and I'm strong."

"Irwin, this is what Rock Hudson died from last year. How could you have let this happen? Why, why, why?" Milt blurted.

Fran was hit by a shock wave. The room began to spin. HIV! She grabbed the back of the sofa, then sat down.

"No! My son couldn't have this disease. Why?"

"Mom, what's wrong?" Cheryl panicked as she ran into the kitchen to get Fran a cold compress for her head. Irwin and Milt stopped talking and helped her into the bedroom to lay down. They shut the lights and closed the bedroom door, but Fran could still hear them talking about her.

"Dad, I think Mom could be heading for a nervous breakdown," said Irwin.

Then Milt added, "This was something we were all concerned about after you were shot. But it didn't happen then and it won't happen now because she knows you need her. You know your mother, she'll do everything she can to get you well. She is stronger than you think."

Fran heard their conversation through the thin walls of their apartment, but this time, there was nothing she could do to help Irwin. He'd contracted AIDS.

The following year, Lee died. Once the cancer spread, it was too late to do anything. Fran helped Lee as much as she could during her final months. Sometimes, as Fran stroked Lee's face or gave her a glass a water to drink, Fran saw her mother's image as she was dying. The resemblance between mother and daughter was uncanny.

Fran didn't want Lee to suffer anymore from the cancer that raged through her sister's body. Unlike Mike and Fran, Lee never spoke about her father's murder. She kept all her grief and anger hidden away deep in her soul. Fran hoped her sister was now at peace and was reunited with her beloved Sidney.

In 1988, as the twentieth anniversary of Robert F. Kennedy's death approached, interest grew once again about that fateful day in June 1968. Several reporters interviewed Irwin, and on April 22, his account of that day, along with Irwin's picture, appeared in the Friday edition of the *Los Angeles Times*.

Right around the same time, Irwin received a personal invitation from Senator Ted Kennedy to attend the twenty-year memorial for Robert Kennedy in Washington, D.C. Ted Kennedy also extended his invitation to Milt, Fran, and Cheryl.

Irwin was honored and ecstatic with the personal invite directly from the senator, but the invitation also brought back a deluge of memories, both good and bad. He decided that they would all go out to dinner and make plans for their trip to D.C. Fran was thrilled that Irwin had received this honor, but Milt was concerned and worried that those painful memories might resurface.

Irwin picked everyone up, and the family went to Lawry's for dinner. They each ordered the same thing—prime rib. As they were waiting for their food, Irwin began telling them about their upcoming trip.

"Mom, Dad, I have everything arranged. We will be flying to D.C. on the first of June and we will spend five days in Washington, exploring all the sites. Senator Kennedy's office is providing us a liaison and will act as our guide, giving us private access to the historical sites. His assistant also asked me if I

wanted to go to Bobby's gravesite by myself in the morning before the official service. I said I wanted to do that."

"Irwin, are you going to be alright reliving this?" Fran asked.

"Mom, I'm thirty-seven years old. That horrible day will be
with me the rest of my life," said Irwin. "I think going to the
gravesite before the actual service will allow me to grieve in private. I need to do this, Mom. Maybe it will finally give me clo-
sure. The best part will be that the four of us will all be together.
I'm so glad Cheryl will be coming with us."

Before they knew it, they were on the flight to D.C. Fran was
so proud of Irwin and was grateful he wanted them to be with
him at the memorial celebration. They were honored the
Kennedy family gave them the opportunity to remember and
pay tribute to Bobby.

They filled their days leading up to the memorial service
with sightseeing trips to the Capital and eating at some fabulous
restaurants. Their emotions were mixed with the excitement of
D.C. and the sadness of why they were there.

A car arrived at their hotel to take Irwin to Arlington National Cemetery for a private moment to visit Bobby's grave.
When Irwin returned several hours later, he wanted to be left
alone.

They went to Arlington for the memorial service held at twi-
light. When they arrived at the gravesite, a crowd of people had
formed on a hillside beyond the sectioned-off area where the
family and invited guests would be sitting. Irwin showed his
pass and they were escorted to the second row of chairs. All of
Bobby, John, and Ted's children and many of the grandchildren
were in the first row. Irwin, Fran, Milt, and Cheryl were in the
second row, behind the Kennedys.

As the remembrance to honor Robert F. Kennedy began,
everyone stood up. The young man who was standing in front
of Cheryl turned around and asked, "Am I blocking your view?"
Cheryl responded, "No, not at all." Then Cheryl turned to her

mother and whispered, "That is John F. Kennedy, Jr."

The speeches and stories that were shared by Bobby's children and family brought smiles, laughter, and tears to all of the onlookers. When Bobby's son Joseph walked up to his father's unassuming grave and began speaking, the crowd was silent.

"On behalf of my family, I want to thank all of you for still caring. Twenty years after my father's death, all of us in our family share with countless others those precious moments of my father's public life, and those moments seem especially clear as we stand here at his grave tonight."

Joseph's speech was very moving. He spoke of his father's concern for all minorities and all Americans who were struggling. He spoke of the hopes and dreams Bobby wanted for all children. As each Kennedy approached the microphone, the emotional stories continued with grace and dignity.

Fran kept glancing at Irwin and saw he was emotional and moved. She wondered what he was thinking. It was a beautiful but sad service under the warm moist air. Most of the onlookers were still crying as they walked away from Bobby's gravesite. Later that night, they got calls from California saying that they saw Cheryl on television sitting behind John F. Kennedy, Jr.

The following year, Cheryl remarried. Fran and Milt were thrilled! Steve was a neighbor of theirs when they lived on Shenandoah Street in 1958. The two of them met again at Santa Monica Beach by chance in 1965 when Cheryl was seventeen. Soon after, Steve joined the Air Force and was sent to Turkey and they lost contact. Twenty-four years later, the two of them reunited. This time they made sure they got married.

Fran tried to keep her emotions intact, but found her mind wandering to a dark place. She couldn't stop thinking about Irwin's fight against his dreadful disease. She couldn't stop thinking about the possibility of losing him. His doctor was one of the best in the country. She prayed every night that the doctors would find a cure for her son and all the other sons and daughters afflicted with AIDS.

The AIDS virus invaded every cell of Irwin's body. At first, the effects were subtle and hardly noticeable. But as one year ended and another year began, Irwin's strong muscular physique started to diminish. He lost weight, and his face looked drawn and tired. But he continued pushing forward, determined to beat the disease. They all tried to keep positive. But as the disease raged on, Irwin's decline could no longer be denied.

As 1994 drew to a close, so did Irwin's life. He was in the final stages of his illness, and the disease metastasized into Kaposi Sarcoma. Irwin was going to die. Flashbacks of her father's death invaded Fran's dreams. Irwin knew that the last gift he could give his parents was to allow them to be near him. This was not something he would normally have done. Cheryl knew that the only way her parents could survive losing Irwin was to be there with him. They all tried to help Irwin as much as they could.

Irwin was extremely guarded during those final months. He was allowing only a few people to be with him. Fran and Milt were with him from Sunday to Thursday. Cheryl flew down and stayed with him from Thursday to Sunday. Marni also flew down to be with her uncle. The family wanted and needed to be with Irwin as much as possible.

During the last couple of weeks of his life, a full-time nurse helped keep Irwin comfortable. During Irwin's final hours, Cheryl carried out her brother's wishes. She had a dozen vases of white flowers delivered to the house. She placed them throughout the master bedroom which overlooked the Pacific Ocean. She lit scented candles throughout the massive impeccably-designed bedroom. She also placed framed photographs of family and friends, many of whom had already passed, around his bed.

Even though it was a brisk winter day, Cheryl opened the carved French doors to the expansive deck. The ocean air slowly drifted through the bedroom. The waves gently crashed over the rocks and Irwin's favorite songs quietly echoed through the CD player. Unlike three days earlier, when the thunder of violent ocean waves crashed against the glass sliders, today the sea was calm.

Irwin died on Thursday, February 16, 1995, as the sun was setting over the ocean. As he took his last breath, Cheryl, Milt, Marni, and Fran held his hands. The rest of the family and friends sat on the edge of his bed. He died with his eyes wide open. Cheryl took his baseball cap which was still on his head, and tilted it down.

Everyone was numb. Fran felt as if a lighting bolt had struck her, paralyzing all her limbs. She needed to be helped up. At some point, the family went downstairs and the nurse stayed with Irwin. They all sat outside under a pitch-black sky illuminated by millions of stars. As the foaming waves broke on the rocky shoreline, everyone looked up. Fran prayed that Irwin and the rest of the family who had past, were getting to know each other.

Irwin and Cheryl had made most of the arrangements several months before his death. Fran couldn't bear to think what it was like for Irwin to select his own casket. Irwin was going to be buried in the family crypt next to Milt's mother Sadie, and then later Milt and Fran would take the last two remaining places. The next couple of days were blurred for everyone.

Cheryl and Marni made the obligatory calls, advising friends and family of Irwin's death and telling them that the funeral was on Sunday. The following day, Cheryl went to Hillside Memorial to finalize all the arrangements. The flowers were to be all white. Irwin wanted doves released at the gravesite and a harpist playing, "Somewhere Over the Rainbow."

As the service came to a close, the rabbi handed Fran a shovel. She hadn't noticed the mound of dirt near the crypt. Milt held Fran's hand and the two of them lifted the dirt together. Because Irwin wasn't buried in the ground, the ritual was ceremonial.

Fran was in control of her emotions. She said, "I brought Irwin into this world and I will stay strong. I will honor him every day of my life."

The reception was held at the Ritz Carlton Hotel in Beverly Hills. Over five hundred people came to remember and honor Irwin. Some were movie stars. Others were athletes, writers, famous chefs, and journalists.

The speeches were touching. The stories were sweet, and some were even comical. All included tears. The tears really flowed when opera singer Rosalina Tantino, sang a rendition of Irwin's request, "Ava Maria." Everyone in the room held hands and was touched by the love and kindness that was shown. Irwin was well loved.

Fran's grief lay upon her like the summer fog, heavy and damp. She passed her days under a shroud of gloom. Fran's identity seeped into the atmosphere like a birthday balloon clipped by a thorny branch, letting the air slowly dissipate.

She tried to be positive and enjoy the life she had left. She still danced and sang and Milt and Fran still played Gin Rummy. But she felt different. She couldn't explain it. It was subtle. Some days she felt as if she was walking through a dark cloud. Other times, everything was clear and bright. Something had changed, but Fran couldn't articulate what it was. She was concerned, but kept her thoughts to herself.

Chapter 58

Cheryl
Monterey, California, 1995-2006

My mother disguised her memory loss. For the next couple of years, she suffered in silence. She made a simpler routine for herself, making lists and schedules to check off as her days progressed. She no longer cooked, cleaned, or washed clothes. My father hired someone to help with those chores. Dad also did a masterful job covering for her, running interference when I questioned what I observed. He always provided a logical explanation for her forgetful behavior and assured me she was fine. But in 1999, when she got lost driving home from her Saturday bridge club, we had to face reality.

The following day, my father called and told me he had made an appointment for Mom to meet with a neurologist. He asked if I could fly down from Monterey and go with them to the appointment. Of course, I told him I would.

I flew into John Wayne Airport and Dad picked me up. My mother wasn't with him. She was at her day program that catered to adults with memory issues. During our ride home, Dad brought me up to speed as to Mom's decline. It was difficult to hear my father's heartache.

When we picked Mom up, she was excited to see me. She ran up to me, hugged me, and gave me a great big kiss. The following day, we met with the doctor. He ran some cognitive tests and confirmed she probably had Alzheimer's.

As soon as we could, Steve and I made arrangements to sell my parents' condominium. Then we moved them to Monterey to be close to us. We found an excellent assisted living community with amenities for both their medical and social needs.

The move was difficult for my father, but he agreed he couldn't handle the challenges on his own.

During the first several years, my parents resided at Villa Serra and my mother learned to follow my father's lead. She made sure her conversations were short and simple. Always active, Mom still tried to do as much as she could, but the disease made it difficult for her to complete even the simplest of tasks.

However, there was still one activity that she was able to do with joy and expertise. She could still dance. When the music played, whether in her apartment or at an event, she transformed into a dancing queen. My parents dancing together was a thing of beauty. Everyone watched them glide over the dance floor, spellbound.

Alzheimer's disease is insidious and degrading. My mother knew she was losing her memory and a part of her mind. But, she faced her challenges with grace, a smile on her face and a hug for everyone she met. She always had a kiss for her loved ones.

Watching my mother's slow decline was agonizing, but we still enjoyed moments of pure joy and laughter. As she lost her short-term memory, her past appeared in bright colors. Her long-term memories jolted free, taking her on an historical journey of her last eighty plus years.

She told me about the time she lived in Brighton Beach, and how she would swim in the ocean and stroll along the boardwalk. She remembered working in the principal's office while a student at Abraham Lincoln High, and going on the rides at Coney Island. She remembered her first date with my father, and how she volunteered for the Red Cross during the war. And she talked about her Papa as tears flowed down her face.

Those years were very hard on all of us, especially my father. He had his fears and apprehensions. He asked, "Do you think your mother will live long enough to celebrate our sixtieth wedding anniversary next year?"

I didn't know what to say. Without thinking about the logistics, I said, "Dad, we don't have to wait until next year to celebrate, let's do something this year. We will call it your sixtieth. Let me give it some thought and try and come up with a plan."

We hugged and cried, and then picked up my mother from day care.

Mom always talked about wanting to see Niagara Falls before she died. My father always talked about going to Cooperstown before he died. And they both always loved a great party. So, Steve and I bought four tickets to New York City.

After arriving in New York and getting a full night's sleep, we met in the hotel lobby. Then we went to New York's famous Jewish Carnegie Delicatessen. After breakfast, we stepped into our rented shiny, black stretch limousine and headed to the old neighborhood. First stop, Brighton Beach.

We pulled up in front of the apartment complex where my mother had lived with her mother, sister, and grandmother. The wrought iron gate into the complex was locked, but we slipped in as one of the residents came out. Mom stared at the rows of mailboxes embedded in the plastered walls and said, "This is where I lived. I remember."

Although the apartment was just a few blocks from the boardwalk, we asked our driver to drive us there. As soon as Mom saw the ocean, she bolted toward the beach. We took our shoes and socks off and let the ocean water trickle between our toes. My mother laughed, and one-by-one, each of us did the same. Walking along the boardwalk, I saw pure joy in her eyes. She was present. She was alert, and she was happy.

Before going back into Manhattan, we made three more stops. First, to Coney Island, where we ate Nathan's hot dogs for lunch. Our second stop was to Abraham Lincoln High School. As we walked up the stairs to the front doors, recognition of past memories crossed my mother's face. Again, Mom was alert and present.

"This is where I went to school," she told the two armed police officers guarding the entrance.

We walked into the main corridor and saw the framed photographs of the graduating classes from 1936 to 2001.

"Dad, which graduation class were you?" I asked.

"My class was the first one to graduate from Abraham Lincoln," he responded. "Where are you in this photograph?" I asked, not seeing his face.

"I was sick that day, so I'm not in the picture."

I knew when my father wasn't telling me the truth, and this was one of those times. I waited until we were back in the limo before I asked again. "Dad, why weren't you in the photo?"

"I was expelled a couple of weeks before graduation," he confessed. "I had this one teacher who constantly walked past my desk and would pull the hair on the top of my head. I repeatedly told him not to touch my hair, but it didn't stop. I finally had had enough. The last time he did it, I threw a punch, he went down, and I was expelled. That's why I wasn't in the picture."

There was nothing but silence until we pulled up in front of the apartment complex in Brooklyn. The tour was almost over.

We got out of the limo and walked toward the brick building where Irwin and I had lived. In my memory, the halls in the apartment were wide, long, and expansive. I remembered learning how to ride my bicycle down those halls. We walked upstairs to what used to be our apartment. My father knocked on the door, but no one was home.

My memories were much exaggerated. The hallway was actually very narrow, but not through the eyes of a five-year-old. As we walked away from the apartment, my mother looked at me and said, "We lived here when you were a baby."

On our second day, September 11, 2002, we went to the site of the World Trade Center. The ground, enclosed by chain-link fencing, still simmered with steam and embers. It was sacred ground. That sight will forever be embedded in my mind. It was hard to believe that exactly one year to the day, New York had experienced the worst tragedy of terror in this country's history, and that three thousand men, women, and children perished. We placed flowers along the fence and didn't speak until we arrived back at our hotel.

After leaving New York, we took a train to Niagara Falls. When we arrived, we were given yellow plastic raincoats to put on. The mist and water spray from the falls doused us, delighting my mother, who giggled with each droplet. She was like a little kid jumping in puddles in the street and getting a good soaking.

The next day, we went to Utica and then drove to Cooperstown. We walked through the museum and went on the symbolic baseball field. This was my father's fantasy, and also my husband's. But for me, the memories were about my father teaching me how to play the game. We stayed overnight before going to Boston to celebrate my parent's "sixtieth" anniversary. My mother enjoyed every moment of our trip.

We had about one hundred people at my parents' sixtieth anniversary party. The grandchildren, nieces, and nephews all flew in for the gala. Many friends also came to celebrate with us. We hired a band and we danced the night away. It was a wonderful celebration of life. A professional photographer captured all the memories on film, now tucked away in my heart and in a photo album.

The following year, Mike passed away with his family by his side. Mike had been the anchor of our family. His death marked an end of an era and the loss of a remarkable man. Mike had always been our compass. It was hard to fathom life without him.

We all flew to Chicago for Mike's funeral. We spent a week with family and shared stories about Mike and all his "connections." We had been afraid to ask him about those connections, but now I wish I had. I miss my uncle and will never forget his generosity, kindness, and love. He was one of a kind.

Epilogue

Fran and Milt

The last nine months of my mother's life were the most difficult for us to witness. Because of her rapidly progressing disease, she was unable to remain at home with my father. We had to move her into an Alzheimer's facility.

We set up a schedule so someone would visit her every day. Some days, we would take her for a ride to Monterey Bay. My mother still loved the ocean. I think she thought she was back in Brighton Beach. Other days we took her to Baskin-Robbins for a hot fudge sundae with whipped cream and a cherry on top. Some days we turned on the music and we would all dance.

On Christmas Eve, 2006, with carolers singing "Hark, the Herald Angels Sing", we said goodbye.

On December 16, 2016, eight days short of ten years from my mother's death, my father Milton died holding my hand. He was ninety-eight years old. I know my parents are dancing together on a soft cloud in heaven with Irwin and the rest of the family.

Three Assassinations was inspired by actual events that took place before and during my mother's life. It is based on my family's oral history, events I witnessed and extensive research, some of which unearthed hand-written notes, numerous newspaper articles and court documents.

I was also struck by the many historical events and coincidences that wove a purposeful pattern connecting the Kaufman family to some of the most horrific political assassinations of the twentieth century.

THE END

Acknowledgements

I have to start by thanking my husband, Steve. He read and edited all my drafts and encouraged me throughout this entire journey. I could not have done this without him by my side.

I also want to acknowledge my weekly writing group and our fearless leader, Ana Manwarring. Their support and encouragement I received was invaluable.

A special thank you to Mary Sheldon for her insight and input, both of which were extremely helpful. Her comments and suggestions not only enhanced the story, but also brought the characters to life.

And a big thank you to my publisher, Eric, his wife Peggy and everyone at Alive Book Publishing. They helped guide me through the process and the entire team they put together was incredible. Their patience and support were much appreciated.

ABOOKS

ALIVE Book Publishing and ALIVE Publishing Group
are imprints of Advanced Publishing LLC,
3200 A Danville Blvd., Suite 204, Alamo, California 94507

Telephone: 925.837.7303
alivebookpublishing.com

CPSIA information can be obtained
at www.ICGtesting.com
Printed in the USA
LVHW031725310323
743063LV00004B/150